T0246283

THE MYSTERIOUS BOOKSHOP

presents

THE BEST
MYSTERY
STORIES
OF THE YEAR

2024

THE MYSTERIOUS BOOKSHOP
presents

THE BEST MYSTERY STORIES OF THE YEAR 2024

INTRODUCTION BY
ANTHONY HOROWITZ

FOREWORD BY
OTTO PENZLER, SERIES EDITOR

THE MYSTERIOUS PRESS
NEW YORK

THE MYSTERIOUS BOOKSHOP PRESENTS
THE BEST MYSTERY STORIES OF THE YEAR 2024

Mysterious Press
An Imprint of Penzler Publishers
58 Warren Street
New York, NY 10007

First edition

Interior design by Maria Fernandez

Library of Congress Control Number: 2024941948

Hardcover ISBN: 978-1-61316-551-5
Paperback ISBN: 978-1-61316-552-2
eBook ISBN: 978-1-61316-561-4

10 9 8 7 6 5 4 3 2 1

Printed in the United States of America
Distributed by W. W. Norton & Company

CONTENTS

FOREWORD

A commonly asked question (probably the *most* commonly asked) posed to authors is "Where do you get your ideas?" One of the most asked questions of me is its cousin, "Where do you find the stories for the book?" and its corollary, asked by beginning mystery writers, "Where can I submit my stories?"

I cannot answer the first question, which to me is one step away from being a miracle, and it's too glib to respond to the others with "Any place that publishes fiction," though it is largely true.

If a writer is just discovering mystery fiction, the most obvious answer is *Ellery Queen Mystery Magazine*, which has been publishing first-rate detective stories for more than eighty years. If they have been working in this literary genre for even a short time, it is too obvious to mention, which is also true of its sister publication, *Alfred Hitchcock's Mystery Magazine*. If we add the third most likely choice, *The Strand Magazine*, the home of most Sherlock Holmes stories during the Victorian and Edwardian eras and brought back to life twenty-five years ago after a long hiatus, I have exhausted all the most prominent candidates.

Sadly, fewer and fewer short fiction works appear in general magazines. Such women's magazines as *Redbook* (which first serialized Dashiell Hammett's *The Thin Man*, among much else), *Good Housekeeping*, and *Ladies' Home Journal* proudly ran stories (many of them mysteries), as did such men's magazines as *Esquire*, *Argosy*, *Stag*, *Gentleman's Quarterly*, and *Playboy* (and some men actually *did* read the fiction, contrary to common belief). Now, if they still exist, the publication of fiction is as rare as a conservative defense lawyer.

There were other mystery specialty magazines in the 1950s, 1960s, and a few held on into the 1970s: *Manhunt* (in which original stories by Ross Macdonald, Mickey Spillane, and Ed McBain first appeared), *The Saint Mystery Magazine*, *The Man from U.N.C.L.E.*, and eponymous digest-size publications named for Rex Stout, Ed McBain, Michael Shayne, Edgar Wallace, and John Creasey (the latter two published in England).

Some years earlier, there were such high-paying and prestigious general interest magazines as *The Saturday Evening Post*, *Collier's*, *Liberty*, *Scribner's*, and *Cosmopolitan* (before it changed its target readership to primarily women).

There were, too, pulp magazines, which flourished in the 1920s, 1930s, and 1940s, before the creation of mass-market paperback books doomed them. Pulps, which in some years saw as many as five hundred different titles at newsstands, contained mostly fiction and featured authors who went on to become successful book writers. In the mystery field, the most notable were Dashiell Hammett, Raymond Chandler, and Erle Stanley Gardner, though some British authors also frequently introduced works in these cheap magazines with their garish covers, notably Agatha Christie.

The New Yorker still publishes quality fiction, including the occasional mystery story, and several others still throw a bone to authors by offering a single story per month. There are numerous other outlets, but not for authors who want to earn a living by the pen.

There are hundreds of literary journals that publish thousands of stories every year but they only provide nourishment for the soul, unable to pay more than a few dollars and copies of the magazine for a work over which a serious writer may have labored for a month or more. And this is princely compared to electronic magazines, e-zines, where payment is largely restricted to a sincere *thank you*.

More recently, a good source of original mystery and crime stories has been anthologies. Whereas anthologies were once relatively uncommon, scores now seem to be published each year, focused on a region or an organization that publishes them, restricting contributors to members of their particular coterie. Some of these modest publications have been especially well-represented in this volume.

A high percentage of stories in this edition were discovered in literary journals, most of whom deny that they publish crime fiction until I'm able to supply the parameters of how to define *mystery*.

While it is redundant to write it again, since I have already done it in so many "Best of . . ." anthologies that I've edited (although it is painful to acknowledge, I do recognize that not everyone reads and memorizes my forewords), it is fair warning to state that many people erroneously regard a "mystery" as a detective story. Though important, detective stories are only a subgenre of the much bigger literary category of mystery fiction (generally referred to in the UK as crime fiction), which I define as any work of fiction in which a crime, or the threat of a crime, is central to the theme or the plot. While I love good puzzles and tales of pure ratiocination, few of these are written today as the mystery genre has evolved (or devolved, depending upon your point of view) into a more character-driven form of literature, with more emphasis on the "why" of a crime's commission than a "who" or "how." The line between mystery fiction and general fiction has become more and more blurred in recent years, producing fewer memorable detective stories but more significant literature.

To find the best of these stories is a yearlong quest, largely enabled by my invaluable colleague Michele Slung, who culls the mystery magazines, both printed and electronic, for suitable stories, just as she does short story collections (works by a single author) and anthologies (works by a variety of authors), popular magazines, and literary journals. As the fastest and smartest reader in the world, she examines somewhere between three thousand and four thousand stories a year, largely to determine if they are mysteries (you can't tell a story by its title), and then to determine if they are worth serious consideration. I then read the harvested crop, passing along some of the best (or at least those I liked best) to the guest editor, and we select the twenty that are then reprinted, with another ten that just missed the cut being listed in an honor roll as "Additional outstanding stories."

It is almost impossible to adequately thank the guest editor for the 2024 edition of *The Mysterious Bookshop Presents the Year's Best Mystery Stories*, Anthony Horowitz, one of the most talented and hardworking writers I've ever known.

He has been remarkably successful in so many areas of crime fiction that it would be difficult to point to a single one as primary.

As a television writer, which is where I became a fan, he created and wrote *Foyle's War*, arguably the most compelling TV series in history. He also created and wrote the vastly popular *Midsomer Murders*, as well as such limited-run shows as *Collision* and *Injustice*.

His young adult novels featuring Alex Rider have sold more than twenty million copies and have been the basis for a much-loved TV series. His adult books have shown his range: two Sherlock Holmes novels, *The House of Silk* and *Moriarty*; three James Bond novels, *Trigger Mortis*, *Forever and a Day*, and *With a Mind to Kill*; the massive bestsellers *Magpie Murders* and *Moonflower Murders* (both also successful television programs); and, perhaps the most fascinating and challenging of all, the most recent series featuring Detective Hawthorne and a sidekick named Anthony Horowitz, *The Word Is Murder*, *The Sentence Is Death*, *A Line to Kill*, *The Twist of a Knife*, and *Close to Death*.

There is much, much more, but the big question is, after more than fifty novels and all those television shows, how he found time and energy to work on this volume.

A word of thanks is also more than appropriate for the previous guest editors of this series: Lee Child, Sara Paretsky, and Amor Towles. I am deeply in debt to all four for their generous participation.

While I engage in a relentless quest to locate and read every mystery/crime/suspense story published, I live in terror that I will miss a worthy story, so if you are an author, editor, or publisher, or care about one, please feel free to send a book, magazine, or tear-sheet to me c/o The Mysterious Bookshop, 58 Warren Street, New York, NY 10007. If it first appeared electronically, you must submit a hard copy. It is vital to include the author's contact information. No unpublished material will be considered, for what should be obvious reasons. No material will be returned. If you distrust the postal service, enclose a self-addressed, stamped postcard and I'll let you know that your submission was received.

To be eligible for next year's edition, a story must have been published in the calendar year 2024. The earlier in the year I receive the story, the more fondly I regard it. For reasons known only to them, some dunderheads wait until Christmas week to submit a story published the previous spring. This occurs every year, causing serious irritability as I read a stack of stories while friends trim Christmas trees, do their holiday shopping, meet for lunches and dinners, or otherwise celebrate the holiday season. It had better be a damned good story if you do this. I am being neither arrogant nor whimsical when I state that the absolute firm deadline for me to receive a submission is December 31 due to the very tight production schedule for the book. If the story arrives one day later, it will not be read. Sorry.

Otto Penzler
February 2024

INTRODUCTION
Crime Fiction and the Truth

I knew I wanted to be a writer when I was ten years old. Telling stories came naturally to me. A lonely, not terribly clever boy in a destructive private school, I slept in a dormitory with six or seven boys on army beds, all of us missing our parents and home life. I told stories and cheered the others up. That was how I made friends and discovered my calling.

By sixteen, I knew that I would be not just a writer but a crime writer. That insight came from a Christmas present I received from my father: the complete short stories and novels of Sherlock Holmes in two volumes. I have them to this day.

What I loved about Arthur Conan Doyle's brilliant creation was not the crimes themselves. In fact there are surprisingly few murders among the sixty investigations, and many of the stories are fantastical to say the least. No. What grabbed me was the idea that mystery and crime had tentacles that could reach out across the entire world, that a story beginning with a treasure stolen in Agra or a forced marriage in Utah could find its conclusion in Croydon or the Brixton Road. If you know London, you'll know that these are not the most exciting holiday destinations, and as a teenager being brought up in Stanmore, which I thought of as an equally uninteresting place, the attraction was irresistible.

And so—*Foyle's War, Midsomer Murders, Magpie Murders,* the *Hawthorne* novels: my biog says that I have committed more fictional murders than any living writer, which may only be the dream of an overimaginative publisher's PR department but does broadly describe my work of the last thirty years.

I love crime fiction. I love reading it and writing it. I devoured pretty much all the works of Agatha Christie when I was traveling the world in a year off before I went to college. I'd pick up and

xviii   ANTHONY HOROWITZ

drop off paperbacks as I progressed through youth hostels and actually read *Death on the Nile* on the Nile, *Murder in Mesopotamia* in Mesopotamia, and *Murder on the Orient Express* in Istanbul (I couldn't afford the train tickets). At college, I devoured Golden Age crime fiction and adored Anthony Berkeley, Dorothy Sayers, Rex Stout, Ellery Queen—all the usual suspects and more. I'm a fan of at least a dozen modern crime writers I could name. Japanese crime fiction in particular appeals to me and I love almost anything published by Pushkin Vertigo (and, of course, The Mysterious Press).

But as I've gotten older, I've become troubled. Why do I love crime fiction? Why does anyone?

I remember working on *Agatha Christie's Poirot*, writing scripts for Sir David Suchet who, for me, has never been bettered in the title role. I would often find myself wrangling with the producer until three o'clock in the morning. How did the fingerprint get on the glass? Could the killer arrive at the house in such a short time? What were the sight lines? Were we making everything clear enough? And as the clock ticked on and bed became an ever more unlikely prospect, a devilish voice would whisper in my ear . . .

Who cares? Does it really matter? It's only a murder mystery. Who will notice?

I had the same dark thought when I was writing *Midsomer Murders*. Each script took me about three months to create. It demanded two hours of a viewer's attention on a Sunday evening. And all of this simply to discover that the butler did it?

What was I doing with my life?

And yet for all my growing doubts, crime fiction has become more popular than ever. You must forgive me if I explore this with reference to my own country, England, but let's start with the pandemic, when, not surprisingly, book buying soared. According to the press at the time, book sales rose by an astonishing 21 percent, with sales of around 3.8 million copies a week. And what was the most successful genre? It wasn't humor or romance or even science fiction, which might have held up a mirror to what we were living through. It was crime. While people huddled behind closed doors, a staggering sixty thousand murders were delivered in a single week.

What is it about murder stories that makes them so popular? The first thing to say (and I've said it often enough) is that it's not the murders themselves. Contrary to what many people seem to think, particularly with the high mortality rate in *Midsomer Murders*, I don't enjoy killing people and as a corollary, it always strikes me how gentle and collegial most of the crime writers I've met have been. The point of murder is simply to introduce character. There is no faster way to open the door into people's lives. A wife kills her husband. But they seemed so happy together! What was the truth of their relationship? What was going on behind those net curtains?

Nor is the detective necessarily the main reason why we pick up a mystery. Of course Rebus, Morse, Reacher, Harry Hole, the Lincoln Lawyer, and all the rest of them have their loyal fan bases, but that doesn't account for the thousands of other successful and even bestselling books with less well-known investigators or single adventures that have never continued into the world of the series. Agatha Christie's most brilliant (and most copied) novel, *And Then There Were None*, doesn't have a detective at all!

It's my belief that crime novels have come to offer something that is sorely missing in real life and that, as human beings, we fundamentally need. And that something is justice, closure, truth.

Consider the template of a thousand whodunits. A community is in trouble, rife with suspicion and fear. It's no coincidence that so many Golden Age crime stories are set in English villages where everyone knows everyone . . . or thinks they do. Somebody has been killed. The detective usually arrives as an outsider, unless of course the village happens to be St Mary Mead. He or she is rather like the Byronic hero ("that man of loneliness and mystery") and finds a modern counterpart in one of those Clint Eastwood spaghetti westerns where the lone rider suddenly turns up in town, settles every score, and then disappears like a desert mirage. One thing is certain. By the time the hero leaves, the truth will be known with every *i* dotted and *t* crossed. The community will be healed.

When you start reading a murder mystery, there can be no doubt that there will be a satisfying conclusion. I'm sure somebody at some time will have written a whodunit without an ending. Josephine Tey springs to mind with *The Daughter of Time*. But a book without that last chapter, all the suspects gathered in the library or wherever and the killer unmasked, would be an act of self-harm, a literary chocolate teapot. And whether you've guessed it or not, that last reveal is what makes it all worthwhile.

Sadly, life in the UK is not like that at all.

You may have heard of the sub-postmasters, more than nine hundred men and women who ran small post offices all over the country and who were wrongly accused of theft when a faulty computer system called Horizon was installed in their businesses. Ironically, it was a brilliant TV drama—*Mr Bates vs The Post Office*—that brought to light what is now being called the greatest miscarriage of justice in UK history. Some sort of compensation may be on the way as politicians, journalists, PO executives, and Fujitsu bosses (who created the technology and lied about its reliability) rush to apologize, effectively covering their asses. But fifty-nine innocent people died with the shame of a criminal record. Four of them tragically committed suicide. And though lawyers made millions from the ensuing court cases, lives have been ruined and the process of justice has been grindingly slow.

And then there is a woman called Michelle Mone who, if the allegations against her are true, could have stepped straight out of the pages of a Chandler novel as a blond glamor queen with a shifty-looking husband, both of them accused of profiteering from COVID-19. These two charmers were given a £120 million contract to supply personal protective equipment to our health service, none of which turned out to be fit for purpose but which earned them profits of £65 million. The National Crime Agency is circling but Mone is still a baroness, elevated to the House of Lords. Her husband, Doug, has just taken possession of a £50 million yacht. It is hard to describe the sense of anger and disgust these two inspire. At least 223,396 people died of COVID in the UK.

I could go on. Brexit, our departure from Europe, is widely seen as a social and financial disaster, yet the politicians who sold it to us have never been held to account and continue to earn huge chunks of money on the speaker circuit around the world. Liz Truss, who was prime minister for just forty-five disastrous days and who cost the country an estimated £30 billion, has cheerfully accepted a yearly allowance of £115,000 for life.

Injustice upon injustice. And as for the sense of truth, even that is being held back from us. Social media provides multiple interpretations of the same events. As in the United States, conspiracy theories abound and we now live in an age of post-truth where what you believe cannot be contradicted because, quite simply, it is your belief. I've mentioned COVID a couple of times in this introduction. Is it not incredible that we still haven't been told the cause of an event that derailed the entire world? Was it a dead pangolin sold in a wet market in Wuhan, an accident in a nearby laboratory, an experiment that went wrong? We don't know—and wherever we look these days, we live in a state of constant uncertainty and I don't think it's good for us.

So it's hardly surprising that crime fiction, with its insistence upon one inarguable ending and a landscape in which the guilty are punished and the innocent freed to continue with their lives, should be so valued now. Just look at the stories in this collection: little nuggets of life that just make you smile and make some sort of sense of the chaos all around.

I was quite wrong to think the genre lightweight or irrelevant. What it offers is kindness, decency, justice, and truth in a world that increasingly seems to have none and at a time when it has never mattered more.

Anthony Horowitz
January 2024

Ace Atkins *is an award-winning,* New York Times *bestselling author who started his writing career as a crime beat reporter in Florida.* Don't Let the Devil Ride *is his thirtieth novel. His previous novels include eleven books in the Quinn Colson series and multiple true-crime novels based on infamous crooks and killers. In 2010, he was chosen by Robert B. Parker's family to continue the iconic Spenser series, adding ten novels to the franchise. He lives in Oxford, Mississippi, with his family.*

STUNTS

Ace Atkins

RED RIVER STREET

*L*ike the old song says, there's nothing like the life of a Hollywood stuntman.

Saturday afternoon, three people were shot and another killed outside a downtown Austin bar. According to police, the altercation started inside the Royale Lounge, 701 Red River Street, at what was supposed to be a fan-appreciation fundraiser for a regular in the local movie scene, retired stuntman Jason Colson.

Colson, 71, is in stable condition at UT Health Austin. Police haven't identified the other two victims or the man who died at the scene.

"I was in line for an autograph when we heard the gunshots outside," said Scott Montgomery, 51, of Austin. *"At first, everyone thought it was part of some kind of Old West show, like maybe Mr. Colson was going to fall backward off the roof or something. But when we walked outside to watch, the police rushed up and pushed us back. That's when we heard someone was dead."*

According to IMDb.com, Jason Colson worked from the early seventies up through the early 2000s on films like Smokey and the Bandit, Hooper, *and the* Cannonball Run *films. He was the go-to double and stuntman for the late Burt Reynolds. In recent years, Colson had been a featured guest at several film festivals and events for the Alamo Drafthouse.*

"I don't know who would make trouble for Jason," said Lars Nilsen, programmer for the Austin Film Society. "He's one of the nicest guys in the business. Always willing to give his time and immense knowledge of the stunt scene in Southern California to fans. Anyone who has ever heard his story about jumping that cherry-red Trans Am over a ravine in Alabama for Hooper *knows that he was the real deal."*

A woman who answered the phone at Colson's home said she didn't want to comment on the shooting. Austin police say no charges have been filed in an active investigation. Any witnesses are asked to call the department at 512-472-TIPS.

"How do I look?" Jason Colson asked.

It was a little after ten Saturday morning and his daughter Caddy was in his apartment kitchen, sitting at his old wagon-wheel table. She had a purse thrown over her shoulder and keys in her hand. Ready to roll even though the show didn't start till high noon.

"Would you be mad if I said the shirt was a bit much?" Caddy asked.

"This shirt?" Jason said. "Hell. Burt gave it to me himself. Had six of 'em made for *Smokey* deuce. Fans will get it. It's real silk and the red roses were embroidered by hand. Mexican woman over on Olvera Street made a dozen of 'em special for the crew."

"I'm sure the ladies loved it back during the bicentennial," Caddy said. "But how about that nice one Donnie and I gave you for Christmas? Maybe tone it down a little, Dad."

"That's not what folks want," Jason said. "They're not payin' twenty-five bucks a head to see an old man in a button-down collar and tie. This isn't some fancy church service."

"That's me, putting on pearls and lipstick before worship."

Caddy worked her tail off for some Christian nonprofit feeding homeless folks and immigrants in need. She had on an old threadbare Johnny Cash T-shirt, bell-bottoms, and hippie sandals.

She rolled her eyes as Jason walked over to the counter, where he reached for his wallet and then headed back to his bedroom. He stood in front of his floor-length mirror and checked out the spit-shined Luccheses, the tight black jeans, and black silk cowboy shirt. He ran a comb over his gray hair and gray mustache and decided his daughter was a fine woman and an amazing person but plain wrong on the shirt. *1976.* Hell, everyone knew that *Smokey II* hit theaters in the summer of 1980.

"Ready, Daddy?" Caddy said, calling out from the kitchen.

"*I was born ready,*" Jason said in his best Roy Rogers.

Jason remembered the Red River District before the place had a name. He used to hang out at the One Knite Club back when it was filled with bikers, hippies, and old blues musicians. The bar had once turned away the boys from Pink Floyd because they couldn't name a Lightnin' Hopkins song. That wasn't long before they were shooting *Outlaw Blues* with Peter Fonda and Susan Saint James. He'd doubled Fonda in that picture, riding a police motorcycle along the concrete path of Waller Creek and up and down North Lamar and Lavaca. Fonda was playing a convict who'd had a hit song stolen from him by a sleazy country-and-western singer. Pretty damn good script written by his pal Bill Norton, who went on to write *Convoy.* Jason did stunts on both.

The shoot wasn't easy. Most days Fonda and a lot of the crew had showed up stoned out of their minds. Hard to believe he was gone. Burt too. Needham. His old pal Charlie Bail, who taught him just about everything he knew about gags. Almost everyone he knew from the old Hollywood days was either dead or tucked and fucked beyond recognition.

He missed old Hollywood so bad it hurt. But it was gone. He'd moved to Austin five years ago because he could make a buck or two as a consultant for young filmmakers. He worked on a vampire flick, some coming-of-age horseshit made with cell phones, and what was supposed to be a western shot on a jerry-rigged set out in Bastrop. The script was so bad it made him physically ill to say the lines. (OLD MAN: *I'm getting too old for vengeance, son. Blood just begets more blood till there ain't no more.*)

Today was supposed to be a celebration. But now he wondered if it might be a crucifixion.

Damn if he wasn't still into Bobby Delgado for ten thousand big ones. At the moment, he only had four hundred bucks left to his name.

Bobby D won't show, right? Even Bobby D wouldn't want to piss on my parade.

The Jason Colson Celebration hadn't even started, the band hadn't played a lick, and already he had folks talking his ear off.

Some big fella in a black duster and black cowboy hat cornered him by the bar, asking him all sorts of questions about his trucker movies. When they'd shook hands, the duster parted like a curtain and he saw the fella was carrying a goddamn cannon under his right arm. Looked like a walnut-handle .44.

"Mr. Colson, I can't tell you how much your work means to me," the big man said. "I drove all the way over from Amarillo in my rig just to meet you. My daddy and me used to watch you on television when I was a kid. Is it true that *The Fall Guy* was really based on you?"

"Well," Jason said, "some folks have made that connection, although the courts saw it different. But like the bard said, partly truth and partly fiction. Just a walkin' contradiction."

"Who was that?"

"Fella I used to know back in the ole days," Jason said. He gave a quick wink and shook the man's hand again, trying to get back to the card table they'd set up by the bar.

"What's he like?"

"Who's that?"

"Burt."

"Third-finest man to walk this earth," Jason said. "After Jesus Christ and Elvis Presley."

"Did he do a lot of his own stunts?"

"When he could," Jason said. "When he was younger. But Burt had a bad back from football at Florida State and when he did his own stuff on *Gunsmoke*. We knew each other a long while. From *White Lightning* all the way to *Cop and a Half*. We shot that one in Tampa."

"He seemed like a regular guy."

"Yes sir."

"No airs about him."

"None at all."

"I knew it," the man said, hitching up his belt buckle. "They don't make 'em like that anymore."

"Broke that ole mold."

Caddy walked up on them, grabbing Jason's elbow, being a real pro at separating her dad from the crazy fans, and said it was time. Fans had started to line up outside and they'd soon be letting them in. Two-dollar beers and dollar tequila shots, as the event was sponsored by the Jose Cuervo distributor.

She ushered Jason over to the table where he eased into a hard chair, feeling that familiar lightning zap up his legs and into his lower back. Both knees. One shoulder too. Caddy had set out a bunch of Sharpies and Jason Colson swag: eight-by-ten action shots, T-shirts, ball caps, and belt buckles.

The band on stage started picking out the first chords of "East Bound and Down," Jason recalling how ole Jerry had come up with that one on the spot for Hal, saying if he didn't like it, give him a few hours and he'd write something else.

"Only one question," Caddy said, giving him the side eye. "What's all this bullshit about medical expenses?"

"You know," Jason said, "I've had a few over the years."

"Mm-hmm," Caddy said.

"I love you, baby," Jason said, "but can you please ease off on the sermon? Just for today?"

Red River.

Jason didn't know if it was his nerves acting up, but he couldn't stop thinking about that film he'd seen as a boy at the picture show in Tibbehah County, Mississippi. John Wayne bigger than shit in black-and-white with a six-shooter on his hip, leading that first cattle drive along the Chisholm Trail. Monty Clift playing his adopted son willing to follow him into the depths of hell and madness until things went off the rails, the Duke killing off two of his cowboys for not keeping their word. Wayne and Clift damn well beat the hell out of each other until a good woman intervened and told them they really loved each other. *Loved each other?* If only it was all that simple.

Jason knew his own son thought about him the same way. Five years ago, Jason had decided to up and leave in the middle of the night in an old Firebird he'd gotten after *Hooper* wrapped. It had stayed in storage for thirty years until he had the time to take it apart and put it all back together after. Ended up selling it for forty grand to a collector in Dallas. He never did get around to explaining to his son why he'd left again. Some things were just too rough and painful to discuss.

Jason knew that him shagging ass sure opened up some old wounds, scars made when he left his first wife back when the kids were little. But given the circumstances, he didn't have any other choice.

When Caddy and Quinn had been kids, there were epic trips out west. Visits to the movie sets. Disneyland, popcorn, and ice cream sundaes till they about burst. Caddy could always see the good. He sure wished his son one day might do the same.

Jason counted almost a hundred heads, hitting over 2K, as the rain pinged on the tin roof above the wide-open cinder block bar. They'd cheered for him as he made his way to the stage after a fine introduction by his buddy Lars, who ran the film fest. Lars was able to name a bunch of his films that most folks had forgotten, like *Billy Jack Goes to Washington* and *Moonrunners*.

Moonrunners hadn't paid well but was a hell of a fun shoot with Mitchum's son James and a real pistol of a gal named Chris Forbes. No woman, except maybe Lynda Carter, looked better in a pair of tight jeans.

"Never in a million years did I think falling off a damn horse or crashing a car would mean so much to folks," Jason said. "Those pictures we made were supposed to run for a few weeks at your neighborhood drive-in and maybe show up once or twice on late-night TV. But seeing so many young people here tonight shows me that we made something real and honest. And not to get up too high on my horse, but I think that's something lacking in pictures today with all that CGI. I don't care how good the picture is, people can tell what's real and what's fake. And I promise you, everything that happened in those old movies happened in real life. I got a file cabinet of X-rays to prove it."

There was laughter and applause. Just as he was about to shake Lars's hand and return to the card table to sign some autographs, he saw Bobby Delgado walk into the bar. He had that short, mean fella, Angel Rojas, riding shotgun with him.

The men wore all black. They looked like maybe they should've worn hoods and maybe carried scythes too.

Delgado had on a black suit over a black shirt and bolo tie. He was thin and hard looking, with black eyes and slick black hair. Angel Rojas was shorter and squatter, walking low to the ground like a bulldog, with a pockmarked face and trimmed mustache.

When Jason locked eyes with Delgado, he was pretty sure he wasn't gonna be leaving the show with a dime.

So he stepped back up to the mic, cool and collected, and took in all the folks with their eyes on him. The beautiful women, so young they could be his granddaughters, and the aging hipster kids with their retro T-shirts and receding hairlines. He could smell the bar funk of weed and piss; there was a poster on the wall for a monthly burlesque show and another for some punk band playing later that night.

"When you get as old as me, you see things different," Jason said, offering a sad, introspective smile. "Y'all stop being fans and become family. I love you all."

People clapped, hooted, and hollered.

As he shook Lars's hand, Jason leaned in and asked, "Just where's the shitter in this place?"

The line wound its way past the bathrooms, the elevated stage, and the extended bar with the longhorn skull above the bottles shining in bright neon. One fan brought Jason a plate of brisket and beans from Ruby's, another wanted him to sign an original half-sheet to *Moonrunners,* and then a middle-aged woman with frizzy hair and tattoos asked if he wouldn't mind signing one of her titties.

"Sure you don't want me to sign 'em both?" Jason asked. "Don't want the other to get jealous."

It wasn't the first time he'd been asked. Or told the same joke.

The woman leaned down and he signed her right cleavage with a Sharpie.

"Headed straight to the tattoo parlor to make it permanent," the woman said. "How about we do a shot later on?"

"I haven't had a drink in ten years," Jason said, "but I sure do appreciate it."

"My husband sure thought you hung the moon," she said. "He always said *White Line Fever* made him want to be a trucker. Hell, he'd be standing right here with me if he hadn't up and died."

"Sorry to hear that," Jason said.

He reached out and patted the back of her hand. She smiled at him while Jason glanced down the line to see Bobby Delgado and Angel Rojas getting closer. Bobby D never had been a guy to wait his turn, but he figured Bobby must've appreciated the drama of him and Rojas getting closer and closer, hoping that old Jason Colson would finally up and wet his pants.

Not a chance. That wasn't the Colson way.

"Happens," the woman said. "I told him to lay off the red meat."

Jason swallowed and looked back up at her. She pushed her right titty back down into her tight tank top. "What can you do but keep on truckin'?"

"Yes ma'am," he said, "pedal to the metal."

"Darlin'," Jason said to Caddy.

His daughter looked over from where she was making change for a man buying two copies of Jason's autobiography, *From Tibbehah to Tinseltown*.

"You mind holding down the fort while I hit the head?"

"Can't you wait, Daddy? That line's stretching out the back door."

"Wish I could, but my prostate is now officially listed as an antique."

Jason stood up. Rojas turned to Bobby D and pointed right at him. Jason ducked his head and passed behind Caddy, smiling at all the people in line.

"If I don't come back," Jason said, leaning down and whispering in her ear, "I'll call you later. Don't worry. Don't worry about nothing, baby."

"Daddy?"

But Jason was already headed to the bathroom door.

The bathroom had a row of six urinals on the wall, two stalls, and no window or other way out.

Jason walked over to the lone sink and ran the faucet. He splashed some cool water in his face and looked into the rusted reflection. He could hold firm, maybe talk his way out of his arrangement with Bobby D. Or have Caddy pull the car around and drive like hell.

Bobby D didn't know about his new apartment. Didn't know a damn thing about his family. He'd get him back. It might take some time. But he needed to rest up and come up with a plan. He'd already sold his old truck, ran down his last few friends in California for some money, and even sold a silver belt buckle given to him by the late, great Chuck Roberson.

Jason was studying the paneled ceiling for an exit when the bathroom door opened and the big man he'd first met at the lounge walked in.

"Mr. Colson, there's two fellas here aim to do you some harm."

"No offense, son," Jason said, "but no shit."

"I think I can help you out."

"You got ten grand in your hip pocket?"

"No sir."

"How about you give me a boost then?" Jason said, pointing at the ceiling over the urinals. "I'm planning on finding an alternative exit."

The man nodded and then removed his duster and cowboy hat. He sized Jason up, then nodded. "Here, take 'em."

"Son."

"Come on. Those fellas want to rough you up good."

Jason started to unsnap the buttons on his black silk shirt with red roses. He took it off and handed it to the man.

"Always been my lucky shirt," Jason said.

"Looks identical to the one Burt had on in *Smokey II*."

Jason winked at him and slid into the duster and put the hat down on his head. It was a little snug but would work just fine.

"Tell my daughter she can find me saddled up to the Driskill Bar."

"You wrote in your autobiography that you quit drinking."

"I did?" Jason said, cracking open the bathroom door and peering back into the Royale Lounge. "Maybe. But today sure seems like the day to start back up."

There wasn't much planning to it. Jason figured he'd walk past the country band and make his way outside into the rain before anyone noticed a thing. The Driskill wasn't too far away and he'd be high and dry within fifteen minutes, sipping on some Patrón. He felt terrible about leaving his own party early but figured folks would think he wasn't feeling well and had to rest a bit. After all, this was all about helping a man down with medical expenses.

Jason pulled the brim of the cowboy hat over his eyes just as the band started into "Slow Rollin' Low," the theme to *Moonrunners*, a film which later became a little something called *The Dukes of Hazzard* on CBS. He and Waylon had worked on both productions. He sure wished ole Waylon was still around so Jason could tell him about Bobby D and Angel Rojas on his ass. He could hear Waylon laughing about the current predicament. Maybe he'd even write a ballad about it. "The Last Days of Jason Colson."

He didn't get five feet from the men's room when Angel Rojas caught his eye and jabbed Bobby D hard in the ribs. But then Bobby D grabbed Rojas's arm and pointed to the man in the black silk shirt with roses on the shoulders. They turned in the opposite direction.

Jason passed the card table, Caddy not noticing as she was making excuses for him, offering half price on all official stunt gear. *Half damn price?*

He spotted two metal doors at the back of the bar. One had a padlock and a chain and the other looked like it might go into the adjoining bar. He didn't think twice, just pushed into it and found himself in complete and absolute darkness, tripping over something and landing hard onto a staircase. Feeling for the wall, Jason made his way up and then around the blackened staircase, spotting light up top at what looked like an exit. He could hear the wind and the rain now, the tin roof panels slapping up and down.

He tried the exit but it held tight. He leaned into the lock with his good shoulder but it wouldn't budge. Hearing voices and music below, Jason stepped back and kicked hard, the door slamming open. He walked out onto the roof, stepping lightly on the slick metal, looking down onto Red River and all the cars passing in the rain-slick street. The whole bar vibrated from the old Waylon tune playing below.

He saw where there was a small gap between the Royale Lounge and the bar next door, maybe five to six feet. He felt if he had a little wind at his back, he might just be able to make it across and slide down the other bar roof to the ground. It was tricky but he figured it was better than a shot in the back by Bobby D or Rojas.

Jason shimmied down to where the roof flattened out over a loading dock. He backed up, took a breath, and was about to make a run for it.

"Daddy," Caddy called out from below, "just what the hell are you doing? We don't have time for you to play around." Hands on her hips, she stared up from the alley separating the two bars. The rain coming down now, tapping hard at the cowboy hat and across his back.

Jason put a finger to his lips and shook his head. He gestured toward the end of the alley where he spotted Bobby D running like hell and yelling in Spanish. He had a gun in his hand. Caddy simply shook her head and walked away.

Bobby D immediately replaced her, peering up at Jason on the roof, and drew his gun. *Holy damn shit.*

More people followed. Jason could see the Royale Lounge emptying, people standing shoulder to shoulder on Red River and in the alley, pointing up to crazy Jason Colson on the tin roof.

The crowd transfixed as they watched some man in a black suit, a villain straight out of central casting, aiming a big silver pistol up at Jason, yelling, "You have two choices, Jason Colson: easy or hard way down!"

The crowd started to laugh. Some clapped and whistled.

Jason raised his hands as if surrendering.

Bobby D wasn't smiling. He looked to where several folks had gathered around him. One was the big man from the bathroom wearing Jason's lucky shirt, the snap buttons about to explode from his chest. Jason could see he had his big gun stuck in the back of his blue jeans. The fella's hand reached back to grab that beautiful walnut handle.

"Oh shit," Jason said. "Oh shit."

The roof exit slammed open again and Angel Rojas came barreling out with a two-by-four in his hand. He was screaming something nasty and blasphemous when the first bullet ripped into his shoulder, and then another caught him in the throat. He fell backward onto the sloping tin roof and slid his way down fast into the alley and a pile of garbage cans.

Bobby D turned to Jason Colson's number one fan and raised his gun. The whole damn thing running slower than Peckinpah on Valium. Bobby D fired and caught the man in the arm and the big fella fired and caught Bobby D in the leg. The man fired again, the *BLAM* of the pistol sounding like thunder above, getting Bobby D in the chest, dropping him to his knees.

The crowd clapped.

Jason took off the cowboy hat and waved, while no one seemed to pay Angel Rojas or Bobby D a bit of attention. *Son of a damn bitch.* That big ole boy was bleeding right through his lucky shirt. This sure wasn't Jason's day.

That's when he felt the bullet slice through his shoulder and heard the crack. Two more shots and hot pain seared his right thigh. Goddamn Angel Rojas was on his feet in the dumpster, unloading his goddamn pistol. Jason didn't waste a second, taking a practiced fall onto his back as if the bullets had done their job.

Down below, Rojas's hammer finally fell on the sixth shot and he wavered on his feet until he tumbled back onto the black plastic bags.

Caddy was the first to reach Jason on the roof. She was twice as strong as she looked, reaching under his arms and dragging his ass off the rainy roof and into the stairwell, the landing now full of bright light. She held Jason's head in her lap and stroked his gray hair.

"What did you do this time?" She was crying hard. "God, your dumbass fans think it's just another show."

"But you know different," Jason said. Damn if he didn't feel like he was trying to stand up with bowling balls in his luggage. "You always knew."

"Will you ever stop?" Caddy asked. "When will you ever stop?"

Jason could hear the sirens and the drumming of the rain across the roof of the Royale Lounge. As he thought on what had just transpired, he wiped the wetness from his face and mustache. "I'm getting too old for vengeance," he said, eyes fluttering closed. "Blood just begets more blood till there ain't no more."

"I love you," Caddy said, "but damn if you haven't always been full of shit."

I wrote "Stunts" as a way of checking in with two series regulars from my Quinn Colson books. In the series, I'd sent Quinn's semi-famous Hollywood stuntman father, Jason, and Quinn's sister, Caddy, riding out of Mississippi and into the sunset in Austin, Texas. Jason Colson (known mainly as Burt Reynolds's longtime stunt double) is an unreformed and unapologetic risk-taker and troublemaker. What could go wrong? I wondered what would happen when Jason's past glories and current troubles collide at a movie fan meet and greet at an Austin bar. I found a lot of inspiration from both Howard Hawks and Hal Needham for this one.

Michael Bracken *(www.CrimeFictionWriter.com) is the Edgar Award-nominated, Shamus Award-nominated, Derringer Award-winning author of more than twelve hundred short stories, including crime fiction published in* Alfred Hitchcock's Mystery Magazine, Ellery Queen Mystery Magazine, The Best American Mystery Stories of the Year, The Best Mystery Stories of the Year, *and many other publications. Additionally, Bracken is the editor of* Black Cat Mystery Magazine *and several anthologies, including the Anthony Award-nominated* The Eyes of Texas: Private Eyes from the Panhandle to the Piney Woods. *He and his wife, Temple, reside in Central Texas.*

BEAT THE CLOCK

Michael Bracken

Detective Robert Highlander had just settled into the rear pew of the Orkley Revival Baptist Church the first Sunday in November when his cell phone vibrated. He unclipped it from its holster, checked the number of the incoming call, and nudged his wife. "I have to take this."

He slipped from the pew and answered the phone as he walked into the vestibule. As soon as he identified himself, he heard in response, "We got us a body."

"Where?"

He noted the address, slipped back inside the nave to let his wife know she would need to find a ride home, and drove across town to the Dunnett residence. There, a dead man tentatively identified as Hugh Dunnett lay face down on the living room carpet, a single gunshot wound in his back, a broken key-wound mantle clock inches from the outstretched fingers of his left hand, the clock key still on the mantle. The clock had stopped at 1:55.

Billy Wentzman, the bearded crime scene photographer, snapped a few last photos and turned to Highlander. "I guess the old man's time was up."

Highlander didn't react to the younger man's joke because the dead man appeared near his own age and, despite what the mirror told him each morning, he didn't like to think of himself as old.

He squatted next to the body. Gray hair, with a few remaining threads of black peppering it and, unlike his own hair, minimal signs of thinning. The right side of the dead man's head lay upon the carpet, and lividity visible on his face revealed that the body had been in that position for more than six hours. Powder burns around the bullet hole in the white dress shirt indicated the shooter had stood close to the victim, and the lack of any blood on the carpet around the body—though some might be found under the body once it was moved—suggested that the bullet remained inside the torso. The edge of a bold red tie peeked from beneath the shirt collar. Blue pinstriped trousers matched the jacket tossed casually over the arm of the couch, and black wing tips over black socks completed what Highlander could see of the dead man's apparel. There was no jewelry on the dead man's right hand, but his left sported a simple gold band on his ring finger, and a gold-accented stainless-steel Bulova watch adorned his left wrist. It displayed the correct day, date, and time, the second hand continuing its relentless sweep around the watch face.

Highlander looked up when his new partner, a young, pear-shaped brunette recently promoted out of uniform and working her first homicide, led Dr. William Pritchard—the county coroner—into the living room. The doctor's sartorial style was the near opposite of the dead man's—a black T-shirt featuring Pink Floyd's *Dark Side of the Moon* album cover stretched tight over his abdomen, faded blue jeans belted low on barely there hips, and scuffed work boots encased in protective coverings—just as Highlander's black brogues were—to protect the integrity of the crime scene.

Pritchard glanced at the body and the broken mantel clock and said, "Ten hours, give or take."

"That's my best guess too," Highlander said.

"Cause of death is likely whatever made that hole in his back."

Detective Jessica Mitchell's gaze darted from one man to the other and then back. "You can't—"

"No, we can't know for certain," Highlander told her, "but if you've seen enough bodies you start to get a feel for the obvious."

Highlander walked the room, sniffed the whiskey residue in a tumbler on the end table next to the easy chair facing the fireplace, saw nothing else of interest, and released the body to the coroner.

Pritchard said, "I'll get this guy on the table right away. I'll have a preliminary report by the end of the day."

Highlander turned to his partner. "Who found the body? Who called it in?"

"Agnes Quinn, the cook," Mitchell said. Like Highlander, she'd dressed for Sunday services, but she hadn't made it to church. She'd taken the call as she was leaving her apartment and hadn't time to change from her floral-print A-line dress and taupe heels into something more comfortable. "She's waiting in the kitchen."

"She told you anything?"

"Not much," Mitchell said. "I was waiting for you."

Highlander followed the younger detective through the dining room and into the kitchen.

The skeletally thin gray-haired woman sitting at the kitchen table had poured herself a tumbler of Glenfiddich 21 Year from the bottle near her elbow while under the watchful eye of a uniformed officer who did not appear to have finished puberty. The tumbler in her hand matched the one in the living room. Likely the Glenfiddich in it did too. Highlander glared at the officer and nodded toward the bottle.

"She said she needed it to calm her nerves," the officer explained.

Highlander turned to Quinn. "Did it?"

Her crooked smile and unfocused gaze indicated that she had calmed her nerves several times.

Highlander removed the tumbler from her hand and slid it and the open bottle across the table, out of her reach. Then he introduced himself. "You've already met Detective Mitchell and Officer"—he squinted to read the name badge on the young man's uniform—"Calloway. We'd like to ask you a few questions about what happened this morning."

Quinn glanced at the Glenfiddich. "I come to work like usual," she said. "I call out for Mr. Dunnett to let him know I'm here, but

I don't get no answer, so I go looking for him. That's when I found him on the living room floor, deader than a doornail."

"You touch him? Check his pulse? Ensure that he wasn't breathing?"

"I didn't need to be touching him," she said. "I know a dead man when I see one."

"How's that?"

"I seen a few in my time, boxed and unboxed," she said. "You don't get to be my age without suffering some loss."

"You touch anything in the room? You move anything?"

She shook her head. Her eyes didn't shake at the same speed as the rest of her face.

Highlander nodded toward the bottle. "The Glenfiddich?"

She blinked several times before answering. "Mr. Dunnett wasn't going to be needing it, and I saw that hole in his back, so I know he didn't drink himself to death."

As Detective Mitchell took notes, they learned that Agnes Quinn had worked for the Dunnett family for nearly twenty years, preparing lunch and dinner Wednesday through Sunday. "Except the first Saturday of the month," she said. "Ever since the missus's passing, he's been going to the Widowers' Club on the first Saturday."

"What's that?"

"A bunch of old men who teach each other how to do things their wives used to do for them, like cook and grocery shop and iron shirts. I think mostly they just drink and tell each other how much they miss their missuses."

"How long has Mrs. Dunnett been gone?"

"Near on a year. She and her sister died in a car wreck," Quinn said. She shook her head. "Mr. Dunnett was supposed to go on that trip up to the lake house, but something happened and he couldn't leave right away, so her sister went instead. He's been grieving ever since, ain't even taken off his wedding ring."

"He have other family?"

"Three nephews," she said. "Sons of his sister-in-law, the one died in the wreck that killed the missus."

"He get along with them?"

She shook her head. "Leeches, all of 'em. The three of them always sucking up to Mr. Dunnett, trying to get his money."

Pritchard took down their names—Andy, Gary, and Larry Royce—as Dunnett's cook shared what she knew about the nephews. Andy, manager of a garden supply store, was the only married brother; Gary, owner of Royce's Rods and Restorations, was single; and Larry, employed by a printing company, was recently divorced. She didn't know much more than that, but she clearly didn't like any of the three men.

After the cook answered his last question, Highlander slid the Glenfiddich and tumbler back to her and turned his attention to the uniformed officer. "See that Ms. Quinn gets home safely, Officer Calloway."

A circumnavigation of the house, examining every door and window from the inside and from the outside, revealed no signs of forced entry. What it did reveal was a security system that required an entry code, with keypads located at the front, rear, and garage doors.

"Have the keypads dusted for prints," Highlander told Mitchell.

While she returned to the living room to talk to the crime scene techs, he went to the two-car garage via the breezeway that connected it to the house. He found Billy Wentzman admiring a 1957 Chevrolet Nomad parked in the far bay. He stepped around the year-old Lexus parked in the first bay, stopped next to Wentzman, and said, "Doesn't seem like his kind of ride."

"I'm surprised I didn't see it at the car show yesterday," Wentzman said. He earned extra money taking photographs for various hot rod magazines, often using his wife as an accompanying model. "If it's as clean inside as it is outside, it surely would have picked up an award or two."

"Doc Pritchard wants to see us," Highlander told his partner as he returned his cell phone to its holster. They had spent the afternoon canvassing the neighborhood around Dunnett's home, had learned nothing, and had met at the station to begin assembling their murder book. "Says he's ready with the preliminary."

The coroner's office, such as it was, operated out of the basement of the county's only hospital, and Pritchard was waiting for the detectives when they arrived. He removed the sheet covering the nude body of Hugh Dunnett. "There're no signs of a struggle, no defensive wounds of any kind, nothing that suggests the victim anticipated his death."

"You think this was premeditated?" Mitchell asked.

"It certainly wasn't a crime of passion," Pritchard said. "He has a single gunshot wound to the lower back, and the entry wound is angled upward."

Highlander glanced at his partner and winked. "He was shot by a midget?"

"Or someone holding the gun low," suggested Mitchell.

Pritchard continued as if the two detectives had not spoken. "The bullet ricocheted off one of his ribs, perforated his heart, and lodged in his shoulder blade. Ballistics has the bullet and they tell me it's a .38."

"Time of death?"

"If you believe the broken mantel clock, one fifty-five," Pritchard said. "Lividity, rigor, and other indications suggest that's not far off. I'd say the window is sometime between one and two A.M."

Highlander's wife reheated meatloaf leftover from Saturday night's dinner, put a slab of it between two slices of white bread slathered with mayonnaise, and put the resulting sandwich on a plate with a handful of barbecue-flavored potato chips. Linda slid the plate and a bottle of beer in front of her husband and, when he began wolfing it all down, asked, "You eat anything today?"

"Not since breakfast," Highlander said.

"Tough case?"

He shrugged. "Don't know yet. We've had fingers pointed at three possible suspects."

"How's your new partner doing?"

"She didn't say much," he told his wife. "Mostly she just followed me around."

"Smart girl," Linda said. "She's learning from the best."

Highlander snorted. Orkley didn't see many homicides in any given year, and for the previous fifteen years he had been the junior detective in every one of the cases. Only with his longtime partner's recent retirement did he step into the role of senior detective.

"How'd Jessica react to the body?"

"Her first homicide," he explained, "not her first body. She's the one who rolled up first on that three-car pileup last summer where the meth head killed that university professor and the barbershop quartet."

Monday morning, Highlander left his new partner at the station to gather background information on Dunnett and his three nephews while he tracked down Arnold Weatherby, the Widowers' Club's eighty-seven-year-old founder. Weatherby confirmed Agnes Quinn's description of the club: a dozen elderly men who drank and told each other how much they missed their deceased wives.

"We began as a self-help group," he explained when Highlander sat with him at his dining room table. "When we first began meeting, we were all of an age where domestic chores were divided by gender. When my wife passed on—heart attack, God rest her soul—I realized I'd never washed a load of laundry and never cooked anything except on the charcoal grill. Many of my friends were in the same boat, so we started meeting the first Saturday of each month to teach each other things we should have learned long ago."

Highlander glanced around the room much as he had examined the rest of the rooms as he'd passed through them. Though not as large nor as well appointed as Dunnett's home, Weatherby's home suggested that he had done well for himself. The detective asked about that.

"We maintain a certain standard among our members," Weatherby said. "We've a doctor, a couple of lawyers, and businessmen of all stripes. In fact, Dunnett's attorney is a member, and he recommended Dunnett after his wife's accident."

"So, I'm not likely to ever be a member?"

"I don't know, Detective Highlander," he said. "What's your stock portfolio look like?"

Highlander smiled and moved on. "What can you tell me about Dunnett?"

"We limit membership to twelve, and Hugh was our newest member," Weatherby explained. "Joined us about a year ago, right after his wife's tragic accident, replacing Jay Sommerfeld, who had passed a few months earlier."

"What was he like?"

"A little better off than some of us," he said. "Hugh has—had—a cook, and I'm fairly certain he had maid service as well, but not all that much different otherwise. Like most of us, he only ever had the one wife, and it was obvious he suffered her loss greatly."

"How's that?"

"Stoic," he said, "but every time he spoke of her you could see tears glisten in his eyes."

"How'd he get along with the other members?"

"We all get along, Detective. We would never accept a new member otherwise."

"Other than his wife, what did Dunnett talk about?"

"The same as the rest of us: investments, politics, ungrateful family."

"Ungrateful family?"

"There's money to be had when one of our members die," Weatherby said. "Sometimes, it's a great deal of money, and some of us have family members circling like vultures waiting for that day to come."

"And Dunnett did?"

"His nephews," he said. "Always asking for money."

Highlander asked, but Weatherby didn't know much else about Dunnett's nephews. So, he asked what the Widowers' Club would do now that Dunnett had died.

"I've been running the club for thirty years, Detective Highlander," Weatherby said, "and death is the primary reason we lose members. Unfortunately, death is also how we gain members. I have to admit, it's a bit gruesome, but we have a few prospects."

When Highlander left Weatherby a short time later, he carried a list of all the Widowers' Club members, but he suspected the remaining ten men would have little to add to what the club's president had already told him.

From Weatherby's house, Highlander returned to the station and collected his partner. Mitchell carried a folder in which she had gathered printouts from her internet searches, and she gave him the work address of the youngest brother.

"The new Walmart is killing us." Andy Royce, manager of Bloomin' Newman's Garden Emporium, had been stacking bags of compost when the two detectives found him. He glanced from Detective Highlander to Detective Mitchell, and then refocused on the senior detective. "So, what was I doing Saturday evening? Working a second job. We closed here at six. I went home, had dinner with my wife, took a brief nap, and then went out to Cumberland's."

Cumberland's was a manufacturing plant on the outskirts of town.

"I work there part-time, Friday and Saturday nights, ten to six, as a watchman." Broad-shouldered, with thick, muscular arms, Royce wore a green apron with his employer's logo embroidered on it, and underneath wore a blue work shirt, blue jeans, and thick-soled brown work boots. He was clean-shaven, with a crew cut in need of a touch-up, and he had the leathering skin of a man who spent a great deal of time outdoors.

"My wife has wet macular degeneration and our medical insurance is terrible. Stella's had experimental surgery and multiple follow-up treatments. She can't see well enough to drive or work, and it's only getting worse. I used the life insurance money from my mother's accident to pay off our medical bills. It's been almost a year and they're already piling up again."

"How much do you stand to gain from your uncle's death?"

"Best guess?" Royce said. "A couple of million."

"Shared with your brothers?"

"No," he said. "Each."

"That'd pay a lot of medical bills."

"We could certainly use the money," Royce said, "but that's not the way I'd want to get it."

"Any witnesses? Can anyone confirm your presence at Cumberland's?"

Royce named the watchman he had replaced Saturday night and the one who replaced him Sunday morning.

"And the hours in between?"

"Nobody," he said. "But the company makes me punch a clock every hour on the hour."

Other than the department-issued sedan in which Highlander and Mitchell had arrived, there were no vehicles on the Royce's Rods & Restorations lot newer than 1966. As they headed toward the office, Highlander stopped to admire a customized 1957 Chevrolet Bel Air.

"She's for sale."

Highlander turned to the man approaching them. He had finger-length black hair oiled back and a full beard that brushed his thick chest. The short-sleeve black T-shirt stretched across his chest revealed tattoo sleeves on both arms. Tight-fitting black jeans and square-toe black cowboy boots completed the look.

"I can make you and your little lady a sweet deal on that beauty."

Out of the corner of his eye Highlander saw his partner stiffen, and he wasn't certain if Mitchell was more insulted by being called "little lady" or by the presumption that she was *his* "little lady."

"We're not here to shop," Highlander said. "We're here to see Gary Royce."

"Well, you found him."

Highlander flipped open a well-worn wallet to display his badge. "We'd like to talk to you about your uncle."

"Come on inside," Royce said.

He led them past three service bays, where a trio of vintage Chevrolets were in various stages of restoration, and into an office barely big enough for the overflowing desk in the center of the room, the three chairs surrounding it, and the six mismatched filing cabinets. Royce settled behind the desk. The detectives settled onto the two remaining chairs.

"I've been expecting you," Royce said. "Andy called after you left his place, said you think one of us killed Uncle Hugh."

"It's certainly a possibility," Highlander said. "So, where were you this weekend?"

"Saturday was the Rods & Broads show." He pointed to a poster thumbtacked to the wall on his left that pictured a well-endowed blonde in a red thongkini draped over the front fender of a customized black 1929 Ford Model A. "I was there most of the day, and I went to the party that night."

Highlander recognized Billy Wentzman's wife on the poster but didn't mention it. Instead, he asked, "Most of the day?"

"We had to transport our cars back to the shop after the show was over."

"Anyone vouch for your presence?"

He named two employees who were the last to leave after securing Royce's Rods & Restoration's five vehicles. "Must have been midnight or so when they left, and I was here doing paperwork until I headed back to the party."

"And you were alone the entire time?"

Royce nodded. "Yep."

"What time did you arrive at the party?"

"One. One-fifteen. Around then. You might check with some of the people there," he said. "I forgot my cell phone—left it here in the office—and had to ask someone for the time."

Highlander asked for the names of the other people at the party and Mitchell wrote them in her notebook, along with contact information for a few of them.

"As we came in, I noticed that all the cars in the shop are Chevys."

"That's all we work on," Royce said.

"So, the Nomad in your uncle's garage, you rebuild that?"

"Yes, sir," Royce said. "That's our work."

"What's it doing at his place?"

"He was"—Royce hesitated—"storing it for me."

Highlander didn't have any more questions, so Royce walked them out. He stopped next to the Bel Air and patted the fender. He said, "I really can make you a sweet deal."

Highland gave the car a wistful examination. "How much?"

"She's been appraised for fifty, but I've been driving it lately. I could let her go for forty-five."

"Too rich for my blood," Highlander said.

"Saturday?" Larry Royce said. He was a customer service representative for a large printing company, and they caught him as he was arriving home. They introduced themselves in the parking lot as he climbed out of his brand new Corvette. He led them up to his second-floor apartment overlooking the pool in a complex of buildings that catered to singles and the recently divorced. He stripped off his jacket and tie while they talked. His dark hair had been styled, and his nose displayed early stages of a gin blossom. "I went out with a couple of the guys from work to take advantage of the extra hour of drinking, and I rolled in around three with a redhead named Lucy—Lucille—Lucinda—something like that. I knew her from somewhere, but I can't remember from where. She was out of here before I woke up Sunday morning, and she took the fifty-seven dollars I had in my wallet. Can I report that?"

"Not our department," Highlander said, "and not remembering her name isn't likely to help."

Royce shrugged.

"So, who were you out with, and where did you go?"

Royce named three coworkers and four bars. "We got separated at Smiling Jack's Bar & Grill."

"That where you met the redhead?"

He nodded. "You guys want something to drink?"

The two detectives declined his offer, so Royce poured himself three fingers from a bottle of Glenfiddich 21 Year. "My uncle's favorite," he said as he lifted the glass. "Couldn't drink this when I was married. The ex was always on my ass about the cost."

"How long have you been divorced?"

"Six months."

"Seems like you're making up for lost time."

"Trying my damnedest," Royce said.

"Did you have your phone with you Saturday night?"

"I did, but I left it at Smiling Jack's when I hooked up with the redhead. Good thing one of my coworkers picked it up and returned it to me this morning. I was going crazy without it."

"This redhead, you remember anything else about her?"

"Nothing much, really—" He suddenly stood and led the two detectives into his bedroom and pulled back the covers of his unmade bed.

"Here," he said as he picked up an eight-inch-long hair and held it out to them. "Red. I told you she was a redhead."

"What do you want us to do with that, run a DNA test?"

"Sure, why not, maybe you can find the woman who took my money."

Mitchell retrieved an evidence bag from her pocket and let Royce drop the hair into it. Then she waited as he plucked several more of various lengths and added them to the bag.

A few minutes later, after they left Royce's apartment, Highlander nodded toward the evidence bag in Mitchell's hand. "Why'd you do that?"

"She's his alibi."

"You take a good look at that bedroom? I don't think he's washed the sheets in weeks, we've no idea how long that hair's been there, and at least two of them are blond with dark roots."

On the return trip to the office, Highlander asked Mitchell what kind of car Andy Royce drove. She thumbed through her notes and replied, "A three-year-old Equinox."

He didn't ask anything else, and when they were back at their desks, Highlander and Mitchell split the list of Widowers' Club members, calling each in turn and learning little more than what Highlander had already learned from the club president. Dunnett had been well-liked by his fellow members, had suffered his wife's loss with stoicism, and had not often had good things to say about his nephews.

Highlander's last call was to Joseph Ford, Esq., senior partner at Ford, Ford, Cowley, and Smith, LLC, the attorney who recommended Dunnett for membership in the Widowers' Club. When Highlander finally worked his way through the labyrinth of underlings and actually had Ford on the other end of the line, the attorney said, "I'd rather not discuss this on the phone."

They agreed to meet later that day. As soon as Highlander arrived at the law firm, he was escorted by Ford's personal assistant past several open areas populated mostly by women of various sizes, shapes, and hair colors, and then through her office to Ford's corner office. The office was large enough that Highlander could envision playing half-court basketball if the furniture and bookshelves were removed.

Ford had a full head of gray hair and wore a bespoke blue pin-stripe suit over a crisp white shirt and a black bow tie decorated with images of classic cars. He rose from behind his desk and met High-lander halfway, offering a warm greeting and a firm handshake.

At the end of the office opposite Ford's desk were a leather couch and two easy chairs arranged around a coffee table. Ford offered Highlander the couch and then settled onto one of the chairs. Though the two men were of similar height, Highlander found himself sinking into the couch and looking up at the attorney. They shared a few pleasantries before the conversation shifted to the dead man.

"Hugh was more than a client," Ford explained. "He was also a friend. We met more than thirty years ago, at a charity event our wives helped organize. He and Daisy were quite supportive after Tina passed away, and so I felt it only appropriate to reach out to Hugh when the Widowers' Club had an opening."

"What was his reaction when she died?"

"Devastated. He was devastated when his wife passed—his wife and his sister-in-law—and blamed himself for Daisy's death. More than once he said the accident never would have happened if he'd been driving."

"Why's that?" Highlander asked.

"Their car's accelerator stuck," Ford said. "He thought he could have handled the problem if he'd been driving."

Highlander considered that for a moment and then said, "I have a few more questions."

"You realize much of what you might want to ask is covered by attorney-client confidentiality."

"I do," Highlander said. "I just want to ask about his relation-ship with his nephews."

"You think one of the Royce boys killed him?" Ford asked. He considered that for a moment. "I suppose it's possible, but that would be like killing the chicken to eat one meal rather than eating the eggs every day."

"Why's that?"

"He was helping all of them in one way or another. The firm handled Larry's divorce, and Hugh paid the attorney fees. He's been helping with Andy's wife's medical bills, and he loaned Gary a tidy sum to keep his shop afloat. You may have seen the old station wagon in Hugh's garage—"

"The Nomad?"

Ford nodded. "That's collateral for the loan."

"And who handled his sister-in-law's estate?"

"We did. Rose died intestate and her sons stripped her place of everything of value before we had a chance to do an inventory and appraisal."

"So what happens now?"

"I'm not looking forward to the reading of the will," Ford said. "I don't think any of Hugh's nephews will be happy with what they hear."

"How's that?"

"It all goes into a trust with annual disbursements to each of them."

After Highlander returned to the station, he and his new partner discussed Dunnett's three nephews.

"They all have financial problems," Mitchell said.

"We suspected as much from what Agnes Quinn and Arnold Weatherby told us."

"Their mother's death postponed the inevitable," Mitchell said. "Between her life insurance and the proceeds from her estate, they each cleared about a hundred grand. Andy paid off medical bills and Gary kept his business open for another year. Larry lost half of his to his ex-wife, and he's drinking and screwing his way through the rest."

"You think any of those is a good reason to kill their uncle?"

Mitchell shrugged.

"So, what do we know about his wife's death?"

Michell told Highlander what she had learned about the traffic accident that killed Daisy Dunnett and her sister, Rose. "Daisy drove an older model Toyota—well maintained, low mileage—and it appears the accelerator stuck. She lost control and drove into a bridge abutment. Both women died at the scene."

"I thought Toyota had issued a recall to fix that problem."

"They had," Mitchell said, "and there were maintenance records that indicated the Dunnetts' vehicle had the recall work done. Still, maybe the repair work was sloppy."

"Anything in the report to suggest that?"

Mitchell shook her head, and Highlander only caught the motion out of the corner of his eye. "The accident happened over in Skittlebrough County, the investigating officer chalked it up as an accident, and the insurance companies paid the life insurance policies without raising a fuss."

"How much?"

"Dunnett collected a million for his wife. The Royce brothers split a hundred and fifty thousand between them."

Detective Mitchell was already at her desk when Highlander arrived Tuesday morning. Before he could sit down, she said, "You won't believe what came in last night."

"A confession?"

"A thirty-eight," she said. "A couple of kids found it below the Finster Creek Bridge, about seven miles from the Dunnett place. It looks like the killer tried to throw it into the water and missed. The kids found it on one of the bridge's concrete piers. Forensics has had it overnight."

"And?"

"The only prints they were able to lift belonged to the boys who found it, and they plan to test fire it later this morning to see if the bullet striations match the bullet pulled out of Mr. Dunnett," she said with a smile. "But here's the kicker: the gun is registered to Rose Royce, Mr. Dunnett's deceased sister-in-law."

They spent the rest of the morning on the phone tracking down everything they could about the three brothers' whereabouts early Sunday morning.

"I asked Doc Pritchard about Stella Royce's medical condition," Mitchell said. "Wet macular degeneration can be quite serious.

It apparently struck her at a younger age than usual, but she's female with light skin and light-colored eyes, all of which put her at high risk."

"That explains his need for a second job," Highlander said. "What else did you learn about him?"

"I talked to the payroll supervisor over at Cumberland," Mitchell said. "They say Andy Royce clocked in at 1:04, 1:59, and 3:02, but the system is old and never properly accounts for the time change."

Highlander tracked down several classic-car customizers, all of whom claimed they knew Gary Royce and all of whom attested to his presence at the after-party. While Highlander was on the phone with one of them, Billy Wentzman stepped up to his cubicle and listened in.

After Highlander completed his conversation and disconnected, Wentzman said, "One of the dead guy's nephews is Gary Royce?" He shook his head. "Small world."

"Do you remember seeing him at the car show?"

"Several times. He'd entered two complete restorations and three custom jobs. He didn't win a thing."

"What about the after-party?"

"Not right away. He came in late."

"What time?"

Wentzman unconsciously glanced at his Fitbit. "About one fifteen," he said. "I remember because he asked me for the time. He said he left his cell phone at his office."

"And you're certain he never left the party?"

"Well, not until three. That's when everything wrapped up and we all headed out."

After Wentzman walked away, Highlander called some of the party attendees he had already spoken to and asked what kind of watches they wore.

Highlander visited the printing company that employed Larry Royce and spoke with the three coworkers who had accompanied him for a night of drinking. They all told the same story. They went barhopping Saturday night, and they lost track of Larry at Smiling Jack's. None of them remembered him leaving with a redhead, but they said they wouldn't put it past him.

"I turned around and Larry was gone," one said. "I realized he'd forgotten his phone, and I couldn't just leave it on the bar when we moved on, so I took it with me. I gave it back to him Monday morning."

A redhead entered the printing plant as Highlander was leaving, and he watched her for a moment. He realized he'd noticed more redheads than usual—at the printing plant, at the law firm, and even at the grocery store the previous evening when he stopped for milk and Frosted Flakes.

Highlander and Mitchell took over one of the station's conference rooms, spread out everything from the Dunnett murder book, and began tying the pieces together. They started with the crime scene and the report from the forensics team that had gone over it.

A report from the security company indicated that someone had entered Dunnett's home through the garage at 1:30. Someone else entered through the kitchen door at 1:50, and no one else entered until the cook's arrival at 10:17 A.M. Forensics found Dunnett's fingerprints on the front and garage keypads. The only identifiable prints on the kitchen keypad belonged to the cook.

"I don't think anyone staged the clock," Mitchell said. "The only prints on it belong to the deceased, so it must have broken when he fell."

"So the killer comes in, shoots Dunnett, and leaves. Why?"

"Simple," Mitchell said. "Money. What if it wasn't the killer's first attempt? What if the accident that killed Daisy Dunnett and Rose Royce wasn't an accident?"

"Meaning?"

"What if the accident was intended to kill Hugh Dunnett?" Mitchell said. "All three of his nephews needed the money just as much then as now. What they received after their mother's death only postponed things. It bought them a little time, and when they cleaned out their mother's house after her death, one of them found her revolver."

The next morning, Highlander phoned Joseph Ford, Esq., and asked when he planned to hold the reading of the will. After hearing Ford's response, Highlander asked if he and his partner could be present.

"You think this will help you identify Hugh's killer?"

"I'm betting on it," the detective said. "We'll join you this afternoon."

After Highlander ended the call, Mitchell asked, "You feel confident with your conclusion?"

"If I'm right, we'll be eating a steak dinner tonight."

"Why's that?"

"Tradition," Highlander explained. "Every time Wilcox and I wrapped up a homicide, we took our wives out for a steak dinner."

"I don't have a wife."

"Boyfriend?" Highlander asked. "Girlfriend?"

Mitchell shook her head.

"Then it'll just be the three of us. I suspect my wife is eager to meet you. She likes to know who has my back."

They cleared off the conference table, reassembled the murder book, and had just enough time to stop for a quick lunch at Smiling Jack's Bar & Grill. When they reached the law offices of Ford, Ford, Cowley, and Smith, LLC, Joseph Ford's assistant met them at the front desk and led them back to his office. Seated on the leather couch and the easy chairs surrounding the coffee table were the attorney, the three Royce brothers, and Andy Royce's wife.

"This is who we were waiting for?" Larry asked.

"I'm afraid it is," Ford answered.

"Who is it?" Andy's wife asked.

"The two detectives investigating Uncle Hugh's murder."

"So, what do you want?" Gary asked.

Highlander looked at each of the brothers in turn before he began. "Your uncle was likely killed for his money and the three of you have been the primary suspects almost from the moment we found the body. You all need the money—or want it. Andy's wife's medical bills are bleeding him dry. Gary's business is floundering. And Larry is trying to live the high life despite losing half his assets when he divorced."

"Tell us something we don't know," Gary said.

"Each of you had means, motive, and opportunity," Highlander said. "Your uncle was shot with your mother's gun."

"Mom had a gun?" Andy sat up straight and turned to his brothers. "Did you know that?"

Highlander continued as if Andy hadn't spoken. "Any one of you could have taken it at any time before or after her death. And each of you had an opportunity, but that's what had us stumped."

Larry snorted.

"Here's what I think," Highlander said. "Your uncle came home from his meeting of the Widowers' Club. He fixed himself a drink and settled into the easy chair. It was the first Sunday of November and shortly before two o'clock he realized daylight saving time was about to end. He reset his watch and then walked to the fireplace. What we don't know is if he turned the clock back or not. Either way, someone entered the house and shot him in the back."

"Who?" Andy asked.

"Someone who knew the security system's access code—but you all did, didn't you?"

Highlander looked at Andy. "Let's start with you," he said. "You work overnight at Cumberland's, and you punch a clock each hour. We checked with your employer, and you punched in at 1:04, 1:59, and 3:02, but the system doesn't account for the time change. So, one minute after you punched in at 1:59, the clock jumped back to 1:00 and you didn't have to punch in again until 3:00. You had a two-hour window in which you could have driven to your uncle's home, shot him, and returned to the plant."

His wife clutched his arm. "Andy?"

"And Larry," Highlander continued. "We haven't seen hide nor hair of Lucy, Lucille, Lucinda—well, actually, I guess we have seen the hair of the redhead you claimed you were with that night."

"She cost me fifty-seven dollars."

"If she actually exists, she might have made a good alibi," Highlander said, "but she might also have been created out of thin air."

"No," Larry protested. "I know her from somewhere. I just can't remember where. If I could remember, I'd tell you."

Ford stood, walked to the office door, and whispered something to his assistant sitting just outside the door.

Highlander turned to Gary Royce. "You have the best alibi of all," he said. "Several people recall seeing you or talking with you at the Rods & Broads show and at the after-party. There's a gap of several hours between when you returned to your shop and when you arrived at the after-party. Still, based on the timeline we put together talking to the other people at the party, there's no way you could have established your presence at the party at one fifteen, then left the party, killed your uncle, and returned, unless—"

The door opened and everyone turned to look at the redhead who stepped through the open doorway. Larry sat up straight. "Lucy?"

"Lucille," she corrected.

"I knew I knew you from somewhere."

Highlander looked at Ford.

"Lucille is one of our paralegals," he said. "She worked on Mr. Royce's divorce."

"Were you with Larry Royce last Saturday night?"

She looked at Ford for guidance.

"Tell the truth, Lucille," he said. "This is a murder investigation."

Lucille's eyes grew wide. "A murder—? We met at Smiling Jack's, had a drink, and went back to his place around one. I left at six.

"Why'd you take money from my wallet?"

"Cab fare," Lucille said. "I don't have an Uber account."

"Cabs take credit cards."

Highlander interrupted them. "I'll let you two sort things out later. Right now we have something more important to deal with."

Everyone returned their attention to Highlander. "This wasn't the first attempt on your uncle's life," he said. "That was a year ago. The accident that killed your mother and your aunt was intended to kill your aunt and your uncle. Your uncle's car was tampered with, but he couldn't make the trip and your mother was a last-minute substitution."

The three brothers sat silently, at least two of them pondering which of the other two might have killed their mother.

"That's why we looked for anything that tied the two events together, other than the use of your mother's revolver. That connection was automobiles. We could go through the effort to get subpoenas to see where all of your cars were that night, but that would only help us with the two that have OnStar—Andy's Equinox and Larry's Corvette." Highlander turned to Gary. "It doesn't help us with your car, Gary. That Bel Air you tried to sell me is beautiful—and too old for a built-in tracking system. Though any of you might have the skill to tamper with the accelerator on your aunt and uncle's car, you're the only one who modifies cars for a living."

Andy and Larry turned to look at Gary.

"And one other thing, Gary," Highlander added. "You were the only one who worked hard to establish an alibi. When you asked the time at the Rods & Broads show after-party, you only asked people with digital watches—Fitbits and Apple watches that automatically update when the time changes. You killed your uncle before the time changed, and then you drove to the party, arriving after the time changed and seemingly before his murder occurred. That fact that your uncle's mantel clock broke when he dropped it was just good fortune. Or so it seemed."

Gary Royce pushed himself off the couch as if he were about to protest, but Detective Mitchell stepped up and snapped handcuffs on his wrists before he could.

"Gary Royce thought he could beat the clock."

Highlander, his wife, and his new partner were finishing dinner at the steak house where he and his former partner always celebrated the successful conclusion of a homicide case.

"Turns out the note was due on Dunnett's loan to Gary. Gary couldn't make the payment, and Dunnett had told him he wasn't going to extend it again. He was about to lose everything. Gary had taken his mother's revolver when he and his brothers were cleaning out their mother's home, and Sunday morning, he drove to his uncle's house. He hadn't expected Dunnett to still be awake, but that didn't stop him."

"He's as tall as you. So, why did the bullet enter so low?"

"Gary carried the revolver hanging at the end of his arm, hidden behind his thigh. As he was raising it, he pulled the trigger."

Linda looked at her husband's new partner. "So, how'd Jessica do?"

"She did fine," Highlander said.

Jessica smiled at her partner's wife. "I still have a lot to learn."

Highlander's cell phone rang and he unclipped it from its holster. He checked the number of the incoming call before answering. After identifying himself, he heard, "We got us a body."

He noted the address, returned his cell phone to its holster, and pointed to Mitchell's half-eaten sirloin. "Finish quick. It's time for another lesson."

Much of my crime fiction falls into the subgenres of hardboiled, noir, and private eye, but for the past handful of years I've been branching out into other subgenres. A while back, my occasional cowriter, Sandra Murphy, and I were batting around ideas for a locked-room mystery in response to a call for submissions from anthologist Maxim Jakubowski. I wanted to play with time but we could not find a way to make the concept work within the structure of a locked-room mystery. Instead, we wrote a story that involved a peanut allergy and an HVAC system.

Still, the concept behind "Beat the Clock" continued to nag at me until I realized it was ideal for a subgenre I'd never previously written: a traditional murder mystery in which the detective gathers evidence by interviewing all the suspects and then brings them together at the end to describe his investigation and to reveal the killer. I tossed in a bit of modern technology—without which the story doesn't work—gave Detective Robert Highlander a spouse and a new partner, and put him to work solving the murder of Hugh Dunnett.

Because expanding my writing into previously unfamiliar crime fiction subgenres has worked out so well, I hope to continue. Now, let's see, which subgenres haven't I tried . . . ?

Fleur Bradley *is the author of* Daybreak on Raven Island *and* Midnight at the Barclay Hotel *(Viking/PRH), the Double Vision trilogy (Harper-Collins), as well as numerous short stories. Her work has been nominated for the Agatha and Anthony Award and has won the Colorado Book Award, among others.*

As an author of mysteries for kids, Bradley is also a literacy advocate and speaks at events on how to reach reluctant readers. Originally from the Netherlands, Bradley lives in a small cottage in the foothills of the Colorado Rockies. You can find Bradley online at fleurbradley.com.

HOW TO TEACH YOURSELF TO SWIM

Fleur Bradley

There was a knock on the door at eleven o'clock Friday night. Sam wasn't going to answer, but at least he could look through the peephole. It was low, on account of his wife Moira's short stature. So Sam had to bend down to look.

It took him a second to realize he was looking right at someone's eyeball. A green eye, with a slightly bloodshot white.

Sam was about to leave the door unanswered when the person stepped back. It was a kid, skinny in a dirty white tank top and shorts that were too big on him. Blond hair over his ears. The boy was maybe eight from the looks of him, but Sam knew he was actually twelve. This was his grandson, Finn.

Sam still thought about not opening the door—his daughter Abby stood right next to Finn and Abby was nothing but trouble. It wasn't a nice thing to say about your own daughter, he knew that. But it was the truth. Sam stood there, feeling the Florida heat ooze in from the other side.

"Dad?" Abby called.

"All right," he muttered, then reached for the doorknob.

Once he opened the door, Abby rolled in like a tsunami. "It's hotter than hell out there," she said by way of greeting. She hit Sam in the leg with a large duffel bag.

The boy stood on the doorstep, like he was waiting for permission. The last time Sam had seen the kid was at Moira's funeral, five years ago. Finn had been rounder, healthier then.

Sam remembered how well-behaved the kid was. How he'd dropped a dandelion on Moira's grave.

"Hi Finn," Sam said. "Why don't you come inside? We're cooling all of Florida this way."

Keep in mind that all drowning persons are maniacs.
Avoid coming within their grasp.

"I'm not hot," Finn said but he came inside. Of course he wasn't hot—the kid didn't have an ounce of fat on him.

Sam felt like he'd lost something already, just letting them flood his space. He was happy alone. Plus, Abby was prone to thievery, depending on where she was on the ladder of recovery.

Moira's ghost just looked at Abby with love, which made the whole thing worse somehow. They had never agreed on how to deal with their daughter when Moira was still alive, so it made sense to Sam that his dead wife would still think Abby could do no harm. Only Moira couldn't talk these days, so she said everything with her eyes. Like Sam needed reminding.

Sam found Abby in the kitchen with a can of beer (his last) pressed to her forehead.

She popped the beer. Finn was already sitting at the table, quiet as a mouse. Sam still stood, feeling like he needed to keep some distance from the whole scene. "How are you, Abigail?" he asked, knowing she hated her full name.

She sighed and took a long sip of beer. At least it was clear where she was with her recovery. About rung number four on the ladder, Sam figured. And slipping.

That's when Sam saw the bruises, large ones in various stages of healing. Some obviously fingers that had clamped around her neck, her arms. Abby took another sip of beer and started crying.

Sam looked for Moira, but she was no good to him here. Moira was a ghost, couldn't talk, so Sam mostly muttered to her (something he couldn't do now). Finn seemed undisturbed by the scene that was unfolding.

"Are you thirsty, Finn?" Sam asked. He opened the fridge, hoping there was something kid-friendly in there. "I have milk."

Abby wiped her eyes and shook her head, then downed the last of her beer. Sam tried not to be irritated. That was a good beer, an IPA he picked up for special occasions only. She was drinking it like it was the cheap gas station stuff. "No milk. Gives him the runs."

Finn shrugged and smiled as if to say, *whatcha gonna do?*

"Just give him some water," Abby said. She threw out her can of beer and sighed. "I'm going to take our stuff back to my room." She looked tired. Drunk, a little.

Sam felt a familiar sense of dread. Drunk Abby wasn't even the worst of it. It was High Abby he worried about. That was rung number two, slipping to number one if things got really bad. Sam still regretted opening the door.

"Your old room's my office now. Just take the guest room," Sam said.

Abby looked incredulous. "You got rid of my stuff?" Like she was here every week. Like she hadn't been gone for over a decade, couch surfing, living out of that duffel bag. But he thought she'd been okay, sort of. With this new guy who'd come to the funeral. Dave, or Dan, or something. A guy who did boat tours for tourists, in Daytona Beach. "Your things are just boxed up, in the attic," Sam said. "I needed work space."

Abby didn't say anything else but took the duffel and disappeared down the hall.

Leaving Sam with the boy. Finn scratched his side absentmindedly. He could probably use a shower, Sam thought. The boy had gotten himself a glass of water, like he was already at home. The kid needed a burger. Or more like five.

Sam sat down at the kitchen table, next to Moira, who had taken Abby's spot. "You want to join your mom?" Sam asked.

"She's going to sleep. For a long time," Finn added, sipping his water. "She always does after a fight and beer."

Sam nodded. Moira's face was sad now. She was going to cry next—Sam could see it coming. "When was the last time you ate?" he asked and stood.

"Cereal, this morning. With soy milk." Finn didn't seem to know he was supposed to have more to eat than that. Especially considering his tiny stature. Abby was lucky Social Services hadn't taken the kid away yet.

Sam opened the freezer. "I started this thing where I cook lots of meals in one go. It's called meal prep." He lifted a few containers and said, "I got chicken parmigiana, lasagna, steak stir-fry, spaghetti Bolognese . . ."

Finn looked unsure.

"You'll like the spaghetti, I bet—it's my favorite." Sam took the container out and put it in the microwave. When it beeped, Sam put in another Bolognese. And a few minutes later, they both sat at the table, eating spaghetti at midnight. It was peaceful.

Finn ate in silence, finishing the whole thing. Then he said softly, "That was the best meal I ever had."

To the average person the art of swimming is shrouded in mystery.

It was six the next morning when Sam got up—he always woke at the same time, no matter how late he went to bed. Sam made coffee for two. Abby could use some sobering up once she got out of bed, he figured.

It wasn't until the pot was done brewing that he heard someone move around. In his office.

Clutching his mug of coffee, Sam found Finn. The boy was browsing the book titles, hands behind his back, careful not to touch any of them.

Sam was a book dealer of sorts, on the side. He would buy old books, ones he knew he could get a buck for, and then he sold them on the internet. It was a nice bit of extra cash, with Social Security being what it was, and his pension not quite stretching along with inflation. The book selling kept him afloat.

"You have a lot of books," Finn said softly. "What are these?" He pointed to the stack of tiny books, leaflets almost.

"They're called Little Blue Books. People would buy them long ago for a nickel, to learn a new skill or a language or what have you." Sam stepped closer and picked one up. The valuable ones were in plastic sleeves because the paper was almost a hundred years old. It could turn to dust right in your hands. "Is your mom still asleep?"

Finn nodded.

Sam had planned to do a yard sale run, see what was out there. It was how he found his books. And he couldn't very well leave the kid behind.

So Sam said, "Are you up for a little expedition, Finn?"

The three great secrets of proper swimming are confidence, correct breathing and relaxation.

They had breakfast. Then Sam helped the kid find a cleanish shirt, and they both got into the car. It was Moira's; Sam liked driving it because the ghost of her would be guaranteed to tag along. Moira was in the back. It wasn't too hot yet, but the humidity already clung to Sam like a wet blanket.

The kid got into the passenger seat and for a moment Sam considered asking him if he still needed a car seat. But then he thought better of it. It would probably embarrass Finn—Sam had been on the smaller side himself at that age. "Your growth spurt will come," he told Finn as he backed out of the garage.

It was eight in the morning by the time they hit Sam's favorite neighborhood. It was in an older, more established section of town with mature trees and cul-de-sacs, like harbors in the sea.

There was a neighborhood-wide yard sale happening and Sam wanted to get there early. He parked the car, then he and the boy browsed everyone's wares. Finn walked with his hands behind his back, looking like an old man as he let his eyes run over the bric-a-brac, old furniture, and piles of clothing. Sam did his own browsing but kept an eye on the boy.

A few stops in, Finn called out and raised an arm, like he was asking for permission to speak. "Grandpa!"

Sam walked over. "What, Finn?"

The boy pointed to a big box full of Little Blue Books.

Now, that was a good find.

On the very top of the stacks of little books, there was an almost-perfect condition Little Blue Book, number 1206: *How to Teach Yourself to Swim*.

Finn reached out, but then thought better of it.

Sam negotiated for the box, then handed the boy the booklet. Finn smiled and held it like it was a prize.

They bought a few more books and some barely worn T-shirts and shorts that were Finn's size.

They headed home with their purchases. Sam wanted to ask Finn if he could swim, but then realized that, too, might be a sensitive subject. So they drove in silence.

The boy was growing on Sam.

Keep legs together, knees straight, and toes pointed well back.

Abby was awake—very much so. Clean and sobered up, she was cleaning the kitchen and smiled as they came in. "Good hunting?"

Finn nodded and took off to the guest room.

Sam put the boxes in the office to be inventoried later and went back to the kitchen.

"I have an interview," Abby told Sam as he surveyed the fridge for sandwich ingredients. "In an hour."

"That's great." Sam mustered up a smile. Moira wasn't around—he could've used the support right now.

"At the Quick Save, down the road. It isn't much, but it's a paycheck." Abby smiled, uncertain. Her hands had a slight tremor—the addict's dead giveaway. Sam knew it well. She said softly, "Eventually, Finn and I can move out on our own."

Sam nodded. They still hadn't talked about the proverbial elephant in the room: her burly boyfriend whose name Sam couldn't remember, the one with strong fingers. Abby had covered up the bruises with makeup. She was good at it, too. Experienced, Sam thought.

"I'm not going back to Doug. Not this time," Abby said. Her eyes were welling up and she dabbed at them with a paper towel. "He's going to kill me."

This had occurred to Sam as well. He missed Moira—she would know just what to say and do. "Has he hurt the boy?" Sam asked softly.

Abby shook her head, but Sam could spot an Abby lie. He tried not to imagine that burly piece-of-something Doug, hitting Finn.

"What about the other stuff? Are you just drinking, or . . . ?" He let the words hang in the air. Tried not to remember the violence Abby had once inflicted against Moira, the stealing, the time she wrapped his car (a perfectly good minivan, great for hauling) around a lamp post. Then there was the rehab. It had taken them years to pay off the debt on three stints at Peaceful Acres. Not that it did any good.

"God, Dad," Abby said, tossing the paper towel on the counter. "It's always about that with you, isn't it?" She stormed away, slamming the door to the guest room.

Sam sighed. Then he thought about Finn and the Little Blue Book.

> *The big bugaboo that the prospective swimmer must over-come is the fear of water.*

They'd bought the house because Moira liked the walking trails, and the community center that had yoga classes, even a doctor who took patients, and a hairdresser who came once a week. Sam hated it now—the HOA fees were almost two hundred dollars a month, money he could be spending on food or good beer on occasions other than just holidays.

But the community center had a pool. So that Sunday he took Finn, after the boy dug a pair of faded swimming trunks from the bottom of that duffel bag. They both stood at the pool's edge now.

"Have you had lessons, Finn?" Sam asked the boy.

Finn nodded at first, unsure. But then he gazed at the glimmering water and shook his head, just the once. You couldn't very well live on the Florida coast and not know how to swim, Sam thought. It was downright dangerous.

Sam stepped in at the shallow part. The pool was of the wading variety on this side; if you walked to the other end, there was a deep section of the pool for swimming laps. There were several people who Sam had seen around the neighborhood. Moira would know their names but Sam never bothered.

He said to Finn, "We'll stay where we can touch the bottom, see?" The boy nodded but stood frozen. Terrified.

"Come on, Finn." Sam looked to Moira, who tried to take Finn's hand but just caught air. But then that's the bugger about not being alive anymore. So Sam reached out.

Finn clutched Sam's hand, with sweaty fingers that clamped on his like a crab.

"You can do it," Sam said, hoping he sounded encouraging.

Finn stepped forward, one foot in front of the other. As he got closer, Sam could see the bruises, still red and screaming, on the boy's bony shoulders. Was it that Doug character who had done this to Finn, just as he had done to Abby?

Sam forced himself to focus on the water, wading in until Finn was up to his waist.

"Have you ever floated, Finn?" he asked. Sam was worried his neighbors might see the bruises on the kid and think it was Sam's doing.

Finn shook his head. He was still looking at the water like it might swallow him whole.

"You can lay back, see?" Sam got in the water and showed the boy how you could float. It was his favorite thing to do, back when Moira would come for her water aerobics and he would tag along. The water made everything quiet.

But Finn wasn't having it. He shook his head.

"Maybe next time," Sam said as he stood back up, realizing that perhaps he was in over his head here.

Sam had a swift memory right then, like a splash of water in his face. He'd been here once with Abby, when she was young and he was trying to give Moira a break. He'd taken Abby (while he was three sheets to the wind, at least) for her first swimming lesson. It had been a disaster, Abby refusing to get in the water. Screaming, *I'm never coming back here again.*

Now, Sam and Finn stood there a while longer, Sam with the water to his knees and the boy to his waist, watching the other (mostly old) people go about their swimming.

After some time, Finn pulled Sam's hand, just a little. "He throws me in, clothes and all," the boy said softly. "Out in the ocean. Into the dark water."

Never dive with your coat on.

Abby didn't get the job. Sam imagined it might have something to do with her criminal record. She was drinking when they got home—whiskey, straight from the bottle. It was his good stuff, the drink he'd been saving for when Moira was supposed to be in remission. Of course, that had never happened.

Finn went right back to the guest room. The kid probably knew better than to stick around for one of these episodes.

The house phone rang. Sam still had a landline—just never got rid of it, even though Moira had kept telling him no one called people at home anymore, back when she was still alive.

"Don't answer that," Abby said, slurring her words. "It's Doug."

Sam picked up anyway. "Put her on," the voice demanded. Doug, thinking he owned everyone. Sam put the horn down with shaking hands, reminded of the bruises on Finn. When it rang again, Sam yanked the cord from the wall.

Finn stood out in the hall, holding his wet swimming trunks.

"Let's wash our stuff," Sam said to him and took the boy out to the garage where the washing machine was.

By the time they got back to the kitchen, Abby was gone.

"She's sleeping again," Finn said.

Don't hold yourself stiff or tense.

Sam spent the rest of the day cataloguing his book haul and by dinner time, Finn was taking two plastic meal containers from the freezer.

"Is your mom not joining us?" Sam asked as he watched the boy operate the microwave.

"She went out," Finn said. "Looking for jobs."

Sam nodded, but that feeling of dread had now set up camp permanently, like a tidal wave sloshing deep in his gut. The dinner (stir-fry this time) gave him heartburn, just like food used to when Abby was at her worst.

Moira was crying at the kitchen table.

Remember that the more you relax the easier it is for you to swim.

Sam decided to take the boy to the community center early on Monday. Why not, Sam thought. At the rate things were going, Finn and Abby would be living with him for a while. Plenty of time to teach the kid to swim.

They stood at the edge of the pool again, staring at the water. Moira was off in the deep end, doing her water aerobics with the class. Not helpful.

After some time, Sam asked, "Would he take you out on the boat?"

Finn nodded. "He said he had to branch out."

Whatever that meant, Sam thought, but he had a suspicion.

"Why would he throw you in?" Sam asked, regretting it immediately. Traumatizing the boy here by the pool was the last thing he needed to be doing.

But Finn said, matter-of-fact, "He does it for fun."

Sadistic bastard. Sam was about to step out of the pool, deciding perhaps this was a bad idea. But then the kid stepped forward.

Finn said, "Fridays are for transport. Then we go out on the boat at night, into the black water."

Sam could guess what they were transporting in the night. Most likely, Doug was using his boat to make some real money. Getting the stuff Abby liked to snort and inject.

Finn said softly, "It's a secret. While we wait to meet the men on the other boat, they laugh and drink. And then they throw me in the water. They count how long I last."

"Who is this *they?*"

"Mom and Doug."

Always remember to take a good deep breath before each dive.

Abby slept the Monday morning away then left around three to go to work. Apparently, she'd gotten a job at a bar.

Not a great situation for an alcoholic and an addict, but at least she was away from Finn.

It was a good thing Abby was gone. Sam was seething, distracting himself with packaging his most recent sales for shipping.

He took the boy to the post office later that day. The kid was thumbing through his Little Blue Book, the paper chipping at the edges.

"*Confidence is seventy-five percent of the art of swimming,*" Finn read. "It says so, right in here."

Sam wondered what the other twenty-five percent was.

Keep your body tense until the dive is completed.

They went to the pool again the next day, their swimming trunks still damp at the waist from the day before. This time, Finn walked ahead into the water until it got to his middle.

"Way to go, kid!" one of Sam's neighbors called from the deep end. "Teaching your grandson to swim, are you Sam?" the guy asked.

Sam couldn't remember the man's name but did vaguely recall a conversation they'd had at one of the community barbecues. Back when Moira was still alive. The man was a retired cop, Sam knew. Better keep him far away, lest he saw the yellowing bruises on Finn. Sam answered, "Yes, working on it!"

Finn gave the man a thumbs-up, though he still just stood there.

Then Sam remembered where he also recognized the cop-man from: his AA meetings. The ones he didn't go to anymore.

He kept the smile pasted on his face and slowly looked away, running his fingers through the water.

> *Can't you feel yourself floating to the surface, how the water is LIFTING YOU?*

Abby came home after midnight, smelling of beer and that familiar bar stink. Sam had spent a good chunk of her formative years in places just like it. Leaving Moira on her own to raise a strong-willed and moody daughter.

Even back then, he knew it was wrong to be hanging out at the bar after work when Moira needed him. But feeling the alcohol—first beer, then scotch—flood his system was all Sam could do to make it through the day. Drowning his feelings.

Maybe this was his penance, Sam thought to himself as he made a grocery list that Tuesday afternoon. After twenty years of Sam's absence, Moira'd had enough. Just months before her diagnosis, she'd threatened to leave Sam. Over the drinking, the absent nature of him.

He went to AA so Moira would stay. Then there were the doctor visits, the chemo hell, and then nothing else seemed to matter. After the funeral, he'd tossed his one-year sober chip in the kitchen junk drawer.

Abby was long gone by then. Only visiting sporadically with little Finn in tow.

Now here Sam was, taking care of Finn while she was falling apart. But was it the drink, the drugs, the bad men like this Doug? Or was it Abby herself who was the bad news? What kind of person throws their kid in the ocean for entertainment?

Moira had never been able to see Abby for who she really was. When Sam was honest with himself, truly honest, he knew his daughter was the real bad news. Like father, like daughter. Beyond saving.

It was Wednesday when Abby came home during dinner, long before her shift would've been over.

"Well, I'm fired," she said, carrying a brown bag with a bottle of god-knows-what inside. "Stupid jerk, couldn't keep his hands off me."

Finn ate his lasagna without a word.

"Don't you have anything to say?" Abby shot at Sam.

He didn't. Sam was so tired of his own daughter that even dead Moira's pleading eyes couldn't get him to speak.

Abby huffed and left the kitchen. But not before she plugged the landline back into the wall.

Think this over. The water is LIFTING YOU!

Doug showed up on Thursday morning, right as Sam and Finn were heading to the community center. Sam watched the guy's outline through the tinted truck windows, from his rearview mirror, as Abby climbed into the souped-up vehicle.

They roared away. Finn didn't even look up from reading his little book.

At the pool, Finn walked into the water without hesitation. He started a breaststroke carefully, all on his own.

Well, I'll be damned, Sam thought.

After some time, Finn even let Sam hold him up while the boy floated and practiced his leg moves.

"It's so quiet underwater, Grandpa," the boy said afterward. "Like you're dead and in heaven."

Sam decided to take the kid for a walk that afternoon. Sure, it was the usual miserable Florida hot, but kids needed time outside. At least, that was what Moira used to say.

They ran into the man from the pool, the retired cop (and AA member) whose name Sam couldn't remember.

"Joining Grandparents Group, Sam?" the guy asked. His grin was big, full of dentures, and his hair perfectly styled and obviously recently cut. Probably at the community center hairdresser.

"Yes," the boy answered for Sam, with a sneaky smile. "Right, Grandpa?"

"Right," Sam answered.

As it turned out, Grandparents Group wasn't all bad. There were a couple of young assistant types in bright orange polo shirts with the neighborhood logo. They were doing crafts with the kids, while the adults chatted over iced tea. Moira would've loved it.

"It's a new thing they started here," his neighbor said. They both worked on writing their names on a sticker label with a marker. FRANK his said, so there was no more awkwardness over not knowing the man's name. The kids were making some sort of kite.

It wasn't bad. Sam mostly listened to FRANK (and later, ANNE and GEORGE) chatter on about grandparenting, and how it was bad to park kids in front of the TV.

"My daughter does it all the time," Anne said with a tone of disapproval.

Sam wondered what they'd think of throwing your kid into the ocean for fun.

They walked home close to dinner time, with Finn carefully cradling the kite he made.

"I'm going to hang it on the wall."

Sam nodded, enjoying the breeze that had decided to roll in.

"Is that okay, Grandpa?" Finn asked.

That's when Sam realized that the kid was planning to hang it on the guest room wall. His room.

Because the boy thought Sam's house was home.

Practice swimming in a suit of old clothes. This will accustom you to being burdened with unusual weight in the water.

Sam couldn't sleep that Thursday night. He tried to think of all the ways of explaining to the kid that this wasn't his home. That once his mom cleaned herself up and found a job (three rungs up the ladder of recovery, but still), they would be moving out.

When Sam made his coffee that Friday morning, almost a full week since he'd erroneously opened his door to Abby and Finn, he realized something was different. It was quiet.

No rustling of the boy, nor sound of Finn puttering around the kitchen. And no Moira, hanging around at a distance, like a buoy offshore.

Sam checked the guest room. The bed was tousled, but there was no duffel bag. No Abby.

No Finn.

Sam stopped breathing and held onto the doorframe like a life raft. Sam wanted a drink but knew there wasn't a goddamned drop in the house, not even his good remission-that-never-came whiskey.

He spent the day cleaning. Washing the sheets he took off the guest bed. Looking for Moira but knowing he wouldn't see her. She was with Finn.

The kite lay in the corner of the room, forgotten. Sam hung it right above the bed.

Fridays are for transport, Sam remembered Finn saying. They would go out to meet another boat, off the coast. *It's a secret.*

Sam made a phone call.

> *Every swimmer should be prepared to act as a lifesaver on a moment's notice.*

Sam picked Frank up and drove to Daytona Beach. Thankfully, Frank didn't mention AA. All Sam could think about was the kid in the deep, cold ocean water, trying to stay afloat, paddling with his small hands, too frail for a twelve-year-old.

Then Sam made a promise, to Moira's ghost and to himself. He would go to those meetings, keep away from all alcohol. He'd even go to Grandparents Group. Just let Finn be alive.

When Sam and Frank got there, they waited on the docks. Frank had made a few calls in the car, getting the Coast Guard moving. Now Sam paced, hands behind his back. Frank was talking to the cops on the docks, his hair mussed by the coastal wind, not once flashing his dentures.

Then the Coast Guard ship came back.

Finn was wrapped in a blue towel, shoulders stooped, all of fifty pounds soaking wet. No Abby.

One of the Coast Guard guys talked to Frank, then met Sam. "The boat was right where you said it was." He added in a low voice so that Finn couldn't hear, "Those assholes left the kid on his own, in the water. Good thing he's a strong swimmer."

Finn gave Sam a wet hug. "They tossed me in the water," Finn said, his voice hoarse as the paramedic checked him over. "And the other boat came. But then the grown-ups got into a fight and the other guys shot Doug. Then Mom jumped out of the boat."

Sam remembered a young, defiant Abby after her first swimming lesson. *I'm not going back.* He felt his blood go cold.

"I tried to teach Mom swimming, Grandpa. Like the little book said." Finn was crying, giant teardrops dripping down his cheeks, his chin. "But she was too scared. And too sleepy."

Sam swallowed. He thought of Abby, now dead somewhere in the depths of the ocean. With Moira.

"But I stayed hidden behind the boat," Finn said, wiping his cheeks. "And I swam, Grandpa. And then I floated for a while. Just like you taught me."

Sam gave him a sad smile. "Of course you did."

---

*I love old stuff and stumbled upon a small box of Little Blue Books at a flea market. They're pocket-sized booklets from the 1930s that are focused on teaching the (working-class) adult reader a new skill; Little Blue Book number 1206 is titled How to Teach Yourself to Swim. *The author was clearly getting lost in the joy of swimming in a lyrical and quirky way that just demanded to be part of a story. These rules for swimming made the perfect framework for me to explore redemption, and how (grand)parenting really brings out the worst—and best—in us.*

Like the Little Blue Book 1206, this story is an odd duck. I'm grateful to Dark Yonder *and this anthology for the recognition.*

Shelley Costa*'s work has been nominated for both the Edgar and Agatha Awards and has received a special mention for the Pushcart Prize. She is the author of several mystery novels; the first two titles in her new series,* No Mistaking Death *and* The Damages, *feature private investigator Marian Warner. Her short stories have appeared in* The Georgia Review, Alfred Hitchcock's Mystery Magazine, Odd Partners, Blood on Their Hands, The World's Finest Mystery and Crime Stories, Crimewave, The North American Review, *and* Cleveland Magazine. *Shelley holds a PhD in English from Case Western Reserve University, where she wrote her dissertation on suspense, and she went on to teach fiction writing at the Cleveland Institute of Art for many years. These days Costa teaches topics in American literature and literary modernism through the Siegal Lifelong Learning Program. When she isn't plotting murder, she swims laps, studies art history, and enjoys time with friends and family. www.shelleycosta.com*

THE KNIFE SHARPENER

Shelley Costa

GETTYSBURG
JUNE 30, 1863

He has a grindstone and a clubfoot. From what she can tell, the grindstone is easier to get around with than the foot. "Keeps me out of this fine mess, though," says the traveling knife sharpener, jerking his head in some indeterminate direction where apparently the fine mess is happening. Then he judges just how dull Mr. Purdy's cleaver is by bouncing his thumb lightly along it.

In the late June swelter of her orderly hometown with its whitewashed fences and lawful skies and fields, Tillie Pierce sizes up this knife sharpener hailing, as he calls it, from Hagerstown, where the folks have enough sense to hedge their bets. To emphasize his point, John Shafer gives the wheeled wooden frame of the grindstone a hefty tug, holds out a hand as though leading a lady onto the dance floor, and shy Mrs. Skylar hands him two pairs of her paper scissors for his inspection.

They line up. The barber, the tailor, three quilters with tiny scissors, the banker with the family turkey carving knife, even Jennie Wade, who comes up with some mismatched kitchen knives just to flirt with this traveling redheaded stranger from Maryland with a grindstone and a clubfoot. Soon it thunders. The knife sharpener hitches at his waistband, and then with his regular foot pumps the treadle and sets the dull blade of the cleaver against the spinning grindstone.

In a way, Tillie thinks, she is glad she is fifteen and has no tools to sharpen. Jennie Wade is twenty and really has no tools to sharpen either, only she likes to pretend she runs her married sister's household, just to show anyone interested what a domestic catch she is, her with her brown hair coiled like a rattler and her hands dotted with bits of dough that didn't make it into the final loaf.

"Who you like in the fight," calls out Jennie Wade's little brother Sam. A challenge to the knife sharpener. "I'll bet it's Johnny Reb." Someone cuffs Sam's head. Someone else shushes everyone in the general vicinity.

John Shafer doesn't even have to think about it. "I like the man who helped me and my tools into the back of his wagon and took me all the way to the bottom of your Taneytown Road." At that, there are murmurs. "That's who I like."

"You don't care about slaves or freemen?"

"Where can you find me some?"

"Slaves?" chirps Mr. Purdy, sliding a watery glance to the others. "Back in Hagerstown, I'm thinking."

"Freemen," says John Shafer, steadying himself on his clubfoot, shoed in a special sheath of hand-stitched leather. "I ain't seen one yet." Glancing the blade's edge against his tanned palm, he springs a sharp line of blood, gives it a look Tillie can't read, and then grins at his customers. "Not of any color, no sir." When the crowd falls silent, pondering philosophy in a knife sharpener, Tillie watches him grit his teeth and swing his leg outward to angle his clubfoot in the right direction. What follows then is a battery of small steps to balance himself. Then he presents the cleaver to Mr. Purdy with a dip of his red head. "That'll be ten cents, thank you kindly."

Just enough manners to get by, wondering, maybe, whether another fellow in a wagon will give him and his tools a ride to a place where folks need their knives sharpened for ten cents. When he bends to get a drink of water from a shiny tin can, Tillie swings her leg outward in the same arc, just to see what every single turn during every single waking moment must be like for this knife sharpener, and she gets tangled up in her skirts. Even a flurry of steps doesn't help her get her balance, and the tailor makes a grab for her arm. Jennie Wade rolls her eyes at the quilter Miss Cardwell with the thin, shapeless lips, as though they agree on just how impossible the Pierce girl is.

As John Shafer runs his forearm across his mouth, his blue eyes meet Tillie's, and he raises an eyebrow and shoots her a small smile. A better one than the big grin you show people when you want to convey no harm done, no matter what you really mean. In that moment, Tillie knows her skirts are her clubfoot. A clubfoot of cotton and muslin.

Dark clouds collide and raindrops spatter in the dry dust of the main street. The customers scatter, dashing from the kind of shower that quits in five minutes, offering shelter to the red-headed knife sharpener from Maryland, running with their dull knives slicing away the heavy air. Tillie watches him quickly fold up the frame, hoist the handles that pull the grindstone up on its wheel, and lurch awkwardly behind, thanking Mr. Purdy kindly for the offer of his barn for bedding down, nothing fancy.

"Can't you just leave the grindstone here?" In that way as head usher he shows worshippers into their pews on Sundays, Mr. Purdy gestures to the grass just off the dusty street.

"My stone stays with me," says the knife sharpener quietly.

Mr. Purdy tries again. "No one will bother it."

"My stone stays with me."

Done with talking sense to a tradesman from, really, Heaven knows where, Mr. Purdy picks up his pace. Hitching up her cotton and muslin handicap, Tillie trots alongside them, fielding the rushed conversations. The knife sharpener has a bedroll, yes, but no, there's no help for a clubfoot other than what he can do for himself, yes, he's about twenty-five, no, he didn't spot any Federals on his way into town, yes, it's a mystery what Lee's Army has in mind, no, never considered spying as an alternative form of service. Here John Shafer adds something about it not being his fight, nothing beyond keeping alive is his fight, the way he sees it. No, indeed, his heart doesn't rise near clean out of his chest with love for our boys in blue, nor for our boys in gray, neither.

She stops at the open gate in the picket fence at her yard. "Well," calls Tillie, "what does your heart rise near clean out of your chest for, then?" It would have to be interesting, more interesting than battles that only move around and never end.

The knife sharpener sets down the handles of the wheeled grindstone.

"Oh, now," says Jennie smoothly, "our Mr. Shafer can't afford to have his heart do that, not when there's work to be done, no help from the likes of you," she finishes in that mean, throwaway manner she has. Her coiled rattler hair is beginning to slip down the back of her head, and she tells our Mr. Shafer she'd bring him a fresh loaf of her best bread in the morning. But Tillie is looking at the knife sharpener. His face is turned toward the sky, watching, she thinks, for raindrops to clear the air, the dust, the hardships, the years, and nothing comes.

Then.

First come the armies.

Later, Rebel raiders thunder through the defenseless town, where people gawp at how goldarn free they make themselves with any unoffered food they can find already inside on dining tables.

Exactly what relation these threadbare, wild-haired skirmishers have to do with the fearsome Army of Northern Virginia, no one can say. At the Pierce house, they steal shoes, the hired boy, and the mare Tillie considers her very own. Her father, James Pierce, has had enough. Tillie always knows when he's had enough when he pushes up his shirtsleeves like the amateur scrapper he was in his life before marriage, family, Quaker meeting, and the Pierce's Choice Meats store. He stalks after the two villains whooping half-on half-off the mare with the hired boy tucked under the winchlike arms of one of them.

"See here! See here!" he demands in his magistrate's voice, grabbing the mare's mane while another raider brandishes a sorry-looking pistol and Tillie's mother staggers backwards. Tillie watches her father make a strong case for keeping what is theirs, and finally, these skirmishers must not have grown to manhood without some Bible verses tucked up somewhere under their wavy, dirty hair. They drop the hired boy in the dust, who scrambles away, terrified, and the thieves clamber off, admiring the stolen shoes on their lawless feet. Tillie's shoulders droop. So do her father's.

What they had really wanted back was the mare.

"The Flower of Dixie," jeers her father, watching the Rebel raiders take off up the main street. His gray eyes narrow, with that soft look she only ever sees when he is picturing their ancestors traveling into a wilderness with William Penn, when any of the tales that come down from cradle to cradle through the years all have large portions of danger and beauty. "We're in for it, my girl. Best to get you away."

Word comes, the way it always does.

Word comes from the dairyman that Buford's cavalry—three cheers!—is arriving.

Word comes from a Union camp photographer named Gardner that scouts place General Lee's Army north of Gettysburg. When a woman in the small crowd cries, well, what in God's Creation is he doing there, a man intones, "Harrisburg!" Tillie watches a chill sweep across the faces when a great, shared fear makes them shiver. "He's here. In the North. Oh, dear God," flies around the town in the same tone as the time the seventeen-year locusts were spotted, or a hired girl came down with tuberculosis. People scatter, some running for shelter from what they can't even imagine, others running toward the center of town where any sight worth viewing you can surely find there.

Down the dusty street comes John Shafer, wheeling his entire life in a trade barrow, his bedroll lashed across the handles, a hunk of Jennie Wade's best bread carried between his teeth. The air feels heavier than Tillie has ever known it. It swallows sounds—Buford's cavalry like an earthquake rumbling up the northside of town to the Cashtown Pike and the action—muffling everything she can see or hear like that brown dog barking up by the dry goods store, or the librarian hammering the shutters closed over that stately little building while she sobs and shakes her head. Tillie offers the knife sharpener a ride to the Weikert Farm, just three miles south, where they can be safe. Waving her on, John Shafer says he will catch up, thank you kindly. With skirmishers and gunfire nearby, and a three mile walk ahead of him, she really doesn't see how.

JULY 1

Overnight the Weikert barn is converted into a field hospital where in the daytime gloom Tillie sits patting a bloodstained bandaged wrist when she looks down and sees there are no fingers. The boy soldier winces, his lips moving, and she thinks maybe she's hurting him, so she moves the patting farther up the ruined arm, which is when she hears him call her Mother. One mattress over from this boy is an older soldier, not by much, the bedsheet flat where his leg ought to be, hoarse from wailing in pain. One mattress beyond that is the only place she can find silence as the man on it, with bandages on his head, around his chest, up and over his hip turn pink with blood that just wants to get the hell out of that poor wreck, dies before her eyes. With no one to sit with him and hold his hand and tell him he was ever so good and brave and patriotic.

She, Tillie, is just a useless girl with no important role to play. She can win no ground, turn back no foe, defend no line. She is tolerated courteously like she is performing a cross-hand piece on the parlor piano for dinner guests. Ladles of spring water are no help. Prayers and curses are no help. Only the killer sharp edges of John Shafer's work helps, as the field surgeons set about their gory jobs.

She sways as she stands up from the mattress of the fingerless boy soldier. "Mother—?" His other hand reaches for her, catches her skirts instead. Tillie bends, lays a palm on his cheek, feels the muscles trembling underneath. What she is suddenly remembering is the story her father once told her about how when he was twelve he pulled a little girl out of the way of the mail coach hell-bent on getting to Philadelphia by noon. In his experience, he told Tillie, the truest decisions are the ones made in an instant. Oh, there was going to be a calamity, all right, but in half an instant James Pierce knew it was going to be either a dead child for sure, or a possibly dead child anyway and a very injured James Pierce. In the other half an instant, he leaped, grabbed, and rolled them both mostly to safety, although it took some time for her two broken ribs and his one broken leg to heal.

Looking down at the boy soldier trying to hold on to her skirts, she strokes his damp cheek. "Now you get some rest. I'll be back soon, son." Tillie stumbles over the dead, the nurses, the Weikerts themselves, as she finds her way out of the barn, her hand clamped over her mouth. From everywhere comes the whistling thunk of shells. The air is a red mist, every atom visible with spent lives. Whizzing bullets, agonized whinnies, clashing steel—she staggers to the back of the barn, and witnesses the Little Round Top alive with struggle, too close for comfort. Someone calling her Girlie—"What?" she yells. "What?"—pulls her back around toward the side. "Sharpshooters!" She stares at the mouth of an aide, the word low and muffled and strung out, like the two of them are somewhere underwater, barely visible to each other, trying to say something that matters. Tillie wonders if this is what going deaf is like. Eardrums blown out like men's eyes and brains.

She hopes for deafness.

She yearns for it.

July 2

Propped up against the whitewashed barn is a dead sentry, picked off right where he stood, slumping into sitting like he'd just had a mighty fine chicken leg at the county picnic. Tillie catches sight of the knife sharpener just inside the hospital tent set up in the Weikerts' front yard. Next to him is a stack of blades and knives and scissors waiting for his attention. He is hunched over the grindstone, his face set. In the setting sun, sweat glistens on his face, and the spinning grindstone feels to Tillie like their whole godforsaken world that makes no more sense than anything else in Gettysburg.

Inside the tent are amputation benches, outside are barrows where limbs are piled. Orderlies wheel them out of sight, like hauling manure to garden plots, returning quickly, their carts empty. Other orderlies circulate from bench to bench, keeping patient records. Tillie heads for John Shafer, where she will borrow scissors.

And they will be as sharp as all the best sins.

From a wagoneer she gets some gloves, from a record-keeping orderly she gets a pencil, from a sutler selling pipe tobacco she gets wires, and from John Shafer she gets the loan of brass-handled dress-maker scissors he digs out of his unclaimed bag and the blank tags he uses to identify customers' goods. These she slips into the U.S. government–issued haversack she pulled from a pile of the belong-ings of the dead and now wears slung over her shoulder. When the wagoneer gave her a skeptical look and asked what a girl like her'd be wanting with work gloves, she shot back, "Burial detail."

Then she slips inside the front door of the farmhouse, finds a shadowy corner out of sight of the officers eating biscuits and gravy standing up, no time for more, not hardly, some with tattered uniforms and maps and shoe leather. Everything smells. Around them women rustle and clatter, setting down platters, refilling water jugs. As Tillie cuts off her fussy sleeves and opens up the neckline, she hears the scraps of conversations.

Twentieth Maine held the Round Top, Lee's going to have to try to break us at the center, madness, oh, but we'll give him one hell of a surprise. More like a thousand surprises, an officer manages to say around a biscuit he works on swallowing. Tired laughs. In the short weary silence one officer pipes up that Longstreet should know better. Someone else tops him with Longstreet does know better. Good at what he does, but that man couldn't coax a hungry mule with a feed bag.

A thousand surprises.

More troops? But where?

With her heart beating faster, Tillie runs the busy scissors clear around the waistband of her dress and steps out of the silly yards of fabric that only slow her down. Now all she wants is deafness and speed. Two things, now. Finally, in four big slices, off comes her hair, which she kicks into a corner, and slips upstairs into the Weikert boy's room, where she trades a pair of his knickerbockers for her bloomers, cutting just enough from the castoff to make a bandana.

As she springs down the narrow steps, she is light and free, she is sleeveless and airy, a girl from some other time and place, emancipated. Outside, the sun is disappearing over the western horizon, known in these parts as Emmitsburg Road, casting them all into a place of ghastly wonderment, a savagery of ideas. She slows as she makes her way unbothered through the hanging heat to the stack of amputated limbs she spots as high as the Weikert's stone fence. A single orderly in half a blue uniform and a limp moustache is stacking more limbs like he's expanding the drystone wall. He gives her a neutral look, taking in a white muslin bandana covering her nose and mouth.

"Any of these from—" here she fishes for what she means "—the newly dead?"

For a second, the orderly glances away, then back, with a weak shrug. "Why?"

"We give the family as much as we can for burial."

His eyes narrow. "On whose authority?"

"I believe," says Tillie slowly, giving him a level look, "on mine."

They stand sizing each other up. Finally, he sets his gloved hands on his hips. "Well, then," is all he says. Together they decide on a new pile, a small pile, just then only three he can say for sure belonged to soldiers who barely made it off the amputation benches before they died. All legs. He gives her their names and companies, which she pencils on tags, and he quickly pierces each with a wire and loops it around the cold, useless toes.

"Coffins," he suddenly raises his voice, "are getting loaded in the wagons alongside the tent—let's go!" With just three body parts in the wheelbarrow, they lope off toward the tent, bouncing their load across the rough barnyard in their haste. Just three limbs. So few. But three more than these families would have if she hadn't tried. How much everything seems to depend, thought Tillie, on knowing what matters. On knowing what matters and deciding in an instant.

Soon she shares a tin plate from a soldier's mess kit at the plank table in the Weikerts' basement kitchen. The Weikerts provide the beef stew, the camp cook the hardtack. A woman from a neighboring farm pours coffee. No one comments on Tillie's clothes. Very likely no one notices. Knife sharpener up top needs a meal, comes a voice from up the stone steps. A weary captain drags himself over to the doorway, where he stands shuffling, then calls up, send him on down. No special treatment here. In the dark, awkward silence, the knife sharpener answers, I have a clubfoot, sir, and cannot manage the stairs.

"I've got it, sir," says Tillie, to the captain already back slouching on a bench. One less task. Tillie slings together a quick plate of stew and hardtack and starts up the stairs, despite the heat the stone steps exhaling a vaporous cold like something you don't want to see come out of hiding. Cannot manage the stairs, he has said evenly, out of a life's worth of sentences that begin with the words I have a clubfoot . . . and cannot manage a Virginia reel, a bent-knee proposal, a forced march, a thrust with a bayonet, a slow steady aim down the sights of a rifle musket—or, for that matter, even the stairs.

John Shafer steps into the last of the light there in the dim back hall of the Weikert farmhouse, and stares in his lonely neutrality at the thick clot of beef and potatoes. He is looking around for a table, when a lieutenant, one with an uncooperative blond beard but a lot of energy, comes up the steps two at a time with directions from the missus for the girl Tillie to show him up to the entrance to the roof. Word has come down from the Old Snapper himself to survey the battlefield and report back how things, well, stand. At that, the lieutenant lets out a shrill whistle, and whispers, "Meade!" Tillie nods tightly. John Shafer grabs her arm and when she turns, gives Tillie a congested look. "The knife sharpener's coming too," she says to the lieutenant.

Across the soldier's face is a moment's indecision while he rotates his field glasses in a jumpy way, and then catches sight of the clubfoot. "Why, of course," he says in that pitying tone Tillie hardly heard since the battle started, even though there was much to pity. Up they go, stew forgotten, a tight, awkward threesome, to a closet on the second floor that houses a wall-mounted wooden ladder leading to the hinged trapdoor. Tillie and the lieutenant, whose name is O'Brien, step out onto the rooftop, and slowly making his way behind them, grunting and swearing, is the knife sharpener.

They look to the north, the lieutenant pointing out Baltimore Pike, the artery into the town itself. There in the last light of the day, Lee's headquarters, Meade's headquarters, Ewell's Corps, to the northwest A. P. Hills's Corps. Then their eyes settled on the sunset side of the panorama, where the encampment seems to stretch forever. "That there's Longstreet," breathes the lieutenant, and with a knowing nod, "he likes that formation for tents, plus flying the Stars and Bars." Tillie comments there are thousands of troops. O'Brien lowers his glasses. "From up here they look like fields of winter rye where I'm from in Minnesota." He sounds wistful.

The three of them turn slowly toward the right, toward the Union encampment. Their eyes sweep what they expect to find, O'Brien names Newton's Corps just there, and Hancock's Corps just there. A few lanterns coming on like scattered fireflies, occasional shouts, slow wagons carrying their fallen loads.

Then, in a low, cold voice, John Shafer asks, "What's that?" He points far to the right, looking southeast from their position to a long low natural depression in the landscape screened from the ground by thickets of trees. O'Brien is estimating troop strength in a murmur, and then stops to look where the knife sharpener points. It takes them all a good minute before they understand what they are seeing from their rooftop gallery. "Reserves," says O'Brien a little too quickly. "Got to be Sedgwick's Sixth." How many troops lie flattened against the conspiring landscape? No tents, no campfires, no lanterns.

"There are thousands," whispers Tillie.

"If Uncle John brought his whole family," says O'Brien slowly, his eyes pressed into the field glasses, "then it's upwards of ten thousand." Tillie catches her breath, her eyes sweeping the Gettysburg battlefield for as far as she could see. While they stare at what O'Brien calls Sedgwick's Sixth, Tillie feels breathless at the strange majesty of it. These are rows of the living, not the dead. Troops passing the night ahead unsheltered, literally lying in wait for their orders. Slowly, they put together the significance of what they are witnessing. "I've got enough," says the lieutenant, finally, who pities a clubfoot, "let's go."

Tillie turns. The knife sharpener is gone.

In the soft and gentle darkness, the darkness before deep night takes away all the points of reference, the roofline of the barn, the path to the outhouse, and whatever flowers overflow their boxes, Tillie searches for the knife sharpener, moving through scattered shouts and shrieks until what answers are those few stars that locate her on sorry Earth. At last she discovers John Shafer near the corner of Wheatfield Road, only the starlight naming him to her. A crossroads, in the starlight that knows no better than who still stands, who still breathes, and who still yearns in the Gettysburg of all time.

Beside him stands the grindstone, and she watches in the near darkness as he pumps the treadle until that stone starts spinning good and proper, and he half turns his head with the red hair that looks no better than black in the dim light, and blinks at her in acknowledgment. She watches in silence, not asking him why he left that fatal rooftop because at fifteen years old Tillie knows somehow it is fatal.

She watches as he sets his bare hands down on the spinning grindstone, his hands just more old, tarnished, and compromised things unless they get sharpened into life. He holds those hands there for a few seconds in something like a benediction. When he lifts them off the grindstone and the wheel slows to a stop she briefly sees a raggedness, an almost bloody roughness from how the grindstone has acknowledged John Shafer, who then steps aside. He says nothing.

Waiting to see what he does, she silently follows the knife sharpener as he heads steadily down the road from the Weikert Farm. Her body grows cold as the distance between John Shafer and the grindstone becomes larger. Lurching along, he still hasn't made up his mind, Tillie can tell, because he doesn't have a father who speaks about true decisions made in an instant. But they come to the crossroads where everything is suddenly left to its own devices. With the three stars lighting her way, and with distant camp lanterns asking her to act, the knife sharpener does the unthinkable and turns west.

Toward General Longstreet's camp.

Tillie trembles as the full understanding of what he is choosing hits her like a minié ball that has brought down so many others. It will be the last thing she says to him, the last thing she knows for sure. "Oh, don't, oh, don't," she hears her own strained voice so she knows he must too, and still he walks, a black shadow now in the path west down the deserted road. John Shafer from Hagerstown, Maryland, who takes no sides at all and keeps alive with ten cents here and ten cents there, is heading for the camp of General Longstreet. John Shafer looked upon the corps of hidden Union troops and finally found his heart.

But where does that leave hers?

Longstreet is a mile away, him with the smart, still eyes and the tall frame and sorrowful way because he knows all is lost, does he not, does he not, and here, lurching along with the clubfoot that has hidden his own heart from himself comes John Shafer, knife sharpener, here to spring the tragedy, here to deliver intelligence that would matter like meteors and shifting river courses.

She follows him at a distance, and as she watches his gait become more like anyone's, as she watches his back straighten, as she watches his pace pick up, she follows. The only light comes increasingly from the lanterns ahead, now just half a mile, from the camp of General Longstreet. "John Shafer!" she blurts, not too loudly, her voice guttural. He hesitates almost imperceptibly and then shows her his very clear intention. In half a mile he'll reach Confederate pickets, guards scattered around the perimeter.

Still he walks, and as she watches he becomes more sure of himself, straighter, stronger, full of purpose, less full of holding dull knives against his grindstone, now abandoned. And in an instant, a tender instant, an instant full of inscriptions on the tablets of her life, she lets him walk. How far can she let him go? She watches as the lonely neutrality slips away from the knife sharpener. She watches as the purpose of mere survival slips away from the knife sharpener. The clubfoot, the careful diplomacy, the halting acceptance of others' kindnesses—North and South—slip away. She cries at its beauty, the silhouette of John Shafer, heading for the place that drives him, that lifts his crippled heart, until she can't let him go any farther.

In that instant.

And with a cry only she, Tillie, Tillie herself, can hear, she dashes, pulling from the haversack the unclaimed item that she now claims forever as her own, racing with the black trees flying behind her on both sides, flying. For one second, he hesitates, sensing her approach, and then continues. But it is her instant, and her true, decision. In that final moment Tillie closes in on him, hearing the dust of his steps, hearing a great white owl, Tillie still not deaf to pain, and as she draws out the brass-handled scissors, she descends on him in the black night, and she raises and plunges them into the back of the newborn Confederate spy.

July 3

Tillie—Tillie—Mrs. Weikert shakes her gently where Tillie sits outside the hospital barn on a three-legged stool, rolling bandages as heavy white as a grindstone. The cannonading, earlier, seemed to last as many years as she has been alive. Now late in the day she notices untagged limbs getting wheeled away, and hatless, shirtless, but still vertical soldiers crisscross the yard, discussing the finer points of the day's new hell. Beautiful, beautiful, they breathe, never forget it, men crumpling, splitting apart, and that damned cocky Pickett, and still the Rebel yell, or what was left, what was left when the fife and drum died away along with everything else . . .

It all came down, Tillie hears, to what was out of sight, did you see? Appearing like vengeance set free, loosed, rising up, eight thousand troops, no, more like ten, did you see, did you see, hidden troops rising up, fresh and blue like Spring we none of us think we'll ever see again, rising up, remember Chancellorsville was the shout, remember it all. Where's that man got to, that knife sharpener? So unreliable, these people. Run off, joined up, clubfoot no problem, that's where we are, Lee as well. What else can he do, that old man, but pull out now, get the hell off our soil for good and ever?

Will it never rain?

What time's mess?

Wait, what's the orderly got there, looks like that slacker's grindstone, well, better the tool than the man, I say. The tool we can use, how hard can it be, the man we got to feed. Wheel it over to Mackay's surgical tent, step it up, now. Tillie rolls bandages, wondering how they will bandage her up, when they can't see the injury.

And now there's Mrs. Weikert's warm hand on her shoulder. *Tillie—Tillie—girl!*

Tillie turns. Mrs. Weikert's lips are cracked. There is a dead bluebottle fly caught in her uncombed hair, and her eyes shift nervously like they can stay no longer in a single place or she will go mad. The cracked lips are telling Tillie that the two of them are leaving for town in ten minutes by carriage to attend the burial of Tillie's friend Jennie Wade.

Word came the way it always does that poor patriotic Jennie was shot dead by a stray bullet, what a freak act, is nobody safe in their own kitchens anymore, goes on Mrs. Weikert, who cradles the dying.

They can't do any better by poor hardworking Jennie, for now just a hurried hole in her own backyard until all this—an impatient sweep of her arm sleeved with dry bloodstains—is over and there's a proper funeral. "She died," announces Mrs. Weikert in a way Tillie knows will be the way the death story is told forevermore, "kneading bread"—Mrs. Weikert bites her cracked lip, since kneading bread is a sacred act of infinite use and transcendent meaning—for the ten loaves she was baking for her boys in blue. Tillie nods solemnly, staring at the dead bluebottle in the woman's hair.

Mrs. Weikert's chin lifts and she goes on. Jennie's grief-stricken mother has let it be known that she will bake those loaves herself—to continue Jennie's work. Some young women, Mrs. Weikert adds, full of meaning, the red-rimmed gaze quickly piercing the girl sitting on a three-legged stool, still hoping for deafness, the girl wearing a hacked bodice and what could only be her own boy's knickerbockers, the girl sitting on a pair of brass-handled dressmaker's scissors—some young women find ways to make themselves useful.

"Now go make yourself presentable."

Just a few years ago, I toured the Gettysburg battlefield, where I learned about Jennie Wade, the sole civilian casualty of those three sweltering days, a twenty-year-old who was kneading dough in her sister's kitchen when she was killed by a stray bullet. Over five years, I tried to figure out how I could write something meaningful from that simple domestic tale. Had she somehow been a Union spy, known J. E. B. Stuart from church camp, and somehow given him the false intelligence that lured him away from Gettysburg, much to Lee's loss? Ah! If she was a spy, was the fatal bullet actually stray? Had Jennie Wade saved the battle? The Union? But I couldn't figure out how to make any of those elements work together and still be a short story.

And then I found Tillie Pierce, a fifteen-year-old whose parents had sent her three miles south of town to what they thought was safety, landing her, ironically, at a farm at the base of Little Round Top. What I learned about the real Tillie, I came to love, and I knew I wanted to write the kind of story I love, wherein great acts of heroism are not always public. I felt I had to keep the story intimate, a counterpoint to all that carnage, so I gave her a new friend, an itinerant knife sharpener—and, finally, a line item on her résumé.

After five years of figuring, I wrote the story in a week.

Doug Crandell *is the author of the Barnes & Noble Discover pick* The Flaw-less Skin of Ugly People, *as well as three other novels, two memoirs, and a true crime book. He's received awards and endowments from the Sherwood Anderson Foundation, the Virginia Center for the Creative Arts, the Kellogg Writers Series, the Jentel Foundation, and the Goldfarb Fellowship. NPR's Glynn Washington chose Crandell's story for the 2018 COG Page-to-Screen Award. Another short story received the 2018 Glimmer Train Family Matters Fiction Award. Crandell's essays appear in the Pushcart Prize collections for 2017 and 2022, and a short story of his appears in* The Best American Mystery Stories 2020. *He's a regular contributor to* SUN Magazine *and* Ellery Queen Mystery Magazine.

DOWN THE FIRE ROAD
Doug Crandell

Deputy Jeff Spickle wasn't taken seriously. Sheriff Dresser was to blame for Spickle's reputation, because the sheriff was compromised. His love of drink left Spickle in the no-man's-land of informally being in charge, which meant undeserved blame. Deputy Spickle had reached what he believed was his breaking point and was ready to do something about it.

In high school, Jeff needed protecting, but Samuel Dresser needed someone to sober him up before football games. It seemed like a neatly arranged exchange, at least back then, twenty years ago. Now, not so much. The sheriff had gotten worse, missing whole days sometimes, Spickle left to cover for him, but that wasn't the worst. Dresser could be a cruel drunk, prone to blaming Deputy Spickle for the department's problems, then showing up again with no memory other than guilt when he'd become oversolicitous, urging Deputy Spickle to go off on a fishing trip, where the man would inevitably become sloshed around the campfire and Jeff would once again have to haul him into the tent, get him covered with a sleeping bag. Deputy Jeff Spickle tried to stay positive, but he'd wrangled and toted his boss enough times from cruiser to house, from back porch to bed, that it felt like the deputy was in a continuous training video. Deputy Spickle had given the sheriff self-help books to read, even printed out some mantras the sheriff could use to stay positive himself, but all the sheriff did was chuckle as he read them out loud.

Deputy Spickle sat at his desk waiting on Sheriff Dresser to arrive at the office. Spickle looked up at the clock on the wall for the tenth time. He repeated in his head that Sheriff Dresser might be under the weather after working three cold nights in a row, the early spring unusually cold. That sounded real, yes?

In addition to all his other problems, the last eighteen months had seen forest fires arrive with erratic, devastating effects. The fires in North Georgia had come as a surprise to Jeff, to Sheriff Dresser too, because while they'd been required to be on a conference call with state officials, the mountains and verdant forest of the north had seemed untouchable, their pines and hardwoods immune to whatever the hell was going on with the ice caps melting, but that was more than a year ago, and things now were much more complicated. It wasn't just the fires, which seemed to pop up every month or so regardless of weather. The thing was, you couldn't only worry about global extinction when your town, its county, and the surrounding areas descended into decadence and crime. There were opioids, and an increasing number of dealers, broken-up families, scant jobs, and ugly violence. It seemed the ties that had bound the place together were frayed, some completely gone. Jeff Spickle had grown up in these umber woods, hunted the grassy fields in the crisp fall mornings, where now soot turned to the consistency of wet cat litter. He didn't tell anyone how he got teary when he drove the isolated fire roads and passed mile after mile of charred black trees, their limbs eerily skeletal. But in the last several months, after Sheriff Dresser had belittled Spickle in front of two rookie firemen at a Lions Club event, the deputy had felt something building in him. The fires seemed to mirror his hot anger, the dry fuel on the forest floors like what was igniting in his brain. Plans began to flare up in his mind, ways to set the sheriff on a straight path once and for all.

Deputy Spickle watched as outside the big pane of glass, waxy with cold, the main street, known simply as County Boulevard, started to catch a wet dusting of snow along the curbs, the weather as mixed up as the sheriff after three pints of rotgut. Spickle was distracted not only by Sheriff Dresser's tardiness but also by the twin sisters, Kara and Kylie, who were due to give their formal statements on a pair of little boy's shoes. Supposedly they'd found them while doing their own search. Kara had lost custody of her son, but was close to getting him back if she found a new place to live. The little boy had gone missing in the early-morning hours from a small backyard playground the foster couple swore was visible from their kitchen window. The Connors admitted they'd gotten distracted when their power went off. When Peter Connor rushed to the playground, the little boy was gone.

Deputy Spickle had to create a spreadsheet to track all the names, the half-siblings and live-in partners, the petty sellers and skinny users who sometimes stayed with the twins in a run-down condo. He called it the K&K list. Sheriff Dresser had admired it. Kara was a belligerent woman with sleeves of tattoos and a penchant for fighting. She was wild-eyed and promiscuous but attended church faithfully at the Presbyterian Rocky Gap congregation, though some had filed statements claiming Kara was high most services, wobbly and eyes lidded by Sunday School. Her twin, Kylie, while never married and without kids, was wild too, but Kara's reputation was the one that sent out tall tales, where once it was said that Kara stole a trucker's speed and coke while he lay passed out in the sleeper cab at a KOA. By dawn, Kara was back home and sharing the trucker's drugs with most of the names on Deputy Spickle's spreadsheet. That had been more than two years ago, and now she was clean and trying to get her son back.

The clock on the cinder-block wall clunked as another minute passed. The phone rang and Deputy Sheriff Spickle answered with his usual formality. It was important to sound as he always did. On the other end, a man from the county road crew told him Sheriff Dresser's cruiser had been found with both its doors open on the fire road. The caller asked, "Do you know if he's out hunting?"

Deputy Spickle spoke clearly into the phone. "Who is this?" He didn't want some jokester to set him up again, play him like a fool.

"This is Danny Hobbs, I'm serious. The sheriff 's cruiser is here, and I've been waiting for twenty minutes. He's nowhere in sight."

Deputy Spickle was able to place the voice on the other end now, and while Danny had been booked on two DUIs, that was more than five years ago. Deputy Spickle liked the guy, even gave him a reference for the county road crew once Danny had gotten sober and settled down with his second wife. Usually no one called when the sheriff was hard to find, mostly because no one knew but Spickle.

Deputy Spickle tried to sound calm, and said, "Danny, you sure it's the main cruiser? The hip-hop kids like to trick out unmarked to look like police vehicles."

"It's his all right," said Danny, exhaling into the phone.

"Don't touch anything," said Deputy Spickle. He was certain now that he might be able to make the sheriff understand how his actions impacted others. "Don't say a word to anyone else."

"Of course," said Danny. "That's why I called you." It sounded to the deputy that Danny was questioning him, already suspicious of his ability to handle a crisis without the sheriff. "Just don't touch anything," Deputy Spickle said again as he hung up the phone and caught the image of the twins crossing the street, their tenebrous figures in lockstep march.

Kara and Kylie breached the front door of the sheriff's department with a clatter, Kara chewing gum and Kylie wearing the expression of one who hates just for being born. The twins gave Deputy Spickle their best expressions of disregard. Kara spit the gum into his empty wastebasket and plopped down in a folding chair the color of rotten avocado. Spickle stood and gave them no eye contact. "Stay right here. I'll be back as quick as I can," he said, rushing out the door. Kara flipped him off but only the secretary, Mrs. Caldwell, saw it. She shrugged, even smiled a little as the twins hurried back out the door. The twins knew they weren't taken seriously by the law. Mrs. Caldwell got up and went to the door and called to the twins, but they were too far away to hear. She went back to the desk and radioed Deputy Spickle. "The girls are on the move," she told him.

Heading home, Kara and Kylie walked in sync and quickly. Kara brought her fingertips to the divots on her cheek without breaking stride. The pocks, and the birth of her baby, had helped Kara stop using, but her son had been taken anyway, mostly because of the company she kept. The twins passed down the block and back toward the duplex they lived in with a half-dozen others. Kara had kicked using hard stuff, while Kylie only liked weed and rum. Kara still had a drug debt, almost $12,000, racked up from a gram-a-day meth habit. Her dealer, a man she'd dated and had swindled, tried to act tough, but Kara pushed it, shrugged off his threatening texts. As they took the corner of General Lewis Street and strode toward the duplex, Kylie asked, "You think Tommy will come again today?"

Kara spit without breaking stride. "Don't matter," she said, mildly. "Let's get out and look. God knows Spickle is more concerned about his drunk sheriff than my Sonny." Kara stopped briefly in front of the duplex and Kylie braked too. Kara took her by the arm. "Tommy can't get over me. He can act like a petty little kingpin all he wants, but if I thought he had my baby, don't you think I'd go after him?" The twins stood still as the curtains on the two long-paned windows of the duplex were slowly pulled back, some of their roommates sheepishly staring out at them from inside the cramped bottom floor. Kara peered up at the figures. They were about to climb the leaning concrete steps to the porch when a familiar car huffed up along the curb, purple lights blinking on the caps and a beat and pulse of reverb so deep the twins both touched their sternums, nearly at the same time. "Damn," said Kara, but she instinctively pushed Kylie behind her. Tommy hopped out of the car; for all his wannabe antics he still dressed like an office intern on casual Friday, his blond hair short and his ankles bare above boat shoes. Even his tattoos were all show, colorful but with no symbolic meaning at all. "What the hell do you want?" shouted Kara, as Kylie edged her way from behind her sister so they were standing shoulder to shoulder.

Tommy jogged from the street onto the sidewalk, then stopped, ran his hand over his stubble. "I want my money," he said and winked, then turned his expression sour. "You're way too late, babe," he said. "There's no family discount." Pine warblers trilled from the sagging deck. There was the smell of oily exhaust.

"We're not family," said Kara, scoffing, rolling her eyes. "Not even close." She raised her eyebrows.

At this, Tommy became irritable and paced in a tight circle; he was ramping himself up, trying to look crazed. He yelled, "That's only because you won't do the DNA test." He sniffed and looked up at the sky. The passenger's-side window eased down a crack and smoke wafted out. Tommy paused, took a deep breath. "Even though I've given you money for it three times and you ripped me off on that too. Way I figure, your bill is now close to fifteen thousand."

Kara laughed and put her hand on her hip. Kylie glanced up at the duplex windows, but all the roommates had retreated.

"I know you can get it, Kara," said Tommy. "I know you got a payout for that fake fall at the speedway. Just give me my money and you'll never see me again."

Kara sniffed, then cut her eyes to her sister. Kara said, "Tommy, now isn't a great time." Kylie watched to see if her sister would say what she thought she was going to. "Sonny's missing," said Kara, and her voice caught.

Tommy froze for just a split second, then stood up straighter. "You're a twisted person to try and use the kid to stall paying. That's sick, Kara." A distant siren called, and it made Tommy nervous. "I'll be back." He jogged to the car and yanked the door open, the music still thudding. He chirped the tires, sped off down the street, running the four-way.

Kylie watched her sister. "You sure you want him to know about Sonny?" she asked.

Kara ignored the question and took her sister's arm as the curtains inside the duplex parted again. "When we get Sonny home, we've got to find a new place," said Kara.

The spillway embankment was lion colored and mushy, the snow and ice melting as the temps rose. Mother Nature was as dazed as the county's drug users, confused about time and order, the proper way to move forward. Danny crab-crawled down the embankment, and Deputy Spickle followed, his gun slapping at his hip. Behind them, the roiling of a cold creek as the silver waters rushed over round rocks. Danny paused and looked back over his shoulder at Deputy Spickle. Danny said, "You know if he's gone again for too long, you'll have to take over." Spickle waved Danny off. They found a low spot and crossed over the water. Deputy Spickle saw the sheriff's vehicle sideways along the worn fire road, the red-clay ruts like a spine.

The cruiser was empty. Deputy Spickle eased behind the steering wheel, pressed buttons, and turned down the static. Danny stood at a distance. The seats in the cruiser seemed damp and the windshield sported a splatter of mud. "You sure you didn't fiddle with anything?" yelled Deputy Spickle. Danny shouted back that he'd called right away, hadn't done anything more.

Deputy Spickle struggled to get out of the cruiser, his duty belt and its rigs catching on the seat, leather squeaking. Spickle used his cell phone to call the sheriff. It went to voicemail. He dialed it again and was met with the same gravelly message from Sheriff Dresser. Danny stepped closer. "He's probably gone on a bender."

"Watch your mouth, Danny," said Deputy Spickle. "No need to put bad energy out into the universe." Jeff Spickle was a positive-thinking enthusiast, mostly because Dresser had driven him to find something to cling to. Deputy Spickle read books about energy and karma, listened to podcasts, and sometimes allowed the language of that particular school of thought to come out in his official role as deputy. Spickle wanted to make sure he sounded calm and added, "Let's keep things optimistic." He took a deep breath and exhaled slowly, just like they said to do on the *It's All Good* podcast.

The horizon held slightly differing shades of blue metal and gray cinder, clouds swollen and stationary, as if the sky itself was about to fall into the earth. "You see any vehicles out here, Danny?"

"No sir," said Danny, putting a finger to his chin, then looking down, thinking. "Might've been a green one."

Deputy Spickle bent to look at the tracks in the fire road, then stood up again. "What make was this green car?"

"No, not green, green, I mean one of those eco-friendly deals. Green as in Greenpeace."

The deputy shook his head, started to say something, then stopped.

"Don't be like that," said Danny. "I'm just trying to help. You're the one who said we should be positive." The wind picked up, died down, and small ticks of ice sputtered from the sky, pinging lightly across the hood of the cruiser. Danny watched as the deputy circled the car, pausing at each wheel, stooping down, running his hand over the tire, tracing his hands around the wheel well as if feeling for palpitations, his head cocked. "What are you doing?" said Danny, the question laced with incredulity, a chuckle added. Deputy Spickle ignored Danny and continued to the last two tires. He stood up and looked out across the tawny grass field to the timberline, where a dark green queue of longleaf pine swayed in the gusts of grainy cold wind. More than a dozen blackbirds soared upward, only to settle again into the filigreed branches with dabs of white snow too high to melt yet.

"Listen to me, Danny," said Deputy Spickle. "I'm going to leave the cruiser here, lock it up and head back to the office as if nothing is different." Danny crinkled his brow and tried to speak but was cut off. "You don't say a word about this, you understand?"

Danny nodded, his right foot kicking at a thick strand of dead kudzu, its long tentacles gnarled and taupe. "Are you gonna at least call in some help?" he asked.

Deputy Spickle raised his chin and narrowed his eyes. "If I was, I wouldn't broadcast it, but what I will say to you Danny Hobbs, is that you better hope to God you're telling me everything you know." Danny looked up and met Deputy Spickle's eyes. The two men stood like that for several heartbeats, until the wind kicked up again and blew the deputy's hat off his head, and Danny went chasing after it as it somersaulted down the embankment. Deputy Spickle watched him and felt ashamed that he'd been so harsh, but he also hoped he sounded convincing, that he had sold his reactions well enough.

It was already dark by the time Kara and Kylie returned to the duplex. After Spickle had left the sheriff's office without meeting with them, they'd decided to search the area again where the shoes had been found. They'd moved from there to larger patches of ground, ash sludge in their tennis shoes. They spent the afternoon picking through the tangles of kudzu and privet along the stretch of Highway 6 and looking at their phones whenever they rested. Kara texted an ex-cop in Chattanooga she'd dated but he didn't respond. Once they had pushed through the tangles of green, tripping again and again, and wound their way through to the edge of a swampy muck and two sagging cinder bridges, the twins sat on the culvert to smoke cigarettes.

Now, as they entered the front door of the duplex, the living room was full of shaggy young men playing a loud video game on a flat-screen nearly as big as the wall itself. Kara stomped past them. They were hangers-on, oblivious to Kara's desperation, and they stunk of sedentary waste, the duplex like a creature unto itself. The twins had long ago made an unspoken pact that whatever they were dealt, from men and people in charge, they'd strive to be tough, stoic, and numb.

In the kitchen, Kara cracked sodas, handed one to Kylie. Music thumped above them. "That Shelley is up there again with Ryan," said Kara. They both smelled of the outdoors, the briny water, windblown hair, traces of minty vegetation from searching the tangled briars. A lanky kid the twins liked slunk into the kitchen. His name was Chance, and he picked at his face and wouldn't look them in the eye. "You find anything else?" he said, head tilted toward the doorjamb, his dark eyes darting quickly to the space between where Kara and Kylie leaned, then back again as he looked at his feet. The twins thought maybe Chance had learning problems.

"No," said Kara, with a sigh, "and Spickle took off on us too." Kara blew her nose, eyes watery. The twins knew Chance liked them both and was one of the few people who could always tell them apart. Chance nodded and ignored the gurgling bong sounds and whoops the others were making in the living room. He was almost ten years younger than them, just out of high school.

"I'm sorry," said Chance, flashing a quick smile. His skin was bad, but his teeth were white and complete. He'd been just fifteen when he had babysat Kara's son, made the little guy a slingshot out of a maple branch, smoothing the forked wood with sandpaper, using two thick rubber bands for the sling. Chance had made tight wads of paper for ammo and put those and the homemade slingshot in a shoebox and gave it to Kara. She'd not wanted to hurt the kid's feelings, but still she said, "Chance, you know he's six months old, right?" Chance had shrugged and smiled and mumbled something about it being a gift for later.

Kara's phone rang and she fumbled as she tried to yank it from her tight jeans. She answered loudly, a crease between her eyes. While she was on the phone, Chance snuck glances at her and Kylie, then receded back into the dark living room. Kara yelled for them to turn down the video game. She stuck a finger in her ear. "What?" she said loudly, and then even louder, "I can't hear you." She stomped toward the back door with Kylie in tow. Outside, it was cold and very dark. "Okay," said Kara, and shoved her phone back into her pocket, wriggling some to make it fit. She spit, then patted her lips demurely with the sleeve of her sweatshirt.

"What?" asked Kylie, wiping her mouth too, sniffing air through her nose.

Kara said, "It was that damn deputy. Wants us to come back in the morning. Says he has some leads." Kara lit a cigarette and passed it to Kylie, then lit another one for herself. It was quiet out, except for the train way off and the sound of the furnace. They stood and smoked. One of them coughed, then the other. The train blew in, and the rumbling sound grew like a thunderstorm, then slowly ebbed away, the clacks pulsing out over the distant darkness, a faint cannon of light showing the way.

Kylie said, "Why didn't the sheriff just meet with us this morning? Deputy isn't the boss anyway."

"You know why," said Kara, and she flipped her cigarette into the darkness where it somersaulted in the air and threw sparks like a lit fuse. Someone's dryer gave off the warm scent of violet fabric softener. The sounds of tomcats vying in the brown shrubs echoed like movie sound effects. Kara believed she could smell something dead wafting from under the unused clotheslines. Kylie nodded as she toed out her cigarette in the wet, patchy grass.

"Because that old bastard is drinking again," said Kara, and her voice held back tears. They grew somber. The twins had always been this way, shared an unspoken language, and in this case, it was a language of hurt, but also a kind of hopeful rebellion. "Sonny'll be all right, Kar," said Kylie, as she patted her sister's back. Kara inhaled deeply for courage. In their shared bedroom in the duplex, they had talked about calling state authorities, but they weren't exactly upright citizens. The duplex contained enough petty-criminal backgrounds that if they did ask for help outside of Spickle, they knew it would only serve to put the twins behind bars, and worse yet, Kara would never get Sonny out of foster care.

They held hands as they went up the steps. Kara and Kylie went to bed. The others in the house erupted in cheers during the night over some score that had been broken, and they partied until the weak sun rose, watery lemon across the teal horizon. Chance had not slept, but instead stood watch over the twins. When their phones went off simultaneously, it was Chance who gently shook Kylie's shoulder first, then Kara's. He got them up and told them he'd drive them to the sheriff's office. Kara was solemn but intense, as she gargled twice and sprayed on perfume. Kylie repeated the tasks. The morning sky had washed out of color as they walked down the duplex steps and got into Chance's pickup.

Deputy Spickle surveyed the horizon, noted how the pale yellow seemed to bleed into the dungy blueness that slipped outward, slowly, as if it were some chemical osmosis in a petri dish. He drank black coffee and prepared himself. One memory had stayed with him lately. Sheriff Dresser had gotten drunk one night while they were working on reports that had to be emailed to Atlanta authorities by morning. He disappeared around nine P.M. and returned smelling of whiskey. Every so often, he left the office, returning each time more belligerent. The reports didn't make it on time, and in the morning Deputy Spickle could hear the sheriff on the phone, lying about why, saying his deputy had come down with the flu and failed to inform him he hadn't completed the reports. In the scope of things, compared to the egregious things the sheriff had done in the past, Spickle tried to decipher why that moment, that particular lie, had been so hurtful, but he could only come up with an incomplete theory that somehow the event had served as a kind of bleak summation of their relationship. If Sheriff Dresser was willing to blame him for something as minor as tardy reports, there was no respect left.

Deputy Spickle sighed and put the empty coffee cup on the rusty stairwell. He gave the sky one last look and walked back inside the abandoned wool mill and into a space where he kept his books, with titles that referenced the afterlife, the energies of decision and purpose, the self-help hardbacks that he read again every year. Spickle had created this little alcove in the enormous delapidated structure to spy on the drug users, the dealers and tweakers, but it turned out they were never actually here, or at least if they had been, that was years before. He used three padlocks to keep the small area hidden. If anyone saw him out here, they'd just believe he was on patrol. He'd put up gray metal shelving, and now he pulled out a book and shelved it again, a paperback about positive vibrations. He turned to address the single cot where a figure lay duct-taped at the mouth, hands and feet bound with the same restriction.

"All these years," Spickle said as he strolled around the arc of the room, right hand slightly grazing the flaky shelving. "And it was you who was always unreliable." The sheriff's head lolled backward, the smell of cheap, burning liquor pervading the area, overriding the space heater's dusty singe. The precipitation had once again turned colder, with snow and sleet, the early-morning skies pregnant with gray doom. "This excuse and that excuse," he said, shaking his head, "and me the one to take the ribbing." Deputy Spickle unwrapped a stick of gum and slowly eased it into his mouth; he chewed and huffed, shaking his head so much that his neck popped. "So many of the botched arrests and mistakes, almost all yours, but Ol' Spickle is the one who's the joke."

The deputy walked in a circle over the cracked concrete. "You've mocked me, used me as a scapegoat, let people think I was the problem. When all along I covered for you, held my tongue, took the abuse, just like the enabler I am."

Sheriff Dresser made his eyes widen with a question: *What can you be thinking?* The eyes were large and brown, the whites laced with bloodshot, the lids forced open by strain and anger.

"Those twins are due at the offices in a bit. They are mine to have to deal with because you are once again drunk." The deputy removed the gum from his mouth and wrapped it neatly into the foil from which it had just emerged, the strands of sugar clinging to his fingertips. Deputy Spickle stared at his boss of nearly a dozen years. Sheriff Dresser begged with his eyes for the tape to be removed. He wore only a white T-shirt and boxers. Spickle had stripped the man while he was passed out. His skin was marbled like meat, phosphorescent at the knobby joints. "All your messes," declared Deputy Spickle as if providing testimony, "and me the one who looks the fool. I'd be in Atlanta by now working in real law enforcement if it weren't for you." Deputy Spickle stretched his back and nodded into the ether, as if some phantom version of himself and the sheriff resided there, lives much more in sync in that plane than this one. "Well, it's over. I'm going to make things right this time." The sheriff kicked his bound feet against the dry brick wall. "Let me tell you a good one on old Jeff," said Spickle, trying to sound like the sheriff. Spickle paused and stood with his back to the sheriff, right hand tight at his side, fingertips less than an inch from the service revolver. "Isn't that how you started all those stories before you got fall-down, sloppy drunk?" Deputy Jeff Spickle cocked his head, the edges of his face in sharp silhouette. The space went quiet, even the coos of the mourning doves stopped, as if they'd been switched off.

"Sheriff Dresser," said the deputy, shaking his head in disgust. Spickle walked in circles again, his hands shoved deep into his pockets, giving him the look of a man with growths on both sides of his hips. "You're probably asking yourself, why's he doing this?" The deputy put his cupped right hand to his ear and pretended to hear a response. "That's right," said the deputy. "Because you've not heeded any of your second chances, which are in the hundreds. It's time for you to change. The fires, and the drugs, and all the lies, someone must stop them. And it's clear you cannot do that on your own accord."

Sheriff Dresser's skin now appeared yellow in the ocher light from a corner lamp. The sheriff widened his eyes again to ask for the tape across his mouth to be removed, but Deputy Spickle did not see and continued his sermon. "Do you even know what anguish you've brought down on me with your ways?" Spickle paused to listen as a car whisked by with music blaring, the old wool mill echoing back the bass. "I drive down the fire roads and all I've thought about is how to set you right." Small flakes from the dry bricks and crumbling mortar of the walls created a constant haze. "You're to blame for this mess," said Spickle, motioning toward the corroded steel beams above. "Maybe if you'd been the type of man worthy of the law, we wouldn't have a child abducted, and meth and pills." Deputy Spickle went to his shelves of books again, half-turned toward the sheriff. He pulled a thick hardback off the shelf, opened it in the middle, and held it in his palms as if it were a holy tome. "Did you read even one of the books I loaned you?" He slammed the heavy book shut and tossed it, the slap onto the concrete floor like a gunshot.

The sheriff burped, but with no place for the air to escape his mouth, his nasal tract skittered and emitted a foul drunkard's fume. The deputy pulled on his peacoat and stood, as if practicing the art of a real-life statue. He went and sat down on the thin mattress where the sheriff lay, the man's willowy chest hairs rising and falling like a sea creature. Deputy Spickle whispered into his boss's ear. "The world's energy thrives on the dreams and hopes of its inhabitants." Spickle explained how this was it, this time was the last, and he aimed to sober up the sheriff for good. "I stood out there by your cruiser after I circled back and just knew you were somewhere nearby, drunk as a skunk, like hundreds of times before, with the old incompetent Spickle to take the blame for your shoddiness." Spickle looked up at the ceiling. " 'Course you wouldn't remember that, now would you?" The old beams above them seemed to exude cold, as if the space had its own weather. "I dragged your drunken, sorry posterior here. But even with my years of experience hauling you from one spot to another to sober up, I dropped you a couple of times. For that I'm sorry, truly." Spickle paused, tried to make sure the sheriff understood his sincerity for the lumps that were surely on the back of his head. "Anyway, this will serve as a kind of homemade detox." Deputy Spickle peered up at cobwebbed rafters, the rusty iron chains, and the old wasp nests that clung like blisters in every corner. Spickle took the sheriff's stubbled chin in his hand. "Those girls are missing a child," he said. "And I plan on finding that boy and doing it myself, and as God is my witness I'll leave you here forever if that's what it takes."

Spickle paused and looked up into the rusted beams again. He leaned down and put his face as close to the sheriff's as he could, their noses touching. Spickle pinched his boss's bare thigh as hard and for as long as he could, but the sheriff scooted away, his eyes shining with anger. Spickle stood up and turned his back, lit a cigarette, and inhaled deeply, blowing the smoke from his sharp nostrils into the chilly air.

Sheriff Dresser, though he could not speak behind the constriction of the duct tape, tried to make himself understood, but Deputy Spickle just sighed and told his boss he didn't know what else to do, then Spickle turned on his heels and left the space, only to return and rip the tape from the sheriff's mouth. "Don't want you asphyxiating on your own vomit, but you'll only embarrass yourself by yelling for help. Go ahead, yell all you want, let someone find you like this." Spickle retrieved a black bucket from the corner and set it beside the bed. He mumbled disgust.

"Jeff," said the sheriff, his voice hoarse, lips crusty, hair wild. He breathed fast and swallowed. "I understand you're mad, but we can talk this out. We can find a solution." The sheriff was slack-jawed, his pale gawp like an icy opening.

"It's a shame it takes my own deceit to counter yours, but what do they say," said Spickle, "fight fire with fire? Forestry told us to dig the trenches, pour in the fuel, light a match, and let it burn. Fight fire with fire is what they said." Sheriff Dresser tried to respond but Spickle was at the door, then on the outside, securing the padlocks. A lone pigeon blasted from the rafters. The sheriff could hear his deputy's measured footfalls on the rusted iron rungs that led down to the ground level, where he could also hear, just faintly, Spickle pause, no more steps.

Deputy Spickle answered his cell phone; it was Mayor Sharon Tillis. After she made small talk, something about the ice and snow, and the summer's inevitable fires being just around the corner, she asked straight-out about the sheriff. "Is it a bender?"

Deputy Spickle didn't speak, the cold wind at his left ear like a bee sting. The mayor asked again. Deputy Spickle said sternly into his cell phone, no, that the sheriff was fine. "That's not what Danny tells me," she said. Deputy Spickle covered his phone and closed his eyes, took a deep breath, then returned to the call. "Just give me today. He'll turn up." He looked at his watch. If he could meet with the twins and make them believe how sincere he was, everything would work out, all of it.

"I can bring in some help," said the mayor. But she reasoned it out and finally told the deputy, before she hung up, that if he needed anything, he shouldn't hesitate to ask. Sheriff Dresser heard his deputy's footsteps grow more distant, and then an engine starting. The sheriff closed his eyes and opened them again slowly, believing he was the only other human life in the vast belly of the old wool mill, before giving in to sleep, his shaking chills lulling him into surrender.

Deputy Spickle drove so fast he had to tell himself to slow down, and he said it aloud. The winding roads climbed by elevated steppes further upward into the small mountains. The blackened forests he rushed past in a blur appeared as if on a sped-up video, erratic and severe. Once he passed Turger's Mount he knew cell phone service would be gone. He sped along the soft gravel road until he reached Mrs. Buker's mailbox, a rooster with maroon tail feathers made of tin. He jumped out of the cruiser, greeted by Chippy, a fat beagle with itchy red ears. Mrs. Buker was so senile she didn't know the dog was hers half the time. She had babysat Deputy Spickle and Sheriff Dresser decades before. Spickle jogged up to the house, took the front steps two at a time. He needed to make sure the old woman didn't falter, that she would follow through on her part. He knocked on the door. Mrs. Buker answered in her flannel pajamas, Sonny behind her. She said, "Hello." The deputy nodded and looked down at the little boy, who seemed ready to accept his new life. He had the twins' eyes, blue and a little wild.

"Mrs. Buker," said Spickle. "Is everything okay?" The old woman was smiling, her disconnect from reality glimmering in her sweet brown eyes. Sonny tugged at her pajama leg. He said he was hungry. She pulled the boy forward and told him to say good morning properly. Sonny looked up sheepishly at Spickle and smiled. Deputy Spickle smiled back as Sonny put a thumb into his red mouth. Spickle told Mrs. Buker, "Remember, don't answer the door for anyone else, just me." Mrs. Buker was already closing the door and waving goodbye at the same time.

Sheriff Dresser woke to strong winds rattling the loose window frames, the shards of glass clinking, pieces the size of jewels falling to the concrete. His head banged unmercifully, and the sting of bile at the back of his throat was hard to extinguish, even after he managed to sit up more. He had to admit that his deputy had indeed done a fine job of binding his hands and feet. His fingertips and toes tingled. The sheriff shook his head as he looked around the space. The wool mill had once employed his father, uncles, and almost all the men he'd known as a boy, but the factory maintained only a skeleton crew as he entered the eighth grade, and by the time he graduated high school the place had made its last thousand pairs of socks and shuttered. His own feet made him think of all of this, his white socks gray at the tips, bought from Walmart and made in China.

He wanted coffee badly. The sun spilt into the old crumbling wool mill, tangerine light bathing the dry, powdery walls. The scent of warm minerals wafted inside the space. The sheriff closed his eyes and sucked in the crisp air, not unlike well water, the scent of old iron as palpable as the rust around him. The sheriff spat.

Deputy Spickle had been correct, yelling for help wasn't an option, but then as the light grew stronger, and the wind died down, there was the sound of footsteps, and a voice calling his name.

Going back down the mountain just as quickly as he'd gone up it, Deputy Spickle fought back the panic that his lies were careening out of control, the tires on the cruiser chirping as he took curves fast. He reviewed the plan again, went over the steps he'd already taken: Once he'd used the keys from the power company to flip the transformer up the road from the foster couple, it was simple to get Sonny into the cruiser. The little fella had spent a good bit of his first years away from his mother, and police cars had been how Sonny moved from one foster home to the next. Spickle checked his watch, and he saw he'd arrive at the office a good half-hour before the twins. He'd have to pick up the pace, be discreet, keep the mayor updated but placated too. Spickle nodded his head at this thought as he drove.

Chance coughed and sniffed as they rolled into a parking space at the sheriff's department. He got out to smoke. Kara touched her sister's wrist. "Kylie," she said. Kara offered up her mild expression, a mixture of resignation and utter fatigue. Kylie stared into her sister's eyes. Throughout the years, they'd found in each other a longing, as if they'd been the other's parent. Kylie nodded but didn't speak a word. Together they lunged out of the car and tramped toward the sheriff's office.

"So," said the deputy, "I've got good news." He stood and walked in front of the desk where the twins sat, both erect.

Kara glanced sideways at her twin. "Tell me right now," she said. Kylie looked at her sister as she talked. "Tell me *please* right now," said Kara, trying to sound appreciative, as if she were appeasing a homeroom teacher.

"I believe I have a lead," said Deputy Spickle as he took a deep cleansing breath.

Kara said, "And?" She scooted to the edge of the chair even more, now almost off the seat. With the two identical women perched before him, Spickle could see them as pupils, their postures ramrod. He had to tell himself he was doing the right thing, by the sheriff, by the twins, and for the town. He pushed away the notion that he was also doing it for Deputy Jeff Spickle.

"Here's what I need you to do," he said. "I need you both to remain calm, stay home, stop your searching. Let law enforcement handle it." Deputy Spickle offered a quick nod. "We can bring Sonny home, but it's time to have just one focus."

"Like hell," said Kara. Deputy Spickle held up a finger, and she forced herself to listen, to stay quiet.

"I have reason to believe Sonny is fine." Spickle walked back behind the desk and sat down. He placed his hands on the blotter, laced his fingers. "I need your word that you'll give me some more time. And to abide by my requests. Can you do that?" He looked from Kara to Kylie and back again.

"No," said Kara. "I want you to tell me who you think has him, where he is, and I want to hear it right now." Kara straightened her shoulders. She said, "The foster parents won't return my calls, and we've gone by there twice and it looks like they're gone. Have you even interviewed them?" Kara took a deep breath. "Are they suspects?"

Deputy Spickle thought about an exercise in one of his books. He pictured an ocean, blue skies, green water, white beaches, the warm sun, and the clean air. He counted to three before responding. "I've taken the Connors' statements, yes." Deputy Spickle smiled and took a deep breath. "Tommy Gates has been to see you several times over the last few weeks. I hear he wants his money, that you have a debt with him." Kylie stood up first and glanced back at her sister who remained seated.

Kara stood up too. "For the record, Spickle," said Kara, "if I truly believed Tommy had my son we wouldn't be here. Tommy does not have Sonny." Kara was seething, as if she might lunge at the deputy. She'd done it twice in the past, at a security guard in a honky-tonk called Twangers, and another time with Sheriff Dresser, who'd laughed and picked her up so her feet couldn't touch the ground before lowering her, cuffing her, and sliding her into the back of the police cruiser. "Now," she said, "don't tell me that's why you believe Sonny is fine. Don't tell me Tommy Gates is your big lead."

Deputy Spickle rubbed his chin and sat back. "I didn't say that, and I really can't say any more, but I can promise you both, you'll have Sonny back by nightfall." The foster couple had been easy to keep quiet, just a little petty cash for them to stay in Chattanooga for the weekend and some convincing that Spickle needed to stake out their place. They'd agreed when he gave them an extra $250 for expenses and assured them all would be fine. He'd told the Connors, acting as if he were trusting them with law-enforcement secrets, that they pretty much knew the little boy's father had him, and being that he was a criminal, he'd likely come back for the kid's clothes and toys. He'd said it all with conspiratorial trust and ended with telling the Connors they had better let the law take care of it.

Kara's face showed her mental calculations, a crease between her eyes as she thought. She'd gotten clean and was close to getting Sonny back. All her life, it was people in authority that held all the cards. She stared at Spickle so intently he had to refocus. He looked at Kara's face and her eyes were as smoky as the fire road, the eyeliner as black as the burnt oaks he passed during patrol. "We'll do as you say, for now," she said, "but if Sonny isn't back by nightfall, I swear I'll hold you and this whole department liable." Deputy Spickle nodded, offered an empathetic smile. "By the way, when's the sheriff gonna be back on his feet?" asked Kara, as Kylie nodded. "We need him on this."

"I assure you, I'll get your son back," said the deputy, pausing then, glancing at both women, and deciding he'd lost track of who was who. "I'd be happy to call you with regular updates," he added. Kara nodded, and Kylie pulled her cigarettes and cell phone from her back pockets.

Spickle said, "Please leave all your details with Mrs. Caldwell and I'll call as soon as I can. We'll have little Sonny back before you know it."

The secretary was busy tapping away at a keyboard, the blue glow of the computer screen steadily reflected in her reading glasses. Outside in the parking lot, Chance was on his phone, his thin neck craned, as if trying to listen for faraway sounds. Kara and Kylie moved to the office door and walked through it, past Mrs. Caldwell's reception area and out the automatic entrance.

Out the back exit, Deputy Spickle rushed to his cruiser and quickly started the car. He was feverish, a sweat at his beltline and around his starched collar. The twins had rattled him. He would need to rush the plan, he understood that now. It reminded him of the one and only time he stole as a child and ended up telling on himself to the Danner's Candy Store clerk immediately. He felt a rush of cold run through his chest, thoughts of details that he might've overlooked. He tried to check them off in his head. The twins knew Sonny was missing, and maybe a couple of their drug-addled roomies, and so did the Connors, but no one else, and it hadn't been long. Mrs. Caldwell believed the twins' presence at the sheriff's office had to do with simple petty crimes. There'd been no DFCS report filed yet, and if the timing worked, it would be a moot point, something done after Sonny was safely back. Spickle focused on speeding up the steps in his plan now, or else all would be lost. He tailed the twins in the pickup driven by the kid with two arrests for petty drug possession, Chance Wilfort. But after the kid seemed to be simply driving the twins back to their duplex, the deputy did a U-turn and went back to the office.

By noon Spickle was pacing in his office. Mrs. Caldwell buzzed him. "Anything you need? I'm about to go home for lunch." He was curt, telling her no, no, and to enjoy her pot roast. "It's lasagna," she said, but he had already tapped the speaker button and he didn't hear her. He watched the clock but felt uneasy. He'd planned on waiting until late afternoon, but something nagged at him, a disappointment in himself hung in his mind too, as if he lacked the patience of a real law enforcer. Deputy Spickle busied himself with a stack of files, then got up and walked to the windows, the weather outside again unsure of what it wanted to do, bleak, with a leaden haze over a dull sun, then back again to more overcast, some wet flakes.

He thought he'd have a panic attack if he didn't act. He grabbed the keys from his desk and pulled on his coat, rushed out to the parking lot, and jumped into the cruiser.

He floored it past the Rainbow Paint Store and the Zelzer's Insurance Company at the edge of the city limits. There was a powdery snow on the blackened limbs of burnt-out trees, the ground beneath like melted dark chocolate. He gunned the motor, and the tires of the squad car squealed against the damp pavement as shiny as onyx. Up and up he went until he reached the summit. He parked close to the log-style home. The swollen beagle brayed and threw its muzzle to the dark skies. Spickle pushed the car door open and called to the dog. "Chippy," he said, and the fat little thing waddled closer, wagging its stocky tail. Up on the porch, Mrs. Buker sat in a swing, knitting and singing along with a gospel station emanating from a black radio. Chippy turned excited circles and ran full speed up the steps to the house. Spickle jogged up them too, his stomach tight, heart racing.

Deputy Spickle paused on the front porch and took a deep breath, all the while Mrs. Buker kept at her knitting. It had been a long morning, but so far, so good. Spickle looked around the front porch, ducked to peer into the windows. "Where's the boy?" The air was redolent of dogwood, purple woodsmoke drifting over the hills, the scent as nutty as roasted pecans.

Mrs. Buker didn't take her eyes from her project but answered matter-of-factly, "Sheriff Dresser came and got him." Mrs. Buker's wrists pulsed with paper-thin skin, dark blue veins underneath. She was relaxed. The cold air whisked into the channel of the front porch. Chippy circled then sat down at the feet of Mrs. Buker, leaves somersaulting along the deck boards.

"Mrs. Buker," said Spickle, pinching the bridge of his nose between index finger and thumb, "please go and get the boy now." His voice was laced with derision. "I'm on a tight schedule. Things have changed. I need to get Sonny now."

Mrs. Buker only grinned. "The sheriff came and got him, I said."

The old woman didn't flinch when Deputy Spickle brushed past her and hurried inside the log cabin, calling for Sonny and tossing quilts aside from the couch and love seat. He ran up the stairs to the loft only to find it tidy, bed made. He pushed open the door to the only bathroom and yanked aside the shower curtain. Deputy Spickle rushed to the small living room, pulled the sliding-glass doors apart, and peered out from the small deck toward the woods. He hurried back through the house and onto the front porch again, where Mrs. Buker had fallen asleep, the ball of yarn at her feet. He shook her by the shoulder and she startled. Deputy Spickle got to his knees so he could look her in the eyes, his hand still clutching her bony shoulder. "Mrs. Buker, focus now. Where's Sonny?" He waited for her to answer but reworded the question. "Mrs. Buker, where's the little boy you've been taking care of for me? Where is he? Think, now, think."

The old woman's hands trembled. She looked up and off to the side but had started to sob. She shook her head and said repeatedly that she didn't know. Spickle helped her off the porch swing and guided her inside. He ushered her to the couch and put a quilt over her legs. As if nothing had happened, she told him, as she pointed a remote at the television, that her favorite game show was about to come on. "Mrs. Buker," he said, on his knees again, his voice like a plea, "you must tell me where the boy is."

She smiled, took her eyes off the television set for just a second, and touched his face. Deputy Spickle patted her hand and rose, hot and sick.

He went out the front door of the cabin and closed it quietly, as if he were afraid he might trip an alarm. All he could focus on was getting inside the cruiser, where he could think, map out some alternative plan. His hands fumbled with the keys as he turned the ignition. He forced the realization of two abductions from his mind. He rubbed his face with his palms and wiped his nose. He took a paper cup of cold coffee from the console, gulped it. "Think," he said softly.

Deputy Spickle got out of the cruiser and went back to the log cabin, eased the front door open. Mrs. Buker was asleep on the couch, a slight smile on her face. He checked the pantry, went up into the loft again, looked under the bed, the bathroom once more.

Deputy Spickle covered Mrs. Buker with another quilt, locked the door on his way out. He walked the perimeter of the property, the sloping yard that turned to a forest of longleaf pine. He could smell ash and taste it in the cold wind as he turned and headed back to the cruiser. Maybe Tommy had tailed him and had convinced Mrs. Buker he was law enforcement? Or the twins and the Chance guy had followed him earlier and talked Mrs. Buker into handing over Sonny? Who else could've? Why had she said Sheriff Dresser had gotten Sonny? Probably because of her old mind.

He started the cruiser again and backed up, and that's when he saw them. The sheriff held the little boy's hand as they walked, casually, as if heading toward a fishing hole. Spickle slammed the brakes, watched Sheriff Dresser wave, as he and Sonny approached the car. Spickle looked around; no other vehicles, nothing but Mrs. Buker's Ford sedan she hadn't driven in years. Sheriff Dresser stooped and tapped on the window, smiled. Deputy Spickle pushed the button and the frosty glass slid down. His throat was tight and for the life of him he couldn't grasp what had occurred, how it'd happened. The air seemed too thin, and Spickle thought he might hyperventilate.

"Open up, Jeff," said the sheriff, "and I'll tell you all about it."

A click and thud and the doors unlocked. The sheriff helped Sonny into the backseat, then got in himself. Spickle's eyes were glued to the rearview mirror, but then, when the sheriff started to speak, he turned in the seat to get a better look. Sonny was yawning and climbed into the sheriff's lap.

"Jeff," said the sheriff, his eyes clear, even a little grateful, a smile as he spoke. "When you abduct your boss it's not a bad idea to make sure there are no witnesses." Sonny rested his head against the sheriff's chest, closed his eyes. A dusting of snow accumulated on the windshield. Deputy Spickle tried to speak but the words wouldn't form, as if his tongue had lost the ability to move. The sheriff rearranged Sonny so the boy's neck wasn't craned, now almost cradling the child. "Danny, as you may recall with his DUIs, is a drunk too." The sheriff looked down at the little boy's face. "Once a drunk, always a drunk, sober or otherwise, goes to meetings. Of course, we're not supposed to talk about that, but you're a sworn officer of the law." Spickle closed his eyes and kept them closed, a defense against the story the sheriff laid out. Danny hadn't figured it out right away, but he had indeed tailed the deputy. "You see," said Sheriff Dresser, "you were right about me not yelling, but once I knew it was Danny on the other side of that wall, well, drunks know drunks."

Apparently, Danny'd had to run home to get clothes for the sheriff, and a sledgehammer, but he didn't have much trouble busting through the brick walls. "I'm not saying he didn't work up a sweat, but like I say, drunks stick together."

Deputy Spickle opened his eyes. "But how'd you know about Mrs. Buker and Sonny?"

"I didn't," said the sheriff, "but once Danny got me free, I figured I'd do a little investigating of my own." Sonny squirmed some in his sleep. "Our dear Mrs. Caldwell is a true confidante, as you know." Deputy Spickle felt the red on his face intensify, and it was hard to keep eye contact with the sheriff, but it was also a relief to hear his words. "She first tried your cell phone but couldn't track it, then she went to the GPS on the cruiser. Once she saw you'd been making trips up the mountain, I knew where you were visiting. I was surprised to see Sonny boy, but as soon as I did, I pieced it together." Larger snowflakes drifted over the blackened hills, piled up on the scorched limbs of the hardwoods. The sheriff said, "But I get what you were trying to do, set me straight, find a missing child and all, earn back some respect, and that last part can still happen, but not the first. I'm going to those meetings, I'm trying, and I'll keep at it. I mess up again, I give you official permission to book me."

Deputy Spickle nodded and started to apologize, but the sheriff cut him off. "Jeff," he said, "if we're going to set this all orderly, we've got to get to work. There are some moving pieces here we need to fit just right."

They packed up what they needed and Deputy Spickle got out, opened the back door, and took the sleeping child from the sheriff's arms. A rucksack over his shoulder, Sheriff Dresser said, "Left an impounded car about three miles down the mountain, right where the worst of the fires was. We'll need to get some food for the boy from the car. There's a leftover charity box from Christmas, mostly canned." They started down the fire road, the air chilling. Along the ditches, they found a small footpath, where some of the old-timers used to walk because they had no car. The path provided enough cover. Besides, the road wouldn't be traveled much until June when the campers appeared. Deputy Spickle started to talk again and was able to get out, "You don't have to . . ." before the sheriff waved him off.

"The plan will have to take us closer to the Connor place," said the sheriff, as he shoved the canned goods from the trunk of the impounded car into the rucksack. "Story goes as such: I was tracking the boy and found him but lost my way, you know, since I was inebriated and all."

Deputy Spickle shook his head, protested, "But all these lies, that's what I was trying to stop, but ended up lying even more."

The sheriff raised a hand as if he might be testifying. "Jeff, I get to tell the story, and don't forget," he said with a grin, "you're the kidnapper, so we do as I say." The deputy nodded, still holding Sonny over his shoulder as the gray skies added a deep purple along the ridge. Sheriff Dresser said, "Besides, us drunks, we bring people down to our level with deceit. These lies, this time, will protect *you*." They removed their coats and wrapped the sleepy boy up snug. Sheriff Dresser carried Sonny, and Spickle strapped on the rucksack.

As they entered the edge of the woods, the sheriff picked up the story from earlier. "Anyhow, I'll say I got turned around and our citizens will have enough sense to take that as I was drunk again." Sonny yawned as they trekked along a straight line of charred elms, their wide trunks like black chalkboards. "It'll take a little finesse with the Connors, but to be honest, they'll just be glad the boy is safe and they can still get paid to foster." They trudged through mucky ground, the acrid scent of burnt grass and scorched pine cones heavy in the air. "We can insinuate the power being cut off was a teenage prank." Deputy Spickle felt queasy at the ease with which the sheriff could falsify. The sheriff added, as if his words were the last on the subject, "The twins, well, I hear

Kara has been clean for six months. I'd like to help her and Kylie get Sonny here back. Might set us all on the right track."

They walked for almost two hours, through more burnt forest, past two small lakes called the Dahlonegas, and along a section of briars where rabbits flitted underneath. The light started to fade. They switched on flashlights in the dusk and kept moving east for another thirty minutes. "How far you suppose we are from the city limits, the Connor place?" asked the sheriff, as Sonny woke up more and mumbled something that sounded like he was hungry.

"I think," said Deputy Spickle, looking at his cell phone, which had service now, "we must be about four miles out." He pointed in the general direction ahead of them. The sheriff placed Sonny down, kneeling so he could talk to the boy. "You a hungry Sonny boy?" said the sheriff, tousling the little boy's brown hair. Sonny nodded and smiled a sleepy grin.

They made a fire, rocks around the edge. The sheriff heated green beans, chicken noodle soup, and opened several cans of tuna. Sonny was small but had a good appetite. "This is nice," said the sheriff as he cleaned up and Spickle made a small pallet for Sonny to sleep on next to the fire. They wiped the boy's face and tucked him under their coats. He was asleep again within minutes. They kept the fire going, the heat from it strong.

"What about the twins?" asked the sheriff. "They holding up?" Deputy Spickle nodded but his face was flat, as if he'd been shown an awful crime-scene photo.

"Listen, Jeff," said the sheriff, "it is what it is, and yes, you could've come up with a better idea, but we've got the hand we've got, and besides, putting a little fear of God into Kara might just help her stay focused on getting Sonny back, you ever think of that?" Deputy Spickle swallowed hard and took a deep breath. The sheriff poked the fire, and said, "Good, now, let me tell you what we need to do at sunrise."

In the early light, they stretched and quietly put out the fire, dowsing it several times from canteens. Both had only caught snippets of sleep. The sheriff knelt and gently smeared Sonny's face

with soot. The boy didn't stir. Sheriff Dresser handed the lump of
black to his deputy. He said quietly, the land around them nearly
silent, "Here, rub it in, so they'll know we've been lost."

When the sun came up fully and the land around them twin-
kled into existence, the silvery hoarfrost reflecting a new blue sky
and clear sunshine, they moved away from the campsite. After
twenty minutes, the sheriff said, "Hand me your phone, I'll call
it in." He took the phone from Spickle and handed Sonny over.
The sheriff said clearly into the phone, "Mrs. Caldwell, you're
in early, as always." He told her Deputy Spickle had found him
and the boy, that she should call the twins, and after that, if she
wouldn't mind phoning Danny Hobbs at county transportation
to come get them at the crossroads of Blue Ridge and Ellijay.
"You'd be mighty proud of Deputy Spickle, Mrs. Caldwell. He
parked his cruiser at the top of the mountain and just set off on
foot to find us, didn't stop until he did, even had a rucksack of
food. Little Sonny probably thinks he's been on a great adventure
and nothing else. Deputy Spickle saw to that. We might need to
get the newspaper to do a story."

Sheriff Dresser handed the phone back. Spickle said, "You
didn't need to do that."

"It's truly the least I could do. From now on, it's gonna be the
straight and narrow, Scout's honor." They stood awhile, Sonny
asleep on the deputy's shoulder, and with the plan complete,
there wasn't much to do but wait. Above them, the cobalt sky
throbbed with sunshine. The sheriff said, "Jeff, what do you say
we come back up here in April and bring Sonny boy with us,
camp by the Dahlonegas, show the little fella how to fish. We
could fry up a mess at Mrs. Buker's." Deputy Spickle agreed,
and they watched as one of the county transportation trucks
climbed the road, Danny behind the wheel. Sheriff Dresser
said, "Beautiful morning," and then added, staring toward the
truck coming for them, "One day at a time, that's what they say
in the meetings."

Danny honked and it woke Sonny. The little boy patted
Deputy Spickle's face as if they might be old friends. The sheriff

laughed, and the deputy did too, as Sonny giggled and threw his head back.

"Yep," said Sheriff Dresser, his eyes pondering blankly, "one day at a time, that's how we'll do it." Deputy Jeff Spickle watched the man, really looked at him, and wondered if this time it might be true.

The setting for this story is the North Georgia Mountains, the same area where parts of Deliverance *were filmed. I had long been a fan of the book and the film, and to be honest, both horrified and intrigued by the author, James Dickey. I knew I wanted to tell a story with the backdrop of the mountains, especially after some fires in that region flared up. It's an area that is at once diverse and welcoming and closed off and insular. The landscape plays a large role in the story, at least metaphorically.*

As for the two main characters, Sheriff Dresser and Deputy Spickle, well, they are loosely based on the iconic law enforcement duo of Andy Taylor and Barney Fife. I have always admired the writing in the show and been moved by the relationship between two lifelong friends who are often in disagreement, while being loving and patient with one another's flaws. Male friendships aren't often portrayed well in storytelling, and I wanted to show the reader how my two lawmen could simultaneously disappoint and show up for one another.

The plot has two major arcs, twin women in search of a child, and the abduction of Sheriff Dresser by his own deputy. When the consequences collide, the story becomes one of only partial redemption since at its core lies more fabrication for the characters to live forward and off the page. I wrote the draft in about four days. At the time, I was reading a nonfiction book called Murders and Social Change, *published in 1974 by James Jenkins. It helped me understand crime in the South.*

Jeffery Deaver *is an international number-one bestselling author. His books are sold in one hundred fifty countries and translated into twenty-five languages. He has served two terms as president of Mystery Writers of America and was recently named a Grand Master of MWA.*

The author of forty-eight novels, one hundred one short stories, a nonfiction law book, and a lyricist of a country-western album, he's received or been shortlisted for dozens of awards.

His The Bodies Left Behind *was named Novel of the Year by the International Thriller Writers association, and his Lincoln Rhyme thriller* The Broken Window *and a stand-alone,* Edge, *were also nominated for that prize.* The Garden of Beasts *won the Steel Dagger from the Crime Writers Association in England, and he has won the Short Story Dagger from CWA, and another story was shortlisted for the award. He's also been nominated for eight Edgar Awards by MWA.*

Deaver has been honored with the Lifetime Achievement Award by the Bouchercon World Mystery Convention, the Strand Magazine's Lifetime Achievement Award, and the Raymond Chandler Lifetime Achievement Award in Italy.

His book A Maiden's Grave *was made into an HBO movie starring James Garner and Marlee Matlin, and his novel* The Bone Collector *was a feature release from Universal Pictures, starring Denzel Washington and Angelina Jolie. Lifetime aired an adaptation of his novel* The Devil's Teardrop. *NBC television recently aired the nine-episode prime-time series,* Lincoln Rhyme: Hunt for the Bone Collector.

THE LADY IN MY LIFE
Jeffery Deaver

U pper New York Bay—a.k.a. New York Harbor—is considered by many to be the best natural harbor in the world.

It can also be among the most beautiful, as was the case today. The water was gunmetal, and the breeze was teasing up whitecaps. A container ship, massive, like a thirty-story building in recline, eased gracefully west, aiming toward the New Jersey docks, where the many-colored trailers would be lifted off and sent to depots around the country, and new ones seated on the vessel for a journey to who-knew-where.

Taking it all in was Miguel Torres, sitting on a bench in North Shore Waterfront Esplanade Park, the northern tip of Staten Island. He was eating his lunch, which he had made himself. It was a tuna-salad sandwich, dressed with cheese and pickles. The bread was homemade white.

Baking was a hobby of his (he could not make a casserole or cook a roast, but flour and yeast were ever at his command). He was drinking hot chocolate from a cup that he had unscrewed from a lengthy green thermos.

He was a compact man with thick, trimmed black hair and a matching mustache. His face was handsome enough to be that of a model. He was five feet eight inches tall. And muscular, thanks not to a gym (he had not been to one in five years) but to his profession of landscaper.

Presently, as often, he was mesmerized as he gazed over the water at the distant, ever-impressive fortress of buildings in lower Manhattan, at Governor's and Liberty Islands, at the no-nonsense docks and warehouses of Brooklyn and, to his left, the bristling cranes of New Jersey's industrial backbone: the cranes that lifted, loaded, and offloaded the containers he'd been thinking of moments ago.

He stretched. Felt a bone pop.

Tired . . .

The alarm had cried out at 4:30 A.M. and, after rolling groggily from bed, he'd had a breakfast of cold tamales and coffee and then driven to Mr. Whittaker's house, a nice brick two-story in Tudor style. Miguel had been hired to "make it nice for spring." Mr. Whittaker was a recent widower and Miguel had learned that his wife had been the gardener in the family. The retired businessman himself didn't have the heart to putter in the yard, given his loss.

Miguel was attending to the man's flower beds, in sore need of hand-weeding (the only way to do it) and nutrients. He still had eight, nine hours of work to make the yard beautiful once more, beautiful in the way that only living plants could accomplish.

A thought landed like a determined bee on a flower—how different was his life here, compared with that back home. The desert had its beauty but could not compare with the endlessly pulsating plane of water that stretched out before him.

This place was very special. Miguel often dreamed—waking and otherwise—about owning a house with a water view like this. There were a number of such residences available, of course, overlooking the Harbor in all of the boroughs, except Queens and the Bronx. But affording one was another matter. And Miguel Torres had another requirement that limited his ability to find his perfect residence: he would never live in an apartment or condo, water vista or not. He thrived on soil and grass and plants. Which meant that prices for even the most modest of places that would meet his standards started over a million. His age was thirty-two. Over a beer at night, or coffee after work, or hot chocolate at lunch he calculated that by the time he saved enough to buy, he would be seventy-four, depending of course on the undependable real estate market of New York City.

Of course, miracles could happen. But for the time being, he was content to stroll along the Esplanade anytime he wished. And for free.

The park was crowded with people who'd flocked here to enjoy the beautiful early-April day, one of the most temperate of the year so far. Curious by nature, Miguel gazed about. To his right, on the other side of a thick stand of boxwood, was a cluster of three or four people engaged in an animated conversation. He couldn't help but play the eavesdropping game.

In front of him on the concrete walkway, joggers trotted past. Most were frowning. In pain? He laughed. He could tell them about muscle pain—after eight-hour days spent doing what he did.

To Miguel's left, on an adjoining bench, a businessman had doffed his jacket and rolled up his shirt sleeves. He sloughed back and gazed upward, as if praying for a tan.

Miguel took in the Mixmaster blend of all of the sounds cascading, swirling, descending upon him—and the laughter, the caw of gulls, the slap of water, the voices . . .

He remained motionless, a man lost in thought, for ten minutes, then rose and tossed his trash into a nearby bin, much to the disappointment—and ire—of a large gull.

Returning to the sidewalk, he paused momentarily and glanced into the Harbor, then walked steadily from the park.

Miguel Torres had work to do.

The next morning, he was on Paxton Street, which was tucked between the Brighton Heights and Stapleton Heights neighborhoods of Staten Island.

He wore what he usually did on the job: jeans and a flannel shirt—today gray and blue—over a black T-shirt. Today was summer scented and even warmer than yesterday and he'd left his jacket in the truck.

Much of the huge island, one of the five boroughs, or counties, of New York City, had been gentrified. These particular blocks had not been—but they hadn't needed much spiffing. The houses were old but masterfully and solidly built. They were kept up well, and little trim was in need of painting. Most had decent-sized yards, both front and back. Miguel was presently hard at work, engaged in his most effective sales effort: walking from house to house and offering the occupants one of his cards or leaving one on the doorstep if no one was home. If he did have the chance to meet the homeowner and they were willing to listen, he'd offer a brief description of what he might do to make their property more beautiful.

And safer.

As was the case now.

He was standing in front of a single-family home in what was called gingerbread style, the gray siding like fish scales, the roof shingled with dark red asphalt. The windows were of beveled glass, the doorknob and hinges polished brass. He guessed the structure was one hundred years old.

The small front yard consisted of carelessly mowed and underfertilized grass. Some dirt beds were home to a few shrubs and flowering plants, looking none too healthy.

What took his attention, though, was the dominant element of the property: a towering oak, sixty feet high. He knew the rate at which hardwood trees grew and he supposed that it had been planted as a sapling when the construction of the house was completed.

Miguel walked to the front door, rang the bell.

He heard footsteps and a moment later a woman opened the door. She was about his age, maybe a bit older, and had a narrow, striking face and abundant blond hair tied up in a ponytail.

"Yes?" she asked. If she was cautious about a stranger at the door, she gave no evidence of it.

"Hi. Good morning." He had studied English from his grammar school days, and he had only a faint accent.

He offered his card.

> *A-One Landscaping*
> *Miguel Torres*
> *Trees, plantings, irrigation, stump removal, carting*
> *Licensed and Bonded.*

She glanced at it, then behind him, at his truck, a twenty-two foot Chevy 6500, which he kept in immaculate shape (the cleanliness was part of his sales pitch—to demonstrate his responsibility and the care he took in his work). The woman was in jeans and a close-fitting light-blue blouse. Her necklace was a cross. So, most likely a Catholic, like him.

"Oh, I'm renting. I can give you the number of the owner. He'd be the one to talk to about any work."

She wasn't from Staten Island. There's a unique way native islanders talk. Her sentences would have diminished in volume at the end and trailed off to silence. And "owner" would likely have been "owniz" and "number" "numbaz." Locals often added an "s" sound to singular words.

She also had a faint accent that was definitely not from the Island: He believed it was Southern.

Miguel said, "Sure. I can call him. But I wanted to point out something. There's a problem." He turned to the oak. "That branch is about to come down."

The twenty-foot limb drooped over her SUV, a black Honda, which was showing a dusting of pollen from the very oak tree that was threatening to cave in its roof.

"I never noticed it." She stepped out onto the front porch and studied the branch, which was about a foot in diameter where it had begun splitting off from the trunk.

"What happened?"

"Could've been anything. Wind or that ice storm last winter. Maybe age. The tree's healthy otherwise."

She turned to him. They were about eye to eye, his deep brown, hers a glowing blue.

"I'm Katherine. With a K." She noted his card. "And it's your company. You're Miguel?"

"With an M."

A beat of a moment and she laughed.

They shook hands. He was always careful about this. His palms were calloused and very strong. But she didn't shy, and her grip was firm too. When their hands retreated, she didn't look away but scanned his face for a moment.

He too held her eyes, with a cocked head, then turned to the front of the property. "I'm thinking this could be a nice yard."

"The owner doesn't do very much. Obviously."

"I wouldn't mind getting a contract." His eyes returned to hers. "Let me propose something. I'll take care of the branch for nothing. If you could tell the owner about it and give him my number . . . What do you think?"

She debated for a moment. Then: "Well, you can't beat the price. A deal. I'll move the Honda."

Katherine turned and with her left hand reached up and pulled some keys off a hook just inside the door. She was not wearing a wedding or engagement ring.

She backed into the street, then parked in front of his truck.

Miguel got his climbing gear from the back bed and one of the smaller chainsaws.

"You mind if I watch?"

He laughed. "Won't be as dramatic as a hundred-foot redwood coming down. But be my guest."

After mounting the climbing spikes on his boots, he slung the canvas strap around the tree and clipped it to the rings on his utility belt. The chainsaw went over his shoulder. He flipped the strap upward so that it encircled the trunk about three feet above his head. He pulled it taut and, flexing his arms and climbing with the spiked boots, moved upward. He kept repeating the process until he was at the branch.

He glanced back and saw her sitting on the porch studying him. She called, "Like Spiderman."

He chuckled and pulled on goggles and yellow ear protectors then fired up the chainsaw. It took only four strategic cuts for gravity to take over and the limb fell to the ground as undramatically as Miguel had promised.

He now descended and removed the climbing gear. He untucked and removed his flannel shirt, folded and set it on a boxwood nearby. The T-shirt revealed his muscular frame and from the corner of his eye he saw Katherine swiftly study his torso and then look back to the branch.

He tugged the saw to life once more and within a few minutes the limb had become six separate logs.

Removing the goggles and earmuffs, he asked, "You want it stacked for firewood? It'll have to dry for a few months."

"I won't be here much longer than that myself. I don't think the fireplace works anyway."

"I'll get rid of it."

In Staten Island homeowners can leave their own yard waste at curbside for pickup, but what professional landscapers generate has to be hauled away by them. One by one, Miguel squatted, lifted the wood, and threw it in the bed of his truck. Each weighed about fifty pounds, he guessed, but they were nothing for him.

"Where will you take it?" Katherine asked.

"We have approved dump sites. Not too far."

He wiped his forehead with his shirt, then replaced it on the shrub.

"Would you like some water?"

"Sure. Thanks."

Inside, the house was quite nice. *Majestuosa*—stately—was the word that came to mind.

It featured wood-paneled walls, leaded-glass panels in the doors, red-and-black oriental carpets, and more brass fixtures.

"You mind if I wash my hands?"

She pointed to a bathroom and Miguel stepped inside. Like in many old houses there were separate hot and cold faucets, with the hot too searing to use alone. He filled the basin, washed with a lavender foam soap, and then rinsed off in cold water.

He joined Katherine in the spacious kitchen, where she moved a stack of papers off the high-top island. This room seemed to serve as an office.

"Take a seat," she said, indicating the stools.

He hesitated briefly and then sat. While customers sometimes offered him water, none had ever asked him to sit down; they usually seemed eager that he finish his drink and leave.

"Or coffee?"

This had never been offered either.

"No, just water's fine."

She got a glass from a cabinet, added ice, and filled it from the faucet. He wondered if she'd sit too, but no. She remained standing and sipped from a coffee mug.

After a moment of silence, he asked, "You're only here for a while?"

Katherine replied, "I work in IT—you know, internet. A four-month assignment. It's usually cheaper to rent a house than pay for an extended-stay hotel." She looked him up and down again. "You done landscaping all your life?"

"No, no. Started five years ago, when I came here from Mexico."

"I only ask because . . ." Her voice trailed off, and not because of a Staten Island dialect. She seemed to regret where her comment had been going. About his excellent English and grammar, he guessed.

"Down there I wore a suit and tie." His shoulders rose and fell. "But my degree didn't mean much here, so I started my own company."

"That's not fair." She was frowning.

"I thought so at first, but I like this better. Much better. I'm my own boss. Outside, working with my hands."

"Why'd you leave?"

His face darkened "Too dangerous. The cartels. A new president comes in. 'Oh, I'll clean it up. I'll make the country safe . . .' A joke. They never do. I brought my parents and sister too. They're in California."

"But you didn't go there?"

"No. I like New York. It's special."

"It is. Very special. I'll be sad to leave when the job's over."

She refilled the coffee mug, which did not seem to need refilling. "You mentioned your family . . . Anybody else come with you?"

"No. Just us." A pause. "There *was* a woman I was seeing." He shrugged. "She could have come. But she wanted to stay. I can't blame her. It's the hardest thing in the world, leaving your family. She couldn't do it."

He thought about Consuela a lot. He tried not to but that usually proved to be impossible.

"You'll meet somebody here."

"I'm in no hurry. My mother always says, 'Just wait and see what fate has in store for you.'"

"That sounds a little . . . can I say? Ominous."

"I always thought that too."

They shared a laugh and their eyes met once more. Was she offering a flirt, perhaps an invitation of some sort?

He wasn't sure.

But what he did know for certain was that *he* was.

The spell broke. He finished the water and rose. "I should go."

Together, they walked to the front door and onto the porch. She glanced out into the yard. "That other work you wanted to do here. Why don't you just come back and do it? If the landlord won't pay I'll get my company to."

"Well . . ."

"No. Really. It's too nice a yard to look like it does now. Gets prettified, it'll be nice to sit on the steps and have a glass of wine."

"'Prettified.' That's a new one to me."

Katherine's eyes were very much the color of Upper New York Bay on a sunny summer afternoon.

Another silence. Neither moved.

He came a second away from easing forward to see how receptive she'd be to a kiss. He sensed: a lot.

But then he told himself firmly: Careful there.

Which he modified to: Take. Your. Time.

"I can start tomorrow?" asked Miguel.

"Tomorrow would be perfect."

Overnight the temperature had dropped, and it was now ten degrees cooler than yesterday. Overcast and windier too.

The oak, one limb less, swayed, and the budding leaves rustled.

Miguel hit the doorbell button and just a moment later he was aware of footsteps approaching.

Katherine opened the door. She was smiling. He reciprocated. And, though it seemed like an odd gesture, he stuck his hand out. She gripped it firmly and the contact lingered.

He couldn't stop his eyes from sweeping down and then back up. Her outfit was of gray, shimmery cloth, silky. Almost like pajamas.

No, *exactly* like pajamas.

"Morning," he said.

"*Buenos dias.*"

He laughed. Her pronunciation was terrible. "So. With the wind, I checked the tree again. All good. You're safe from falling branches." He noted she'd kept her car parked on the street overnight.

"My hero."

"I've got lime and fertilizer and some acid for the hydrangeas. Rose food too. Where would you like me to start?"

A frown, a tilt of her head. "Here." She took his right hand and put it on her breast.

Miguel was motionless for a moment. One had to be careful nowadays of course, but if this didn't qualify as "consent" he didn't know what might. So he slid his other hand around her waist to the small of her back and pulled her to him, kissing her hard.

She gripped his lips with her teeth. Then opened her mouth and kissed him back just as passionately.

Katherine turned and led him into the hallway, closing the door behind them. Then, still gripping his hand firmly, led him into the bedroom. The lace curtains were partially open, and you could see a portion of the gardens surrounding the backyard. They were in even worse shape than those in the front.

Miguel Torres didn't care.

He opened his eyes to find her dressing.

It was noon. Two hours had passed since he'd arrived, and only the past fifteen or twenty minutes had been devoted to sleep.

She noticed he was awake and smiled.

He did too.

And told himself not to think of Consuela. Though he did, concluding that, as good as such times had been with her, none had risen to this level.

He sat up, swung his feet to the floor. Sipped from the bottle of water on the bedside table. She'd set it there while he dozed.

Katherine walked close and kissed him. She whispered, "Sleepyhead."

"I'm awake now."

She glanced down. "You certainly are."

He lifted an eyebrow. It was an invitation. To accept or reject as she wished.

She clicked her tongue and her face registered disappointment. "I've got an associate who'll be here in ten minutes."

"Well," Miguel offered, "maybe tomorrow."

She frowned.

He shook his head.

She said, "What's wrong with tonight?"

His answer was a firm kiss.

Miguel rose to wash up and dress while she made the bed.

Together they walked into the kitchen.

"Coffee now?"

He'd been just a water-drinking handyman yesterday. His status had changed.

"Black."

As she poured two cups the doorbell sounded.

"That'd be Tim," she said, handing him the brew. He took it and sipped. Strong. He liked it.

She walked to the front door and opened it, letting inside a stocky man in his thirties, dressed in jeans, a white dress shirt, and a navy blazer. He was blond, his hair longish. He carried a backpack on one shoulder, a computer bag over the other. It dangled at his side like a large purse.

He said to Katherine, "Morning," though his eyes were on Miguel.

She introduced him and added, "He's a friend."

Miguel had wondered if she'd say, "My gardener."

"Nice to meet you."

Miguel's impression, however, was that he didn't feel it was so very nice. A smile was on his face, but it was one of *those* smiles—of questionable DNA.

The men gripped hands. Tim's fingers were long but were the digits of a computer person, not an outdoor worker.

Miguel was careful not to exert too much pressure.

She poured Tim some coffee as well, and added cream and sugar.

He took several sips and then set the cup down on the island and opened the computer bag. He extracted his laptop, a big one, the seventeen-inch model. He set this on the kitchen table, tugged open the lid, and booted the Dell up. After loading some documents or diagrams—Miguel couldn't see clearly—he scanned the screen and pointed to some portion of it. Katherine bent down and read.

She said, "Good. They delivered on time. We're right on schedule."

Tim nodded but his face didn't register the same satisfaction hers did.

Which had nothing to do with their project. Tim was jealous.

As Tim looked over Katherine, Miguel studied him. He was not an attractive man, but round and fidgety, unathletic—a high school student who'd kept waiting to flower, to slip from nerd to cool, but had never been able to get beyond the video-gaming, candy-sneaking, girl-ogling years.

His crush on Katherine would run deep and he knew she would always be interested in the Miguels of the world. He would have talents, important ones—like making sure things ran "right on schedule"—but that was different.

Tim, of course, couldn't resent her, not openly, given the infatuation and the obvious fact that she was his superior.

So he'd suck it up when on the subject of Miguel Torres and offer the smile that perhaps he honestly believed would really be taken for one.

He was just wondering whether he should tell her he was going to get to work on the yard when her phone rang, and she took a call. As she listened a frown blossomed on her face.

"Well, that's not going to work. How would that work?" Her voice had an edge he hadn't heard before. She held her hand over the phone and said to Tim, "The trucking company. An accident. They can't do it."

Tim was frowning. He stammered, "They . . . they have to."

She said, "It's not happening. Their other trucks're on the road." She returned to the call. "You'll just have to find another way. We've paid you twenty percent . . . I don't want the money back. I want the shipment delivered like you're contracted to do . . . No, I don't want you jobbing it out. We vetted *you*. We don't have time to screen anybody else. Oh, never mind." She hit disconnect and it seemed she regretted not being able to slam a landline receiver down into a cradle.

She stared at the floor for a moment, her beautiful face registering dismay. She looked to Tim. "So. What do we do? They have to go on board this afternoon. There're no options."

He muttered, "We have to call corporate."

"Oh, great. I can't *wait* to have that conversation."

Miguel asked, "What do you have to be delivered?"

"Computer racks for crude oil tankers' navigation systems."

Tim added, "They're algorithms that measure wind, current, depth of water, draft, dimensions of ships, a hundred other things. They find the most fuel-efficient routes whatever the seas are like."

Katherine was staring at the computer screen. "The contract . . . They *have* to be dropped at the boat we've chartered. Today. In the next few hours."

She looked to Tim, who grimaced.

Miguel asked, "Where are they? And where do they have to go?"

She waved to the computer. "They were just dropped off at a warehouse in Brooklyn. Red Hook. We have a boat at Emerson Dock on Staten Island. That's where they're going."

"I know it," Miguel said. "How big are these things?"

The two regarded each other. Tim said, "Probably fifty pounds."

"How many?"

"Twelve. What are you . . . ?"

"I can do it," Miguel offered.

Tim said, "What, in a landscaping truck?"

Miguel looked him over closely. "The suspension's just like any other thirty-footer."

"But—"

"No," Katherine said, smiling. "I like it."

"Well," Tim said slowly, "How much'd you charge?"

His face suggested he did not want another man to save the day and impress fair Katherine.

Miguel thought for a moment, calculating in his head. Staten Island to Brooklyn and back again. "Make it two fifty."

Katherine laughed. Tim stared at him. She was the one who said, "The job we contracted for is two thousand. That's what we'd pay you."

Miguel lifted an eyebrow. "I think I'm in the wrong line of work."

Tim said to her, "You sure? I mean . . . Security?"

"You have any other options? Those ships sail without the modules, they cancel our contract and buy from Allied Atlantic or Bermuda Systems."

The man nodded.

He gave Miguel the address of the warehouse where he was to pick up the modules and the specific pier at Emerson Dock where the boat to deliver the products to the ships was located.

The captain and crew were on their way. If they weren't there by the time he arrived he should stow them on board, in the hold.

"Don't just leave them on the pier. We couldn't afford to have them stolen."

Miguel gave a laugh and said with some pride, "Staten Island's not like *some* places around here. But we're still New York City." He said he'd be sure to leave them out of sight.

"You're a lifesaver," she said warmly and with obvious gratitude.

There was a beat of a moment as he wondered how she would say goodbye to him.

But there was no hesitation on her part. She walked straight up and kissed him on the mouth.

This was right in front of Tim, who tried unsuccessfully to mask the irritation, if not anger, at his rival.

Miguel said, "I have one condition."

"Name it." She offered a seductive smile.

"I get that rose food on the bushes as soon as I'm back. Can't wait another day."

An easy job.

The drive to the Red Hook warehouse took thirty minutes. Once there, he displayed to a bored manager the bill of lading that Katherine had printed out. The man's spirits improved considerably and he grew more than happy to help load the *cartos* when Miguel held up two twenties and a ten.

Fifty or so minutes later he arrived at the dock. It took no time at all to find the ship, or boat, or whatever you call a craft that was about thirty feet long. It seemed old but the construction was solid, the wood varnished and clean. Like Katherine's rental, the fixtures were polished brass. The captain and crew weren't present. He borrowed a hand truck from a sailor on another craft and three at a time wheeled the cartons to the side of the vessel. He lifted them to the deck, which was a few feet above the pier and then, jumping on board, carried them down into the hold.

He had a thought and laughed. Of *course* that's what the large diesel-smelling space was called—because that was where the cargo was "held."

After returning the hand cart he walked back to his Chevy and looked out over the Harbor, gray and dotted with more whitecaps than the other day, but magnificent still.

He started the truck and drove back toward Paxton Street.

Thinking once again:

I'm in the wrong line of work . . .

Katherine and Tim had been joined by three other men.

They were pale of complexion and in good shape. There was a military air about them, an impression aided by the fact that they wore similar outfits—tan tops and slacks. They almost appeared to be uniforms. Their hairstyle was similar too: cropped short. He wondered if they had been soldiers.

"It went well?" Tim asked.

"Fine. They're loaded. Inside. When I left, the crew still hadn't gotten there."

"Not a problem," said Tim. He nodded at one of the three men, who pulled out his phone and quickly made a call. Something was different about Tim. He was more confident than earlier. Much less of a nerd. Katherine might be in charge, but Tim was a strong second in command. The three newcomers were respectful of him. Maybe even intimidated.

Miguel spotted another difference too. Looking past the hallway, Miguel noted that the bed was no longer made. The blazer that Tim had worn lay on the chair beside it.

And Katherine had changed clothes yet again, now wearing a skirt and a blue cotton blouse.

She took in his face, aware that he understood what had happened. She handed off a look that was very different from the others she'd offered over the past two days. It was the glance you would give to a busboy passing you in a restaurant.

Then Tim said to the trio of men, "All right."

They turned and, before Miguel could even swivel and start for the door, they were on him.

"Wait . . . what . . . ?"

This had all been planned—like choreography.

One pulled a pistol from his back pocket and pointed it at Miguel, who blinked. His eyes turned to Katherine. She gave him another restaurant-help glance and then took a packet of alcohol wipes and began scouring the laptop—the keys, the top, the sides, the battery charger. She nodded.

With the gun still on him, the other two dragged him to the laptop and forced his hands open. They pressed his fingertips onto the keys and parts of the computer she'd scrubbed.

Resisting was impossible, even if he hadn't been at gunpoint; the two planting his fingerprints were strong as bodybuilders.

"What is this? I don't understand!"

Tim pulled on latex gloves and sat at the computer. He began typing.

Miguel turned to Katherine, his eyes imploring her to explain.

"We're patriots." She shrugged. "Government's a perversion. It's grown into a cancerous behemoth that's destroying true values of what America should be. It's driving us toward the poison of globalism. We're not going to put up with that. We won't tolerate foreigners or their influence, and we won't tolerate a *government* that supports them."

"Spare me bullshit speeches. What did you get me into?"

Tim said absently, "Those cartons?"

Miguel whispered, "Not computer racks. They're bombs or chemical weapons, aren't they?"

"Twelve hundred pounds of C-4," Katherine said as she watched Tim—her boyfriend, her lover—type away at the keyboard.

"There never was a delivery problem. You saw 'carting' on my business card, you saw my truck, and planned to set me up." Then he frowned. "A suicide mission . . . Ah, no, the boat. It's remote controlled."

Tim didn't bother to confirm. "Launching it now." He hit return.

Glancing at the screen, Miguel could see a window of a bobbing image, a live feed. It would be from a camera mounted to the front of the boat. Slowly at first it cruised forward, aiming away from shore into the Harbor.

He closed his eyes briefly. He opened them and raged to Katherine, "You set me up! I'm the one on video picking up the packages and loading them on the boat." He gave a sour laugh. "And my fingerprints." A nod at the computer. "It'll look like I was steering the boat!"

Nobody had anything to say.

Miguel Torres had merely stated the obvious.

"And that?"

Katherine looked his way to see what he meant.

He was staring into the bedroom.

She shrugged.

Which meant that, obviously, she needed to seal the deal. And, with a man, what better way to cloud his judgment and make sure he didn't speculate too much about the curious job—picking up cartons for a big computer operation and loading them onto a small boat all by himself.

Miguel looked them over. "What exactly is your point? I mean, *I* wasn't born here. I immigrated legally and I've worked every day of my life in this country. I love America. I'm a citizen."

"Not a real one," muttered one of the tan uniformed thugs.

The word that came to Miguel's mind was: Nazi.

He asked, "And what's going to happen to me? I'll kill myself?"

Why even bother? Of course that was the plan.

"What's your target? A container ship from Brazil or China or Europe?"

"Something much better than that," Katherine said.

"Are you going to tell me?"

Tim said, "We'll let you watch."

Miguel said, "Planes and drones'd be monitored. A small boat in the Harbor. Nobody would pay it any attention."

He glanced at the three clones, then asked Tim and Katherine, "Where are you all from?"

Tim said, "Outside of Birmingham." He glanced to Miguel. "And, okay, just to let you know: we think some of you are okay."

"What?" Miguel whispered.

"Somebody's got to cut the grass and iron the sheets and fix the roofs. Stay in your place and it's all good."

Miguel stared back, his face expressionless. Was the man taunting him? Or serious?

Katherine said to the Hitler Youth, "Let's get on with it. I want to be on the road in a half hour."

While the gunman kept his pistol thrust forward, the other two walked to the stairway, where a length of clothesline lay on the landing. One end was a loop, like an impromptu noose. The other end one of them tied to the banister, so that the loop ended about seven feet off the floor.

"I'm going to hang myself," he whispered.

Both Katherine and Tim were staring at the screen as his long, weak fingers typed commends which ended up as directives to the ship's rudder.

The two placed a chair under the noose and walked Miguel toward it.

He looked back at her. "Ah, Katherine . . . Katherine . . ."

There was something about his tone that caught her attention.

Her ocean-blue eyes stared into his brown, as he shook his head slowly. His face would have to be revealing a hint of sadness—though for her, not himself.

"Oh, no," she whispered.

He nodded.

It was then that the FBI tactical team smashed open the door with a battering ram and a dozen agents with machine guns and pistols at the ready charged into the house, screaming—literally—for everyone to drop to the floor and keep their hands in sight.

The alternative, the agents made clear, was that they'd be shot where they stood.

The quintet quickly complied.

The terrorists had been carted away to federal detention in lower Manhattan, and a crime scene team was scouring the house.

Miguel Torres stood outside with the lead special agent on the case, a tall, dark-skinned man of around fifty. His short, white hair was distinguished. Despite the tough job Special Agent William Nichols would have, his eyes sparkled constantly. He asked, "The cavalry cut it too close?"

Miguel replied, "I had every faith in you. If for no other reason than you'd have a lot of explaining to do to your attorney general if your confidential informant got himself hanged."

He hadn't in fact been too worried. Nichols had assured him that there would be two dozen agents surrounding the house and listening to every word uttered inside, through the microphone sewed into Miguel's pockets.

They would want to get as much incriminating information on the cell as they could, but of course, since the plan was to kill Miguel, at the least overt action or command to do so, the tactical team would rescue him.

Already the press was gathering, but other agents and NYPD officers were keeping them back. Miguel knew there would be a press conference at some point. Hero though he was, he would not participate. For one thing, he was a reclusive man by nature. For another, it was obviously not a wise idea to be identified as the man who stopped a terrorist attack by the infamous Patriot Enforcers Militia. Five had been arrested, but Nichols told him that the outfit had a half dozen branches and numbed close to fifty members. Once the full extent of the plot was known that number would shrink considerably. But even then, anonymity was the better course.

"I think this is the fastest operation we've ever put together," Nichols said and he stepped away to take a phone call.

Fast indeed. It was only two days ago—at his lunch on the Esplanade—that he had overheard the conversation among Katherine, Tim, and several others, probably the three Nazis, who were unaware of Miguel's presence and assumed no one was within earshot. It was this crowd on which he was eavesdropping.

They were on the waterfront to plot out the route their explosive boat would take to its target.

They were not the most brilliant of perpetrators; they should have come up with code words for what they actually said, like "transporting the C-4," "explosion," "body count," and "the day after tomorrow."

He had also heard Katherine—tell the others to meet that night at her house, which was apparently the base of the operation.

After disposing of his lunch trash, Miguel had followed her home to the house on Paxton Street. It was not far from the water, and he could trail on foot.

He had then gone straight to FBI headquarters in Manhattan with the story and was ushered immediately into Nichols's office. He was the head of a joint FBI/NYPD anti-terror task force. He convened a number of officers and together, in the space of only a few hours, they had concocted a takedown plan, Miguel himself suggesting that he work his way into the cell to learn exactly what they were up to.

He had an idea of how he would do so: When he'd followed Katherine back to her house, he'd noted a large oak in the front yard. That night, he'd snuck onto the property with a handsaw, climbed the tree, and cut through much of the branch that over-hung the driveway.

The next day he'd gone to the house and offered to take down the dangerously dangling limb for free.

But meeting her was only part of the plan. There was an impor-tant refinement. At the meeting on the Esplanade he'd heard them talk about transporting the explosives from a warehouse to a dock but were worried about exposing themselves to CCTV cameras. So when he made his offer to cut the branch, he'd proffered his card, which stated that among other services he provided carting.

This got him inside the cell.

He didn't share with Special Agent Nichols that a bit more had unfolded between him and Katherine. Miguel understood that she was using the time in bed to snare him. What she didn't know was that he was using her too; it had been a long time since he'd been with Consuela.

This morning he had picked up the explosives at the warehouse in Brooklyn but instead of delivering them to the dock right away he'd made a fast stop—a garage where NYPD and BATF bomb squad teams rendered the devices safe. He'd then continued on and loaded them onto the boat per the terrorists' instructions.

Nichols finished his phone call and disconnected. "The mayor wants to meet you. The governor too. I told them you're in deep cover. They're going to send you a letter or something." Eyes dancing, he added, "Maybe an Amazon gift certificate. That's a joke."

"How long will they go away for?"

"Attempted murder, attempted destruction of federal property, conspiracy, maybe sedition . . . I guess fifty years."

Miguel nodded with satisfaction.

Nichols gave a laugh. "Figured you'd left your prior life behind, did you?"

One of the reasons the agent and his team had so readily agreed to Miguel's suggestion that he go undercover was his old job in Mexico: He was a senior detective investigating the Chihuahua and Sinaloa drug cartels and a political liaison officer.

After assassination attempt number three down there, Miguel had said enough was enough—they'd get him sooner or later. With the help of the U.S. authorities he'd worked with in Texas, he'd immigrated, along with his parents, his sister, and her husband.

The issue of Consuela Ramirez's joining him had never arisen; it was she who'd set him up for the third hit.

And so America became his new home.

Miguel noted that the reporters were antsy, like racehorses just before the gates open. They wanted their facts. Or if not facts then something that approximated them.

"Have a thought, Agent Nichols."

The man lifted an eyebrow.

Miguel continued, "You'll need my statement, but I'll come into your office tonight."

"Fine. But why?"

A nod toward the press. "They'll be wondering what I'm doing here, how I'm connected. You act like there's nothing I can tell you and walk away. I'll get back to work—I'm just the gardener who happened to be here, taking care of the grounds."

"Smart. Good plan." The agent did as he suggested.

Miguel walked to his truck, collected what he needed. A few reporters asked a question or two but he simply frowned and said with a thick accent, "Nobody tell me nothing."

He returned to the yard.

Yes, it was true that this was a good cover to keep him out of the story.

But just as important, vines threatened to strangle the camellias, and the beds of gypsophila, delphiniums, and buddleia had clearly not been treated with lime in forever.

Those were both sins, and Miguel Torres would make certain they were remedied as soon as possible.

The next day, having tidied up the grounds on Paxton Street and finished "prettifying" the beds at Mr. Whittaker's, Miguel was once again eating lunch on the Esplanade—this time a meat loaf sandwich on rye, one of his signature loaves.

His name had successfully been kept out of the press, though of course he had shared with his parents and sister the entire story.

"*Dios mío*," his mother had gasped. "What a risk you took!"

He assured her that he'd been under the careful eye of the police and FBI, and the Patriot cell was more foolish and less dangerous than the cartels.

"Ah, well, I suppose. But you won't do it again?"

"The odds of my stumbling across a second band of terrorists are pretty small."

Not sharing that Special Agent Nichols had wondered if he might be open to more work, the consensus at the task force being that gardening was not a bad cover story for a confidential informant. Miguel was keeping the option on the table.

He promised he would be out to visit out West soon, and they disconnected.

Now, sipping his hot chocolate, Miguel Torres thought: of *course* he risked his life. He had to.

He would have helped the authorities bring them down, no matter what their plan. But he had a personal stake in Katherine's operation: the target that the cell had selected was none other than the Statue of Liberty, despised because she was a gift from a *foreign* country to America.

When he'd come to this country, he had not gotten his first sight of her from a ship, as had so many immigrants before him, but from the sky, as his airliner settled toward Newark airport on final approach from Mexico City.

It had been at that moment that he'd fallen in love with her and with everything she meant. She was why he often ate lunch here, why he occasionally strolled along these walkways even after a grueling day of work . . . simply so he could glance across the huge expanse of the Harbor for a glimpse of the majestic sculpture, which was, and would always be, the most important lady in his life.

Don Bruns, writer and editor, has a wonderful concept in creating anthologies. He picks a popular music album and invites authors to write a short story based on one of its songs. Last year the album was Thriller, by Michael Jackson.

Interestingly, when he invited me to contribute, I knew exactly what I wanted to write—a story based on the song "The Lady in My Life."

Can I say any more about it?

Alas, no. Because, as is typical of my short stories (this one is my 101st), it contains a big twist at the end.

This is what I feel short fiction should deliver. My novels are about complex characters confronting increasing levels of conflict, in an emotional roller coaster, with some (I hope) fascinating information about topics that vary from book to book (mini reactors in Hunting Time, data mining in The Broken Window, the power grid in The Burning Wire). Yes, they have surprise endings—a necessity in any work of fiction—but those are simply a part of the entire emotional experience of the novel.

A short story, on the other hand, exists for one reason only.

A breathtaking shock.

They're like an illusionist's tricks. Setup, shocking reveal, and the thought: How the hell did the author do that?

Not character studies, no important messages.

Just an unexpected blow to the gut.

Anyway, that's what I strive for.

Read "The Lady In My Life" . . . and let me know if I hit the mark!

John M. Floyd *is the author of more than a thousand short stories in publications like* Alfred Hitchcock's Mystery Magazine, Ellery Queen Mystery Magazine, The Strand Magazine, The Saturday Evening Post, The Best American Mystery Stories, *and* The Best Mystery Stories of the Year. *A former Air Force captain and IBM systems engineer, Floyd is also an Edgar finalist, a Shamus Award winner, a five-time Derringer Award winner, and the 2018 recipient of the Short Mystery Fiction Society's lifetime achievement award.*

LAST DAY AT THE JACKRABBIT
John M. Floyd

EXTERMINATION

Elsie Williams was always in a bad mood when she was working, and since she was almost always working, she was almost always in a bad mood.

Except for today.

Elsie had been employed at the Jackrabbit Diner for the past two years, and although she was usually running the place alone, while her worthless boss was at home drunk, he had made it clear many times that her job description and pay grade was and would always be "waitress." Well, not for much longer. At eight o'clock tonight—five hours from now—Elsie planned to take her final day's pay out of the cash register, turn off the lights and lock up, slide the key and a farewell note to her boss (his name actually was Jack) under the front door, jump in the passenger seat of her boyfriend's blue Camry, and put the Jackrabbit Diner in her rearview mirror forever. She had very little money—the proceeds from yesterday's sale of her twenty-year-old car were laughable—but thanks to recent events, her boyfriend *did* have money, which was her ticket out of here. It was a good feeling.

In the back of her mind, Elsie knew she should leave right now, and to hell with her boss. But despite believing she had a rebellious nature, her work ethic remained stubbornly intact. She would stay and finish the day before starting her new life.

It was right about that point in her thoughts—as she came back from refilling her only two customers' coffee cups while humming a little tune under her breath—that Vito Corleone walked through the front door.

Sixty or so, balding, Italian, jowly, sleepy eyes, deep frown, tiny mustache. He was dressed in brown pants and a tan shirt with the sleeves rolled up—not exactly mafia attire—but that only strengthened the image in her head. He looked like Brando in the tomato-garden scene with his grandson, near the end of the movie.

Elsie had once heard that waiters and bartenders are among the best judges of character, and over time she had come to believe that. And right now, all her instincts were telling her this man was dangerous.

He sat down on a stool at the counter, looked over at her, and mumbled in a raspy voice, "I'm looking for somebody—guy named Mike McCann."

One of her other customers—a man four stools down—rose and began counting change onto the countertop beside his cup.

Elsie studied the guy who looked like Vito a moment before replying. "Sorry. I don't know the name."

He turned to the other two patrons and called out. "Either of you know him? Mike McCann?"

The man who'd stood up shook his head. "Just passing through. But I wish you luck." He paid his bill, walked out, and a minute later she heard a car start up and pull out of the parking lot.

"How about you?" Vito asked the other customer, a tall blond fellow seated at the table in the corner booth.

"Don't know him. Sorry," the man answered, and went back to his coffee and sweet roll.

Vito seemed about to say something more, but before he could, his cell phone rang. The too-loud ringtone was the first eleven notes of *The Sound of Music*, and as weirdly out-of-place as anything Elsie could've imagined. He fished the phone from his pocket, listened a few moments, said, "Calm down. I'm working on it," and disconnected. He frowned at both Elsie and the man in the booth before putting the phone away.

"You up here from the city?" Elsie said.

He gave her a dark look. "Yeah. Why?"

"Just askin'." She was still holding her coffeepot. "You want a cup?"

"Yeah, I guess. And a ham sandwich."

"We only got coffee and pastry," she said, pouring.

He studied her a moment. "What kinda diner don't serve ham sandwiches?"

"The kind that doesn't have a cook. We're not really a diner, we're a coffee shop." She saw him examining the name painted on the wall behind the counter and added, "Don't believe everything you read."

Vito was still squinting at the name of the café. "'Jackrabbit'? How'd that happen?"

"The owner's name. Jack Hopper."

"You're kiddin' me," he said.

"Wish I was."

He shook his head. Both of them stayed quiet while he sipped his coffee and took a long look around. His gaze lingered, she noticed, on the patron in the corner booth, who was now staring absently out the window.

"Why you looking for this McCann guy?" she said. "If you don't mind me asking."

Vito turned and focused on her. "Business," he said. "I went to the address I was given, but I musta wrote it down wrong. I was headed back when I saw the sign for your place. Figured I'd stop and ask."

Elsie nodded. "What business are you in?"

This time he took so long she thought he wasn't going to reply. At last he said, "I'm an exterminator."

The word hung there in the air. "You mean, like, pest control?"

He took another slow swallow from his cup. "Yeah. That's what I mean."

But she didn't think so.

From the corner of her eye, Elsie saw the man in the booth watching them both. A deep silence dragged by. It was so quiet she could hear birds singing outside, the hum of the refrigerator in the back, the thudding of her heart in her chest. Somewhere nearby, a dog barked.

"Excuse me a second," she said, and walked through the old-fashioned swinging door to the diner's back room.

Less than a minute later she returned, wearing a long plastic apron. When she reached the counter across from him, she took a small revolver from behind her back and shot Vito Corleone right between his two sleepy eyes. He froze for a moment, his mouth wide open in surprise, and then fell slowly backward off his stool.

REDIRECTION

Mike McCann, already scared stiff, sat there in the corner booth and gaped. Finally, on legs that felt like chunks of firewood, he rose and stumbled over to join Elsie at the counter.

"What have you done?" he whispered, looking down at the body.

Elsie had tucked the smoking revolver into the pocket of her waitress uniform and shrugged out of the apron. McCann could see why she had put it on, but it turned out to be unneeded; there was very little blood.

"What choice did I have?" she asked. "We figured they'd come for you. I just didn't think it'd be this soon."

McCann had hoped they wouldn't come for him at all. But she was right. You can't steal a hundred grand from the mob and get away with it, even if you hadn't known that's who you were stealing it from. McCann had been told it was just a high-stakes poker game between big shots at the local casino, and had popped into the smoky room with his mask and gun and taken all the cash from the table and from the seven players' pockets as well. And got away clean. But not as clean as he and Elsie had hoped. Turned out there were cameras outside, and far too late he'd started wondering if they'd seen his car and his tag number. And now here they were, in broad daylight. McCann tried to control his trembling arm long enough to look at his watch: half past three. What kind of crooks did their killing in the daytime? Couldn't they have waited till nine o'clock or so? For that matter, couldn't Elsie have agreed to leave with him today like he'd planned, and not insist on waiting till *tonight*?

"What do we do now?" he asked. He hated to be in a position like this, hated to have to ask his girlfriend—*girlfriend* sounded better than *mistress*—for guidance, but Elsie was smarter than he was, and they both knew it.

"We get rid of the body, that's what, and his ride too." Elsie hurried around to McCann's side of the counter, dug a moment in the dead man's pants pockets, and came out with a set of keys. "Here. Take these, drive his car around back, then come in and help me drag him out too. We'll put him in the trunk and then roll him and his car into the bog down by the creek."

"What if a customer drives up, while we're getting ready to do all this?"

"We'll lock the place, put the CLOSED sign on the door, and move your car around behind the building with his, until we're done." She pointed. "Go. I'll clean this up."

But McCann didn't get far. When he opened the front door he stopped in his tracks, staring at the parking lot.

Elsie must've seen him looking because he heard her cross the room to stand there beside him in the doorway.

The only vehicle in the diner's lot except for McCann's was a white commercial van—with the words BRUMUCCI PEST CONTROL printed on the side.

He stood frozen and heard Elsie gulp aloud. When his heart started beating again, he heard her say, "It could be a cover. Maybe it's a cover." And she was right; it could've been. Except for what happened next.

McCann felt his cell phone buzz in his pocket. When he took it out, he saw the word SUSAN on the display. Dazedly he said into the phone, "What is it, honey?"

"I got a problem," Susan McCann said. "I heard a rat in the attic again and called a guy Judy Caldwell told me about to come take care of 'em." She paused. "Where are you, anyway?"

"What guy?"

"I don't know, a funny name. Brenouli, Baruzzi, something like that. The problem is, he said he'd come right away, and he's still not h—"

McCann disconnected. He felt all the blood drain from his face.

Elsie frowned and said, "What?"

He turned to look at her. "You shot the wrong kind of killer."

COVER-UP

Elsie Williams had never believed she could be this calm in the face of disaster. But she had to be. Mike was about to freak out, she could see that, so somebody had to stay cool. After hearing about his wife's call to the bug man and realizing *this* was the bug man, Elsie swallowed hard and took careful stock of the situation.

Okay, she'd shot an innocent bystander. That was really too bad and she was sorry about it. But nobody else knew. They could still make it out of this.

"Listen to me," she said to McCann. "Listen and do what I say. Okay?"

He didn't answer, but he did look at her.

"Back to the plan," she said. They were still standing in the doorway. "Go pull his van around back and I'll—"

She stopped midsentence. She heard a car approaching. "Inside, quick, till it passes."

Both of them ducked back into the coffeeshop and waited. Elsie peeked through the crack in the door.

The car didn't pass. It slowed down, pulled into the lot, and stopped. But that wasn't the worst of it.

"It's the sheriff," she said, closing the door. "Personal car, not his cruiser—but it's him."

McCann looked ready to pass out. She shook him, hard, and put her nose in his face.

"Come on, Mike. We got time, barely, before he comes in."

"Time for *what*?" Then he blinked, and his eyes widened. "Let's do what you said—lock the door, put up the CLOSED sign. He'll think nobody's here—"

"Won't work. He knows your car. It's sitting right there. And this guy's van is too." She turned and looked at the body, thinking hard. "Help me get him into the closet there."

"The closet?"

"There's no room in the back. We can stash him here in the closet till the sheriff leaves."

"What about the van?"

"Leave that to me. Come *on*!"

And somehow they did it. Moving fast, the two of them dragged Brumucci's wide body into the closet just past the end of the counter, grabbed his coffee cup and wiped up what little blood was around—thank God it had only been a .22 slug—and stashed the plastic apron and his cup in there with him. Elsie pushed the closet door shut two seconds before the front door opened and a man in a cowboy hat, khaki pants and an untucked golf shirt sauntered in.

"Afternoon, Sheriff," she said, strolling back behind the counter. "Got the day off?"

Mike McCann, still pale, had only just settled onto one of the barstools.

"Hey Elsie. Mike. Yep, five days off." The sheriff spread his hands. "No patrol car, no uniform, no radio."

"Joe Average," Elsie said. "You fit right in."

Actually, he didn't. Sheriff Joe Sargent was about Elsie's and McCann's age, early forties, but looked ten years older, probably because he'd spent a long stretch on the police force in the city before coming to his senses and moving here. Maybe also because of that, he had a military bearing in both his dress and his posture, with every hair in place, every button buttoned, every crease straight and sharp. Elsie was also aware, although not many people here were, that he had reached the rank of sergeant in his previous job, which had made him Sergeant Sargent. At least he was now shed of *that* awkward title. Sometimes a career change, even for less pay, helped in more ways than one.

He chose a stool next to McCann and said to Elsie, "You running the place again?"

"Jack called in sick."

"Right." The sheriff and everyone else around here knew what kind of sick Jack Hopper was. He took off his hat and set it crown-down on the countertop. "How fresh is the coffee?"

"Brand new." She took an almost full pot off the burner behind the counter, poured him a steaming cup, and put it back. "What brings *you* here today?"

"Killing time. Nancy and the kids are at her sister's, I'm supposed to pick 'em up at five." He paused and jerked a thumb over his shoulder at the door. "What's the deal with the van out there?"

Elsie looked in that direction, as if she could see through walls. Casually she said, "Guy came in this morning, asked if he could leave it there awhile so he could ride with one of his coworkers to a job. Said he'd come back and pick it up after dark. Fella named Brumucci."

The sheriff nodded. "I know him. He sprayed my back-yard for mosquitoes last month. Gave us sort of a package deal—treatments for termites, roaches, everything but horseflies. Kept him there most of a day. Nice enough guy, we thought, maybe a little grumpy. Big fan of musicals, always humming some show tune."

"That was him all right." Elsie threw a quick glance at McCann, whose color was still a little off. Thank God he hadn't had to pull up a chair and play poker with the high rollers he'd robbed, she thought. The truth was, though, she was getting worried as well. Were they going to have to sit here and entertain the Law for another hour while an innocent and extremely unlucky pest-service owner who happened to look like a movie star lay dead in a closet twenty feet away? Elsie felt sweat trickling down the middle of her back.

Just as she was deciding the day couldn't possibly get any worse, the door opened again, and it did.

KILLING TIME

The second thought to go through Elsie Williams's exhausted brain after she'd found out the guy she'd shot wasn't really a hit man sent by the mob to murder her boyfriend was that shooting him hadn't accomplished a damn thing. A hit man was probably *still* coming to murder her boyfriend. Except that maybe it wouldn't be today, and she and Mike would be long gone by tomorrow.

But then the door had opened once again, while she and McCann were chatting with the county sheriff about spraying for insects, and the two grim-faced men who walked into the café were (she discovered later) one Frank "Big Ears" Corelli and one Albert "The Mortician" Mortimer. Except for their business attire—black suits and ties and white shirts—they looked as different as night and day: Corelli was tall, dark, skinny, and calm and Mortimer was short, sandy haired, stocky, and nervous.

Neither man bothered to take a seat or otherwise waste time. They marched in, pulled a pair of heavy black automatics from their shoulder holsters, and stood side by side, facing their three victims-to-be. Elsie couldn't help thinking of *Pulp Fiction*.

"Which one of you's driving the blue Toyota?" Mortimer asked.

For a moment, no one spoke. Elsie stood frozen in place behind the counter; McCann sat stock-still on his stool looking away from the gunmen; the plain-clothed sheriff, seated also, had turned half to his left to watch them. When Elsie glanced at him, it occurred to her that something about Sheriff Sargent had looked off ever since he walked in. Something important. But she couldn't pin it down.

"Who belongs to that car?" Frank Corelli asked, louder this time.

McCann, once again pale as a bedsheet, swiveled his stool toward the two men. He was positioned between the sheriff and the two strangers. Less than ten feet separated the good guys from the bad. McCann took a deep breath, rose from his stool, and said, "It's mine."

Elsie gasped. "Wait a minute—"

"So you're Mike McCann?" Mortimer asked.

"Don't do it!" she said. "Don't tell them anyth—"

"It's okay, Elsie," McCann said. Then, to the two men: "Yes. I'm the one you want. And my friends here weren't there that night. They aren't a part of this."

Clearly amused, Corelli said, "Too late. They are now."

Both men raised their weapons.

In her peripheral vision Elsie, as scared as she was, noticed that Sheriff Joe Sargent seemed to have turned a bit farther toward the gunmen but was still keeping the right side of his body hidden from their sight. In that instant she knew what it was that had seemed different about him earlier. And she knew what she had to do.

"Didn't you idiots see the van out front?" she blurted. As she spoke, she turned a bit also, to her right, to grip the handle of the almost-full coffeepot on the burner behind her.

Guns pointed and ready, both men hesitated. "What about the van?" Mortimer said.

Smiling, Elsie looked past them and called, "Come on in, boys!"

It was an old trick, but Corelli and Mortimer still turned, their heads swiveling to look behind them at the front door—and when they did, Elsie threw the coffeepot, as hard as she could, at Frank Corelli. It hit him solid, just behind the ear, broke, and spilled its blazing-hot contents all over both gunmen.

In the next two seconds, Corelli fell, scalded, to the floor, Albert Mortimer, burned also, turned and fired blindly at her, and the sheriff pulled his service pistol from beneath his shirttail and fired back. The gangster's shot missed; the sheriff's didn't. Mort the Mortician fell face up on the wet floor beside his writhing partner, dead before he landed.

For a moment, no one said a word. Steam rose from the tiled floor, and the smell of coffee and gun smoke filled the long, windowless room. The only sound was the heavy breathing of the three people still standing and Big Ears flopping around on the floor. Elsie realized that at some point she had drawn her little .22 and was aiming it needlessly at their attackers. The sheriff saw the revolver, took it from her gently, and went back to staring at the gunmen on the floor. Then he slid the hit men's weapons out of reach across the room, holstered his automatic, took his phone from his pocket, and called an ambulance.

"So much for my day off," he said.

TERMINATION

The next hour was hectic, but by six o'clock everyone except Elsie, McCann, and the sheriff had left the scene, taking the dead body and the whimpering Corelli with them. Some time after that, as the sheriff and the waitress and her boyfriend sat at the corner table where McCann had been earlier in the afternoon, Sheriff Sargent handed Elsie her .22 and gave her a thin smile. "I'm not sure what would've happened," he said, "if you hadn't thrown that coffeepot."

"I am," McCann said. It was the first time he'd spoken since just before the shootout.

"Yeah, I guess I am too." The sheriff let out a breath. "What I mean is . . . I was in street clothes, Elsie. How'd you know I had my gun?"

She smiled back. "Your shirttail was out, to cover it. Your shirttail's never out."

He thought that over and nodded. After another sigh, he rose from the booth and looked at McCann. "I don't know why they were after you, Mike—whatever happened between you and them must've been pretty bad. Bad enough to almost get us all killed. It's something I ought to ask you about, and you ought to tell me."

The two of them studied each other a moment. "But?" McCann said.

"But whatever it was, it happened outside my county, and I don't figure any of that bunch will be charging you with anything. You understand what I'm saying?"

"Not really."

"I'm saying I don't want these people coming back. And if their bosses really want you, they'll try again."

"So . . . I should get out of town."

"I would if I were you."

McCann nodded, and Elsie fought to keep from smiling. *That's just what we want to do*, she thought. *Free at last*.

They stood also, and the three of them walked to the front door.

Sheriff Sargent paused there, his hand on the doorknob, and smiled again. "Busy place, the Jackrabbit," he said.

He was opening the door when they all heard it. A phone was ringing. A phone with an odd ringtone: the beginning of *The Sound of Music*.

Everyone froze. The sheriff stared at the closet near the end of the counter, and Elsie and McCann stared at the sheriff. After a long wait and another burst of music, Sheriff Sargent took a careful step back, looking now at both of them. McCann was sweating, his face once again the color of wet chalk—Elsie saw it, and so did the sheriff. Slowly, for the second time that day, he drew his pistol.

He aimed it at a spot between Elsie and McCann and held out a palm. Without a word, she handed him her .22. He took it in his free hand, and this time he sniffed the barrel.

"Okay," he said to both of them. "What's in the closet?"

One thing I've always enjoyed, for some reason, are crime stories set in a diner. Maybe it's because of my memory of Hemingway's short story "The Killers" or of the fact that a roadside café is such a good place to find all kinds of different people. Another thing I like is a strong female lead, no matter which side of the law she happens to be on. In the case of my story "Last Day at the Jackrabbit," these two preferences come together when a tired waitress named Elsie finds herself in the middle of a deadly battle between a local off-duty sheriff, her amateur-thief boyfriend, and a pair of hit men who've been dispatched by their boss to track her lover down and deliver their kind of justice.

To this already-strange scenario I added another fictional element I've come to love: the mid-story plot reversal—several of them, in fact—that can take a supposedly normal storyline and, at the drop of a waitress's cap, turn it in a completely different direction. Since I knew editor Andrew Gulli at Strand Magazine *is fond of that kind of thing also, I submitted this twisty story to him, and—lucky for me—he published it.*

I hope you'll like it as much as I enjoyed writing it.

Nils Gilbertson *is a writer and attorney. He has lived in California, Washington, DC, and now resides in Texas with his wife, son, and German shorthaired pointer. Gilbertson's short fiction has appeared in* Ellery Queen Mystery Magazine, Rock and a Hard Place, Mystery Magazine, Guilty Crime Story Magazine, Cowboy Jamboree, *and others. His work has also appeared in a variety of anthologies, including* Prohibition Peepers, Mickey Finn: 21st Century Noir, Gone: An Anthology of Crime Stories, *and* More Groovy Gumshoes. *His story "Washed Up" was named a Distinguished Story in* The Best American Mystery and Suspense 2022. *You can find him online at nilsgilbertson.com.*

LOVELY AND USELESS THINGS
Nils Gilbertson

The harsh, useful things of the world, from pulling teeth to digging potatoes, are best done by men who are as starkly sober as so many convicts in the death-house, but the lovely and useless things, the charming and exhilarating things, are best done by men with, as the phrase is, a few sheets in the wind.

—H. L. Mencken

The strike of a match lit the alleyway, casting a long, pistol-wielding shadow. Pat Boyle paused before raising it to the cigarette on his lips. The flame danced and the shadow turned from darkness on brick to dimly lit flesh and steel, then back again. Boyle drew from the cigarette and tossed the match to the gutter.

"You mind stepping into the light?"

The trembling pistol came first, then the young man wielding it. Boyle waited until he could see the whites of his eyes, ignoring the chatter of the men at the dock behind him as they unloaded cases from the Potomac.

"Can I help you, son?"

"Don't *son* me, mister."

"We're all someone's son." Boyle took a long inhale and looked back to the dock.

The young man thrust the pistol toward him. "Why don't you take your eyes off the booze for a change."

Boyle's stare drifted back. "Either shoot or tell me why you're pointing that thing at me."

The young man glanced down his arm to the pistol as though he'd forgotten he was holding it. "My father's name is—was—Willard Reynolds. He used to frequent the speakeasy—Sixteenth Street spot—that you work at."

Boyle nodded. "I'm sorry, son."

"Don't call me—" He squeezed his eyes shut for a moment, as though frustrated by the dim alley light. "Sorry for what?"

"Sorry you sprung from the seed of Willard Reynolds."

Before the young man had the chance to process the indignity, another man emerged from the shadows. Boyle asked, "How long we got?"

"'Bout ten minutes and we'll be good to go."

"We're square with our friends?"

"All paid up."

"All right. Get out of here."

"But—"

"I said get out of here."

The figure retreated to the shadows and made its way back to the dock.

"What's your name?" Boyle asked, turning back to the man with the gun.

He swallowed and his forearm quivered, tired, unaccustomed to the pistol. "Willard Jr."

"Willard Jr.," Boyle said, shaking his head. "Give me one guess."

"Guess at what?"

"Guess at what reduced you to this. See, I knew your old man. Used to be a decent fella. Drank now and then but held a steady job. Paid lip service to the Anti-Saloon League but lamented their stubbornness in private. But once they got their way—once the political tides shifted—he didn't speak out. No, that takes courage. Instead, he started frequenting our place. Why? The continental clubs reserved for the congressmen and their cronies stopped allowing nobodies like him. The casual imbibing turned heavier." Boyle snuffed out the cigarette and lit another. "I had a front-row seat from there. It's funny you coming here, Willard Jr. Your old man died with a hell of an unpaid tab." He took a step toward the trembling arm. "But I couldn't bear calling in that debt. I see the debt in your eyes—the debt of being the seed of that man, dead from choking on his own sick in a gutter."

"But I—but you—"

"What, it's *my* fault? Your father never drank like that before Prohibition, correct?"

He paused. "It's not right what you and Johnny Dunn are doing at that place. It's nothing but a refuge for skanks and sinners."

Boyle chuckled. "You want to talk about sin? Let's talk about the sons of bitches down the street who voted this madness into law but got bootleggers hand-delivering Canadian booze to the Capitol for briefcases of cash. Let's talk about the clubs for the politicians and industry men that stocked up on a decade's worth of hooch before the law kicked in. They take kickbacks and send people like me to jail on a whim, but *we're* the sinners." Boyle continued toward the retreating young man. "Meanwhile, they turn fellas like your old man from ordinary, flawed men to devils. I'm not the devil, son. The devil and his cronies live at the big domed building on First Street. If you want to kill someone over your father's death you better—"

Before finishing the sentence, Boyle leaped forward, grabbed the barrel of the pistol, and slammed the grip into the bridge of Willard Jr.'s nose. He crumpled and Boyle watched blood paint the road crimson black. He flicked his cigarette and said to the figures he felt behind him, "Bring him back to the club."

Pat Boyle followed the truck through downtown Washington, DC, reflecting on his mortality. Never once did he think the boy would shoot before he got to him, but the throb in his chest told him he didn't know a damn thing about the boy. Hell, he didn't know anything at all. He didn't know about right versus wrong or good versus evil or moral versus immoral—same as the boy—same as everyone. But at least he knew he didn't know, and at least he knew he didn't need to. The best men, he thought, didn't command their fellow man from a giant domed building. The best men disregarded the commands of those who sought power and control and instead basked in the plenitude of life and the abundance that this world offered, in all its forms. He felt his heart in his chest and smiled.

The Moonlight Club sat on the third floor of a narrow building squeezed between two luxury hotels a few blocks north of the White House. Upon arrival, patrons entered on the desolate ground floor level and would be stopped by a fella dressed as a security guard, who informed them it was private property, and they ought to leave. If they shared the password—any sentence incorporating the phrase *lovely and useless things*—the guard would direct them to a concealed staircase.

The truck pulled into the lot at the back of the building, surrounded by tall fences. Boyle followed it in. He parked and watched as fellas started unloading the cases. Two men dragged Willard Jr. from the truck to the back entrance.

The club was brimming with drunken regulars. Men sat at the bar trading slurred ramblings and downing cocktails concocted by Leroy, the bartender. Thick smoke hung like fog above the tables before the small stage, where a man crooned along with a jazz ensemble. The Moonlight Club wasn't the sort of spot you'd find the congressmen and other bigwigs toasting to their reckless use of government power, nor was it one of the hundreds of gin joints that dotted the back alleys where, upon entrance, there was a serious risk of taking a knife between the ribs or going blind from bad hooch. The clientele was made up of regular folks. Everyone from schoolteachers to shopkeepers to lawyers and everything in between. It was also the drinking spot of the local authorities. And when it came to enforcing the Volstead Act and its accompanying laws, if the clubs paid off the cops and DC government, there was little concern the feds would bother interfering. Even the mayor stopped by the Moonlight Club for a rollicking good time now and again. Not to mention, Johnny Dunn, the fella who ran the place, made for damn sure every cop on every corner in a two-mile radius of the joint was getting a generous monthly cut.

Boyle found his usual spot at the corner of the bar and flagged down Leroy.

"Hey, Leroy. I'll take a rye, neat."

"I'll make it a double for ya, sir. Considering the night you've had." He pulled a glass and popped the cork from a bottle and poured generously.

"Word gets around that fast?"

"You know how it is 'round here, Mr. Boyle. Word travels faster than influenza."

"Only question is if it travels accurately." Boyle took a long gulp of his drink and Leroy filled it back up. The bartender was a middle-aged black man who, before Prohibition, had worked as a porter at The Stinson, a hotel that Johnny Dunn had frequented on business trips to Richmond and that Boyle had once visited—at Dunn's recommendation—while tracking a congressional aide's runaway wife. Dunn and Leroy had gotten close enough for Leroy to share some cocktail recipes. When Prohibition hit and Dunn got into bootlegging, he invited Leroy up to DC as head bartender at the Moonlight Club.

Leroy leaned forward on the mahogany bar. "I hear it was the boy of Willard Reynolds—the fella who died in the gutter after drinking here. That true?"

Before Boyle could answer, he felt a hand on his shoulder and turned to see Mick, one of the fellas who ran errands for Johnny. "Mr. Dunn wants to see you in his office."

Johnny Dunn was taking laps around his desk, mumbling numbers under his breath.

"Hi, Johnny," Boyle said. "I—"

But the short, balding man raised a stubby finger in his direction and continued with his routine. Boyle stood and waited.

When he finished a few minutes later, Johnny Dunn nodded toward the solitary leather chair sitting atop a spotless hardwood floor at the center of the office. Once Boyle sat down, Johnny Dunn said, "Do you know what makes me successful in this business?"

Boyle shrugged. "By the time we were fifteen, you might as well have been selling earplugs to the deaf, Johnny. You got a knack for it."

His boss shook his head. "Not even close. It's because I'm *careful*. Because I imagine everything that could go wrong with the operation before it happens, and I plan for it. But I don't *re*act. No. I see where our competitors or government busybodies will strike next, and I *act*. I act in a way that *max*imizes profit and thus, by necessity, *min*imizes violence." He paused. "Do you know me to be a violent man, Boyle?"

"C'mon, Johnny," he said. "We both know the answer to that. *Nine times out of ten, violence is bad for business*, that's what you say. Anyway, can we skip the spiel tonight? I got a date with a bottle that I hope is strong enough to spin me to sleep."

"Postpone it. We got this Willard Jr. issue to deal with. What concerns me is that a sniveling little shit like him can get that close to my number two man, sticking a pistol in his face while he's overseeing a supply pickup."

"Number two, huh?" Boyle still carried his PI ticket, but since the beginning of Prohibition, his client list had dwindled to one. As long as the Moonlight Club was in business, he didn't need surveillance jobs for suspicious spouses to pay the bills.

Johnny Dunn ignored the quip, instead licking his finger and rubbing out a smudge at the corner of his desk. "Irv's in there now with Willard Jr. I don't like it, but sometimes what's hard is necessary, like pulling teeth."

"You talking literally or figuratively? 'Sides, shouldn't I be the one working on the kid after he stuck that piece in my face?"

Johnny Dunn shook his head. "Irv has a taste for that sort of thing. I want you to find out who's behind this. In my experience, beating it out of them doesn't work as well as you expect."

"What's there to figure out?" Boyle asked. "Willard Jr. and his old man were close. The boy went nuts when his pa drank himself dead in our joint. He said it himself."

Johnny Dunn sighed. "One thing I've learned in this business is that it's rarely that simple. There are powerful interests out there who would like to see this place reduced to rubble with us inside. I know you have some contacts who can help you find out if this was petty revenge or something worse. I see something bigger in the works." Johnny Dunn closed his eyes and inhaled through his thick, red nose. "I can *feel* it."

Before Boyle could respond, Irv Redding stumbled through the office door. Panting, he looked at Johnny Dunn, then Boyle, then back to the boss. "You better come see this, Johnny."

"This ought to be good," Johnny Dunn said.

"It's Willard Jr., sir. He's dead."

Swollen, purple veins bulged in Willard Jr.'s pallid neck like worms burrowed beneath the skin. The whites of his eyes were now red, drained of life, and his cheeks were puffy and crisscrossed with a maze of burst capillaries. His hands were tied behind his back and his head tilted backward, Adam's apple prodding cold flesh, threatening to pierce through.

"The hell happened?" Johnny Dunn asked.

"I ran out for a second to get some supplies," said Irv. "I come back and find the son of a bitch dead as his old man."

"And looking like his old man, too," Boyle said, examining the body. "I remember Willard Sr. had the same discoloration of the skin, swollen veins, red eyes."

"That's bull," Irv said. "The old man died choking on his vomit. He was a drunk, it happens. Willard Jr. hasn't had a drop of booze since he's been here." He paused. "My best guess is Willard Jr. had something on him to take in case things went sideways. He knew what we'd try to get out of him, and he knew he'd squeal."

"Suicide is your theory?" Boyle asked.

"Yeah. I was the last one with him and it's the only possibility that makes sense."

Boyle leaned toward the young corpse. "Making sense can be a wonderful thing," he said. He turned his gaze to Johnny, then to Irv. "But, sometimes, aren't things more interesting when nothing makes sense at all?"

A few silent moments later, Mick joined the three men in the windowless room deep in the belly of the building. "Christ," he said, examining the body. "Looks same as those dead folks at the joint over in Dupont where they had a batch of booze cut with wood alcohol."

"The Rooster Room poisonings?" Boyle asked. "You sure this looks the same?"

Mick nodded. "Sure. I was meeting a gal there and watched half the place stumble out confused, veins bulging, struggling to breathe."

Boyle turned to Johnny. "That stuff's no joke. Any reason to shut down tonight?"

Johnny Dunn closed his eyes and recited numbers in his head with subtle, noiseless movements of his lips. It was as though he were calculating every variable in all of history that had led to that single moment. Then he said, "No reason to think someone spoiled our hooch. We know our sources and there's no indication that Willard Jr. had a drink here. Irv, clean up this mess. Boyle, find out what the hell's going on."

The night was dwindling and, despite the free-flowing drinks and raucous jazz ensemble, the clock on the wall suggested that soon the place would empty and all that would be left were those who ached at the notion of being alone.

Boyle sat at the corner of the bar sipping rye whiskey. "You plan to perch yourself on that stool all night, Mr. Boyle?" Leroy asked with a grin.

"What, I'm not good company?"

"Company got nothin' to do with it. I get to rest all day before I'm back at it tomorrow night. My guess is Johnny's got you running 'round town solving problems."

"Bartenders know all, don't they?"

He topped off Boyle's drink and said, "Ain't a damn secret in this joint that folks can keep from me for more than an hour."

"I don't doubt it." Boyle lit a cigarette and waited for the distinguished lines of the bartender's face to crease from a smile to a portrait of regret.

"It's about the Willard fella and his boy, ain't it?"

Boyle nodded.

Leroy glanced over each shoulder. "I remember the night Willard Sr. died. I was the one serving him. Sure, he came in with whiskey on his breath already, but he only had a few drinks here. For a fella like him, last thing I expected to hear the next morning was that he'd died from too much booze. I'd seen that man drunker than a sailor every Friday and Saturday for half a year." He lowered his head. "But then I think, ain't that only a way for me to make amends for the role I played in his death? I don't know, Mr. Boyle. Way things are these days, it's like any decision we make can lead to a man's downfall. How do you carry on in a world like that?"

Boyle took a drink. "What do you think has existed longer, Leroy, guilt or alcohol?"

"Excuse me, sir?"

"I'm no sir. Which one?"

The bartender pondered the question before answering. "Booze has been around awful long, but I imagine guilt has been there since the start of man. Bible times. It's inherent in us."

"Wrong," Boyle said. The flickering candlelight set his eyes aflame. "The intentional fermentation of alcohol for purposes of ingestion dates back to the Stone Age. Tens of thousands of years ago. The invention of guilt—by weak men who sought to order society as they saw fit but lacked the strength to do it by force—occurred much later."

Silence filled the club as the jazz ensemble finished their final set, the wail of the trumpet evaporating into the smoky, window-less room. "I'm afraid I don't follow," said Leroy.

"As you reflect on the choices you make, I want to remind you which plays a more fundamental role in our civilization. When guilt wins, *they* win. When alcohol wins—when liberty wins—*we* win." He lifted his whiskey glass. "I can feel it, Leroy. I can feel life in all its wonder when this elixir burns my belly. It isn't sin; it's life itself."

At that, both men turned and saw a woman with a narrow nose, thin lips, and bobbed dark hair fill the doorway. The pin affixed to her dress signified membership in the Woman's Christian

Temperance Union, but he had met her years earlier when she
hired him to tail her wayward husband.

Boyle waved her over.

She took the seat and said, "Leroy, darling, be a doll and fetch
me a Corpse Reviver."

"Yes, Miss Rebecca," he said, already prepping the glass.

"Thanks for coming," Boyle said without looking up.

"Oh, it's not like I have anything better to do at this hour."

They sat in silence until Leroy served the drink. She had a sip
and relented to a smile that she couldn't have fought off with every
ounce of will in her.

"What's the latest with your teetotaling friends?" asked Boyle.

"That's it? Right to business?"

"Business is all you get at four in the morning."

She stuck out her lower lip, imitating a pout. "But we agreed,
didn't we, that this was the safest time for me to stop by? So
that my teetotaling friends, as you call them, don't catch wind of
our meetings?" Her drink was half gone, and she signaled with
a dimpled smile for Leroy to start fixing another. "They're not
wrong on everything you know," she continued. "If their husbands
weren't such brutes coming home drunk and doing Lord knows
what to them every Saturday night, they wouldn't have it out for
you and your spirits."

"Plenty of blame to go around for the ills of the world," Boyle
said.

"I must say, my life has improved since my husband died."

"I'm sure he's in a better place."

"Hell?" She shrugged. "It might give this desolate rock a run
for its money."

Leroy lifted the rye bottle to Boyle, and he shook his head
and pushed the empty glass forward, as though betraying an
old friend. "I'm tired, Rebecca. I spent part of my evening with
a pistol in my face and I'm trying to figure out why. What do
you got for me?"

"There's no question that the Anti-Saloon League is hiring
undercover agents to get involved with some of the saloons and
speakeasies. It's their thinking that the feds aren't enforcing

anything so it's their holy duty to act by any means necessary. I'm not privy to the details nor have I heard anything specific about your establishment."

"That connected to the Rooster Room poisoning?"

"Can't say for certain but I'll keep my ear to the ground."

"What about Willard Reynolds?" Boyle asked.

"The dead one?"

"I mean his son, Willard Jr."

Rebecca started on her second drink and slid a generous bill across the bar toward Leroy. "I've observed him with some of the others, part of the groups of young men who want to join the ranks. He seems to be quite involved."

"With anything in particular?"

She shrugged. "I can look into it. Why? Would you like me to speak with him?"

"Sure," Boyle said. He stood and adjusted his hat and nodded to Leroy. "You can check in with your husband while you're at it."

As he walked home, Boyle watched the orange glow of dawn rise above the Tidal Basin and saturate the waning night sky. The majestic monuments reminded him of man's obsession with legacy, but the apathetic manner with which night traded shifts with day assured him that no stone structure could memorialize the fleeting nature of existence. We were meant to disappear, he thought. Only once we accepted and embraced that fundamental truth could we truly live.

When he returned to his cramped apartment, he fried an egg and drank a warm glass of milk and slept for a few hours. He dreamed vigorously. As though his subconscious was alarmed by the listless manner with which he carried himself by day and sought to shake him from his waking slumber by presenting its vilest concoctions of the mind. That night, his subconscious shunned the strictures of reality and Willard Jr.'s bullet pierced Boyle's brow. At once, he was a boy again, his mother at the Sunday night dinner table trying to wipe the wound from his forehead, insisting he was making a fool of himself showing his face to their church friends like that. Boyle tried to sit still like a good boy, but he couldn't help but squirm as his mother's finger excavated the shards of skull and rubbery brain matter beneath.

He woke to the midmorning sun and scratched his forehead and, after the customary internal quarrel, rose to face the day.

The only person in the bar that morning was Gordie, Mick's eighteen-year-old cousin whom Johnny paid two bucks a day to do chores. Boyle found the young man, built like a lineman and already balding, emptying cases of liquor behind the bar.

"Hey, Gordie."

"Mr. Boyle," he said with a wayward smile.

Boyle pulled a cigarette from his pocket and lit a match. "You were around last night, yeah?"

"Sure was."

"You help out with the Willard boy?"

"Dragged his ass upstairs and tied him up."

"How'd he seem to you?"

"How do you figure?"

"Drunk? Acting funny?"

Gordie shook his head. "Sort of dazed, but sober." He paused. "Irv was acting funny about it."

"How so?"

Gordie scanned the room before responding. "Made sure he was in there alone with him. I stood outside and waited. Didn't hear much. Then Irv came out and said no one in besides for him."

"Then what?" Boyle asked.

"He came back about twenty minutes later. Went in and came out white as a sheet. Said Willard Jr. was dead."

Boyle nodded. "He seemed surprised?"

Gordie shrugged. "Far as I could tell."

Boyle smoked his cigarette and Gordie wiped his sweat-dampened brow and grabbed a soda pop. Boyle closed his eyes and felt the hot smoke in his throat and keyed in on the unique creaks, like fingerprints, signaling the descent down the stairs from the offices above. He took one last drag—resisting the allure of the clinking bottles—before opening his eyes to find Mick staring at him.

"Thank God you're here, Boyle," he said. "Johnny's losing his shit. You better get up there."

Before following, Boyle turned back to the bar. "Hey Gordie, you ever seen a snake shed its skin?"

"Say what?"

"It's a hell of a thing. They leave the dead part behind but come out just the same."

Irv was already there. He stood in the corner and watched Johnny Dunn, on his hands and knees, scrub the crevices of his desk with a toothbrush.

"Shoes," he hollered as Boyle opened the door. "Take off the damn shoes."

Boyle slid them off and approached the chair before the desk. "What's the problem, Johnny?" he asked. "Besides for dust buildup."

Moments passed with no response but for vigorous brushing and Johnny's quickening breaths. When he emerged, he was beet red and sweating. "Got the message this morning—there's a blown still out at our source near Leesburg."

Boyle shrugged. "Pain in the ass, but we've got other sources."

Johnny shook his head. "That's just the start. An hour later, word comes through that a truck expected in this afternoon had an axle snap and the whole shipment's busted. We don't even have enough supply to get us through the night."

"Hell of a coincidence," Irv offered from the corner.

Boyle turned to him. "Mark Twain was born and died in the years Halley's comet appeared seventy-five years apart."

"Shut up, Boyle," Johnny said. "There's no question the Anti-Saloon League is behind this. Word is out that the mayor's stopping by tonight—the perfect time to target us. And you know Congressman Buckner, one of our few allies on the Hill? He was an old fraternity man with Willard Reynolds. I already got a call from him saying we need to stop bringing attention to the joint—and that if he finds out there's any funny business behind Willard's death, we're dealing with the teetotalers alone." He paused to catch his breath. "You learn anything last night?"

Boyle still had his eye on Irv. "Nothing. Those pious types are a crafty bunch. Lotta hours of the day with unsullied minds. No surprise they come up with a clever idea or two."

"I can handle the supply problem, boss," Irv said.

Johnny glared at him. "Yeah? How's that?"

"You know Geary, the fella in Baltimore who we get a shipment from every few weeks?"

"Yeah."

"He keeps a stash on hand and uses it in situations like these to strengthen connections. Jacks up the price for short notice but nothing crazy."

"How do you know this?" Johnny asked. "And why haven't I heard it before?"

Irv shrugged. "Never had this issue before."

Johnny grumbled as though half-satisfied with the answer.

"It's never smart to pay up for a last-minute batch," Boyle said. "You know what those bootleggers will do to the stuff to make some extra bucks."

"He's trustworthy," Irv said. "Besides, we already buy from him."

Both men turned to face their boss. After a heavy breath, Johnny said, "Irv, set it up. We can't afford to go dry this weekend."

"It'll be here," Irv said. He headed for the door.

Once he was gone, Johnny turned to Boyle. "You got something to say, smart guy?"

Boyle lit a cigarette and shrugged. "Can't be right without risking being wrong."

A note waited for Boyle at the bar. "You see who left this?" he asked Gordie.

"Some kid," he said. "Said it was for your eyes only."

Boyle cracked the seal. It read: *Prescott's at noon. You're expected. RB.*

The thick heat made the midday walk to Logan Circle a pilgrimage. As he walked, sweat dampening his linen suit, Boyle considered that his livelihood had turned him into a man of the night. A creature who emerged only to poison and be poisoned in the wee hours under cover of darkness. The sun's glare an enemy, he yearned for the comfort of the shadows.

Prescott's was a speakeasy housed underneath a pharmacy that served a high-end clientele. Inside, Rebecca sat at a lonesome table drinking champagne and nibbling on crab cakes.

Boyle joined her and the barman greeted him with a whiskey. "Anything to eat?" he asked.

Boyle shook his head. "Hope I'm not picking up the bill," he said as Rebecca slurped an oyster with as much grace as possible.

She tilted her head and cleared her throat, and, in her soft features, Boyle recognized her shameful delight in knowing something he didn't. "I've caught wind of a plan tonight at your spot. I take it you've had issues with your regular supplier?"

Boyle took some drink.

"Of course, you have," she said. "I know Johnny's careful, but the replacement booze will be adulterated. Same MO as the Rooster Room. You have to shut down tonight."

Boyle chuckled.

"Is this funny to you?"

"They say in the midst of suffering is when men prove their worth."

She leaned forward. "What are *you* worth, Mr. Boyle? Far as I can tell, nothing is worth much to you."

"I have an acute fascination with lovely and useless things."

"Well fascinate yourself with this—there's a plot to target the poisonings to particular patrons at your joint tonight."

He pondered for a moment. "How could they target the poisoning without help from the bartender?"

Rebecca shrugged. "Men are creatures of habit—they drink what they drink. A marking perhaps? Otherwise, it seems it would require direction."

"Men drink what they drink," Boyle repeated. He downed the last of the whiskey and rose. "Thank you, Rebecca."

"I'll hear from you tomorrow?" she asked.

"I hope so."

Boyle returned to the Moonlight Club at seven that evening—an hour before it opened. As expected, he found the barroom empty but for Johnny and Irv at a table, Mick and Gordie unloading the new shipment, and Leroy tending bar.

"All whiskey and gin?" Boyle asked Irv.

"You bet."

"Well done," he said. "Plenty to get us through the weekend."

"My pleasure."

Boyle selected a couple of new bottles and took them to the bar. "Shall we see if it's any good? Leroy, fix us a round. What'll you have, Irv? Johnny?"

"I'll pass," said Irv.

"Nonsense," said Johnny Dunn. "Boyle's right, you earned it. Let's have a round."

Irv dabbed the sweat in the valleys on his forehead with his handkerchief. "All right. Gin martini."

They watched in silence as Leroy fixed the drink, the only sound the clink of ice against glassware. "You fellas joining me?" Irv asked as Leroy served it up.

"Sure," said Johnny. "But only if you break out the special reserve you were bragging about. You know, the good stuff for the mayor?"

Irv chewed his lip like it was steak fat, forehead scrunched as though he was pondering every decision he'd ever made.

"Special reserve?" Boyle asked.

"Uh-huh."

Boyle returned to the cases and went through the inventory. He noticed that several of the whiskey bottles had a small diamond-shaped marking on the neck.

"Ones with the diamond?" Boyle asked.

Irv's face was still. In the background, Boyle saw that Leroy's wasn't.

"Can I see that?" the bartender asked.

Boyle brought it over and Leroy examined the bottle like a precious artifact. His worn face reflected a keen familiarity with evil, but a simultaneous exasperation with its ubiquity.

"The mark," he said, eyes on Irv. "It's the same as the one on the bottle for Willard Reynolds Sr. the night he died." Leroy's gaze shifted to Boyle. "He said the same thing then—that it was a special reserve bottle for old man Reynolds."

"You watch your mouth, boy," Irv spat, rising from the table. "You watch your mouth spreading nonsense like that."

"Sit down, Irv," Johnny belted. "*Now.*"

Irv shot one more look at Leroy and complied. He took a breath. "Look, Johnny, I don't know anything about whatever's going on here. Leroy's lying through his crooked teeth, and I can't say why." He turned to Boyle. "Unless *you* put him up to it."

"Tell me," Boyle asked, "why is it that the truth is often so hideous?"

Irv didn't respond.

"Because the truth reflects reality and, in reality, people do hideous things. And they do the *most* hideous things in the name of good." He picked up the bottle and pointed to the small diamond. "Does this mean anything to you, Irv?"

"Not a thing."

Boyle retrieved a glass, uncorked the bottle, and poured two fingers of the golden liquor. "Care for a taste?"

Irv shook his head. "I can't stand whiskey. The damn stuff makes me sick."

Boyle swirled the liquor in the tumbler, eyeing it with wonder. "I'm sorry, Johnny," he said. "We better shut things down tonight."

"Why's that?"

"Irv's with the Anti-Saloon League. He's a member of their undercover army trying to bring joints down from within."

Irv's mouth fell open but, by then, Mick and Gordie hovered behind his chair.

"You can thank Leroy's keen eye for confirming it," Boyle continued. "See, the mark signifies bottles poisoned with wood alcohol. Irv's first victim was Willard Sr. He instructed Leroy to give him the so-called special reserve—a targeted killing. Irv knew that Congressman Buckner might go sour on us if his old college buddy croaked here. But that wasn't the only reason he did it. Willard Jr. was already involved with the Anti-Saloon adolescent army, and it was a way to turn an eager young man into a devoted fanatic. A mad dog to sic on their enemies. That way, when Willard Jr. came for me, it would look like vengeance—a crime of passion—not a choreographed political killing."

"But Willard Jr. botched the job," Johnny Dunn said.

"He sure did, poor kid. And after we dragged him back here, Irv knew he wouldn't stand up to our questioning. So, he slipped him the same medicine his old man got so he wouldn't spill."

"This is all horseshit," Irv said, hunched in his chair, voice shaking.

Boyle ignored him. "Next step wasn't as original: blowing up stills and jacking trucks. See, Irv needed a way to substitute the shipment with one he had control over. Can you imagine the shit storm if—on top of the Congressman's buddy dying—the *mayor* did? Or a few of DC's finest? We'd be finished. We'd crumble and they'd move on to the next target in their holy war, God knows how many bodies in their wake."

At that, Irv's face contorted to a smirk which turned into a jubilant howl. "That's all you got, is it? No proof at all? Only wild accusations from a freak like Boyle?" He turned to Johnny Dunn. "Johnny, you can't be buying this. How long have we known each other? You wouldn't do me in without a shred of evidence, would you?"

Johnny eyed the bottle with the mark before turning to Boyle. "How do you know all this?"

"Tips from friends in convenient places." Boyle had lots of friends in convenient places, all relationships he'd cultivated during the years he'd gumshoed for anyone willing to pony up a retainer. "I'd be happy to bring them in to corroborate. Some of them are right here—Leroy, Gordie." Johnny glanced at each, and they gave their boss a solemn nod.

Irv took a long inhale, as though unsure of how many he had left. "If this is all true, Boyle, you know who my friends are. The most powerful men in the world down the street. If you kill me, they'll come for you."

Boyle lifted the tumbler and swirled the whiskey in his palm. "Who said anything about killing?" He presented the glass to Irv. "All I ask is that you take a drink."

Writing fiction set in another time period can be tricky. It is difficult to capture the essence of a bygone era and to write a story that is more than an imitation. When esteemed editor Michael Bracken invited me to contribute to Prohibition Peepers, an anthology of Prohibition-era private eye stories, I wanted to avoid these pitfalls. After all, what do I know about life and times in the 1920s?

Times change, I thought, but people don't. So, I started with a character—a reflective yet ruthless PI who believes that the fight against Prohibition is a fight for the human spirit. I then dropped this peculiar PI into our nation's capital, where factions are all too ready to sin in the name of virtue; to clash in the name of peace. From there, the story fell into place.

I highly recommend the Prohibition Peepers anthology, edited by Bracken and published by Down & Out Books. It explores a fascinating era of our history that is fertile ground for crime fiction. While most of my stories are set in the present, I enjoyed visiting the past for this one.

Peter W. J. Hayes *was born in Newcastle upon Tyne, England, before moving to Paris and later immigrating to Pittsburgh, Pennsylvania. After college he drove delivery trucks and bartended, then lived in Taiwan for a year before backpacking across mainland China. Returning to Pittsburgh, he moved to the other side of the bar to begin a long career in marketing. Following a six-year stint as chief marketing officer for one of the world's largest investment houses, he retired and turned to crime writing.*

Hayes is the author of the Silver Falchion–nominated Vic Lenoski mystery series. His short stories have appeared in Black Cat Mystery Magazine, Crimeucopia, Mystery Magazine, Pulp Modern, The Literary Hatchet, *and various anthologies, including three Malice Domestic anthologies and* The Best New England Crime Stories.

His short stories have been finalists for the Derringer and Al Blanchard Awards, and he was a finalist and highly commended for the Crime Writers' Association Debut Dagger Award.

Visit Hayes at www.peterwjhayes.com.

EL PASO HEAT

Peter W. J. Hayes

John still wakes sometimes in the night, sweating, reliving that moment at the bagel shop near his offices. In his dream—before nausea forces him awake—he sees again his daily order of orange juice and a sesame bagel on the table in front of him, untouched. He knows it's Friday because he smells walnut cream cheese—his favorite. He always reserves that spread for the last day of the workweek, as a treat to start the weekend.

Which is when the two men slide into his booth, directly across from him.

One is young, his face scrubbed shiny. He wears a pink polo shirt; just another suburban dad returning from his young daughter's soccer game.

The second is older, with a flattop John remembers from 1950s photos of his grandfather. That man's face is weathered, the bags under his eyes swollen. John straightens and opens his mouth to protest, but the older man lifts a large, vein-skeined wrist and shows his palm.

"Hear us out." His voice is calm. Authoritative.

The younger man slides a business card across the table to him. John recognizes the round blue logo of the FBI.

From that moment on, for the rest of his life, John will never eat walnut cream cheese. Even the smell of it turns his stomach.

Truly, the arrival of the agents was a relief. Until that moment he'd been trapped. He was only a few years out of college, still in his first job at an accounting firm. He didn't know where to turn, how to extricate himself.

Two years into his job, he'd been promoted to one of the firm's largest accounts. While reviewing their cash flow, he'd noticed that some cash deposits appeared regularly, as if they were timed and structured. He'd then spotted how the deposit totals exactly matched overnight transfers to offshore accounts—while a few vaguely titled line items adjusted as if *they* were accepting the deposit amounts.

For John, it was like lifting his eyes from hand-hewn stones and lines of mortar to see the inside of a cathedral.

At first he was excited, but a few guarded questions revealed that his more experienced colleagues didn't see the shell game concealing the overseas transfers. He wondered for a time if he could be wrong, but he knew he wasn't.

Then came the proof. Not long after his discovery, his boss, Mario Coom, tapped him on the shoulder after their weekly staff meeting. Mario, a fit, middle-aged man with wavy black hair and a permanent five o'clock shadow, led him into his office.

John still remembered that office, with its tall windows and city views, the shelves of acrylic awards and photos of Mario with city council members and sports stars. At that time, it was the type of office he desperately wanted to inhabit one day. His dream office. Mario closed the door and looked him up and down. Then, his brown eyes burning in a way that made John uncomfortable,

Mario told him they had a snitch in the company. How their largest client, a Mr. Volkov, was concerned. That John needed to be loyal, now more than ever.

Mario didn't explain why a legitimate accounting firm might have a snitch. Or the coincidence of their largest client having the same last name as the city's biggest crime boss. Or why—and this part truly worried John—Mario even trusted him with this information.

John wasn't the snitch, and he understood Mario might be testing him. But common sense told him if he quit the company, Mario would assume he was guilty. Worse, the large amount of cash moving through the accounts meant the stakes were high. He also knew that if he stayed and the money laundering was discovered, he would be complicit. Perhaps arrested.

Which was why, when John saw that round blue logo on the business card, despite a shudder of fear, he pulled the card and his bagel closer as if they were life rings tossed to him as he drowned.

Eighteen months after that first FBI visit, John slid into a booth at a bagel chain in El Paso, almost two thousand miles from his last job. He placed his orange juice and sesame bagel—slathered with the plain cream cheese he always chose for Mondays—on the table in front of him.

His first day of work, his second chance.

Behind him were months of secret depositions and closed grand jury testimony. His arrangement with the FBI was simple. He knew his company's bookkeeping practices, and Volkov's accounts in particular. The snitch in the company passed along copies of spreadsheets to the FBI, and John explained them. He worked with an FBI forensic accountant, a plump, balding man with oddly modern eyeglasses that looked out of place on his pale face. His last name was Crane, and he talked as he worked, turning their sessions into an unexpected masterclass in money laundering. John was fascinated. By the time they finished—and Volkov's trial was underway—John knew Mario's laundering techniques were, at best, mediocre.

No wonder he'd spotted them so easily.

He mentioned that to Crane, who laughed.

"You'd be good at this. And you should know, each launderer has a signature. It's in the techniques they use to hide false transactions. I'd recognize an individual's work anywhere, Grasshopper."

When John stared at him in confusion, Crane added, "Never saw the old *Kung Fu* television series, huh? And you're right. Mario's work is shoddy."

But where was Mario?

The day the FBI served their arrest warrants, Mario's penthouse was empty, his luxury car gone. The FBI mounted a short-lived search. Volkov was the FBI's real target, and Mario's role was just an office boy, as one of the agents put it. There were serious bad guys to catch.

John didn't really care, and now he had a second chance. He stared at his orange juice and sesame bagel with its plain cream cheese, and stood. New beginnings meant ending old habits, he decided, and tossed his breakfast into the garbage receptacle. He bought a take-out coffee and muffin and drove the last mile to his new office.

The U.S. Marshals' WITSEC program had placed him in a midsize accounting firm that specialized in bookkeeping for car manufacturers. A retired U.S. Marshals Service commander sat on the company board, which told John, now living under the name of John Craft, that the Marshals were as tightly knit as the mob. As he crossed the parking lot to his new job, the sun reflected off the building's glass windows, hurting his eyes. It was barely eight fifteen, yet the heat of the asphalt seeped through the soles of his shoes. Of course they didn't relocate me to Hawaii, he thought. It was safer to place people somewhere no one wants to go.

His new boss, Walt Tierney, walked him around the office and did introductions. At the end of a series of low-walled cubicles he met Susan Sanchez. Suzy stood in a single fluid movement and offered her hand. Her black hair fell just below her shoulders, her brown eyes were so bright John had trouble meeting her gaze. Her hand was refreshingly cool after the outside heat.

He didn't want to let go

Suzy worked on the team handling the company's largest client. John could tell from the way Walt introduced her that he respected her work. As Walt led him to his new office, John glanced over his shoulder. Suzy was watching him, her head above the low cubicle partition. If eyes could smile, hers were certainly doing so.

That Friday, he asked her out.

And just like that, seven years passed and dawned on the Saturday of their five-year-old son's birthday party.

John couldn't imagine not being married. He loved Suzy and their two children, even the small suburban house the Marshals Service had provided. He even liked Suzy's extended family. Her aunts, uncles, and cousins enveloped him, dismayed that his parents were dead and he had no siblings. It was as if those facts made them want to protect him all the more.

It was all a lie, of course. John's parents lived in a small suburb outside Boston in a white Cape Cod that leaked around the stone chimney, no matter how many times John's father caulked or replaced the flashing. John's only communication with them was through Linda Fesco, his case officer. Each month, he wrote a letter and enclosed several photos of Suzy and the kids. All hard copy, email was out of the question.

He'd been surprised when the FBI suggested witness relocation. He wasn't the snitch and didn't think he needed protection, but the FBI introduced him to Linda, who gave him a gut-wrenching presentation about the likelihood of retribution from Volkov's gang. Grudgingly, he'd agreed to a diluted version of WITSEC lasting ten years. Controlled communications with his parents would be allowed. To Linda and the FBI, he acted as if WITSEC was unnecessary. Secretly, he liked the idea. He imagined dates and job interviews after the ten years were up, and letting slip—in a hushed voice—burnished anecdotes from that period of his past he really couldn't discuss.

Linda Fesco was with him the day he visited his parents and explained he was leaving, that communications would be rare and monitored. His mother barely said a word, fighting not to cry. His father, an accountant himself, had followed the Volkov trial in the news. As Linda skated past topics best left unsaid, John saw his father making the links anyway, his gaze flicking from Linda to John and back. As Linda and John prepared to leave, his father grasped his hand and pulled him close. Not a hug, really, his father rarely hugged, but close enough for John to hear him say, "I'm proud of you, son. You did the right thing. Take care of yourself until we see you again."

In the car with Linda, he fought back tears. He was his parent's only child, and he suddenly understood how terrible this must be for them. For the first time since the bagel shop and the arrival of the FBI agents, everything felt real and final. Worse, his father was wrong. He hadn't done the right thing. He hadn't done anything but desperately grab the life preserver thrown to him.

And now he was running away to hide.

He tried not to relive that pain and self-recrimination now, waiting for the oven to finish warming pizza bites for the five-year-olds at his son's birthday party. Parents were still stopping by, dropping off his son's day-care friends. Suzy's family was out in force, swarming the house, their voices raised in excitement. It was a rush of noise and warmth. John thought about how his mother would love to be here. He could see her distributing paper plates and warning the children not to spill their punch. It saddened him.

The doorbell rang and Suzy bumped him with her hip, her cheeks flushed and eyes sparkling. "I'll do this, you get the door." She was almost breathless with excitement, and John felt a rush of happiness for her, followed, as he headed to the door, by a surge of gratitude. Despite everything, he was glad for his life.

His son, Toby, had answered the door and was grinning at a girl offering him a brightly wrapped gift. The girl's mother spotted John and smiled, her teeth surprisingly white, as her husband pivoted from closing the door. He and John locked eyes.

For John, it was like being shot with a low-voltage Taser.

It was Mario Coom. His dark hair was thinner, the jawline softer, but it was Mario. Right down to the five-o'clock shadow. John was so mesmerized he kept walking toward them, as if Coom was a magnet and he was no more than iron filings.

Mario was the first to snap out of it. He blinked, looked around the living room, and spotted Toby. He dropped a hand to the back of Toby's neck and stared at John, as if asking whether he needed to crush Toby's pale neck in his hand.

John stopped dead, unable to look at what might happen to his son, and turned to Mario's wife. He introduced himself, both first and last name, and managed to hide the quiver in his arm as they shook hands. He turned to Mario, who in a deft move transferred the covered dish in his right hand to his wife and reached for a handshake. He didn't release Toby's neck.

"Mario Rabino," he said, and squeezed John's hand so hard John thought his fingers might rearrange themselves. "Can you show me where to put this dish?"

John eked out a yes. Mario released John's hand and Toby's neck and took back the covered dish. Dazed, John led him to the kitchen, just as Suzy disappeared into the living room with a plate of pizza bites.

Mario slid the casserole onto the countertop, turned to John and showed him the blade of a paring knife. It took John a split second to realize it was his own knife, from the block knife holder on the countertop. Mario scanned the kitchen and looked at him. "Phone. Give me your phone." His voice was compressed. "I won't say it again."

John understood in a rush, his mind finally working again. Mario hadn't spotted a landline, and all he needed was John's cell phone to stop any calls for help. He handed it over. Mario pressed one finger to his lips in a signal to stay silent and disappeared into the living room. Not knowing what else to do, John followed.

Mario was talking urgently to his wife. John moved close enough to overhear her say, a surprised look on her face, "But we were going to the mall, to look at couches."

"We're staying," Mario replied harshly, leaning closer. She tightened, as if she expected to be slapped. The tone of Mario's voice, and their movements, were so intimate and practiced they left John cold.

"Are you okay? You look like you've seen a ghost." John flinched and found Suzy standing next to him, a quizzical smile on her lips.

"No, yes, I'm fine. Just overwhelmed by all the kids." He tried to smile and knew he failed.

Mario raised his phone to his ear, watching John and Suzy together. He stepped close to Toby, the blade of the paring knife sticking an inch or two from his right fist. John looked down and saw Suzy holding her phone. He turned to step away, but Mario's wife approached them, a bright smile on her face.

"I hope you don't mind if Mario and I stay for the party?" She touched Suzy's forearm with her fingertips. "We do so love children's parties."

"It's not a problem at all," Suzy replied, and glanced at the silk scarf Mario's wife wore around her neck. "And that's a beautiful scarf."

"Oh." She touched it self-consciously. "I burn so easily from the sun. I have to be careful when I'm outside."

John sidestepped away from them, impressed at how easily she lied. He'd already overheard their original plans, and from the angle where he stood, he'd spotted a heavy dose of makeup edging out from underneath the scarf. Together, the makeup and scarf were meant to hide something, and John guessed it was bruises. He moved a few more steps away, watching Mario. Mario finished his phone call and pocketed his phone, saw John was free of Suzy, and backed away from Toby. He gave John a toothy smile that said, "Gotcha," and pointed at his fist, where the paring knife was hidden.

For two hours Mario never strayed far from Toby. John examined every possible permutation of why Mario might be in his house. Perhaps Mario was the original snitch for the FBI and was relocated to the same city by the Marshals Service? But if that was the case, they were on the same side and Mario wouldn't threaten him. He discounted that possibility. That left only the raging coincidence that Mario fled to El Paso, and the Marshals Service blindly relocated John to the same area. It was insidiously bad luck, as if Mario was the rainwater his father couldn't keep out of his house. But John's mind kept shifting to how the day might end.

He was sure Mario wouldn't just herd his wife and daughter into his car and drive away, never to be seen again.

There was more to come.

He was right. As a stream of parents arrived to collect their children, Mario took a call and came over to him.

"Outside. There's someone you need to meet."

Mario placed his hand in the small of John's back and guided him through the late-day heat to a white SUV waiting in the driveway. Mario opened the back door and gestured John inside. When John hesitated, Mario leaned close and said, "Just a conversation. Do you really think we'd grab you in the middle of the day with everyone watching? We just need to be clear on a few things."

John glanced about and saw Mario was right. Several parents stood in a group in front of the house. Two of Toby's friends chased each other around the large purple-blooming Texas Ranger plant by their front window. Suzy was standing with another mother, her hand shading her eyes, watching what he was doing.

John clambered into the back of the SUV. The door slammed shut behind him and Mario took the front passenger seat.

The man waiting for John in the back seat reminded him of the young FBI agent from the bagel shop, all those years ago. Like him, this man wore a polo shirt (yellow, this time), but instead of wrinkled chinos he wore blue jeans ironed to a knife-edge crease. One leg was crossed over the other, displaying expensive loafers and no socks.

"So you're John," the man said, looking him up and down with piercing blue eyes. He was in his forties, his sandy blond hair cut short above a chiseled face. John stared back, thinking the man looked like an unusually virile spokesman in a perfume ad.

"I'm Alfred," the man said.

Deep in his subconscious John smelled walnut cream cheese and fought down a surge of bile. He knew the man's name wasn't Alfred. Somehow he would have preferred this Alfred to be overweight, swarthy, and drowned in tattoos, like the driver.

"I'll keep it short." Alfred smiled, his teeth straight and white. "I always liked a child's birthday party. Do you like your family, John?"

John nodded.

"Now, Mario told me you worked for him back in Boston, and I'm guessing the Marshals Service was kind enough to move you here. A bit of bad luck running into Mario again, isn't it?"

John thought the man's tone was oddly mechanical. Almost bored.

"I was getting ready to bring John into the business," Mario said from the front seat. "He had potential. I told him we had a snitch, to see how he'd react. I didn't know we actually had one. But John kept quiet. That's potential." Mario twisted around in his seat to make eye contact. "I was ready to bring you in. Where the real money is."

John wasn't sure what to say. Mario was grooming him? That's what the snitch conversation was about?

"Well, isn't that nice and all," Alfred said. "But we're here today, and the three of us are going to work something out." He pegged John with his gaze. "You keep quiet about Mario, okay? Anything happens to Mario, arrest or otherwise, and your wife and kids disappear. It will be your worst nightmare, and we'll let you live for the rest of your life to think about it. Do I make myself clear?"

John heard every word and felt let down. Despite not admitting it to himself, on some level he'd known this was the outcome. His family was the best leverage they had. Now that he heard the words, they sounded almost anticlimactic.

"And remember this," Alfred added. "We're watching you. You try and run, and you'll be the only one left alive."

"Okay." John summoned the courage to look him in the eye. "Is that it?"

Alfred gave him a cold smile. "I don't think we need more."

John turned to Mario. "Give me my phone back."

Mario glanced at Alfred, who nodded. Mario rummaged in his pocket and held out the phone.

John took it. "You don't have to worry about me." Before anyone could say anything more, he opened the door and slid into his baking hot front yard. Toby was standing by the front door, and John walked to him, placed his hand on the back of his neck and massaged gently, as if he could make the pressure of Mario's hand disappear. He knew he couldn't. He knew it would always be there, as it was on his own neck. A slow boil of anger started inside him.

Suzy, of course, wanted to know why he got into the SUV. He passed it off by saying he'd met Mario at the driving range and they were talking golf. The car was just to keep cool. Suzy offered to invite Mario and his wife over for dinner and John declined, admitting in a soft voice that he didn't really like Mario. Suzy eyed him, but didn't bring it up again. And then John settled in to wait. He was quite sure Mario would call, he just didn't know when or how. No one threatened to murder your family and then walked away as if nothing happened.

But, when his phone rang at work two days later, it wasn't Mario. It was Linda Fesco from the WITSEC program.

"Just checking in," she said jauntily.

"It's not the end of the month," John replied, guardedly.

"What, I can't check on my charges?" She said the last word as if he were a fourth grader.

John stayed quiet, to let her think he was considering her question. "Nope," he said finally. "Same old, same old. Had my son's fifth birthday party over the weekend."

"I bet that was fun."

"Kind of crazy, house full of five-year-olds, but yeah."

"That's it?"

"Pretty much."

Now it was her turn to be silent for a few seconds. "Uh-huh. Well, if anything unusual comes up, give me a call."

"Will do," John said, and hung up. He stared at the phone for a few seconds, trying to remember the last time Linda Fesco called him off schedule. He already knew the answer. It was never.

Two days later his office phone rang, and when he picked it up, Mario was on the line.

"John, you play golf, right?" Mario asked, without preamble.

"I do."

"Okay. Saturday morning, tell your wife you're going to the driving range with some guys. Get to this address by ten o'clock." Mario listed a place that was surprisingly close by. "Come up to suite thirty-two hundred. And John?"

"Yes?"

"Take a long look at a photograph of your wife and kids before you come. Just so you and I are clear."

John didn't need to be reminded. He went to bed every night and woke up every morning thinking about it, the time in between punctured by dreams of the bagel shop.

John arrived at the suite at ten o'clock on Saturday, to find himself alone with Mario in an office space of low-walled cubicles and offices. The name on the door was Potter Accounting. Mario ran an electronic wand over him to check for microphones. He inspected John's cell phone, to be sure it was turned off, as instructed.

Mario handed back John's phone. "On your way home, turn it back on when you pass the driving range." He waved at the office. "This is where the real magic gets done. Potter Accounting, get it?" He directed John to a desk with a laptop. "From now on, you work for us." He studied John carefully. "And you know what that means, right?"

John did. He was there to cook the books and hide whatever money Alfred was laundering. He'd expected Mario and Alfred to do something like this—to incriminate him—and he knew he had no choice but to go along with it. Worse, this time there would be no FBI agents sliding into his booth one morning at breakfast. If he wanted out, he would have to do it himself. And he was quite sure he would have only one chance.

John stayed patient for five months. Sometimes Suzy complained about his golf and he shifted the day of the week or time. Mario was surprisingly flexible about it. What Mario wouldn't change was his approach to hiding offshore transactions. John spotted them just as easily as before, which led him to question how to make them harder to trace. Thinking up ways to disguise the transactions became a game to him, something to relieve the boredom.

He tested each new idea against what he'd learned from Crane, the FBI forensic accountant. Slowly, a method formed. He could camouflage the offshore transactions by randomizing the amounts and frequency of the deposits and corresponding transfers. He kept the approach in his head, never putting it to paper. He told himself it was just a way to keep himself interested and challenged, nothing more. Until the day he walked out of the office at his regular job to find Linda Fesco standing next to his car.

He didn't recognize her at first. Normally she wore a dark suit and white shirt with her hair pulled back in a severe bun. Today, a short sun dress barely reached a quarter of the way down her supple, tanned thighs. Her bronzed shoulders were bare and large sunglasses sat atop a head of shiny hair that tumbled halfway down her back. She was shapely, smiling, and looking to all the world as if she was waiting only for him.

John stopped a few feet from her, his entire body jangling. "What are you doing here?"

"Just thought I'd stop by. See how you're doing."

"Are you on vacation?" John knew it was a ridiculous question, but he couldn't reconcile this seductive woman with the Linda Fesco of the Marshals Service. Panic struck him. Any moment Suzy would leave the office building for their drive home. After they married she'd kept working, the company simply shifting her under a different boss. Suzy couldn't see him talking to a woman who looked like this, a woman obviously waiting for him.

He looked at the office building. It was worse than he thought. Twenty feet away, Suzy stood motionless between the double doors leading into the lobby. Her hand was on the door handle, as if she'd turned to stone midmovement.

"You have to go," he said, turning to Linda. He heard desperation in his voice.

Linda glanced in Suzy's direction, reached out a hand, took him by the collar and rose onto her toes. She placed her lips near his ear. "You need to do the right thing here, John." She let go and dropped back to her usual height.

"What are you talking about?"

She smiled, so broadly he knew she was doing it for Suzy to see. "You know exactly what I'm talking about. Do the right thing, John, and it will all work out okay. And I suggest you tell Suzy I'm an old girlfriend passing through town, and that I decided to surprise you. It might work. But if I don't hear from you, she'll see me driving by your house a few times." She twirled and crossed the parking lot to a convertible parked in a fire lane. She slid into the driver's seat, blew him a kiss, and zipped out of the lot.

John turned toward Suzy, who was walking toward him. The despair on her face broke his heart. A delirious anger overtook him. He was being used. Set up. Played

He tried to control the turmoil inside him. "Hey," he said, as she drew close.

She stopped several feet from him. "Who was that?" Suzy's voice was fraught and thick.

"Oh. An old girlfriend. From college. I didn't even know she was in town. I guess she's passing through."

Suzy pressed her hand to her abdomen where she once carried his children. She didn't say anything, just walked around the car and got into the passenger seat.

John turned to the driver's side door, willing his hands to stop shaking.

That night, once the children were in bed, John and Suzy went around and around, arguing about Linda. John invented a name and backstory for her, and stuck to his tale about her passing through town. Suzy kept returning to how much time he spent playing golf, and finally reached a point where she asked if it was golf at all. Exhausted, they both fell asleep at five in the morning. Nothing was resolved; they were just too tired to continue.

They drove to work in silence. In his small office, John swilled coffee. He had to act. He knew it. If Suzy spotted Linda again, she would never believe his lies. His anger shifted and swelled. What Linda had done was no different than Alfred. Worse, really, because Suzy knew about it. He swigged more burnt, bitter coffee, already well past his two-mugs-a-day routine. He'd thought WITSEC would burnish his life, make him mysterious and dashing. In truth, he felt cheap, dirty, and desperate. The Marshals Service had promised they would protect him, but Linda had weaponized the program and didn't care if his family was within the blast circle.

But Linda was right about one thing. It was time to do the right thing. And he would.

Over the next few days, he and Suzy settled into a prickly stalemate, talking only about their children and family logistics. Out of deference, John waited until Saturday to say he was going golfing again, and drove straight to Potter Accounting. Mario showed up for the first hour and John did what he asked. As soon as Mario returned home, John opened a new offshore account in Panama, then installed the methods he'd worked out over the past few weeks to camouflage the transfers into it. He also added a new sub-account to one of the payables line items and backdated two years of payments from it into a collection of local bank accounts. He doubted Mario would spot it. Lately, Mario paid less and less attention to details.

During the middle of the week, he called Linda and left her a message.

"I've been thinking about what you said," he told her, when she returned his call.

"I knew you would."

He didn't like the arrogance in her voice, but he asked for a meeting in a week.

"Why so long?" she asked.

"I need time to put something together," he said quietly. "I'm being watched. And we need to meet somewhere safe. My family is in danger."

"I'll send you the details." Her answer was brusque, the tone take-control. The call ended.

I bet you will, John thought, as he put down his phone.

⚊⬩⚊

John hadn't quite lied when he asked for time to put something together. That something was cash, which needed time to channel through his randomized system of transfers. He had specific cash totals in mind for both of the accounts he'd opened.

A week later he met Linda at, of all places, a bagel shop. It was Linda's suggestion, and he wondered if she'd picked it on purpose after reading his FBI file. It fit a pattern about her that was obvious to him now. She was so blindly ambitious that if the FBI met sources in bagel shops, in her mind she should as well.

They'd argued over the meeting time, John holding out for early evening. He had his reasons.

"What do you have for me?" she asked, as soon as he sat down. She was professionally dressed again, her hair severely tied into a bun.

He uncapped his bottle of iced tea and took a sip. When he was finished he held up a flash drive for her to see, but slid it into his shirt pocket. "I have some questions before I give you that."

She pulled her gaze away from his shirt pocket and met his eyes. "I'll answer what I can."

"You picked El Paso for a reason. It was no accident. You sent me here."

"That isn't actually a question, but yes." She didn't hide the derision in her voice.

"You thought I would bump into Coom?" John fought down his anger. "How is that even possible? The probability is no better than the lottery."

She tilted her head back, looking down at him, scorn in her eyes. "Is it, though? We had reports he was here, which makes sense. I mean look at this place. Half the city is in Mexico. There's fifty large accounting firms here, more than two hundred little ones. I bet half are laundering cartel money. Guys with Coom's skills run to places like this. On top of that, accountants like certain neighborhoods, which means their kids go to the same schools and day care. We dropped you into the middle of all that. Was it a long shot? Of course. But I placed people in cities all along the border. I call the program Retread. The truth is, people gravitate to what they know best. I took accountants, mobsters, drug smugglers, guys who ran illegal gambling, you name it. Placed them where they were bound to meet their own kind. And when they do, they join up. Can't help themselves. All I have to do is lean on them and boom! I have an informant in a crime network."

John struggled to understand the enormity of what she was saying. How many people like him had she put in danger? "But I'm not a crook. I don't want any of this."

She shrugged. "And yet you're working for Coom again."

He stared at her, fighting anger. "They threatened my family."

She gazed at him, a half-smile on her lips. She didn't believe him. He could see it.

He tamped down his anger and tried to think through her viewpoint. "If I was bait," he said slowly, "you were watching me."

"Not really. We don't have the budget for that. But we knew you wouldn't run into Coom or anyone at your day job. So once in a while we'd follow you on a weekend. And one Saturday, guess who's having a birthday party? We took photos of everyone going in and out. And who do we see, but Coom?" She snapped her fingers. "Then we did start following you. Okay, enough of this. Hand over the flash drive. I've got the FBI on a string. You need to understand, this is my ticket to Quantico. After this I'll be working for them and done with this carny job babysitting people like you."

"And all this was your idea?"

"Damn right. My baby. Took me two years to get my boss to go along with it. I checked who might go into WITSEC, convinced them if they needed it, like you, and decided where to send them."

John's mind flashed to Coom's hand on the back of Toby's neck, to the paring knife in Coom's other hand as he hovered behind his son. All because Linda wanted to job hop.

"What happens now? To my family?" John asked.

"Nothing. You give me the flash drive. In my reports you're just a confidential informant. Your name never comes up. The FBI take down Coom and his boss, and you stay here for the next two-some years of your ten-year deal. Then you do whatever you want."

"Okay," he said slowly. "And you understand if the arrests are messed up, my family will be killed. That's the threat."

She waved a hand as if she was shooing away a fly. "Oh, for goodness sake, grow a pair. You'll be fine."

He didn't believe her for a second, but that was okay. Carefully, he placed the flash drive on the tabletop and slid it over to her. "If you can, give it to the forensic accountant I worked with at the FBI. Crane. He knows Coom's work."

She picked up the flash drive and tapped it on the table. "Well done, my friend. We'll all be a lot better off." She slid out of the booth.

No, he thought, the plan here is for *you* to be better off. He watched her leave the shop.

He waited thirty seconds and followed her outside. As she climbed into a nondescript Chevrolet sedan, he cut over to his own car. She headed north and he followed, staying as far back as he dared. He had one shot at this, and he couldn't lose her.

Fifteen minutes later, Linda left the highway and threaded through a suburban plan of tightly packed homes built along Spanish lines. The Franklin Mountains loomed in the distance, the sky above them purple and pinpricked with stars. She finally turned left, slowed, and swung into a driveway as a garage door lifted. John continued through the intersection and circled the block. The road took him past the far end of Linda's street. He took the next left, and driving slowly, squinted between the houses until he spotted the back of Linda's house. He took his foot off the gas, memorizing the back of her house and what he could see of her backyard. Just before the next house blocked his view, he spotted a small roofline in Linda's backyard. A shed. He goosed the gas.

Perfect.

For the next month, nothing changed. John called Mario once a week and set up a time to meet. He and Suzy continued their cold war, talking only when they needed to. But the following week, Mario didn't answer John's call. That weekend, John drove to Potter Accounting to find the door padlocked and a note pasted to the door, asking anyone with information about Potter Accounting to contact the FBI.

Two days later, at work, his phone rang.

When he answered it a male voice introduced itself as Steve Carryer. "John," he said, "I just want you to know that I'm your new case officer. We should meet, I'm thinking next week."

"Oh," John said carefully. "What happened to Linda?"

"Just some reorganization at our end. Nothing to concern yourself with. And I see you barely have two more years left with us."

"Right, it was ten years from the start."

"And you've been busy. Married and a couple of kids. I've got a boy myself. And this whole business with Mario Coom. I just want you to know you have nothing to worry about. FBI rolled up the whole network. The few who got away were low-level, and they ran to Mexico. They won't be back. I think there's a commendation in the works for you."

"What I'd really like is to tell my wife the truth. Why I'm here. What's going on."

Steve was silent for a few of John's heartbeats. "Well, let me bounce that upstairs, but I'm thinking it shouldn't be a problem. When we meet I'll give you the final word. Don't say anything until then. Okay?"

He agreed, and when he met John the following week, he was given the go-ahead.

That night, the children in bed, John took Suzy into their bedroom and closed the door. Slowly, he told her the whole story. About the Volkov trial, the move to El Paso, Coom showing up at the birthday party and forcing him to work weekends, all under the cover of golf outings. Who Linda really was, how she had set him up, and that it was finally over. She listened to him, her knees drawn up to her chin on the bed, her eyes half-closed. Then he told her about his mother and father and their Cape Cod house in Boston. He even told her about the chimney leak his father was unable to repair.

What he didn't mention was his series of withdrawals from banks in El Paso. The one hundred thousand in cash and the glass Mason jar. How he slipped out of the house at three A.M. and parked in the driveway of a house a block from Linda's house, one with five newspapers lying jumbled by the front door. And he certainly didn't tell her about hiding the glass jar of cash inside Linda's garden shed.

When he finished, Suzy said she needed to think. The next day, after dinner, he saw her on her laptop, reading newspaper stories about Volkov's trial.

The following morning, the newspapers exploded with the story of Mario Rabino's arrest, his real name of Coom, the charging of his boss and colleagues, and the end of a cartel money laundering operation That night, once the children were in bed, he and Suzy lay in the dark next to each other, staring at the ceiling, until Suzy rolled onto her side, facing him, shifted closer and slid her arms around him. He took a chance and kissed her lightly. He tasted the damp salt of tears. She burrowed against him and tightened her arms so hard he could barely breathe, as if she would never let go.

Several weeks later a short follow-up article in the newspaper described how the FBI's review of Potter Accounting's financials revealed two years of monthly bribes to a member of the Marshals Service, and how the cash was found hidden in a glass jar in the garden shed behind the Marshal's house. Her hearing was imminent.

John didn't give it much attention. He didn't think Linda would get a harsh sentence, if any at all. The evidence was largely circumstantial, although it was there in the documents on the flash drive. But she would lose her job and never again endanger the people she was charged to protect simply to further her career. That was all he really wanted.

Three months later, returning from the driving range one Saturday, John stopped at one of the El Paso public libraries. Inside, he sat at a public computer and visited the website of a bank in Panama. He entered an account number and waited as the site churned. He knew he shouldn't check the account, but he couldn't help himself. The account was his fail-safe. If the FBI hadn't arrested Coom, or something went wrong, his plan was to take

Suzy and the kids and escape in all the confusion of the arrests. He didn't need the money now, but there was something he couldn't let go. He wanted to know if the FBI's forensic accountants had found the account, if Crane had discovered it. He wanted to know how well his camouflaging techniques worked. That, more than anything, made him risk a peek.

The account balance appeared. He'd set the deposits to cut off once the account reached five million dollars. It was all there. Had they really missed it? He searched the screen and saw a red dot next to the notifications link. A message. He clicked.

Well done, Grasshopper. I almost missed this. Almost. This is your work, Coom doesn't have the brains. I only know of one other who uses these techniques, a Spanish launderer I named El Capo. We almost had him once, in a hotel in Marrakech, but he escaped. As you have. I read the report and saw your case officer used you. Put your family in danger. And she was taking bribes. For what, I wonder? Interesting, how the payments were so easy to find. I think I'll give you a choice, Grasshopper. I'm going to leave this account here. You've earned it, and after what happened, you deserve it. Take it, if you want. Or, come and work for me, here at the FBI.

Keep in mind I know your signature now, my friend.

The note wasn't signed, but John knew it was from Crane. He saw Crane's natural skepticism in his question about the bribes. He reread the note and a door opened inside him, not to the big shiny office with the city views and rows of acrylic mementos. He didn't care about that, he realized. It opened to something better, to the columns, crypt, vault, and rose window of that same cathedral he'd seen years earlier when he first understood what Coom was doing.

He sat back. Crane offering him the five million was likely a trap, or at least a test. He knew that, although he had an odd feeling that Crane was serious.

He would decide later. It wasn't about the money, he knew that now. It was about being good at something. Doing the right thing in the way he thought best. Not running away. He'd done that, and he knew it because the dream about the bagel shop no longer woke him at night.

He deleted his browser history and shut off the computer. On the way to his car, he called Suzy.

"Hey," he said, when she answered. "I'm finally on my way home."

The opening of "El Paso Heat" came to me unbidden, and I was taken with the way the young protagonist—just at the beginning of his business career—was overwhelmed by circumstances he lacked the confidence to control. Making the best of poor choices, he soon finds himself in El Paso, only to discover that he and his new family are the victims of a much darker force—the naked ambition of someone charged to protect him. Whether he can find the wherewithal to protect his family and extricate himself from this new danger, of course, becomes the existential question of the story.

Shells Legoullon *is the author of numerous publications, including contributions to the* Chicken Soup for the Soul *series and* Thrill Ride—The Magazine: Best of 2023. *She is a former San Francisco North/East Bay regional advisor for the Society of Children's Book Writers and Illustrators and a current member of Sisters in Crime and the Pacific Northwest Writers Association. Her passions are thriller fiction, red wine, and dark chocolate. Legoullon is the mother of four boys and lives with her husband and two crazy dogs on a misty lake in Northern Idaho.*

THE BACKWOODS
Shells Legoullon

THEN

Daddy dragged the body toward the backwoods. Charlotte crouched behind a heap of old tires, flies buzzing thick and loud, something stinky in the tall grass she couldn't see. She plugged her nose with her fingers and sucked back a sticky August breath. Holding as still as the Virginia air, she prayed Daddy wouldn't catch her out of bed. But the shiny car's headlights had woken Charlotte. Then she heard Rose crying. Daddy yelling.

Charlotte's eyes adjusted to the night and locked on Daddy's strong hands gripped around a man's ankles, slouched dress socks and the reflection of fireflies in two polished shoes. Even at ten, Charlotte knew Daddy was up to grown-up business. She stayed put while Daddy and the struggling figure disappeared into the thicket of trees.

A funny tickle itched deep in Charlotte's belly. Curiosity. Daddy had strict rules about going into the backwoods uninvited. But even as her tiny heart pounded like a frightened rabbit, she crept forward in her red rubber boots and Cinderella pajamas. Keeping a safe distance from Daddy, she followed behind him and the stranger, and slipped inside the eerie blackness.

That's the night Charlotte discovered there was a hungry monster living in their backwoods and if you fell into its slick, muddy mouth, you'd disappear forever.

Now

Simon pads into the kitchen with bare feet, his pj's too short for his growing legs. He's tall for six, like his father. I'm at the table under the bay window where Mama and I used to sit together when I was Simon's age.

"Am I too late?" Simon rubs his fists against his eyes.

I set down my coffee and motion him over. "Too late for what, Bug?" He slips inside my open arms and I wrap him up tight. Drinking in the scent of him, little boy, sleep, and hints of smoke from our fire last night. It was magical, roasting marshmallows and catching lightning bugs with my son on the farm I grew up on.

"The chores," Simon says with a tired whine.

"You're right on time. Breakfast first though."

He tips his chin up to meet my gaze. "I'm not hungry. Let's do the eggs first, then eat breakfast."

I grin at my son, a complicated blend of Peter and me. He loves this farm almost as much as I do. "I'll compromise," I say.

He frowns. "I hate compromises," he says, showing Peter's determination.

"We all do sometimes," I laugh. "Go get dressed and I'll make you a piece of toast. If you eat it all, we'll do our chores."

Simon springs from the kitchen and up the stairs. His feet tromp overhead as he makes his way to my old bedroom. I open a loaf of bread and plunk two pieces into the toaster. While I wait, memories from my childhood wrap around me like a weighty quilt. I picture Mama sitting at the table, her cheater glasses balanced on the tip of her nose while she mends one of our torn items of clothing. Rose is on the phone in the other room gabbing dramatically with one of her friends. And Daddy is outside working. Always working. He was my hero and my best friend after Mama died and Rose left. He was bigger than life.

Now, without him, the house seems smaller but I swear I can still feel his presence in every corner.

"Ready," Simon squeals, bursting back into the kitchen in old clothes and my red rubber boots in hand.

He sets them down as I butter his toast. I sneak a long glance at him as he stares out at the farm, and I'm certain I've made the right decision. This is what Simon needs. In Daddy's words, a boy needs to be outside, exploring and getting his hands dirty. Peter doesn't understand why I insisted Simon and I stay at the farm for the summer. Then again, Peter was raised in the city. He doesn't see the same beauty in these backwoods.

Simon rips off the crust from his toast and gobbles up the inside section. "Done," he says, then rubs the crumbs on his jeans and takes a swallow of orange juice.

I love how eager he is to be here and honestly, I'm just as excited. Even if it's not much of a farm anymore. In the last ten years Daddy took care of the chickens and made a good little side business for himself selling eggs to locals or passersby. After the horses died, he never replaced them. Our one cow is nearly fifteen and no longer produces milk.

Simon slips on the rubber boots and pushes the screen door open.

"Hold on Speed Racer," I say and follow him outside, where my own rubber boots are waiting. "Let's go over the rules again."

Simon wrinkles his nose. "Again?"

"Again," I say. "These rules are very important. I need to know you understand them."

He huffs, then recites them back to me. "Always wear my boots in the summertime, because of the copperheads and rattlesnakes. Never go down by the main road. Don't play near the creek unless you're with me." He rolls his eyes, then finishes. "And never, ever, ever go into the backwoods unless you invite me."

"Why not?" I wait patiently.

Simon rolls his eyes. "Because of the sinkhole," he says as if I'm an idiot. "If I fall in, I'll drown."

"Good," I say. "Now let's go collect eggs. We might get some customers this morning."

Simon grabs a basket and runs to the barn. I pull the heavy door to the side for him and we head for the chicken coop, the hens flutter and cluck, but move aside as Simon plunks the eggs into his basket. It's the third time we've done this together and his timidness is gone. He talks sweetly to the hens and thanks them for their eggs, which makes me smile.

When all the eggs have been collected, I close the coop and we make our way through the barn.

"What's that?" Simon points to the steel bar of metal hooks hanging overhead, just noticing it for the first time.

"It's a type of gambrel. It's used for hanging an animal once it's dead so you can skin it."

"Yuck." Simon looks at me. "Why would you want to skin an animal?"

I imagine the image my son has conjured up in his head. He's grown up in the city after all. "It's used for hunting, Simon. After Grandpa shot his game, he'd hang it on this hook to prepare it to eat."

Simon makes a face. "Gross."

"You don't think it's gross when you're scarfing down a hamburger or roasted ham at Thanksgiving." I ruffle his hair and think of Daddy's similar explanation when I was Simon's age. "Are you ready to put the eggs in the cartons?"

He tugs his worried gaze away from the scary contraption and heads out of the barn. I make a mental note to take the gambrel down this weekend while he's away. I have no use for it, haven't hunted since Daddy was alive. Daddy would say I've grown soft, shopping at my fancy grocery stores where everything's done for me. I laugh at the thought. He's right in a lot of ways. There was something about growing our own food and living off the land that was special. I was just too young to appreciate it back then.

I follow behind Simon and close the barn doors, taking in the expansive green lawn in front of the house and Mama's overgrown garden of weeds to my right. Maybe Simon and I will clean it up and plant some vegetables this summer. If Peter had it his way, Simon would be signed up for sports, the Boy Scouts, and chess club, every second of his summer scheduled. But I'm my father's daughter.

Simon loads the eggs into the cardboard cartons behind the little egg stand Daddy built. A cloud of dust billows up the dirt drive and I glance at my watch. Peter isn't supposed to be here for another hour.

"I think we have a customer, Si," I say and my son's face lights up. I lift my hand to shield the sun from my eyes as a black diesel truck rumbles to rest behind my Range Rover.

Something about the way the two men inside the cab stare at the house brings me pause. They aren't here for eggs. I feel it in my bones. "Stay put," I tell Simon and approach the strangers. Both truck doors swing open at the same time. My body hums with a warning. Daddy says the gut has no use for lies, so I plant my feet between my son and the truck, waiting for them to reveal their intentions.

"Can I help you boys?" I use an authoritative tone like I'm generations older than they are, which I'm not.

The driver sidles around the front of the vehicle pushing his hands into his front pockets. His attempt to look harmless, an "awe shucks" sort of swagger in his step. I keep my eyes on the passenger, who leans against the truck and doesn't try to hide his menacing appearance. His long greasy hair falls past his shoulders, a serpent tattoo on his neck disappearing beneath his shirt collar. I assume the inconsistency between the two men is either on purpose or one of them is trying too hard.

"Howdy," the driver says, like Virginians talk this way. "We saw the sign on the road." He points to the eggs.

"You're here for eggs, are you?" I was never good at pretending. Daddy's voice is crystal clear in my head. *Don't show your hand too soon, Charlotte.* "Well, you've come to the right place," I say.

The passenger rocks off the door of the truck and steps closer. I twist my head and see Simon's big grin. His first customers. I'll have to teach him how to read people better. I back up, so that I'm closer to Simon.

"We'll take a dozen," the passenger says, looping his hair behind his ears, and it's then I hear the accent. My eyes flit to the plates on the truck. New Jersey. I'm right.

Simon hands the passenger the carton. "That's seven dollars," he says.

Both men look at one another, then the passenger says, "Shit, are they magic eggs?"

"They're organic and fresher than you'll find anywhere else," I snap.

"You owe me a dollar for the swear word," Simon says to the man.

The driver chuckles, then turns his attention back to the house.

The passenger hands Simon a ten-dollar bill. "Keep the change," he says. "I said a couple of swear words on our way up the driveway."

Simon takes the money and gives the stranger his widest grin, his missing front teeth reflecting his age.

I cross my arms. "You gentlemen passing through?"

"Nope," the driver says. "We're staying in town at a little bed-and-breakfast."

"Martha's Place," I say.

He shrugs. "I don't know who owns it. Haven't checked in yet."

"That's the name of the inn," I say, again with a sarcastic tone. "The owner is a man named Lyle and I'm pretty sure it's just rooms. No kitchen available to cook those eggs."

"The eggs are for my aunt," the long-haired passenger says too quickly. "She only eats farm fresh."

"What's her name? I probably know her."

The driver interrupts. "Just you and your boy live out here?"

"No," I say as Simon chimes in.

"My grandpa died. So, me and Mom are staying here for the summer."

I shoot Simon a look. He stops talking.

"My husband's on his way with more family. Should be here anytime." Even as the words fall from my lips, I know how pathetic I sound.

The driver tips his chin. "Well, you take care. Our aunt's going to love these eggs."

"You didn't mention her name," I say again, but I know why. There is no aunt. They're here for another reason, I just don't know what it is yet.

For a long beat the men stare at me and I at them. The air between us is charged, my heart drumming between my ears.

In my head, I gauge how long it would take me to run to the house for the shotgun. But I can't leave Simon. Daddy's literally rolling over in his grave. *You've grown too trusting, Charlotte.* He's right. I'm off my game. We're too far from the road for anyone passing by to see a struggle and even if I was able to call someone for help, it would take them over fifteen minutes to get here from town.

I square my shoulders. "Well, thanks for stopping by."

The driver glances at the passenger, and there's a brief exchange between them I recognize. Debate. I don't know what they want or why they're here, but every cell in my body screams.

"Simon," I say, keeping my eyes on the men. "Can you go inside please."

Thankfully, for once he doesn't argue. He senses it too. As he starts for the house, a familiar sight catches my eye. My husband's shiny silver Mercedes pulls up the drive. Both men glance at the car then back to me.

"Look forward to tasting your eggs," the driver says and they climb into their truck as my husband's car comes to a halt in front of the house.

I wait, as the men pull away from the property and I can no longer see the taillights. A tickle wriggles low in my belly. It's not the last I'll see of them. Daddy's words purr in the back of my head. *Fool me once.*

Now

Peter swoops Simon off his feet and tosses him over his shoulder. He heads toward me, and I'm struck by his casual appearance. Clad in worn Levi's, a T-shirt, and a Red Sox baseball cap, he looks like he did the day I met him in the UVA bookstore. An easy smile pulls across his lips as he sets down our son and wraps broad arms around me.

"Hi," I say, my nerves settling. I hadn't realized how rattled those two guys made me. "You're early." I'm grateful, but don't tell him why. He'll just worry.

Peter kisses my forehead. "Wanted to beat the traffic. You know what a bitch that is on a Friday," he says.

"You owe me a dollar, Dad," Simon says. "I already made three extra dollars from the guys who bought our eggs."

"You're right, Buddy." Peter's brow furrows. "Go get your stuff."

"Okay." Simon skips toward the house, the screen door slamming after he's inside.

Peter glances around the farm with an air of distaste. He just doesn't get it.

"Charlie." His expression is serious. "I hate the idea of you and Simon out here alone. You're what, twenty miles from town?"

Here we go again. "We're safe," I say. This is mostly the truth.

"Come home with Simon and me for the weekend. I can take next week off and help you clean out your dad's things. We'll get the place ready to sell."

There's an arrogance in his assumption I've decided to sell the farm when I haven't. Besides, this place may be buried so deep in debt, selling won't be an option. I won't know anything until I get to the bank.

"It'll be good for me to go through Daddy's things by myself. While Simon is off having fun, I can take my time." I glance at the white two-story where I was raised. "Who knows what Daddy has squirreled away in that house."

"You shouldn't be doing this alone." Peter shakes his head. "Where the hell is Rose anyway?"

My sister. We haven't really spoken much since the day she left. I didn't even recognize my own niece and nephew at Daddy's funeral. Rose didn't want a thing to do with the farm. She'd flown in the night before the service with her kids, then flown right back out when it was over. She didn't even bother coming by the house for the potluck. Too many painful memories. I can't blame her.

"She's busy with her business and her daughter starts college in a few months," I say, making excuses for her like I always have. "Anyway, Daddy left the farm to me, not Rose. It's my responsibility."

He exhales, "Will you at least take down that sign on the road?" He narrows his eyes. "Give the damn eggs away." His gaze drifts to the end of the driveway. "I saw the guys who just left. Something off about them." His lawyer brain. Always skeptical. "You know what, I think Si and I should stay. I'll call Luke's mom and tell her Simon can't go to the birthday party tomorrow."

"No. Simon's excited for the party. I'll take the sign down."

"Good." He pulls me into his arms. "I don't know what I'd do without you."

I tip my chin and kiss him, the deep romantic kind of kiss that's often forgotten over years of marriage. It surprises Peter too.

"Ew," Simon says and we pull apart, smiling at him. "I'm ready, Dad."

I take in my son; his backpack slung over his spindly shoulders and I miss him already.

"Say goodbye to Mommy," Peter says.

Simon flings his arms around my hips. I bend down. "I love you, Bug. Have a fun weekend."

"Don't do all the chores without me." He grins and climbs into his booster in Peter's backseat.

I kiss Peter one last time. "Drive safe," I say, a lump in the back of my throat. "See you Sunday."

A few minutes later, my husband and son are gone and for the first time in my entire life, I'm alone on the property. Just me, a handful of hens, a very old cow, and only God knows how many buried secrets.

I spend the rest of the morning cleaning out Daddy's closet. He didn't have much. I'll drop it off at the church when I'm in town today. As I gather his boots and place them in a box, I notice the corner of carpeting raised in the back of the closet. The house used to be all hardwood, but Mama said she needed some cushion beneath her feet on those cold mornings and a week later, Daddy had all the bedrooms carpeted. Not with the cheap stuff from our local hardware store but the thick, luxurious kind with the fancy pad underneath.

The landline downstairs rings and I push to my feet, taking the box of boots with me.

"Hello." I answer on the sixth ring, out of breath.

"Ms. Wildwood?" The woman's voice has a little draw like Mama's did.

"This is Charlotte Maxwell, used to be Wildwood," I say.

The woman on the other end of the line chuckles. "Of course. This is Ruth from Chadwick's Mortuary. Your daddy's ashes are ready."

"Thank you, Ruth," I say, picturing the slight woman who's worked at the mortuary since Mama died. "I can swing by this afternoon."

"I'm here until three o'clock."

"See you soon."

Once I've loaded the donations into my car, I lock up the house and head out. As I'm pulling down the long narrow driveway, an image of Daddy on the front porch the day I left for college flashes in my mind's eye. He was happy I'd chosen the University of Virginia. It was close to home and somehow he'd saved enough money to cover all my expenses. I didn't think much about money then. Daddy always provided. Now that I'm an adult, I don't know how he did it.

I stop at the end of our driveway, keeping my promise to Peter and wriggling the post from the dirt. Tossing the *Wildwood Eggs for Sale* sign into the backseat, I can almost hear Daddy mocking me with one of his many metaphors. *If the wolves want in, Charlotte, they're coming whether you want them here or not. And it's your job to protect the henhouse.*

THEN

Two months after the glossy car and slick stranger brought her sister home late, Charlotte and Daddy waved goodbye to Rose as she boarded the midnight Greyhound to California. Daddy pretended Rose was going to visit Mama's sister, but Charlotte wasn't stupid. She had a pregnant teacher at school. She knew there was a baby growing inside of Rose's belly. She also knew, deep down in her bones, Rose was never coming back.

Things changed around the house after Rose left. Daddy's dark moods lifted. He and Charlotte spent their days working the farm, fishing, and at night, catching lightning bugs in Mama's canning jars. It was also the summer Daddy taught Charlotte how to shoot a gun.

One Saturday morning, he woke her early. She'd wiped the sleep from her eyes, dressed quickly, and met Daddy in the kitchen. The sun was barely awake itself when they slid on their tall rubber boots and trudged into the forest.

Charlotte wasn't sure if she was more excited about learning to shoot or that Daddy had invited her into the backwoods. As they moved quietly through the dewy forest, Daddy held up his hand and pointed to a huge dark pool of mud between a circle of towering pines. "You see that, Charlotte?"

She tipped her head up to look at Daddy, eyes squinting from the sunrays bleeding through the branches. "The mud puddle?"

Daddy shook his head. "It's no mud puddle. It's a sinkhole, close to twenty feet deep. It's been here since I was a boy.

"How did it get here?" Charlotte was fascinated.

"Rock separated and caused a cavern to open. Over time, with all the rains and continued moisture, the soil rose to the top. Now it's like a swimming pool of wet sludge. If you fell in and I wasn't here to help you, you'd drown. No one would ever find you." Daddy looked thoughtful. "I never understood why my daddy didn't shore it up all those years back but I've come to respect it as part of nature's gift."

"What if a poor animal stumbles into it?"

Daddy nodded. "Animals know better. Now you do too. That's why I don't ever want to catch you playing out here without me." Daddy's voice was serious. "Not until you're older."

Charlotte nodded. "I promise, Daddy." Maybe it was the way the shadowy light fell across the film of moisture on the sinkhole that took her back to that night, reminding her of those shiny shoes slipping beneath the surface. A shudder whipped up her back. She had so many questions for Daddy but she wasn't ready to ask them.

Now

I park on the corner of Main and First Street in front of the church. An older gentleman sweeping the sidewalk waves a teenage boy my way to unload the car.

"I have an appointment at the credit union," I call to the man. "Can you make sure he closes the car up when he's done?"

The man nods. "Thank you for the donation and I'm awfully sorry to hear about your daddy," he says, then continues sweeping.

There's not a soul in town Daddy didn't know. It's the little things like this I miss about home. I'd forgotten how Mayberry it is around here and how people take care of each other. I stride across the street, past The Rusty Spoon, a diner that's been on Main Street since I was a little girl. Daddy and I ate in that diner many nights after Rose left. Daddy said it was because Rose did all the cooking, but I think he missed her and eating at home was too painful. For both of us.

I stroll into the credit union.

"Good afternoon," a woman in a tailored suit says as she approaches.

"Hi," I say. "I'm Charlotte Maxwell. My father Russell Wildwood passed away a few weeks ago and I'm here to discuss his accounts." I reach into my bag. "I have the power of attorney and a copy of the will. The death certificate is taking longer than expected."

The woman pats my arm. "I was so sorry to hear about your daddy passing. He was a joy around here," she says, motioning me toward a windowed cubicle in the back corner of the bank.

A joy? Aren't you full of surprises, Daddy.

"I'm Phyllis Hawthorne," she says, taking a seat behind a narrow desk. I pull out the chair across from her. "Let me pull up your accounts."

I slide the documents she'll surely need across the desk as she works her computer, then I dig out the safety deposit box key and set it down next to my phone.

Phyllis pushes the paperwork back to me. "Russell added you to all his accounts, dear. Don't you remember signing the paperwork?"

Daddy must have forged my signature. I stifle my amusement. "That's right," I say. "I must have forgotten."

"Ten years will do that to you," Phyllis says. "I just need to see your identification so I do my job," she smiles, apologetically.

"Of course," I say. I slide my ID across the desk. Phyllis glances at it then hands it back to me. She taps a few keystrokes on her computer and turns the screen. I hold my breath, not sure I want to know how deep in debt Daddy really is.

"These are your two account balances, a savings and a checking," she says as I stare at the numbers on the screen. It can't be right. There's over $400,000 in the checking account and the savings sits at nearly $1 million. Where did Daddy get this kind of money?

"Are these the only two accounts?"

"Only ones with us, and knowing your daddy, I'd be shocked if he had an account with another institution." Phyllis laughs. "He told Carl if he ever sold the credit union to one of those big banks, he'd pull out all his money and run."

"Sounds like Daddy. What about the mortgage on the farm?"

Phyllis scrunches her forehead like a flesh-colored accordion and I prepare myself. Hopefully, the money in the combined accounts is more than enough to take care of what we owe.

"Charlotte, your daddy paid off the farm years back. Didn't he tell you?"

"He never mentioned it." But what I want to ask this woman is how. How did my father, a farmer who really hasn't done much farming since I left for college, pay off our property and manage to save almost a million and a half dollars?

Phyllis closes her screen, pushes up from her chair, and motions for me to follow her. I loop my purse over my shoulder, grab my phone and the key from the desk. I pad behind her, still reeling from what I've learned.

Phyllis unlocks the door and steps inside a room with another security door. She closes the one we just came through, locks it back up, and works through bank procedure for entering the safety deposit box area.

A bank of drawers lines the walls of the small room. Phyllis glances at me, obviously waiting for me to give her the number of Daddy's box.

"Box 285," I say.

Phyllis inserts her key and I insert mine below hers.

"Take as much time as you need," she says. "Just replace everything and close the door when you've finished. It'll self-lock."

Then she leaves and I'm alone in the room. I open the tiny door and retrieve a weighty metal container, laying it on the table.

Unlatching the lid, I draw the box open and gasp. Three cylinders of what look like gold coins stare back at me. I've seen these before. Not as many, but when Daddy and I use to take road trips, he'd always let me hold a couple of gold coins. The only other item in the box is an envelope with my name on it. I run my nail beneath the seal and slide out the letter Daddy's left me.

> *Dear Charlotte,*
>
> *If you're reading this, it means I'm off to visit your mother. I know you're wondering about the money and where your Daddy got three cylinders of gold coins. You might want to sit down, Darlin, because this is just a drop in the bucket. Before you go getting all riled up, you need to know, everything's on the up-and-up. Don't you dare go thinking your Daddy's some kind of crook.*
>
> *Truth is, I found it buried on the property that's been in our family for nearly a century. It's Confederate gold from the 1800s. Stolen at the time and buried. And there's more of it. You'll find five ammo cans in my closet beneath the floorboards filled with five cylinders each. This is yours and Rose's inheritance. I know your sister doesn't want anything to do with the farm. She wanted you to have it. Part of me hopes you'll keep it in the family, raise your beautiful boy here, but I understand if you have to let it go. I love you, Girlie. You are a blessing.*

Hot tears well in my eyes, but I keep reading.

> *Let's get down to business. This gold is very old and because it's so old and valuable, you're going to want to cash it in slowly, over time. There's over five million dollars in those ammo cans and you don't want to draw attention, so go out of town, out of state even, and look for shops that don't require identification. That was my biggest mistake. Take three to four coins per shop, say they've been in your family forever. Use a lot of different coin shops to convert it over time and if you have to give your name, use a false one.*
>
> *I've used Al's Coin Shop in New Jersey for years, but old Al died not long ago and now his shady son and nephew run the place. DO NOT use them. And for God's sake, Charlotte, don't tell that husband of yours. I like him, don't get me wrong, but he's too damn righteous. Lawyers are all the same. He'll try to convince you that gold doesn't belong to you. Anyway, I know you'll do what I would do. Just be careful.*
>
> *Love, Daddy* ☺

My hands are trembling when I return the box to the drawer. After I've secured the lock, I slip Daddy's note into my purse and wave to Phyllis on my way out of the bank. Pushing into the sunshine, I think of the secrets Daddy's kept from me.

I'm halfway down the street when a familiar voice sparks the vellus hair at the base of my neck. Outside the diner, the two men from New Jersey are having lunch. And I know. It's too coincidental for them not to be who I think they are.

"If it isn't the egg lady," the guy who was driving the truck says.

I glare back at them, their cocky demeanors contrasting our small town. "And how'd your aunt like the eggs?" My tone borders on antagonistic although I'm well aware I'm anything but dangerous looking.

The long-haired guy tilts his head to the side as he swallows the bite in his mouth. "She wants another dozen."

"What's her name again?" Daddy always said, the body language of someone up to no good will always give them away.

Sure enough. Long Hair chokes into his fist and the other guy shifts uneasy in his seat and says, "Sorry to hear about your father passing away." He thrusts his hand forward. "I'm Robert, by the way."

I glance at his hand. "Did you know my father?"

He lowers his hand. "Nope. Your boy mentioned it this morning," he says. "Just being polite."

"Are you?" I narrow my eyes.

"You're a frosty one," his partner says. "You treat all your customers like this?"

I raise my chin. "Only the ones I don't trust."

Robert grins. "Ignore my cousin. He means well." With a sharp glance and a scolding tone, he says, "Don't you, Alex?"

Tension hangs between them for a beat. Alex wipes his greasy smile with a napkin. "Didn't mean to offend."

"You boys take care," I say and turn to go.

"We'll see you in the morning," Robert says.

"Excuse me?"

"Another dozen eggs. For our aunt."

I shrug. "We're sold out."

Robert tilts his head. "Won't those chickens lay more eggs tonight?"

Stupid city slicker. "Not enough," I say. "A lot of family at the house."

Alex laughs. "Lady, we know it's just you and your boy out there. All alone. Cute kid by the way. Kind of young to leave by himself while you run errands, don't you think?"

The subtext is deafening, his threat in everything he doesn't say. Something instinctual snaps inside of me. "Don't talk about my son," I snarl.

Robert studies me, rubbing his finger across his bottom lip. "No, Mama Bear would never leave her cub on his own. Kid must be gone for the weekend with his dad." He twists in the metal chair to face me. "I've heard a lot of scary stories about the backwoods behind your farm," Robert says. "Aren't you afraid, pretty woman like you all by herself?"

Taking a deep breath, my heart thundering behind my rib cage, I lean in close. "I was raised in those backwoods," I say, doing my best to sound brave. "Maybe I'm the scary thing you've heard about."

There's a pause before they both break into a fit of laughter at my expense. I turn on my shaky legs and head for my car. Daddy's voice is so loud it's like he's right beside me. *No one threatens mine.*

I climb into the car, toss my purse on the passenger seat, and start the engine. As I back into the street, I keep my eyes on the men in the rearview mirror. They're watching me. My first thought is to call Peter, ask him to come back to the farm. But I'd never hear the end of it.

Instead, I dial up Sheriff Atwater, and as the call rings through my Bluetooth, I take a left off Main Street and onto County Road 28.

"Charlotte Wildwood," he answers with a smile in his voice, calling me by my maiden name. "What do I owe the pleasure?"

"Hi Sam," I say to the man I've known my entire life. "I just finished taking care of a few things in town and I'm headed back to the farm—"

"You should have stopped by the house," he interrupts.

"I will next time," I promise. "This is more of a business call."

"What's going on?"

"There's two men outside The Rusty Spoon. They bought a dozen eggs from me earlier and kind of gave me the creeps just now. They're up to something, Sam."

"What did they do to make you feel uneasy?"

"They know I'm alone at the farm. They said as much," I tell him.

"I'm on it, Dolly," Sam says, calling me by the nickname he's used since I was five. "You . . ."

Damn service always gets tricky at this point. "Sam, I'm going to lose you. Thanks for following up."

"You must be on your way home," he says, crackly but audible. "Don't worry. Talk soon."

I end the call and release a nervous breath. If anyone's on it, it's Sam. He's been the sheriff of Monroe County forever, not to mention the best friend Daddy and I could ever ask for all those years when it was just the two of us.

My body settles into the seat leather as I realize I forgot to swing by the mortuary for Daddy's ashes. Glancing at the clock, there's no way I'd make it back in time. Besides, I have bigger things on my mind. Daddy has nearly a million and a half dollars in the bank, plus the gold in the safety deposit box and another five million under the closet floorboards. I can hardly wrap my mind around the idea of it.

But now it all makes sense. Those road trips we took when I was a girl. The improvements to the farm, the new equipment, the house upgrades. Daddy always telling me that Rose was fine, he was taking care of her financially. And although he was always busy, working the farm, I never really understood how we made money. But I was young and naïve. I guess as I got older, I assumed Daddy had the place mortgaged to the hilt. He'd paid for my wedding, which was no small affair. And all this time, he'd patiently used only what we needed, never lived extravagantly.

I turn onto our gravel driveway and hop out of the car. Pulling the heavy metal gate across the entrance, I connect it to the steel post then loop the bulky chain through to secure the lock. The last time we locked the gate was the night Rose's coach drove her home. My childhood brain couldn't understand then how he'd hurt my sister. But after Coach Bale disappeared, six additional girls came forward. Some younger than Rose. As a mother, I believe Daddy did what he thought was in his child's best interest.

I consider Simon. There's nothing I wouldn't do to protect him.

Now

I'm lightheaded when I reach the house. I should eat but I climb the stairs instead, two at a time. I flip on the light and plunk down on my knees to the raised corner of carpet at the back of Daddy's closet. Then I tug until the entire floorboards beneath are exposed. Running my hand over the rough grainy wood, I feel for a loose board or something out of place until my fingernail catches in a groove.

I rush downstairs and retrieve a knife then hurry back where I work the tip into the groove until the little panel pops out. Retrieving my phone from my back pocket, I turn on the flashlight and shine the beam into the hole where five metal ammo boxes sit side by side. It takes both hands to pull just one box up from its hiding place. My fingers tremble as I open the rectangular metal canister. Like Daddy promised, five cylinders of shiny gold coins line the interior. Five million dollars. Holy shit!

The landline rings downstairs and I jump. I lower the ammo can back beneath the floorboard, push the panel into position and smooth the carpet back into the corner. I make it to the kitchen just in time.

"Hello," I say, breathless.

"Charlotte, it's Sam. You okay?"

Does he know about Daddy's gold? "Yeah, I'm fine," I say, keeping it simple.

"Wanted to let you know, those boys from Jersey were long gone when I showed up."

Did I mention their New Jersey plates? I don't think I did.

Sam's tone goes serious. "You call if you get spooked out there. I'll come with guns blazing."

"Thanks Sam," I sigh, thinking I must have mentioned them being from out of town. Low blood sugar makes me scatter-brained. "I closed the gate and the doors are locked. I'll be fine."

"Okay, Dolly. Let's have dinner while you're here."

"Sounds good," I say.

"Bye now."

I pull Daddy's letter from my purse and reread it, paying special attention to the part about Al's Coin Shop. Daddy said he'd made a mistake giving his real information out. This must be how they found the farm and how they know Daddy's gone.

I toss one of Simon's frozen macaroni and cheese dinners into the microwave. Talk to me, Daddy. What do I do? Between the sizzle and popping sound of my meal, I hear Daddy's velvety voice in my head. *People think it's perfectly fine to take what doesn't belong*

to them, Charlotte. Look what happened to your sister. Do what you
have to do to protect what's yours.

The microwave beeps but my eyes are fixed on Daddy's gun case. I cross the room and tip up on my toes, reaching for the small key nestled into the molding of the cabinet. The glass door swings open. There are two rifles, a shotgun, and an antique revolver I fired once as a little girl. I remove all the weapons from the case and the boxes of bullets Daddy stores in the locked drawer at the bottom. After I've loaded each gun, I strategically hide them near points of entry. Then I pull the steamy container from the microwave and devour the creamy pasta.

As I eat, I think about Daddy and the hundreds of dinners we had right here at this table. His essence is everywhere and his wise words reverberate through the rooms like it was yesterday. *Do you want to be the predator or the prey, Charlotte?*

I know with all certainty those men are coming back here tonight. For Daddy's treasure. And they will not hesitate to hurt me or even kill me.

I will not be the prey.

THEN

When Charlotte was in high school and most of her friends were at cheerleading practice, band, or doing an afterschool sport, she was at home. Daddy's orders. He would never allow someone to take advantage of Charlotte the way they had Rose. It got to the point where she stopped fighting and gave in. Besides, Charlotte didn't hate the farm like her sister did. She loved everything about it, especially exploring the forest. By fifteen, Charlotte had spent so much time in the backwoods, she could weave her way through the hundred acres with her eyes closed and not even stumble.

She fished and foraged, read books and wrote in her journal. Not once did she feel afraid out there all alone. In fact, it's where she felt the safest. Sometimes, because her childhood memories nagged at her, she'd sit near the sinkhole and wait. Not quite sure what she was waiting for. Maybe a hand to break free of the sludge. Reaching for someone to take it. To pull them out. She knew what her answer would be. Because by then, Charlotte was old enough to understand there were good and bad people in the world. And if Daddy put someone in their sinkhole, they were probably not worth saving. Not to Charlotte anyway.

Now

I drag Daddy's heavy chest of drawers into the closet. It fits perfectly, almost like it belongs there. Then I dress for the evening. Black leggings and a long sleeve dark shirt despite the summer heat. Sure, I could pack my things, including the gold, and tuck tail for DC. But it would only buy me time. In the end, I'd end up leading those boys straight to Peter and Simon.

I won't put my family in danger. I have to handle the problem here. Tonight. Or die trying.

Before heading up to bed, I stack five soup cans in front of every door. Daddy called this a hillbilly's alarm. If I fall asleep and the house is breached, I'll at least have a warning. I release the weighted breath lodged in my breastbone and shake my head. All that money for all those years, sealed just beneath the floorboards.

It's after midnight when I startle. My eyes fly open. I swing my feet off the bed and creep to the edge of the window. Moonlight bleeds through a slice of inky black sky. Bright enough to spy the two shadows skulking up the driveway. If I called the police or Sam, I could have them arrested tonight for trespassing. But they'd be released by morning and I'd always be looking over my shoulder. I don't do loose ends.

Slipping my feet into the boots I've left by the bedroom door, I loop the rifle over my shoulder and ease down the stairs. Daddy told me once that men like the ones lurking outside my home underestimate women, mostly because we're not as strong as they are. But Daddy reminded me in the same breath that brute and brawn pale in comparison to intelligence.

I slink through the living room and into the kitchen. I'm sure Robert and Alex will split up. Try to ambush me from both sides of the house. But my vantage is the backwoods. Easing the stack of cans away from the back door, I peek onto the porch, then open the door as a crash of toppling cans sounds from the front room. At least I know where one of them is at.

The crunch of footsteps snags my attention to my left. My heart thunders behind my rib cage. Alex snakes around the side of the house and our eyes lock for half a breath. Daddy's voice booms. *Run, Charlotte!* I turn on my heels and sprint for the tree line, irrationally hoping my predator follows.

Memory is a clever thing and despite the years since I've raced through these woods, my steps are light and knowing. Alex clambers after me, cursing with every tree root he stumbles on. He's faster than I thought he'd be, closing our gap too soon.

"You can't outrun the devil, lady," he calls.

I keep moving. One misstep, a second off, and my plan will fail. Then I reach my mark and spin around, lifting the rifle to my shoulder. Adrenaline courses through me like a rushing river. Alex stops dead in his tracks, a gun pointed in my direction.

"Drop the rifle, Dolly," he says with a twisted grin.

"What did you call me?" The sting is sharp and sudden. I can't breathe. Is Sam with them? I level the rifle so it's trained on Alex's forehead.

"Come on now," he says. "We don't want you hurting yourself with that big gun."

I'd like to shoot the arrogant expression right off his face, but I hold steady, digesting what I've learned. Sam's betrayal is like another death I have to hold. Alex takes a slow step forward, inches from the slick surface between us. I hold his gaze.

"I know why you're here," I say. "You're wasting your time though. He spent it all."

Alex shakes his head. "I know your father. He's a frugal son of bitch, piecemealing those coins one by one. My best guess, it's buried out here in these backwoods and you know exactly where it is."

My legs tremble. "You're right," I say. "And if you shoot me, you'll never find it." I force a calm into my voice. Then I say a silent prayer this greedy asshole does what I expect him to. "But you'll have to catch me first." I whip around to run when I hear it. The sound reminds me of meat slapping against a chopping board.

"You bitch!"

I turn around to find Alex sprawled belly down on the mucky surface of our reliable sinkhole. He claws for purchase, which will only move him deeper into the sludge. Daddy says it's human nature to kick and paddle to stay afloat, but this is nothing like water. Soon he'll tire and be swallowed up, then drift below the surface to join the other evil dwelling there.

"Help me," he pleads.

I shake my head. The gun he was holding is out of reach and sinking too. Watching him struggle, I'm drawn back to the night I watched Rose's monster descend to Hell and I wonder if somehow it prepared me for this very moment.

"Please," he says, more desperate now. The venom in his tone all dried up.

I turn away, before my conscience can stop me. When I step into the clearing and out of the woods, Alex's last scream pierces the night. Robert must hear it too. He bursts from the front porch.

"Alex?" He calls out. I wedge inside the parted barn doors as Robert takes in the quiet farm.

I lift the rifle, line up the sight, and think of Daddy. *Don't aim at something you aren't prepared to shoot, Charlotte.* Robert's a big man. From this distance, I'll need to be accurate. But I've never hurt another person. Daddy whispers in my ear. The same words he used the first time he took me hunting. *There are only two reasons to take a life, to feed yourself or to save yourself.* I hesitate then pull the trigger. Robert shifts as the bullet strikes the metal bracket on the porch post. He's a blur as I move away from the door and scramble up a ladder to the loft. I crawl behind the stack of hay Daddy keeps stored up here despite the fact the horses died years ago. My breaths follow in a ragged rush.

The barn door slides open and I press my body against a hay bale, close my mouth to still my panting. I've always been good at hiding. I'm weightless as I reposition and brace my rifle on top of the straw. Lights illuminate from outside, no idea where they're coming from. Robert's shadowed outline looms up the barn wall.

"Alex?" He clicks the scope light on his gun and shines the beam around the barn. "Are you hurt?"

My trembling finger loops around the trigger as his light strikes my face. I freeze and he's up the ladder before I can fire. He rushes me, knocking the gun from my sweaty grip. It falls to the concrete below with a loud clank. Robert mounts my hips, pushing me onto my back.

I punch at his face, but he's quick. "You'll never find the gold if you kill me," I say.

"I'm not going to kill you." His grin is sinister. "I'm going to have a little fun first. Then you're going to show me where Daddy hides his fortune."

I buck and twist, my fists connecting with his chin, then his ear.

"Stop hitting me," he snarls, smacking me hard in the face.

He sets the gun on the hay bale. I glance at the open ledge not two feet from us. Daddy always meant to build a rail. Robert fumbles to unbutton his pants with one hand, the other pressing my wrists over my head. Sweat drips from his forehead. I go limp beneath the weight of him. He smiles at my submission. Then he unzips his jeans.

My eyes flit to the hay door Daddy installed during one of the upgrades, again noticing the lights outside of the barn. I manage to free one of my hands and work my fingers around the metal loop for leverage. Robert's too interested in finding the waistband of my leggings to notice. I wait for his weight to shift. As he wriggles his pants lower, I buck my hips and knock him off balance. I twist from beneath his legs and as he attempts to right himself, I don't hesitate. I push.

The look on his face as he falls over the ledge sears into my brain. I brace for impact, expecting the thunderous mass of him to strike the unforgiving surface below. Instead, I hear bones crack. Flesh split. The familiar sound of Daddy mounting his kill on the gambrel. I wiggle my leggings up and retrieve his gun, then carefully move down the ladder of the loft. Robert moans in pain, his eyes finding mine. But he doesn't beg for my help like Alex did. Not yet anyway. He's probably in shock.

Moving to the wall, I turn on the power and lower the skewered man to the floor. When he's on his knees, I get closer. He fell at an angle, so that one of the hooks went through his shoulder blade and the other, his ribcage. Blood pools around him.

There's movement in my peripheral. I whip around, pointing the gun at the figure. It takes a beat before it registers. Sam. Thank God. I almost didn't recognize him out of uniform. I can count on one hand how many times I've seen him dressed in shorts and athletic shoes. Then, I'm reminded. He betrayed us.

"Good work, Dolly," he says, continuing his game. "Put down the gun. You're safe now."

The lights outside are from Sam's cruiser. Robert was going to rape me with Sam right outside. "Am I safe, Sam?" The question hangs between us like a sticky spider's web and through it, I see him differently. This man I've trusted and loved for as long as I can remember, Daddy's best friend. Sam was going to let them hurt me. Then what?

Sam tries again. "Charlotte, I'm here to help you."

"Get these fucking hooks out of me, Atwater," Robert growls, and I'm certain.

"We were like family, Sam?"

Sam shrugs and at least has the decency to look ashamed. "It's a lot of money, Dolly, and your daddy hoarded it like a miser. How much do you think a sheriff makes around here, anyway?"

"He loved you like a brother, Sam and I . . ." Daddy's voice fills my ears. *Charlotte, you bring your heart to a fight and it's sure to get broken.*

I back up toward Robert, his gun still held in my hand and poised on Sam's chest. Lining up behind the big man, I crouch down, careful to stay clear from the blood. Sam watches with interest until he understands.

"You're not a killer, Dolly. I know you won't shoot me."

He's right about one thing. I'm not a killer. There's only one choice. I pull the trigger.

Now

Sam recoils. "Shit. You shot me, Charlotte."

But I hit his shoulder, not enough to take him down. He lunges for me as I pull the trigger again, the bullet striking the wood post. The gun slips from my hand and I run. Sam runs after me. Out of the barn and into the backwoods.

Sam might be one of the few people who know these woods as well as I do. He knows about the sinkhole. My only hope is to outrun him and hide. Hope his bleeding shoulder slows him down. I sprint over roots and felled trees, but Sam, despite his age, is close.

"Charlotte," he calls. "There's enough money for both of us."

I dare a glance back at him and my boot gets caught in a vine. Falling face first, into the leaves and forest debris, I scramble to get up. Sam looms only feet from me.

Shaking my head, I think of Simon. "Okay, Sam," I say. "You win. We'll split the gold and never talk about this again."

With the precision of a man who's been enforcing the law forever, he whips out his gun and flashlight. *I'm sorry, Daddy, I tried.*

Sam cocks his head to the side, studying me. "On second thought, I know you too well. You'll go tattle to that attorney husband of yours and ruin everything." Sam's face pinches. "I think this has to be goodbye, Dolly."

My heart sinks at the thought of leaving Peter and Simon. I take a deep breath in as movement next to Sam's foot catches my attention. Sam rolls his wounded shoulder as I take a deliberate step to the left and back. Move Sam, just a little.

"Stay still. This is hard enough," Sam orders, but I shift again and this time, Sam repositions his stance. The lurking copperhead, hidden in the dry leaves, strikes like lightning. Sam yells. I bolt from where I'm standing and run until I've reached the barn. The bite won't kill Sam, but it should slow him down and buy me enough time to call the police, figure out my next move. *Think, Charlotte.*

I find Robert passed out. Most likely from the pain. I bend down and wipe Robert's gun clean of my fingerprints, then use my shirt sleeve to position the gun in his right hand. I fire once, then scoop up my rifle from the floor, climb the ladder and crouch behind the hay bales. Waiting for Sam.

Minutes later, he returns dragging his right leg. As Sam steps inside, I line the sight onto his chest. The rifle shakes in my hand. I have the perfect shot. Daddy's voice is sharp. *He's not the man we thought he was, Charlotte.*

Bang! I startle. Sam stumbles and folds to the concrete.

My finger is still soft on the trigger. It wasn't me. I scramble to the edge of the loft and look down. Robert's trembling hand drops the gun at his side.

Now

The timer sounds and I lift the roast from the oven. Peter's favorite. Herbs and garlic fill the kitchen as the front door slams.

"Mommy," Simon calls. "We're home." Tiny feet scamper up the stairs.

Seconds later, Peter rushes into the kitchen and scoops me into an embrace. "Oh my God, Charlie. Are you okay?"

I squeeze him tight. "I'm fine," I say. "Sad, of course, about Sam."

"Random, right?" Peter pulls back. "So, tell me again what they think happened."

I shake my head and turn toward the stove, so I don't have to look at my husband when I lie to him. "I mentioned to Sam those boys who bought eggs from me were in town and acting shady. He must have followed up and I guess there was a car chase. I woke to gun shots. Obviously, there was a struggle, not sure what happened, but by the time the police arrived, it was over." I shrug as I place the roast on a platter.

"And you said one of them fell into the sinkhole?"

I nod. "Sam's final words as sheriff. They managed to pull the body out pretty easily since he hadn't been there long."

Any longer and they may have had to troll deeper, exposing all of Daddy's secrets.

Simon flies into the kitchen. "Hi Mommy," he says. "You didn't do anything fun without me, right?"

I wrap my arms around my boy and bury my face in his soft hair. "Nope. You didn't miss a thing."

As I sit at the table with my family, my thoughts drift to Daddy. I couldn't have survived this without him. My partner in crime. And in a few weeks after everything has settled, I'll tell Peter about the gold and Daddy's wishes.

"We should probably shore up that sinkhole, Charlie. And for God's sake, don't let Simon ever play out there. It's too dangerous," he says, stuffing a potato into his mouth.

I'm my father's daughter. I repeat the words I've heard a million times. "The backwoods are only dangerous if you don't respect them. Just like the ocean," I say. "Those backwoods built me, Peter. Shaped the woman I am today. You have no idea what I'm capable of."

He takes me in, suppressing amusement as I lift my knife and slide it through a tender chunk of meat. Hopefully, he'll never have to find out.

My inspiration for this story stemmed from countless visits to my in-law's home in Faber, Virginia. It was a sprawling, sixteen-acre parcel nestled into the side of a rock outcropping and surrounded by creek beds and backwoods. It was beautiful and mysterious, and I often suspected it held incredible secrets.

An idea sparked when my husband, a gold coin enthusiast, shared a story about missing Confederate gold from the Civil War. According to history, Jefferson Davis left Richmond, Virginia, in April 1865 with millions of dollars in gold, silver, and bullion. He held only a few dollars when he was captured a month later in Georgia. Where did it all go? Historians, treasure seekers, and the FBI believe millions of dollars remain buried and unaccounted for.

Coupled with this intriguing gold legend and my in-laws' enigmatic property, "The Backwoods" sprang to life. Although I took many fictional liberties, from the town to the county, I hope I've captured this special place's essence, leaving the reader with a curiosity and heightened respect for the Virginia backwoods.

At the age of thirteen, when his best friend was interrogated by the police for over eight hours and confessed to a crime he didn't commit, **Victor Methos** *knew he would one day become a lawyer.*

After graduating from law school at the University of Utah, Methos sharpened his teeth as a prosecutor before founding what would become one of the most successful criminal defense firms in Utah.

In ten years Methos conducted more than one hundred trials. One particular case stuck with him, and it eventually became the basis for his first major bestseller, The Neon Lawyer. *Since that time, Methos has focused his work on legal thrillers and mysteries, earning a Harper Lee Prize for* The Hallows *and an Edgar nomination for Best Novel for his title* A Gambler's Jury. *He currently resides in Southern Utah.*

KILL NIGHT

Victor Methos

1

He looked like a scarecrow drenched in rain.

The man was cast in shadow from the headlights of Ryan Hooper's Jeep. Rain drizzled through thin gaps in the windows where the roof didn't attach properly. Ryan felt the droplets hit his face as he watched the man move into the middle of the road and wave both arms.

He slowed the Jeep. Off to the side was a white Toyota with its emergency lights blinking into darkness. Beyond, rain pummeled the barren sands of the Utah desert.

The man wasn't wearing a jacket. He ran to the driver's side.

He was older than Ryan, maybe in his midforties, with a thin face that looked like a skull. He wiped at his brow with the back of his arm.

"Ran outta gas," the man said. "Mind giving me a lift?"

Ryan checked the clock on his dash. "I gotta be in Vegas soon. My wife's due date is tomorrow and she'll lose it if I'm not there."

The man tried to block the rain from his eyes by holding his hand up. "My motel's on the way. Up the road about thirty miles. My wife's waiting for me there."

Ryan hesitated. The man flinched as rain pelted his eyes.

"I just need a ride, friend."

Thunder crackled in the inky-black sky above them.

"Okay, hop in."

The man ran to the trunk of his car, took out a small duffel bag, and ran back. He opened the door, tossed the bag into the back seat, and climbed in. Ryan began to drive. He glanced at the man and saw water droplets dribbling down his nose. The man slid fingers through his wet hair and sighed with relief.

"I'm Ryan."

"Jim."

The darkness outside was accentuated by the looming canyons beyond. The road was two lanes of blacktop with white lines; besides that, Ryan couldn't see much, just amber and red taillights in the rearview on the rare occasion a car raced past him on the opposite side of the road.

He'd never taken this road before, and the drive was long, but the interview he'd had yesterday at a hospital in Provo, Utah, was worth the trip. The job would be fewer hours than he worked now. Nurses could be worked to the bone in big cities like Las Vegas, but small towns were more laid-back. With a son on the way, he wanted as much free time as possible to spend with his boy. His own father had left when he was ten, and he swore he would do better.

"Your Jeep's leaking," Jim said.

"Yeah, I screwed up putting on the roof once, and it's never been the same."

He glanced at Jim again. It was too dark to see many features, but he was unusually thin with closely cropped hair.

"No coat?" Ryan asked.

Silence.

Without a response, Ryan felt the awkwardness of two strangers forced together with nothing to talk about. Awkward situations made him anxious, and when he was anxious, he talked too much.

"Not the best place to run outta gas, huh? Literally the middle of nowhere."

No response.

The vast, empty landscape and a silent passenger made him feel claustrophobic. He wished it weren't raining so he could open a window.

Jim stared forward as the sound of rain intensified from a gust of wind. Then the sound subsided to droplets hitting the roof and the slush of tires through puddles.

"Where you coming from?" Ryan asked.

"Nowhere."

"Oh," he said with a nod of his head. Fear tickled his belly. Suddenly, all he wanted was to get this man out of his car. "Sorry, didn't mean to pry."

To his relief, a sign flew past them that said:

GAS AND FOOD
NEXT EXIT

Jim was staring straight ahead, and if he had seen the sign, he didn't react.

"How 'bout some music?" Ryan said. He picked up his phone, and Jim's hand went around his wrist. The fingers felt bony.

"I like the sound of the rain," Jim said.

"Okay, not a music fan. That's fine." Ryan cleared his throat and pulled his hand away, relieved when he felt Jim let go.

Ryan glanced at the road and then back to Jim's face. He could see his eyes in the headlights of a passing car. They were black and steely. After a few moments of silence, Ryan realized Jim wouldn't talk unless he spoke first. Talking, at least, made the awkwardness slightly more bearable.

"Could you not get reception?" Ryan said.

"Reception?"

"Yeah. On your phone. Is that why you asked for a ride instead of calling someone?"

"I don't have a phone."

"You don't have a phone?"

He shook his head slowly, his eyes on the road. "I don't have anyone to call."

"I thought you said you had a wife?"

Jim looked at him, and a grin slowly came to his face. "Except her."

The road narrowed to one lane on each side, and Ryan felt the desert closing in on him.

"That wasn't your car, was it?" Ryan said without taking his eyes off the road.

"No," he said flatly, "but I don't think the owner's gonna miss it."

"Why won't they miss it?"

"Because I cut her hands off and buried her in the desert while she was alive . . . and I'm gonna do the same thing to you."

2

Nick Collins sat at a table in the district court's attorney/client conference room in downtown Las Vegas. Since graduating from law school a few years ago, he had been coming here one morning a week to donate his time to victims of domestic violence who couldn't afford attorneys.

The young woman across the table had a black eye that spread down her cheek. Her hair was pulled back, and her nails had been chewed down.

"I'll file it right now," he said. "I just need your signature here." He slid a document and a pen toward her, and she signed. "And here," he said, flipping a page over. When that was signed, he said, "There's a seventy-five-dollar filing fee."

"Oh," she said, averting her eyes. "I, um, I don't have any money. I didn't take anything when I left. Just some clothes."

Nick could feel her embarrassment.

"You know what, don't worry about the fee. We'll get it taken care of."

"How?"

"I can pull some strings."

She gave a shy grin. "Thank you."

"It's okay. You'll get some documents at the shelter with the hearing date. Make sure you don't miss it."

"I won't."

The woman just looked at the floor as she left. Nick stretched his neck from side to side and then gathered his things. He took his suit coat off the back of the chair and went out into the hallway. The clerk's desk was on the way out.

"What can I do for you?" the clerk said.

"Got a divorce petition to file."

"All righty."

She stamped the file and punched some buttons on the computer. "Just need your Bar ID and the seventy-five-dollar filing fee."

He took out his wallet. His credit card was maxed, but he had a hundred bucks he'd been saving for a new pair of running shoes. He hesitated a second but handed her the hundred.

She gave him a sideways glance. "You shouldn't feel like you need to pay their filing fees, you know. Everybody's got a sob story to sell."

"I don't think her eye was just a story she was selling."

Nick got his receipt and stopped at the vending machine on the way out of the courthouse.

He waited at the rail station near the court for the train. Though he had an old Kia, he hated driving and avoided it as much as possible. Instead, he preferred to read old science fiction novels on the train.

The law office of Anthony J. Angelo was behind a Burger King in a gray brick building off the Strip. A billboard in the Burger King parking lot had a picture of him with the words, INJURED? WANT CASH FAST? CALL FAST CASH TONY across it in bold lettering. The nickname arose after he ran a TV commercial proclaiming himself able to get cash faster from insurance companies than any other attorney in the state. A claim no one had bothered to verify.

It was the first legal job out of law school Nick could get, mostly because the pay was so low no one else wanted it, but he liked the slow pace of suing insurance companies, and as a small-time personal injury lawyer, he could come and go as he pleased. Freedom, he'd decided, was more important to him than money.

Another attorney, Stephanie Brown, someone Nick had gone to high school with, worked in the first office near the entrance, and Nick saw her behind her glass desk. Though they had gone to different law schools, they had graduated the same year, and he felt she, unlike him, could get a job at any firm or clerk for any judge she wanted, but she chose to work here with Tony. Nick had asked her about it once, and all she said was, "The grass is always greener."

Today, she wore a thin green cropped sweatshirt, revealing the navel piercing on her flat, milk-white stomach, with black pants and white sneakers. Her hair was pulled back—except for a few strands that fell over her green eyes.

He hoped his voice wouldn't crack like a teenager's when he said, "Hey, Steph."

She gave him a grin and said, "Hey, you. How was your pro bono?"

"One divorce petition and two stalking injunctions."

"That's a lotta work for free."

He shrugged. "What can you do?"

"Not take them."

A voice down the hall said, "Nick, is that you? Come 'ere, I want you to meet somebody."

"Duty calls," Nick said.

"Good luck."

He went down the hall to Tony's office. Sports memorabilia hung on the walls, along with his score on the law school entrance exam, the LSAT, which proclaimed he got a perfect score. Nick was almost certain the document was altered.

Seated across from Tony was an enormous man who overflowed from the chair. He was tall and wide, and his shirt pulled up tight over his prodigious belly. Tony sat behind his oak desk with his cowboy boots up, the rhinestones shimmering.

"Nick, this is Mr. Hank Crawford. He's a new client you're going to be working with."

Nick held out his hand, and they shook. "Nice to meet you."

Tony said, "You know that all-you-can-eat place on State Street? The Bottomless Plate? Well, Mr. Crawford was put through a traumatizing experience there. Halfway into his meal, they escorted him out."

"For what?"

"Saying he ate too much. Humiliated him in front of the entire restaurant."

"Oh."

"And I'm sure it's happened to a lot of people. So I want you to put out an ad in the papers and radio. Tell them the Law Office of Anthony J. Angelo is looking for claimants for a class-action suit against those harmed by the unfair practices of the Bottomless Plate and its owners and subsidiaries." He looked at Crawford. "Hank, it takes courage to be the first one to step forward. You're an American hero for doing this."

Crawford held his head a little higher with a slight nod.

"We'll stay in touch," Tony said, holding out his hand. They shook and Crawford left with a nod toward Nick.

When Crawford was out of earshot, Nick said, "Um, I'm pretty sure they can do that, Tony."

"Yeah, maybe. Who cares?"

"That's a frivolous lawsuit. I can't file that."

Tony wiped a tiny speck of dirt off his boot. "That restaurant pays for insurance to cover things like this. If we don't sue, that money stays with the insurance company as profit so their executives can buy another beach house for their mistresses. So you ask yourself, where's that money better spent? With working folks like us busting our asses or the bloodsuckers screwing the little man in their Bentleys and private jets?"

"Well, I guess if you put it that way . . . maybe a suit for fraudulent advertising?"

"There's that brain I hired. But I want you to hold off for a bit. I got something else for you." He took a thumb drive off the desk and tossed it to him. Nick missed and dropped it.

"You didn't play sports, did you?" Tony said.

"No. I was in chess club."

"I can tell. Anyway, the case is in Bailey, Utah. I filed a motion to pro hac you in so you can appear there. Trial starts in two weeks."

"Trial for what?"

"Murder."

"What!" he said, almost laughing. "You're kidding, right?"

"I don't kid about things like this, son. The defendant is Ryan Hooper. You know who that is?"

"No."

"He's my banshee of an ex-wife's little brother. But family's family. She said the public defender down there is two hundred years old and kept falling asleep at the hearings. She's scared Ryan's gonna be locked up for life. He claims he didn't do it, but the victim's hands were found in a duffel bag in his Jeep, along with traces of cyanide in there. He isn't a bad kid. I always liked him. Go down and see what you can do for him."

"I'm not a criminal lawyer, Tony."

"It's all the same. Trying to get disability from the government, suing an insurance company, murder . . . it's all elements, and you gotta point out the weakest one to the jury. You're smart. You'll be fine."

"I don't think I can do it, man."

Tony inhaled and watched him. "Well, I was gonna send Stephanie down, too. She's had some criminal experience at the public defender's office. Maybe I can just have her handle it."

"Oh, she's going?" Nick asked as casually as possible.

Tony grinned. "Yeah, she's going."

"Then why do you need two of us?"

He switched his feet around. "Lemme ask you something. Little quiz. You got a bat and a baseball that cost one dollar, ten cents total, and the bat costs one dollar more than the ball. How much does the ball cost?"

Nick thought for a moment.

"Five cents."

"Why?"

"Because one dollar *more* means the bat costs $1.05, and the ball has to cost five cents."

"Right. But do you know almost everyone gets that wrong? Know why?"

"No."

"Because we're not as smart as we think we are. We're not meant for cities and complex laws and smartphones. We're meant to live out on the plains hunting mammoths. So the brain gets easily confused, and we rely on gut instinct without knowing it. Our gut instinct tells us the answer is ten cents. Just like our gut instinct tells us two lawyers are better than one. The jurors think this guy must *really* be innocent if he's got two lawyers sitting there. So, I'd never order you what to do like those rich bloodsuckers at the big firms downtown, but I would really, *really* appreciate it if you took this case with Stephanie."

Nick stared at the thumb drive in his hand and considered his options. He could turn it down, and what he had waiting for him was preparing a lawsuit against a buffet, or he could spend a week with Stephanie . . .

"Yeah," he said, hesitation still in his voice. "I guess I can go."

3

Two weeks later, they took Stephanie's Honda down because Nick wasn't sure his car could make the five-hundred-mile drive. The driver's side window was down, and the wind whipped Stephanie's hair as she hummed along to a song.

"So why couldn't we continue this to prepare more?" Nick said.

"The public defender continued it like eight times. Tony filed a motion to continue and the judge denied it, saying the case has been pending too long."

"Seems unfair to make us go forward without adequate time to prepare."

"Life's not fair. So why should the law be?"

He looked at her, and she laughed at his expression.

"We'll be fine. You need to relax and have more fun with this job, Nick. We're not suits in an assembly line. We're out on the road fighting the system like revolutionaries or something. Granted, really low-paid revolutionaries. But that's criminal law. It's not like those fake-ass slip-and-fall cases you do all day for the paycheck."

"Speaking of paycheck, know what I can't believe? That Tony's not getting paid for a murder case. Especially for his ex-wife."

She chuckled. "Oh, he's getting paid."

"He said it was pro bono."

"It's not pro bono. It's alimony. His ex came to him to defend her brother, and he said he would do it if she ended his alimony payments. She finally agreed when she saw the public defender wasn't doing anything. Tony doesn't take a piss unless he gets paid."

Bailey, Utah, was in Pyute County, which to Nick looked like little more than deserts and red rocks. One little town in the center of an environment that could be mistaken for Mars.

They got off the highway, and Nick noticed the town had only one exit.

"One-exit town," Nick said.

"What?"

"I grew up in a small town in Idaho before I moved to Vegas. My grandma used to say we lived in a one-exit town and that people in one-exit towns shouldn't mingle with people in big cities."

"Eh. I think people are the same everywhere."

Outside town was a gas station with three pumps. Gas n' Things. Stephanie parked and said, "I need to walk around. Even my ass is numb."

The cashier was a big guy with a red cap and a white beard. Nick bought a bottle of water while Stephanie went to the bathroom. The man's name tag said *Merch*, and he scanned the water and said, "Where you headin', son?"

"Here. Bailey."

"What business you got here?"

"Going to court. Why?"

He shook his head. "Don't get many people that stop in Bailey. Just curious."

The town was laid out in a flat area and surrounded by the red rock hills. Their motel was an ugly brown building with a pool and cracking pavement in the parking lot.

Nick got out his gym bag full of clothes and a few law books about murder trials, and they went to the front desk. A man with stringy hair and glasses was bent over a magazine on the counter.

"Help you?"

"We have a reservation for two rooms," Stephanie said.

"We got one open."

"I booked for two."

"Great. We got one open. You want it or not?"

"I guess we'll take it."

"One bed?"

They both said, "Two," at the same time.

"Uh-huh," the clerk said, glancing at them both. "Couch is a foldout. It's forty-eight a night."

Stephanie said, "Why forty-eight?"

"Excuse me?"

"I mean, why not forty-nine or fifty?"

The man got a set of keys off a board behind him. "Air conditioner don't work, so I gave you a two-dollar discount. You're welcome."

The room was small and dirty with one window. It looked like it hadn't been cleaned . . . really ever.

Stephanie said, "Do we even wanna know what those stains on the carpet are?"

"It's not so bad. The sign out front said free HBO, so, you know, it's got that going for it."

They hadn't eaten since they left and decided to try the diner across the street. It was packed. Probably because it was the only place to eat lunch in town.

They were seated by a window, and a waitress took their order of two cheeseburgers.

"You ever been here before?" Stephanie said.

"No. You?"

She shook her head and took a drink of water. "I barely have time to go anywhere. Any extra time I have I spend with Max."

Max was her ten-year-old son from a previous marriage that lasted six months. Nick knew her ex, Mike, who he had gone to high school with as well. The main thing he remembered about the guy was that he once thought it would be funny to lock Nick in auto shop overnight.

He said, "Do you know this case didn't even really make the news out here? I checked. There was one little blurb in the local paper and it didn't even go into detail about it."

"So?"

"So you don't think it's weird that such a gruesome murder doesn't get any media attention?"

"Nick, we're in the butthole of the desert. The 'media' out here is probably some high school kid hoping to make extra pot money off of clicks. I wouldn't read too much into it."

A man came up to their table. He wore a white shirt with a red bow tie and a white mustache matching his hair. He lit a cigar, though a large NO SMOKING sign was behind the register.

"Mr. Collins and Ms. Brown. Welcome to Bailey, Counselors."

They glanced at each other.

"Saw your pictures on the Nevada Bar website. You'll have to excuse the little intrusion, but I like to know who's appearing in my court."

"Oh, you're Judge Goodman," Stephanie said. "Nice to meet you."

"Nice to meet you, young lady."

Two men who'd had lunch with the judge stepped out of the booth. One was in a green police uniform with brown pants and had a patch on his shoulder that declared him the sheriff. The other was a tall man who looked like a bird, and the judge introduced him as Christian Young, the county attorney who was prosecuting their case.

"You guys are eating together before a trial you're adjudicating?" Nick said. The judge's eyes fixed a stare on him as he puffed his cigar.

"Son, how long have you been practicing law? Couple years? Lemme let you in on a little secret; judges like people that go along to get along." He took the cigar out of his mouth. "Lunch is on me. See you tomorrow morning, Counselors."

After the men left, Nick said, "They're, like, buddies. That's clearly ex parte communications they shouldn't be having."

Stephanie shrugged. "He paid for our burgers. How bad could he be?"

4

The meeting room at the Pyute County Jail was just a conference room with a table and wooden chairs. Paintings of sunsets and deserts hung on the walls. Stephanie and Nick sat on one side of the table, and a thin, younger man in a beige jumpsuit sat across from them. He had frizzy hair and a wide-eyed expression.

"You guys are the lawyers?" Ryan said.

"We are," Stephanie said. "I'm Stephanie Brown and this is Nick Collins. We'll be defending you in your case going forward."

"My sister said Tony was going to defend me."

"He is, in a sense. We work with him and he sent us down."

Ryan looked between the two of them. "How old are you guys?"

"Does it really matter?" she said.

"Well, I guess not." He looked at Nick. "How many murder trials have you done?"

"Um, none."

"What about you?" he said to Stephanie.

"If I tell you zero or a thousand, does it make any difference?" she replied. "The evidence is what it is, and not to be rude, Mr. Hooper, but beggars can't be choosers. So if you'd rather keep Sleepy McNight-Night as your lawyer, I'm happy to go home to my son. Keep in mind you're looking at life in prison without the possibility of parole. You'll die in a cell."

Ryan looked down at the table and sighed. "You're right. I'm sorry. I just, um, this isn't exactly how I saw my life playing out. I didn't even get to see my son being born. It just messes with your head."

Stephanie said, "Let's just go through some of the events, okay? We've already watched your video interview and read all the transcripts of everything that's happened so far, but we should hear it from you."

He leaned back in the chair. "What do you wanna know?"

Stephanie said, "You described the man you gave a ride to as blond with short hair and maybe in his forties, is that right?"

"Yeah."

"Did they get a police sketch artist in with you at any point?"

"No. No one believed me. Not even my lawyer."

Nick had called the previous lawyer to get caught up on the case and was shocked to learn the old man didn't do any investigation on his own. Even on simple fender benders, Nick would interview all the witnesses several times and go out to where the accident had occurred to better visualize the case.

"What happened after you picked him up? I'd like to hear it in your own words."

Ryan shrugged. "He was acting super weird, and then outta nowhere, he says that the car I saw on the side of the road wasn't his. That he cut the owner's hands off and buried her in the desert, and that he was gonna do the same thing to me. I pretended like it was a joke and laughed it off, and like a minute later, we were at an exit with a gas station. I told him I needed to get gas and pulled in. I ran inside to call the cops, and when I came out, he was gone."

"And there were no video cameras at the gas station, correct?"

"No. I mean, my lawyer said the police didn't find any."

Nick said, "Anybody see this other guy that maybe the cops missed?"

He shook his head. "It was the middle of the night. And the cashier wasn't even paying attention. He was watching something on his phone."

Stephanie said, "You didn't know the victim, Jasher Phelps, in any way, right?"

"None at all."

"They found her body using a methane probe about a mile from where you said you picked this man up. They got the Utah State Crime Lab to do what's called an x-ray diffraction on mud that was found in your Jeep. The mud in your Jeep matches the mud found on Jasher and had traces of her blood in it."

"And like I told the cops, the guy must've had the mud on him. They didn't find blood or mud on my clothes, just in my Jeep. How could I cut someone's hands off and not get blood on me?"

Nick said, "Is there any reason you can think of as to why traces of cyanide were found in the mud in your Jeep?"

"I don't know. Maybe he tried to poison her."

Nick shook his head. "No cyanide was found in her system. Her killer didn't get the chance." He hesitated. "You're a nurse, right?"

He scoffed, "Why? Because I must know how to poison someone 'cause I have medical training?"

Stephanie said, "That's what the prosecutor is going to tell the jury."

"You don't believe me either, do you?"

Stephanie folded her arms and leaned back in the seat. "Guilty or not, we'll fight just as hard either way. So stop with the attitude. We're on your side. Now, is there *any* reason you would have traces of cyanide in your Jeep?"

He looked between the two of them. "No."

Stephanie said, "Why would he leave the duffel bag in your Jeep?"

"He probably panicked and forgot it or wanted me to get blamed for it." He leaned forward. "What about all the other missing people?"

They glanced at each other, and Nick said, "What missing people?"

"I've heard from some guys in here that people coming through Bailey go missing all the time. That nobody really talks about it but that it goes back years."

Stephanie made a note on her phone. "I'll look into that. We haven't heard anything, though."

They spoke awhile longer, and then Stephanie said, "I think we have what we need for now. We have court in the morning and will meet you there. Tomorrow's just some final motion hearings and beginning the process of jury selection. So we won't be doing a whole lot."

"You've looked at everything, though, right? All the evidence?"

"We have."

"What do you think's going to happen? Are you going to get me out of this?"

"Well, the circumstantial evidence against you is fairly strong. The victim's hands and the hatchet used to cut them off were found in a bag in your Jeep; trace evidence found in your Jeep matched trace evidence found on the victim; and judging from the hemorrhaging, inflammatory-cell infiltration, and formation of granulation tissue in the wounds, the coroner estimated Jasher had her hands removed around nine to ten P.M. You were driving right past where she was buried a little before that time."

Nick added, "But the fact that you called the police doesn't make sense if you just killed someone."

"That's what I kept telling them! Why would I call the cops if I'd just killed somebody?"

Stephanie said, "They think you did it to throw suspicion off yourself, which isn't as good an explanation as they think it is."

Nick nodded. "But we're in their territory. The jury will be from here, and you're not. It's a bigger disadvantage than you would think."

Ryan exhaled. "This is a nightmare. I can't believe this is happening to me." Then he scoffed, "I was just trying to be a nice guy. And now I'm going to die in a cell for it." He shook his head. "I feel like everybody would be better off if I just wasn't around."

Stephanie said, "Hey, look at me . . . you have a son now. So do I. And if there's one thing I know about being a parent, it's that you don't get to just give up. No matter how bad it gets, you have a person in this world that needs you now. I'll do everything I can to help you, but you don't get to give up. This fight's not over yet."

5

The motel room felt cramped, and Nick had to leave the door open to create the illusion of space. The air conditioner spewed nothing but warm, stale air that smelled and tasted like dust. Darkness, at least, fell quickly, but the temperature didn't drop much.

Stephanie sat on the bed in shorts and a tank top with beads of sweat rolling down her neck as she reviewed documents. Nick was standing outside in basketball shorts when he heard her answer the phone with a sigh.

"What?" she said. Then, after a minute of silence, she added, "Mike, you haven't taken him for like three weekends in a row . . . I don't care. My mom's planning on having some time to herself. He's your son, too, and believe it or not, he actually thinks you're a good father."

Nick felt bad eavesdropping and walked a few paces away.

A couple of minutes later, Stephanie appeared at the door and said, "It's too hot in there. Let's go to the pool."

"I think it's closed."

"So?"

"You wanna break in?"

"We rented a room. It's not breaking in."

They got to the pool, which was surrounded by a black metal fence. The sign said it had closed at 8:00 P.M., and Stephanie started climbing over it.

"Come on," she said from the top of the fence with one foot over the other side.

"I'm good."

"Quit being a baby. How many times do you get to break into a pool and go swimming?"

"You said it wasn't breaking in."

"I lied."

She stripped down to her underwear and dived into the pool. It looked refreshing. Nick could feel the desert heat on him like hot glue.

"I'm going to jail," he mumbled as he carefully scaled the fence.

He stripped down to his boxers and jumped in. The water was warm. He came up to the surface and Stephanie was in the shallow end, leaning against the side and staring at the stars. He turned to his back and floated.

Nick swam up to her and let his head rest on the side of the pool. A breeze blew, and it felt good against his wet skin.

"You nervous about court tomorrow?" she asked.

"Yeah. I mean, I've done some personal injury trials, but it's weird having someone's life in your hands instead of trying to get them a paycheck. Are you nervous?"

She shook her head. "No. You get used to it."

A beat of silence passed.

"Was that Mike on the phone?" he said.

"Yeah. Sorry you had to hear that."

"It's okay. I shouldn't have been listening."

"I forget we all went to high school together. Were you guys friends?"

"Well, he used to take my backpack and throw it on the roof of the school, and he locked me overnight in auto shop once. So I guess that's kind of like friendship."

She chuckled. "I'm so sorry."

She smiled as she kicked out her feet, making little waves. "It's weird we never hung out. Did we have any classes together?"

"Yeah, geology. I actually paid Danny Sanchez to switch seats so I could sit behind you."

"Seriously? Why?"

He kicked his feet out like her and enjoyed the sensation of warm, splashing water.

"I, um, really wanted to ask you to a dance. One day I actually worked up the courage to tap you on the shoulder. When you turned around, I chickened out and asked if I could borrow a pen."

"Hey!" a man shouted from beyond the fence. "Pool's closed. You not know how to read!"

"Oh man, I think we're in trouble," she laughed.

They grabbed their clothes and ran out, giggling as the man continued to yell.

6

The courtroom reminded Nick of something from the early twentieth century. Wood paneling and polished chairs. He and Stephanie sat at a big brown table, and behind them were the audience pews with the jury box across the courtroom next to Christian.

A bailiff said, "All rise; Eighth District Court is now in session, the Honorable Wilford Goodman presiding."

Judge Goodman came out and said, "Please be seated," without looking up. He nodded to the bailiff, who disappeared into a back room and came out a minute later with Ryan Hooper. Bags under his eyes and messy hair. He was sat at the end of the table. Nick felt for him. He looked like someone on the verge of having a nervous breakdown.

The judge said, "We are here for the matter of *State of Utah v. Ryan T. Hooper*, case number 223656. Counsel will state their appearances."

"Christian Young for the State."

Awkward silence in the courtroom.

Stephanie nudged Nick. "Oh, um, Nick Collins and Stephanie Brown for the defendant."

"Very well, good morning, all. Mr. Collins, now is the time set for any motions in limine you may wish the Court to hear. Do you have any you'd like to present?"

Nick took a deep breath and then rose. "Yes, Your Honor." He went to the lectern with his stack of motions and said, "We'd first like to—" The motions all slipped to the floor because the paper clip had gotten loose, and when he bent down to get them, his shoulder hit the microphone and caused loud feedback.

"Sorry," he said.

"How about you give me a brief outline, son. No need to read them; I've read the motions prior."

"Oh yeah, um, we had the first two motions to exclude the blood evidence found in Mr. Hooper's Jeep based on violations of the Fourth Amendment as laid out in *Utah v. Strieff*. The responding officers did not—"

"I find the actions of the officers in response to sections one, three, and six of the motions in limine to be within the bounds of *Utah v. Strieff* and its progeny. I therefore deny Counsel's motions. Next issue, please."

Nick looked at Stephanie, who spun her finger, indicating to go on. In civil law, everything had to be laid out by the judge because, since money was involved, everything would be appealed, and the judge needed a good reason for any ruling, no matter how small. Nick wondered if criminal court was more seat of your pants. He hated the seat of his pants.

"Um, well, the next motion is to exclude prior convictions unrelated to—"

"I find Mr. Hooper's prior convictions to be admissible character evidence under Rule 404a and b, as the State is not using it to show that Mr. Hooper acted in conformity with that character on this particular occasion. Next issue, please."

A slight twinge of agitation ran through Nick.

"Your Honor," he said, forcing his voice to stay calm and even, "we would move to exclude statements made by the defendant under Rule 403 due to being unduly prejudicial in light of—"

"I find sections four, eight, and—"

"Your Honor, may I finish what I was saying?"

The judge's face went stern, and he leaned back in his chair. Nick glanced over and saw the prosecutor grinning.

"Mr. Collins, you submitted these motions as quickly as you could, and I appreciated that. However, I have read them and the State's motions in response and your rebuttals. The oral arguments are a formality for the record."

"So, what you're saying is that you've already made up your mind without even hearing us out?"

"Nick," Stephanie whispered. He looked at her, and she gave a slight shake of her head.

"Counsel, let me explain something: We might just be backwoods yokels to you, but out here, we follow the letter of the law. And the letter of the law states that I can decide these motions based on the briefs without oral arguments. I have done so. If you wish to keep speaking and waste everybody's time, go right ahead. But I'm presuming Mr. Hooper would like to resolve this matter."

"Not if you're going to railroad him."

"Mr. Collins," the judge said with a raised voice, "I don't know what kind of judges you're used to in Las Vegas, but down here, we expect decorum at all times. Now I would—"

"I have a new motion. Motion to recuse you as trial judge based on inappropriate ex parte communications with the sheriff and county attorney."

Christian Young chuckled, and Stephanie groaned.

Judge Goodman turned bright red and looked like his head might explode. "Motion denied," he spit out.

"Then I would ask that this trial be stayed, as I will be filing a motion for interlocutory appeal to the Utah Court of Appeals to have you removed as trial judge."

"File your appeal and ask the appellate court for a stay. As far as this court is concerned, we are moving forward today."

Nick and the judge now stared at each other with venom from both sides.

"No," Nick said.

"Excuse me?"

"I said no. I won't move forward. I made a valid motion to recuse you and notified you of an interlocutory appeal. I would ask for a different judge. Otherwise, I'm not going forward with the trial."

Stephanie said, "Nick, sit down."

"I won't."

The judge nearly shouted, "You will go forward with the trial or we will hold a contempt hearing. Is that clear?"

"Yes, it's clear. But I'm not doing it. Hold me in contempt if you want."

The cell behind the courtroom was small but clean. It held two bunks on each side, and the sheets and pillows were surprisingly stain free. A sink and toilet were near the back of the cell, and a plant sat near the lone window. It was withered and dry, dead.

Nick sat upright against the wall. He rarely lost his temper, but it had boiled to the surface a few times in his life. What pushed him over this time was that Judge Goodman had clearly made up his mind about Ryan's guilt and wanted to move the trial along. But all Nick could think about was Ryan's kid growing up without a father. Like he had.

He wished he could go for a run right now. It was about the only thing that completely cleared his head.

A bailiff brought Stephanie back. She glanced around the cell and said, "As first criminal trials go, I'd say it's going pretty well, wouldn't you?"

He didn't say anything.

"Come on, Al Capone. I got you out."

7

While Nick was locked up, the judge, Christian, and Stephanie had agreed that the issues Nick raised would be noted for appeal, and an interlocutory appeal would be filed the next day, along with a request to stay the trial. The judge would sign off on a request for emergency relief, meaning the Court of Appeals had to approve or deny the trial getting stayed within two business days. In the meantime, they would have to wait and see if they were going forward or not.

Nick didn't speak on the drive to the motel. When they got back to their room, he started packing.

"What are you doing?" Stephanie asked.

"I'm going home."

"It's only two days. Might as well stay here."

He shook his head as he stuffed some clothes into his bag. "I'm not coming back."

"Why?"

"Why?" he said, stopping and looking at her. "How about because the judge locked me up on the first day and our client's kid is gonna grow up without his dad because I don't know what I'm doing? I'm not good at this. I'll stick to fake slip-and-falls and ambulance chasing. I never should have come down here."

He kept packing.

"Nick, stop."

He didn't, and his anger bubbled to the surface again as he tried to shove law books into a bag they didn't fit in, so he threw them on the floor.

She touched his hand. "Nick . . . stop."

He exhaled and stood there, staring down at his bag.

"You think you screwed up, but you know what I saw? I saw a guy who really cares about everybody getting a fair shake. That's really rare in our profession. It's what I would want in a lawyer."

He looked at her and she smiled. She smiled with her eyes, too. She was someone whose joy came through every part of her body.

"So look," she said, "we have two days before the trial gets going or we get a new judge. Why don't we go through the discovery again and dig in and see what we can come up with? It sounds like the cops thought they had their man right from the get-go and didn't spend time looking for other suspects. If Ryan's telling the truth and someone else really did it, maybe there's something the police missed?"

He hesitated and then nodded. "Sorry."

"No worries. I think we all have the right to freak out sometimes."

"I'll, um, grab the files. But let's go somewhere that has air-conditioning."

Bailey had a public library that shared a building with a small store that sold trinkets to people passing through.

They got a table by the windows and piled the stacks of documents on it.

Nick had gone through all the reports, test results, re-creations, drawings, videos, photographs, and interview recordings half a dozen times in two weeks. He'd found it difficult to sleep and stayed up reading detectives' narratives and autopsy conclusions to see if it would help alleviate his anxiety. It didn't. But he did understand the central issue in the case now.

Ryan as the killer just didn't make sense. How could a mild-mannered guy with no background of violence suddenly commit the most horrific murder Nick had ever heard about? To be buried alive without hands to even attempt to claw your way to the surface was about as close to hell on earth as he could imagine. And calling the police after would have been the stupidest thing Ryan could have done if he were the killer. The body was found hundreds of yards away from the road. No one would have found it if he'd said nothing. Then again, if the prosecutor's theory was correct, if he felt he'd screwed up somewhere along the way and left evidence behind, being the one to call it in and blame a hitchhiker would be a good attempt to throw suspicion off himself.

Nick and Stephanie pored through the reports in silence. The only sounds in the building were pages being flipped and the occasional click of the air conditioner turning on.

It was afternoon when Nick went to the diner to get a couple of sandwiches.

Stephanie paced in front of the building on a call to Max, and Nick sat on the stone steps.

When she was done with the phone call, she sat next to Nick. She looked across the street at some children playing outside the gas station.

He handed her a sandwich and a bottle of water and said, "I was thinking about something. Who's the best lawyer you know?"

"Tony."

"Me too. He's got a bad reputation, but he's really good at what he does. He told me before I left to look for the one element in the crime that's weakest for the prosecutor and focus on that."

"Yeah, he's said that to me, too."

"So what's the weakest element here?"

"Motive."

"Right. If Ryan did kill Jasher, why not toss the stuff, clean up the Jeep, and keep driving? It makes no sense that he called the cops after killing someone. No matter what the prosecutor says about him wanting to seem innocent by being the one to call it in." He thought for a moment. "Do you know the only thing I had trouble understanding in the discovery? It was the x-ray spectrograph. You good at reading those?"

"Yeah, I interned at the state crime lab as an undergrad. Come on, I'll show you."

They went back to the table in the library, and Stephanie took out a few graphs with large spikes drawn on them, the pages coated in numbers. It almost looked like a different language.

"So these are the trace elements they found with their relative frequency and quantity. The bigger the spike, the more of it was found. On the left is the normal stuff you would find in mud, like silt and clay particles, and on the right is the abnormal stuff."

Nick examined the elements on the right side. "So the biggest spike is in cyanide?"

"Which is why they think Ryan tried to poison her first before burying her."

"But none was found in her system, right?"

"Right. But a nurse might just have some handy in case he needs to kill one of the victims fast and get away. Like an insurance policy or something. And maybe the vial or whatever broke open during a struggle and didn't get into her bloodstream?"

"If his plan was something as clean as poison, it doesn't seem like he'd go from that to cutting off her hands and burying her, does it? If you're panicking and the plan changes, you want something quick and efficient, like strangling."

"Then where else could the cyanide have come from?"

Nick thought a moment. "I had a case once where I sued a gold mine. Gold miners use cyanide to bring gold to the surface. If it's raining . . ." He had butterflies as he went to the librarian and said, "Excuse me." She looked annoyed, and he figured it was the volume of his voice, though no one else was there. "Excuse me," he said quietly. "I need to find out if there's any gold mines around here. Where would I look?"

"In the mining claims at the county recorder's office."

"And where is that?"

"I'm the county recorder. The county recorder's office is the next desk. I'll meet you there."

8

The drive to the Turquoise Valley Mine, the only gold mine within fifty miles of Bailey, took much longer than it should have. The roads twisted through canyons into dead ends or forks that weren't on Google Maps. The landscape was sand and rocks in every direction, and Nick could imagine walking for a week and not seeing another person.

The road twisted up a canyon, and they finally reached an open space. The mine had to be hiked to from here. They sat in the car with the air-conditioning on full blast.

"Driving that was way harder than you'd think," Stephanie said.

"Now imagine it in the dark," Nick said with his face buried in the file. "ME said Jasher's hands were removed between nine and ten. Only someone who's driven this road before could make this drive in the dark. And Ryan's never been here."

Stephanie rummaged through the glove box and said, "Ha. Here it is."

She took out a used plastic bag. "We need a dirt sample to see if there's cyanide here. I have friends at the crime lab that can get it analyzed for us."

"You don't think Christian will have a problem with the defense attorneys handling that evidence?"

"Yeah, he's not just gonna accept evidence I put in a bag I used for lunch like a month ago. But if we show him the results, he'll have to have SIS come out and do their own thing." She closed the glove box. "Hope you like hiking in dress shoes."

The entrance to the mine was up a steep incline. There was no shade. Both their shirts were stained with sweat. Nick tried to hide that he'd forgotten to wear deodorant this morning but was so miserable after a short while he no longer cared.

"I think I'm having a heart attack," he said from behind her.

She trudged a few paces without responding and said, "I can almost see it. Just like five more minutes."

"How can you *almost* see something?"

"Just keep walking."

He walked for three breaths before he said, "Did you look into what Ryan said at all? The disappearances?"

She nodded but didn't turn around. As though the motion would take up too much energy. "I talked to Christian while you were a jailbird. He said they get a lot of missing-persons cases from people driving through. It's been happening a long time." She took a breath. "He said a lot of people think the town is cursed."

"Cursed?"

"There's rumors it was built on an old Lipan Apache cemetery. Sounds like BS to me."

"I don't know. A lotta people believe in ghosts. There's gotta be something to it, right?"

"Or we're all crazy."

Another fifteen minutes and Nick's cell phone no longer turned on because it was overheated. Fifteen minutes later, he felt faint and his shirt clung to him as if he'd dived into a pool.

"I gotta take a break, Steph."

She stopped and put her hands on her hips, breathing deeply. "I thought you were a jogger?"

"We're in hell's microwave. Jogging can't prepare you for this."

He leaned against some rocks, but the sun was angled in a way that provided little shade. He had to squint and noticed he couldn't hear any cars on the road from here.

"What's that?" she said.

He looked over to where Stephanie was gazing. The mine was up a bit around a bend, but the edge of it could be seen.

Nick took a deep breath and pushed himself off the rocks.

9

The entrance to the gold mine was narrow but opened up into an ample space and then went farther back into darkness.

"You sure you wanna go in there?" she said.

He peered into the dark, and it looked like it went on forever. "What if he really didn't do it? He's got no one else helping him. It's just us."

She sighed. "Fine. You go first then."

Nick ducked his head a few inches and went through the entrance. The mine was cool and dark. He enjoyed it a minute. His skin felt cooked, and he knew he would have a bright-red sunburn come morning.

When he looked around, he caught a glimpse of something farther back in the mine. A shape. He took a few paces toward it and could make out a table or a desk with a chair. Some items lay on the table.

Nick took out his phone, but it was still overheated and wouldn't turn on.

"Steph, does your phone work?"

"Yeah."

"Can you turn on the flashlight and come here, please?"

She did.

"Eh. It's better than some apartments I've lived in."

"Me too. Can you point the light over here?"

Several old knives and a blade curved like a crescent moon lay on the table. Hatchets were lined up in a row, speckled with dark rust.

A noise came from the darkness beyond.

Motion against dirt and gravel. The sound made both of their heads whip toward it.

"Nick, I'm thinking maybe it's time to go."

He didn't move his eyes from the direction of the sound, though he couldn't make out anything. "I think I'm cool with that."

She bent down and scooped dirt into the plastic bag. They hurried out of the mine.

While they were driving back, Nick held up the bag and looked at the dirt inside. By establishing that the cyanide could have come from the ground in the mine, maybe they could show Ryan wouldn't have had time to commit this murder? The mine was only a few miles from where the body was found, and if they could find a credit card receipt, photograph, video. . . anything that showed Ryan was far enough away he couldn't have made it here in time, they might have a shot at an acquittal. At the very least, they could argue that whoever lived there—if someone did live there—was the one that actually perpetrated this crime. Was it possible that a bag of dirt could save a man's life?

"You think someone lives there?" Nick said.

"That's too creepy to even think about. We need to talk to Christian and have someone look at—"

An eruption of force shoved the car forward with so much power the bag of dirt exploded all over the vehicle.

The Honda was rocked by a convulsive seizure of screeching tires as it careened off the road. Nick's head whiplashed against the dashboard, his seat belt tightening against him like a pulled rubber band.

Stephanie screamed.

Nick looked behind him and saw the back windshield view filled with the front grille of a massive van. It rammed the car again. Stephanie's Honda slid into the other lane before the tires straightened and regained traction.

The van sped alongside the car as Stephanie slowed down. The van's windows were darkened, and they couldn't see inside. Stephanie suddenly hit the gas, trying to get in front of it, but it dived across the lane, lunging toward the car.

Stephanie managed to slam the brakes as smoke rose from the tires, and the pair was thrown forward again. The van continued on, speeding down the road. Its taillights disappearing in a trailing cloud of brown dust.

Stephanie grimaced. Her forehead was bleeding from the steering wheel.

"Are you okay?" Nick said.

"Yeah," she said. Her eyes were glossy. She tried to open the door, but it wouldn't budge. So she rammed her shoulder into it while pulling the handle, and it cracked open. The metal groaned as she pushed it. Nick got out and tried his cell phone.

"My phone won't turn on. Is yours working?"

She leaned against the car. Nick looked at the wound on her forehead. "You're bleeding."

He got a bottle of water and some napkins out of the car. Dousing the napkins, he lightly dabbed her forehead.

She dialed 911, and Nick could hear someone say, "Nine one one, what's your emergency?"

Before she could say a word, they heard a rumble up the road. The van was shooting at them like a rampaging bull. Rocketing at top speed, the van shook and rattled.

Nick grabbed Stephanie's hand and pulled her out of the way as the van smashed into the car. They dived onto the dirt as the grinding snarl of metal on metal filled the air. The van slammed the car so hard it sent it across the lane into a ditch. The two vehicles joined into a messy heap of metal, but the van's tires screeched as it pulled back into a cloud of exhaust.

"Run!"

10

Nick ran with strength he didn't think he had. The desert sands were so hot the heat rose up into his shoes. They ran straight in one direction, away from the road. The driver had to have seen them but didn't follow. The van bulleted down the direction they had been driving from, toward the mine, and disappeared.

They stopped and sucked in air, Stephanie's hands on her knees. Nick surveyed their surroundings. Nothing but tumbleweed and cacti. The road was the only reprieve, a cut mankind made across the alien landscape.

The van was gone. It couldn't drive out here in this terrain to follow them, but Nick was worried about a rifle crackling the silence.

Stephanie said, "I dropped my phone. We need to go back for it." She looked pale, and blood dribbled down her cheek.

"There's a gas station like two miles up. You wanna go for that or your phone?"

"Phone. It's right there."

"Why don't you wait here and I'll go look for it?"

"I can take care of myself, thank you."

They slogged back in silence with their eyes on the road. The one advantage they had was that the environment was flat and barren; they could see someone coming at them from any direction. But it wouldn't matter if the man had a rifle.

The dirt and dust had settled and the road was still. They searched for her phone.

"I dropped it when you pulled me away."

They searched another minute before Nick said, "Found it."

Beaten into the dirt, cracked with spiderweb fissures in the glass, was her phone. He picked it up and it was bent in half, almost snapped.

"Oh, goody," she said.

He dropped the hunk of metal and plastic.

"Gas station?" he said.

She nodded as though she had agreed to jump off a cliff.

It was afternoon and the sun was starting its descent, but the heat didn't let up.

The desert didn't get any less barren the more they walked. Nick realized he hadn't seen a single animal out here, and they'd been walking for what must've been half an hour.

"If he circles back, we need to run."

"I don't think I can run again, Nick."

"If we don't make the gas station in time, we won't have a choice."

A few minutes of silence passed between them as they focused on their steps.

"I wonder how many of those missing-people stories are true?" Nick said.

"I don't even want to think about it."

The Gas n' Things—with its three pumps in front and a small, fenced-in parking lot with brown wooden slats in the back—came into view.

Stephanie said, "I never thought I'd be so happy to see neon beer signs."

"I'm getting the largest Sprite I can with a barrel of ice."

"You can keep your Sprite. I'm getting a bucket of slushy."

Near the fence, Nick heard something. The hum of a revving engine.

The van exploded through the fence in an eruption of splintering wood. The tires screeched. It charged like a shark homing in on a blood trail.

Stephanie jumped out of its path, swan diving into the dirt and rolling on her belly. Nick dashed for the pumps. The snarl of grinding gears echoed as the van lurched forward with more speed. Nick faked left and went the other way, as the driver slammed on the brakes and smoke poured out from the tires. The van smashed headlong into the first pump. The pump twisted into crumpled metal and plastic. Shooting jets of fuel into the air. The stench of gasoline burned Nick's nostrils.

He was soon drenched in the stuff. The van didn't move, but he couldn't see through the windshield with the gallons of fluid shooting out of the underground tanks. Finally, the door opened, and he saw black pants. The driver stepped out. His hands were blackened with dirt and grime, and a small axe dangled from his fingers. He didn't seem to mind getting doused in gasoline.

Nick could see where he was heading: in Stephanie's direction. She pushed herself to her feet as she noticed him.

Nick glanced inside the station and saw the clerk, Merch, staring out at the carnage with wide eyes, a phone glued to his ear. He considered running in and asking Merch to come out and help, but there was no time. The figure had almost reached Stephanie.

Nick bolted in their direction, his shoes splashing through puddles of gasoline. The figure turned just as Nick slammed into him and threw his full body weight behind the impact. They both flew off their feet. Nick rolled on the ground and the wind was knocked out of him. The axe banged against the concrete.

Nick could see the driver clearly. Skin wrapped around a skull. Black eyes that didn't seem to recognize him as another person. Just taking him in as though he were meat.

The man reached for the axe. A fear gripped Nick, but he knew he'd die in the next few seconds if he didn't act. He lunged for the axe and both of them grabbed it. The man was paper thin but had a wiry strength that Nick couldn't match. He ripped the axe away and lifted it to put it into Nick's face.

Merch stepped out of the station and cocked a shotgun.

The man looked up at him, and their eyes locked.

"I don't want to, son," the old cashier said, "but I will."

The skull face didn't show any reaction. Instead, his expression was passive as he stared at Nick, and the axe fell from his hand and clanked onto the pavement.

11

Two days later, after what seemed like a dozen hours of interviews, Christian Young came by Nick and Stephanie's motel room when the sun was setting. He didn't come inside the room but instead smoked while he leaned against the railing outside and said, "Just wanted to give you this."

It was a copy of the motion to dismiss the case against Ryan Hooper.

"Who is he?" Stephanie said, folding her arms and leaning against the door.

"We don't have any idea. No fingerprint hits in IAFIS, no identification, and he won't talk to tell us his name. So we're going to send his mug shots up to the FBI to have it run through their facial-recognition database, but that's like winning the lottery."

Nick said, "What about the mine?"

"We found items from at least eight individuals and some remains that haven't been identified yet."

"Remains?"

Christian nodded. "He would keep their hands." He dropped the cigarette and stepped on it. "I think you kids really got lucky. A lot of people didn't get away."

The following day, Nick sat outside the jail on the hood of their rental car. He hadn't slept that night. Dreams of eyes in darkness constantly woke him. One time, he saw Stephanie wide awake sitting in a chair with a book, her eyes not moving across the page.

Ryan's wife, Sarah, and his infant son were in a Prius near the jail entrance. Nick and Stephanie had spoken with Sarah for a while this morning, and she'd cried and thanked them several times.

The sun heated Nick's already sunburnt neck as he looked over to Sarah now and waved at her. She gave a shy grin and waved back.

Stephanie sat on the hood with him. A thin line of stitches on her forehead.

"You sunburn like a beluga whale," she said.

"Do they sunburn easy?"

"No idea." She looked out over the desert to the road leading back to Nevada. "I can't wait to go home. And I bet you're ready to get back to ambulance chasing."

"Actually, I'm thinking I might ask Tony for more criminal cases."

"Seriously?"

He shrugged. "It was nice actually helping someone. Feels like I'm spinning my wheels most of the time."

"Well, send me your fake-ass slip-and-fall cases, 'cause I think I need a break from criminal law."

The sunlight was making him squint. Finally, he took a deep breath, as though inhaling courage, and said, "I'd like to take you to dinner and a movie."

Stephanie laughed.

"Ouch. That wasn't the reaction I was hoping for."

"No, it's not that," she said. "You just look like you're about to pass out."

"So . . . is that a yes?"

She smiled. "Yes."

"Good, because that would've been an awkward six-hour drive back if you'd said no."

The doors to the jail slid open, and Ryan Hooper walked out to his family with the biggest smile Nick had ever seen.

---

*About fifty miles from my house, on the border of Arizona and Utah, a young family was driving through on their way to California. Darkness had fallen and a long stretch of empty road separated them from the California border. A credit card charge showed they left a Maverick gas station around 8 P.M.

Two hours later, the family was dead. Their Dodge minivan was run off the road, and each victim was killed with a single gunshot wound to the head.

This incident, which I stumbled upon in college, haunted me. Nothing was stolen, no one was assaulted other than the shootings, no motive ever uncovered; they were seemingly chosen by fate to die.

Terror, true terror, I think, is this realization that the universe doesn't discriminate in its atrocities between the guilty and the innocent, the brave and cowardly, the good and evil.

I'd always wanted to write a story about such atrocities in that little patch of desert. The inclusion of "Kill Night" in The Best Mystery Stories of the Year 2024 *is not just an honor; it's an opportunity to share this meditation with kindred spirits who aren't afraid to look into the abyss and maybe realize something is staring back at them.*

Leonardo Padura *(Havana, 1955) is a novelist and screenwriter. He has authored fourteen novels, several of which feature detective Mario Conde as the main character. His books have been translated into thirty languages. He has been awarded, among many other prizes, the National Literature Award of Cuba (2012) and the Princess of Asturias Prize for Literature (2015).*

A FAMILY MATTER
Leonardo Padura

Translated by Frances Riddle

I

As soon as he saw his friends Anselmo Bris and Martica Ojos Bellos at his door, Mario Conde confirmed, once again, that his instincts were as inscrutable as they were infallible: this would not be an ordinary day.

He'd suspected it from the moment he woke up and saw the trees in the garden petrified by the heat, too blistering even for the imperturbable sparrows. Although it was still only April, a sticky, sweltering day surely lay ahead, one in which, at the very least, nothing good would happen. Did he dare to brave the streets, scouting for people desperate enough to sell their old books or anything else? He couldn't shake the feeling that something strange was in store for him, and this intuition manifested, as always, as a throbbing pain on the left side of his chest, a burning sensation that was worrying but, up to now, had not yet managed to kill him. So before drinking his coffee and slipping into his pants, stiff with accumulated sweat, he ripped last year's calendar off his bedroom wall. It had been hanging across from his bed for several months, still showing the month of October, as a way to torture himself with the numerical proof that the ninth of that month—circled several times—had come and gone, meaning he'd arrived at the advanced age of sixty and was now officially a shitty old man with few years left to live.

His finances were in such a sad state that he needed to go out and scrounge up some cash, as he'd done every day since leaving the police force, all those years ago. But considering the unseasonably warm weather, combined with his weighty premonition, Mario Conde decided it would be best to stay at home. He could practice one of his regular pastimes: sitting around lamenting his miserable life, the disastrous social-civil-economic situation of his neighborhood, his city, his country, his continent, and the world as a whole. Or, if he could muster the energy, he could sit at his typewriter and knock out another page (or more, with luck) of the sordid, disquieting tale of a man very similar to himself with a few (likable) friends and many fellow countrymen (many of them assholes) very similar to the people he knew.

But then the knock at the door pulled him out of his thoughts, and one look at Anselmo and Martica, his old high school classmates, widely considered to be an enduring and indestructible couple, confirmed his intuition.

"Did we wake you?" Anselmo asked, shaking Conde's hand.

Martica, meanwhile, leaned in to plant a kiss on his cheek. "You need to shave," she said. Her face showed her age, the same age as Conde, but her eyes, always so beautiful and expressive, were clouded with worry and sadness.

Conde's detective instincts, still alive and well, had kicked in, so he neither responded nor objected to her comment. "What's wrong?" were his words.

In the kitchen over cups of coffee, Conde learned the reason for his former classmates' unexpected visit: Juan Miguel.

Juan Miguel was the couple's only child and had been like a nephew to Conde, Carlos, Conejo, and Candito. Juanmi, as they called him, was beloved by all of Anselmo and Martica's friends thanks to his natural charm: he was kind, clever, mischievous, cheeky without being spoiled or annoying, able to talk to his parents' friends almost as an equal in the frequent gatherings around food and drinks during the period of relative bonanza they'd enjoyed. More than a child, he was an accomplice. Juanmi was intelligent, exuberant, and, on top of everything else, a beautiful boy: thin, with corkscrew curls and his mother's eyes set in the face of an angel. He was constantly playing diabolical pranks that never altered the saintly expression on his face. His parents and adopted uncles predicted a bright future in which Juanmi would rule the world.

But things changed when Juanmi went out on his own. It was the 1990s, a time of devastating crisis, when everything was scarce and people had to fight for survival as the youth of Juanmi's generation began to leave the country. In the boy's case it manifested as a kind of bipolarity: He married his girlfriend and, swapping things from his grandparents' family home, managed to set up a small apartment for himself in the La Víbora neighborhood. But at the same time, he abandoned his studies, believing that a university degree would do nothing to improve his life. That's when he descended into the world of shady yet highly profitable business dealings, converted to Afro-Cuban Santeria, and became a babalawo priest. But his newfound faith didn't fool anyone who knew him: Juanmi was pragmatic and had discovered mysticism as a way to collect money from unsuspecting believers seeking help from the beyond. He was called "godfather" by many Mexican and Spanish tourists who had fallen into his trap, bringing him gifts whenever they visited the island.

Everything was going fine until Juan Miguel's parallel lives began to converge and his loved ones seemed to resent it. Conde had heard that Lulú, Juan Miguel's girlfriend of many years and now wife, disliked the young man's lifestyle and that the marriage was in trouble. The breaking point came when Lulú, sent to Canada on a professional development course for her job as a geologist, left the university that was hosting her and crossed the border into the United States, seeking asylum. The news came as a heavy blow to Juanmi, who'd been unaware of his wife's intentions. The happy-go-lucky huckster became focused on a single objective: finding his wife . . . But, as one of the most famous lines of Cuban poetry rightfully reminds us, we have "the cursed circumstance of water everywhere."

II

Anselmo and Martica had last seen Juanmi a week ago and he'd phoned them five days prior.

"He called to tell me that he loved us very much and to say he was sorry," Martica told Conde. "And when I asked why, he said I'd find out . . . That left me very worried, and that same night, almost by chance, I discovered that the jewelry box in my dresser was missing my grandmother's engagement ring, Anselmo's father's gold chain, and a Patek Philippe watch that my dad found ages ago on the floor of the Payret Theater."

"When things were at their worst," Anselmo added, "we almost sold it all but ultimately decided not to. It was like selling off our family . . ."

"I remember," Conde nodded. "How much did they offer you at the time?"

"Five thousand dollars," Anselmo said, "but we knew we could've gotten more. Seven, eight thousand . . . Who knows . . ."

"He knows what that jewelry means to us! If he stole it, he plans to use the money to leave Cuba," Martica declared. "And we're sure that's it because the day after he called us we went to his house and it was almost completely empty."

"And you haven't heard from him again?"

Anselmo and Martica shook their heads in unison, as if running on the same battery.

"And we're scared to go to the police to see if they know anything," Anselmo added. "He might still be in Cuba and it could cause trouble for him . . . But if he left by boat he should've sent some sign of life by now. We called Lulú again this morning and she claimed she hadn't had any news from him either. But I thought she sounded very odd, like she was nervous . . ."

Martica let out a sob, and, mustering all his tenderness, Conde placed a hand on her shoulder: the woman feared the worst. Attempts to flee the island across the Straits of Florida all too often ended in tragedy, and traveling through Mexico to cross the U.S. border was risky as well.

"And now you want . . . ?" Conde began.

"We want to know what happened," Anselmo said, completing the thought. "And you know how to find someone, Conde."

Mario Conde nodded. All he could do was nod, remembering Juanmi, who, at age four and thanks to him, was able to recite a string of thirty-two curse words without repeating a single one.

Juanmi's spiritual godfather was one of the most well-known babalawos in the country. In addition to being a priest of the Yoruba rituals, he was a member of the secret Abakuá sect and an active Freemason. And Conde knew that no one initiated in the prophetic art of Ifá's divination tray, not even Juanmi, would dare to take an important step without consulting that deity, who could see the future and predict destiny.

Lorenzo Antúnez was a mixed-race man with a solid build and a changeable personality: he could be loquacious when he wanted to be, or as closed as a padlock that had lost its key when he didn't. He'd risen to prestige thanks to the seriousness with which he practiced his beliefs and his deep knowledge of the stories, rites, and functions of the religion.

Antúnez received Conde in his living room. If not friends, they were at least cordial acquaintances; Conde had visited on more than one occasion, offering books he thought might be of interest. Seeing that Antúnez was a true man of faith and not some scam artist trying to take advantage of people, Conde had always given the priest a more than reasonable price.

"Yes, Juan Miguel came to see me," Antúnez said when the bookseller explained the reason for his visit.

"Do you remember when that was, Babalawo?" Although the man was only a few years older than Conde, he always addressed the priest in the most polite terms: something in Antúnez's bearing seemed to command respect.

"He came to see me often after his wife stayed in the United States . . . He was very upset and needed to talk . . . Then he didn't come around for a while, but he turned up about ten days ago asking for a spiritual consultation."

"And did you consult for him, Babalawo?"

"Of course . . . Juan Miguel is a madman, but he's one of my godsons."

"And could you tell me what Ifá said?"

Antúnez smiled, his gold tooth lighting up the small room decorated with African and Catholic religious symbols, along with diplomas for merits within the Freemasonry system.

"That is personal and—"

"Antúnez, you know who I am and what Juan Miguel means to me. He might have gotten himself into some sticky situation . . . or the worst could've happened. He's out looking for money and . . ."

The man nodded, his gaze fixed somewhere above Conde's head, weighing esoteric loyalties against earthly necessities. Finally, a sense of responsibility to his disciple seemed to win out. "Ifá told him that it's not always a good idea to go chasing after a skirt . . ." he began.

"His wife," Conde translated and the babalawo nodded.

"He also reminded him that the sea is beautiful, but that its beauty hides a treacherous nature."

"Because he asked about leaving by sea?"

"Yes . . . but Ifá also told him that man is even more treacherous than the sea . . ."

Conde nodded. "And did Juan Miguel tell you, Babalawo, what he was planning to do after hearing Ifá's warnings?"

The priest nodded. "He said that even though things had been rough for a while, he couldn't live without his wife . . . Some men are like that, my friend."

III

Conde ordered a double rum at the Bar de los Desperados and went to sip the infamous spirit in the shade of an almond tree on a low wall far from the other drinkers. He needed to decide which of the two paths that had opened before him would lead more directly to a clue about Juan Miguel's whereabouts. He could either follow the trail of the jewelry, or delve down into the darker world of migrant smuggling. But what if the jewelry, along with the money from the sale of his belongings, was a direct payment for a spot on a boat destined for Mexico or Florida? Conde knew that the trip cost about ten thousand dollars and that, with the jewelry he'd taken from his parents, Juanmi could've easily obtained that amount, possibly more.

As he smoked and drank, the fiery liquid intensifying the dogged midday heat, Conde thought about all the factors that shape a person's destiny. Juan Miguel, with his supportive family and innate intelligence, should've had a good life. Anyone, even Ifá, perhaps, would've predicted that he'd complete his engineering degree and begin to earn an honest living. But the country's painful economic collapse marked a different course for Juanmi, and the young man chose a more lucrative life in the margins over near starvation as a respectable engineer, like his father, trapped in a career that provided barely enough to survive. Only his love for Lulú had spared him a more drastic descent. But Lulú had been unwilling to accept his incursion into the world of dishonest dealings. And now, it seemed, Juanmi had gone in search of that lost love. His many years' experience with criminality could perhaps spell his salvation: Juanmi had learned to swim in rough, dangerous waters where large sums of money changed hands, where loyalty and honor were nonexistent.

Conde, ill-informed and disconnected from the depths of the Havanan underworld, felt incapable of finding his way to any of the doors Juan Miguel might've knocked on or even walked through. His best option, as always, was Yoyi Palomo, his partner in the secondhand book trade, skilled at swapping whatever was necessary to go on living, drinking, even eating.

Yoyi was only a few years older than Juanmi, and, in every sense, a perfect example of that pragmatic younger generation. When Conde explained the search he wanted to undertake, and why, Yoyi immediately halted his commercial activities and placed himself at his friend and colleague's disposal.

"We should start with the jewelry," said Yoyi as they approached his powerful, elegant 1957 Chevrolet Bel Air. "A Patek Philippe from the fifties has a very specific set of buyers in Cuba. And I know all of them . . ."

The first stop Conde and Yoyi made was at the home of Tata La Manta, a watch dealer. All the most exquisite examples of Swiss watchmaking had passed through his seasoned hands. The old mansion in El Cerro where La Manta lived, restored from top to bottom, looked to Conde like a monument to the bad taste of the new rich born from crisis and poverty: walls hung with tapestries depicting pastoral scenes, polished tile floors, furniture upholstered in gleaming vinyl, a bar with baroque aspirations in one corner of the main room built from ornately carved wood.

After Yoyi introduced Conde as his business associate and someone who could be fully trusted, the exchange between the younger man and La Manta was quick and tense, reminding Conde of scenes from a nature documentary in which a tiger and a lion fight over a gazelle: both were fierce businessmen and Conde accepted his role as a fly on the wall.

"A Patek Philippe from the forties or fifties, with a crocodile-skin band, possibly original," said Yoyi, kicking things off.

"I haven't seen a Patek in a couple months. The well seems to have dried up. That'll happen if you take and take and never replenish the supply . . ."

"If it wasn't you, who could've bought it?"

"Who knows," La Manta said and shrugged his shoulders. "Millán the Madman or Ramón from La Lisa maybe . . . Just about anyone would buy a Patek Philippe. The trick is to find a good buyer . . . but that depends on how eager you are to get rid of it. Was it stolen?"

"Yes and no."

"How does that work?"

"Someone stole it from their parents, but the parents haven't reported anything."

"And what did he want it for? Drugs? Gambling debts? Cash? To get out?"

"It seems like it was to get out. By boat. Direct to Miami, preferably," Yoyi added.

"That's not my scene. I deal with diplomats, businesspeople here in Cuba, or regular buyers who fly in every few months to pick things up."

"But you know everything that happens in Havana, down to which dogs have ticks," Yoyi said. "This isn't a business deal, Tata. It's . . . a family matter."

Tata La Manta's reddish eyes stood out from his dark face. His many years of successful business dealings had sharpened his ancestral instincts, acquired over generations of survival through hardships and horrors, hunger and persecution. "Gabriel Quintana," he said, looking to Conde. "Gabito. I don't know where he lives but he runs his business in La Güinera. He's a dangerous guy. And I know a dangerous guy when I see one."

IV

La Güinera slum had sprung up many years prior and had seen little improvement since then despite concerted efforts to combat the evils of poverty and marginality. Conde remembered that in his childhood, mentioning La Güinera was like mentioning hell: a place no one would willingly enter.

Conde trotted out his most convincing arguments and persuaded Yoyi to stay behind as he descended into the depths of the city. He still knew how to look out for himself, and, going alone, he'd have better chances of an encounter with Gabito. Yoyi grudgingly agreed, on the condition that he would remain on hand as backup, parking his Bel Air at the top of the road leading down into the slum.

Conde walked the shantytown's main artery, surprised at the number of people of all ages, races, and appearances crowding the streets or gathering on the corners to buy, sell, or offer whatever service they could in exchange for a quick buck. Did anyone here have a steady job? Their opportunities for earning an honest living, thought Conde, couldn't be very promising.

Conde stopped several people to ask if they knew Gabito and where he lived, but everyone said that they'd never heard of such a person and so obviously had no idea where to find him. So Conde took out a cigarette and sat on a boulder in the shade of an old laurel tree to wait for Gabito. The message had surely been relayed.

Twenty minutes later he saw three men approaching. One was mixed-race, one was Black, and the other White. Several paces from Conde, who remained seated, the White man stepped forward and asked: "Why are you looking for me?"

Gabito was a tall, corpulent man in his thirties. If a face can reflect a person's character, his was an open book: the dark scar across his chin and the fierce intensity in his eyes showed his violent relationship to humanity.

"I was hoping you could shed some light on something," Conde responded, still sitting, drawing lines in the dust with a stick.

"I'm no lighthouse. Who are you?"

"I'm Juan Miguel's uncle. I'm trying to find out where he is. And I think you might know."

Gabito smiled. Conde was surprised by the gleaming perfection of his teeth.

"I don't know any Juan Miguel . . . Or do you mean Juan Gabriel, the singer?"

Now it was Conde's turn to smile and shake his head as he finally stood. He threw a glance at Gabito's acolytes, tense as coiled springs.

"Gabito . . . I was once a police officer, years ago, now I'm a nobody . . . just a shitty old man. But I don't like to be reminded of it. I don't care about whatever business you're involved in, although I could make things difficult for you if I wanted to because I still know plenty of officers who could write a doctoral thesis on you."

"Are you threatening me?"

"No, because I know that you and those two bulldogs behind you could get rid of me in under a minute and no one would have seen a thing. I'm simply explaining that I have no intention of butting into your business, even if I don't like it very much. I just want to know what happened to Juan Miguel. It's a family matter," said Conde, and, seeing that Gabito looked away, pensive, he decided to press further. "Lorenzo Antúnez is looking for him too. Juan Miguel visited his godfather a few days ago and he received a bad omen: Ifá told him to watch out for the sea and I know what Juanmi was thinking . . . Aren't you one of Antúnez's godsons too?"

Gabito looked away again. Conde knew that he was dealing with an intelligent man, more intelligent than most of the people around him, who owed his success to his cleverness. But intelligence doesn't always come with sensitivity. The man was making calculations, weighing odds, taking stock, and Mario Conde could only hope he'd pressed the right button.

"No, Antúnez isn't my godfather . . . Juan Miguel is my godfather."

The afternoon sun hung over the calm sea, bathing it in a blinding patina of gold. Conde and Yoyi stood in an empty bend of the coastline, several miles beyond the Santa Fe beach. They were beginning to think that Gabito had wasted their time when the outline of a man appeared against the setting sun, dodging reefs and rocks. As his image came into view, Conde sighed with relief.

"It's him."

"I'll wait in the car," said Yoyi Palomo, placing a hand on Conde's shoulder before moving away along the shore. His part of the mission was now complete and what was left was a family matter.

V

It had been many months since Conde had seen Juanmi, who looked thinner through his long-sleeved shirt but also more mature, maybe because the young man now wore a thick black beard that somehow managed to highlight the beautiful eyes he'd inherited from his mother.

"How many curse words are there?" Conde shouted as soon as he thought Juanmi was close enough to hear him.

The young man's mustache twitched into a smile. "Thirty-two, officially. Would you like me to recite them?"

Conde took a few steps toward Juan Miguel and hugged him. The young man smelled bad.

"How are you, Juanmi?" he asked, without releasing him.

"Good, Conde . . . And how are my parents?"

"Worried . . . That's why I'm here."

Juan Miguel nodded. "Do you have a cigarette?" he asked. Conde handed his pack to the young man, who took one and lit it. Conde did the same, taking a long drag. "Can we sit?"

Even under that intense sun, it was cooler on the beach than in the city center. And Conde loved the smell of the sea. He'd once dreamed of having a house, small and modest but right on the water. That dream had faded many years ago but he still loved the salty scent of the ocean.

"What are you going to do, Juanmi?"

"I'm leaving. Someone's coming to get me . . . Tonight."

Conde shook his head. "Why didn't you tell your parents?"

"I couldn't talk about it with anyone. Much less them."

"And what if they turned you in for stealing the jewelry? Or reported you missing?"

Juan Miguel smiled and threw his cigarette toward the sea but the wind lobbed it back onto the rocks at Conde's feet.

"The police aren't going to bother looking for me . . . And if they did, they wouldn't find me. You know good and well, Conde: unless you're a politician or a murderer, no one will find you here."

"I found you . . ."

"You're different. You can track me down by smell."

"That's true . . . but it was easy. You smell terrible."

"I haven't been able to bathe for four days." Juanmi smiled again. Then he stretched out a leg and put a hand in his pocket. He opened his fist to show Conde the engagement ring crowned with little diamonds and the gold chain: the inheritance from his grandparents.

"Give these back to my mom and dad. I didn't need to sell them," he said, handing the jewelry to Conde.

"What about the watch?"

"I'm keeping the Patek Philippe. Remind my mom that my grandfather gave it to me when I started at the university. And I want to have it with me," the young man said, pushing back the left sleeve of his shirt to show Conde the small watch, glimmering in the fading sun.

"And you're not going to say goodbye to Anselmo and Martica?" Conde asked as he put the jewelry away.

"No. I can't . . . I can't look back, Conde. You understand, don't you?"

Conde gazed out at the sea and nodded. "And where did you get the money to get out?"

Juan Miguel turned serious. "I'm not going to tell you that. Not because you used to be a cop, but because you've always been such a puritan . . . And I don't want you to think badly of me."

Conde nodded. "I couldn't think badly of you, Juanmi."

"And you're not going to the police to report an illegal transport tonight?"

"I should. Migrant smuggling is illegal and—"

"And what if it's my wife coming to get me because she realized we're still in love in spite of everything?"

Conde looked at the young man. Then to the sun, slowly sinking into the sea and the horizon.

"I didn't need the money because Lulú paid for everything. But I wanted the jewelry and some money because you never know how these things are going to turn out, or when they'll happen."

Conde nodded and took out another cigarette. He lit it and handed the pack to his nephew.

"No, I don't smoke . . . That cigarette I bummed from you was my last. I wanted to smoke it with you because, if you recall, you're the one who gave me the first one I ever smoked."

Conde stared at the burning tip of his cigarette. "No, I didn't remember that."

The two men fell silent. The last rays of day were fading into an evening that would soon be night.

"I have to go," said Juan Miguel, but he didn't stand up.

"And what about the advice the saints gave you? About the skirts and the treachery of the sea?" Conde wanted to know.

"Those saints spent their lives taking crazy risks. Why wouldn't I take my own? . . . Have you ever fallen in love, Conde?"

Conde smiled. "A thousand times, you know that . . ."

"Well, I've only fallen in love once. Almost twenty years ago. With the woman who's coming to pick me up today."

Then he stood up and it seemed to Conde that the boy had grown taller. The former policeman stood as well, with the slight difficulty that came with age.

"Any message for your parents?" Conde asked.

"Yes . . . that I love them. But that I love—"

"Don't say it, don't say it," Conde interrupted. He took Juan Miguel by the forearm and pulled him into a hug. He definitely smelled bad. But he felt sturdy, like a man. "Have a safe journey . . . and take care of that watch. I hope you'll be happy. That's what matters."

"Thank you, Conde," said Juan Miguel and he hugged him.

"Can I tell your parents that I saw you?"

"Of course, tell them . . . but give me a few days. If everything turns out all right I'll be able to speak to them first."

"Okay . . . Well, go on, you don't want to miss the boat," Conde said and he clapped the boy on the shoulder. He began walking to where Yoyi stood waiting for him, but after a few paces he stopped and turned around. "Juanmi, what was curse word number thirty-two?" he shouted.

"Resipinga," said the other man, without stopping.

"Where did you get that one?"

"You made it up, Conde!"

Conde smiled and waved goodbye to the silhouette disappearing into the growing darkness. And then he couldn't hold it in any longer: tears fell from his eyes. How the hell could he not cry when the whole situation was so damn resipinga!

Mario Conde has a life of his own. And he increasingly does whatever he wants to. Since he has now appeared in so many novels, he's developed his own likes and phobias. Also his own world of connections, among them his friends, since friendship is, for him, one of the fundamental values of the human condition. And this story is essentially about friendship—in the way that Conde understands and practices it.

Dan Pope *is a 2002 graduate of the Iowa Writers Workshop. He has published two novels,* In the Cherry Tree *(Picador, 2003) and* Housebreaking *(Simon & Schuster, 2015). His short stories have appeared in numerous print journals, including* The Gettysburg Review, McSweeneys *(No. 4),* Iowa Review, Bellevue Review, Bennington Review, Shenandoah, Harvard Review, Witness, Post Road, Crazyhorse, *and* Greensboro Review, *as well as many anthologies, including* Best New American Voices 2007 *(Harcourt) and* the Pushcart Prize Anthology *(2020).*

SNOW OVER HARTFORD

Dan Pope

Peering through the glass door into the ICU, Mulvaney recognized the kid instantly. He was twenty-two, according to the incident report, two arrests for possession, a couple of misdemeanors, breaking and entering. A thief, like all junkies, but still that same face, the sleepy brown eyes, the splash of freckles across the cheeks—a child's face. Mulvaney had never forgotten him, one of the cases that he still pondered sometimes at night, even now, ten years later, though it hardly seemed that long ago.

The kid looked up from the bed when Mulvaney entered the room; his eyes flared in recognition, and he smiled, just a flash, but that same gentle smile.

"They sent you," he said, his voice raspy.

Mulvaney turned on the recorder and placed it on the table by the bed. "I gotta read you this, Ronny. Is that okay?"

The kid cleared his throat, twice. "Go ahead."

Mulvaney pulled the laminated card from his pocket and read the form. "Do you understand? Are you able to make a mark on the paper? I can see your hands are wrapped—"

"I can't move them. I have no feeling."

"But you understand your rights? And you wish to speak with me?"

"They just took the tube out. I need—"

"Water. Yeah, you sound hoarse. This will help."

The kid leaned forward and Mulvaney put the plastic cup to his mouth, angling the straw so he could sip.

"I want to talk to you about what happened on Friday. Today is Sunday. You've been in the hospital for a couple days. You've had a couple surgeries, right? You remember that?"

"I guess."

"You had that breathing tube in your mouth. You know that, right? You know why you're in the hospital? You're shaking your head no, but you gotta say it for the recorder."

"I don't remember."

"You don't remember? Okay. Were you shot by the police?"

"I'm gonna go with yeah."

"How many times were you shot?"

"I don't know. Nobody's told me anything. You're the first."

"Do you remember being in Hartford? In your grandma's car?"

"Yes."

"Okay. What I want to know is what led up to that. I want to know how you ended up in your grandma's car in Hartford."

The kid blinked a few times with those hooded eyes of his, bloodshot. His arms and chest were wrapped in gauze, two IV lines attached to veins in his wrist, a larger blue tube leading under the blanket toward his stomach; his neck and upper torso were stained with a yellow-brown disinfectant, the skin pale. Under the sheet, his abdomen was wide open, the nurse had told Mulvaney, a midline incision packed with gauze and plastic wrapping to keep his intestines from spilling out.

Mulvaney refilled the water glass. "You've been staying with your grandma and grandpa. So on Friday morning, what happens? Walk me through your day."

The kid took a long, raspy breath. "I was lying in bed most of the day. Then my girlfriend came upstairs and said, 'Grandma said we can use the car.'"

"What time was this?"

"Afternoon, around four. And I said, 'I'll go warm it up for you,' 'cause you have to warm it up before. I go warm it up. That was it. She came out and we left for Hartford."

"Why'd you go to Hartford?"

"To cop drugs."

"Do you remember where?"

"Evergreen Street."

"You remember who you copped from? I see you're shaking your head. Listen, Ron, I'm not here worrying about that, I promise you that. I can't do anything about drug dealers in Hartford. I work in Manchester. You know that. I just want to get all this straight in my mind."

"A guy named Juan."

"Okay. What happened after that?"

"We went to Stop & Shop. Then the cops rolled up."

"Where were you?"

"Sitting in the car. I went to pull out and the lights went on. I didn't know what was going on. So I hit the gas and I remember hearing, *Pop pop pop. Pop pop pop.*"

"What happened after that?"

The door opened and a nurse came in. Mulvaney frowned. He had a rhythm, and he needed to keep it going, like a drum beat. He waited while the nurse checked the kid's blood pressure. Pretty girl, Eastern European accent, Polish probably. She noticed the audio recorder on the table. "You're not recording, are you? We've just taken out the breathing tube."

"Yeah," Mulvaney said, offering a weak smile. "We're recording."

"His chest is packed—"

"Yeah, I know."

"He's on heavy painkillers—"

"I know. Your supervisor gave me—"

She frowned, shaking her head. She took her time checking the kid's vitals and meds. She went through some questions for him. Ever been in a car accident? Any metal in your body? Allergies to iodine?

Finally, she took her kit, giving Mulvaney a long look, shaming him. Sure, the kid was on painkillers, he probably wouldn't even remember this conversation. But that was for the lawyers to work out later, that was their job; he was a cop, his job was to investigate. Hartford wanted answers, they wanted to get the kid on the record, and they'd called him at five A.M. on a Sunday.

When she left, Mulvaney took a deep breath, starting over. "You remember the last time we spoke, Ronny? Almost ten years ago now, wasn't it? In your mom's apartment? We talked about some pretty heavy stuff back then, right? I'm talking to you today because you've been about as honest with me as a person can be. Well, I need you to be that honest again. Okay? Let's go back to the beginning. You've been staying with your Grandma. Why?"

"My mom kicked me out a couple of years ago. I stayed with Dylan for a while. But there wasn't enough room after I met my girl. So we moved in with Grandma."

"Okay. Tell me about your day on Friday."

"I just did."

"I know. But let's start over. Try not to leave anything out."

"I was lying in bed and my girlfriend says, 'Grandma said you can—"

"Grandma doesn't usually let you use the car, right?"

"No, she does. I've been using it for months. Ever since I moved in."

"Okay. So your girlfriend—Elena, right?"

"Yeah. She told me to warm up the car. So I walked downstairs. I said, 'Thanks, Grandma.'"

"Was Grandpa home?"

"Nah. He goes to work at three."

"What time's he come home?"

"Midnight. He works second shift."

"Okay. You warm up the car. Elena comes out. Who's driving?"

"Me."

"Where do you go?"

"Hartford, like I told you."

"Straight to Hartford? You sure?"

"Yeah. We go to Evergreen Street, like I said."

"And you meet a guy named Juan."

"Yeah."

"You called him on your phone? So, there will be a record of you calling Juan, right?"

"Yeah, it's under something else, but that's his name."

"How much did you pick up from him?"

"About a gram."

"You had rigs with you?"

"Yeah. We wanted—we were trying to kill ourselves."

"Trying to kill yourself? Why?"

"I'm a fucking junkie."

"I've known you for a long time, Ronny. You and I go way back. You were only a kid then, but you got that creep off the street. He was hurting a lot of kids. And you were the one who stood up. That took a lot of guts. Now you want to kill yourself? That doesn't make sense to me. Why?"

"Let's talk about this when you're not recording."

"Well, it's pretty serious. Why don't we talk now? We talked about that other stuff on a recording. That was tough as it gets, right?"

"Yeah. And I still feel—I still feel fucked on that deal."

"Fucked how? He's serving time. And if he gets out, he's gonna have a suspended sentence for the rest of his life hanging over his head. And he's gonna be registered. And it was your work that put him there."

"Yeah, I did what you asked and then everybody disappeared. I didn't get no help. Nobody did a thing for me. Not a single thing. I'm just sick of living like this. And I want to die."

The kid cleared his throat with a dry, hollow cough, like nails rattling around in his neck. Mulvaney passed him the water cup, directed the straw toward his lips. From the hallway he heard the yelp of a police radio—the Hartford cops, pacing the floor, waiting on him, drinking hospital coffee.

Mulvaney asked, "Did you tell anybody you wanted to die?"

"Just my girlfriend. We wanted to do it together."

"Did you tell Dylan?"

"Can't trust him."

"He's a good friend. He cares about you. I already talked to him."

"You know, any other cop, I wouldn't say shit."

"I appreciate that." Mulvaney let a few moments pass. "How long have you wanted to kill yourself?"

"A while now."

"How were you gonna do it?"

"Gonna OD."

"You were gonna OD? You went to Evergreen, you got dope. After you got the dope, where'd you go?"

"We shot up in the park."

"Is that where you wrote the note?"

"Yeah."

"Do you remember what you wrote?"

"No."

"Did you write it before you used or after?"

"After."

"After? It's risky, though, right? What if you OD'd right away?"

"Yeah, well, I didn't really care. Obviously."

"Then what? Where did you go?"

"Stop & Shop. For cigarettes."

"You bought cigarettes at Stop & Shop. Then what happened?"

"We were sitting in the car in the parking lot. The cop rolled up. At first I didn't think nothing of it. But I go to pull out and all of a sudden another cruiser comes out of nowhere, lights on. I panicked. I figured fuck it. I wanted to die anyway . . ."

The kid drifted off for a moment, his mouth falling open. Mulvaney touched his shoulder.

"Stay with me, Ronny. This is important. You took off. Where'd you go?"

"It was snowing. I took a turn and slid into a bank. And then that's when they opened up on me."

"Did you get out of the car?"

"No, I was in the driver's seat. Like, literally, I hadn't moved."

"Were you thinking they were gonna fire?"

"No. I thought you guys had procedures."

"And then?"

"*Pop pop pop. Pop pop pop.* That's all I remember."

Mulvaney refilled the water glass and held it out for Ronny, who shook his head. Okay, he thought. The nurse had thrown him off, spoiled his rhythm. And the kid was drowsy. They'd operated on him twice in the past two days. Five gunshot wounds. The girl had come away clean, not a scratch. They'd emptied fifteen bullets into the car. Three cops approaching the vehicle from the rear, one on the left, the other two on the right. And then they'd pulled the Keystone Cops routine, Hartford policemen, fifty years active duty between the three of them. The one on the left slipped in the snow and fell on his ass with his finger on the trigger, spraying bullets into the air. The other two, hearing the shots, opened up. How they didn't kill him and the girl both, Mulvaney didn't know. A total shit show. Internal Affairs wanted to interview the kid, but Hartford had put them off until Mulvaney could get him on the record. Five A.M., his day off, face down in bed, hungover and drooling, and his beeper goes off. Ronald Leclerc, they tell him. The name ringing in his head, like he'd been expecting to hear it. What'd he do? he asked. He hit the jackpot, they say.

"Okay, Ronny. Take me back to Friday. What time do you usually wake up?"

"Lunchtime."

"Okay. You're up late and you sleep late. You're stuck on that cycle with the dope. Were you able to get any on Thursday? We had that big blizzard on Thursday."

"I had some from the day before."

"So, when you wake up on Friday, how long has it been since you've dosed?"

"Late Thursday night, two in the morning."

"Elena, too?"

"Her too."

"How long do you usually go between doses?"

"Sometimes a couple of days."

"You can make it that long? And you don't get sick?"

"We do, but we can tolerate it."

"So, you wake up in the afternoon. Who's home? Was Grandpa home Friday?"

"No. He was already gone."

"Okay. Where was Grandma?"

"On the couch. Where she always is."

"She's sick, right? Is she on medication? What's she take? Fentanyl, right?"

"Yeah."

"What else?"

"Blood pressure pills, stuff like that. She's always on the couch, watching TV."

"Did you text anybody during the day?"

"Dylan. I talk to him every day."

"What were you texting him about? Did you ask him for a ride to Hartford?"

"Honestly, I don't remember."

"So you may have? You wake up, you talk to Dylan, you maybe ask Dylan for a ride. Where did you need a ride to?"

"Wells Fargo."

"Why there?"

"'Cause I had a check for there. My girl did."

"Elena had a check? Okay. You needed a ride to cash her check. All right. Let's go over it again. You're home, Grandma's home. Was Grandpa home?"

"Yeah. I remember now. Grandpa was home. Cause I remember him yelling."

"He was yelling? At who?"

"Grandma."

"What were they yelling about?"

"I don't know."

"Where were you when this is happening?"

"In my bedroom upstairs. Where I always am."

"Okay. You're upstairs in the bedroom, Grandpa's yelling downstairs. Walk me through it. What happens next? Don't leave anything out, even stuff you don't think's important."

"I had a rinse."

"Just a rinse?"

"Yeah."

"So, walk me through it, talk me through it like you're explaining a TV show and I don't know what's coming."

"We're lying in bed, me and Elena. I'm talking to Dylan. Grandma and Grandpa are arguing downstairs. I'm like, 'What else is new.' They're always arguing."

"What happens next?"

"Elena says, 'I'm gonna go down and use the bathroom.' I just lay there. She goes down. She comes up. She says, 'Grandma says we can use the car.' And I say, 'Really? How did you manage that?' And she's like, 'I sweet-talked her.' I say, 'All right. Cool.' So I take the key. I get dressed. I run downstairs. I go outside. I warm up the car."

"Now, who's in the house?"

"Elena and Grandma. Grandpa's gone to work."

"This is after three o'clock?"

"Yeah. So then Elena comes out and we go."

"And you go right to Hartford?"

"Right to Hartford."

Mulvaney blinked a few times. His eyes felt heavy, the right eyelid drooping like it always did when he was tired. He'd shared a bottle of wine with his ex-wife last night after dropping off his fifteen-year-old. The last of the brood. The four Mulvaney boys. He and Megan had brought them up right, despite their own problems. They'd ferried them back and forth to a thousand ball games, all four of them triple-lettermen, like their dad. Sure, the boys had had their moments, the eldest especially, like the time he'd totaled the Taurus wagon. Aidan calling from the side of the road at two A.M., *Dad, don't be upset okay, Dad, I know I fucked up.* Mulvaney knew it was okay, because the call had come from his son, not Manchester or State Police. Mulvaney had counted twenty-four dead soldiers in the back seat, Corona Extra. Aidan had come away with a few bruises from the airbag, his best buddy with a broken arm in the passenger seat. Four boys, some sleepless nights, waiting for the cars to come home after curfew, but that was the worst of it, one totaled Taurus. Aside from that, a few broken bones on playing fields. Now the three were on their own—two working, one in college studying criminal justice. Never any real problems, only joy watching them and cheering from the sidelines. Never anything close to the heartache he'd felt that day with Ronny, the kid sobbing, hugging him, a boy who'd never known his own father. Christ. That same child's expression looked at him now, a bit sheepish, because they both knew he was holding back.

Mulvaney sighed. Might as well get it over with, he figured.

"You've always been honest with me, Ronny. So I'm gonna ask you to be honest with me again. I know you might think that leaving stuff out is gonna help you or someone else, but it won't. It's Sunday. They've had two days to collect all the information as to where you and Elena were and what happened. Me coming here is not trying to add to your difficulties. Me coming here is trying to give you a chance to get out in front of this thing. You know that, right?"

"We went straight to Hartford."

"You never went to Wells Fargo? Because I know you did."

"Oh, yes, I did. I'm sorry, I forgot about that."

"Why?"

"To cash the check."

"Whose check?"

"My grandmother's check."

"Not Elena's. Okay. Did Grandma give you the check?"

"I took it."

"You tried to cash the check at Wells Fargo, but what happened?"

"They said the signature didn't match."

"What happened to the check?"

"They kept it."

"And where did you go after that?"

"Hartford. That's when we went to Hartford."

"Okay. Keep in mind, I've already talked to pretty much everybody. I talked to Elena. And now I want to hear it from you. So you tried to cash one of your grandmother's checks. Do you remember how much the check was for?"

"Four-fifty."

"Okay. And where was the checkbook?"

"In her room."

"In her room? The checkbook wasn't with you?"

"No, that's right. I had her checkbook."

"But you took it from her room."

"Yeah. The day before."

"How did you get in her room?"

"She has these inflammatory pills that I was taking for my hand. And I went in there and I was like, 'Grandma, can I have some?' She said, 'Yeah.' So I snatched the checkbook from the desk. There's a pile of papers where she does the bills. It was right there on top."

"So you took the checkbook on Thursday?"

"Yeah."

"Okay. Let's go back to Friday. You wake up, you text Dylan, trying to get a ride to cash the check. Elena goes downstairs and gets permission to use the car. Listen, I can tell you that nobody else in the family says you had permission to use that car. Grandma doesn't want you to use the car."

"We've been using the car for months. We just do."

"Okay. Elena comes back upstairs and tells you she got permission. When you go downstairs, where's Grandma?"

"On the couch as usual."

"On the couch. And how do you know that?"

"I glanced over."

"You glanced over and saw her?"

"I didn't really look. I just kind of went down the stairs and headed toward the car."

"When Elena came out to the car, did she lock the door?"

"I don't know. I was on the phone trying to call Dylan."

"What were you trying to call him about?"

"To see what he was doing. See if he wanted to come for a ride."

"Did he want to go for a ride?"

"He didn't answer. I called him, like, five times."

The kid started coughing, straining to breathe. Mulvaney reached over. "You just gotta move the nasal tube." He loosened the device on the kid's face.

"I wish it was laced with enough candy to kill me."

"Listen, Ronny, stay with me. Let's get through this. You left the house. You went to Wells Fargo and tried to cash one of your grandmother's checks. Then where did you go?"

"Evergreen Street, like I told you."

"Did you pawn any jewelry on Friday night?"

The kid stared back at him with those droopy eyes.

"You see how this is working, Ronny? I've done all the legwork on this already. I know it all. I was kind of hoping that by seeing me, you'd just tell me everything on your own."

"Yeah, I did tell you."

Mulvaney gave the kid a look, the disappointed dad look, play-acting. He was letting him down, he was disappointed, he was sad. He felt like a shit doing it, a liar like all actors. *You know the kid,* Hartford had said at five A.M. *You got the prior relationship. He trusts you. He'll talk to you.* All true. But was that any reason for him to do it? Mulvaney could hear them out in the hall: Hartford and IA, their phones ringing and radios squeaking, their voices, their shoes on the floor. They were itching to get in here. Mulvaney, looking at his hands, figured maybe he'd let them take it, hand it over, let them try.

He felt himself frowning for real now, a true disappointment sinking over him. Disgusted with himself. At leaning over the kid's hospital bed with a sippy cup in his hand. What the fuck was he doing? He didn't need that pretty Polish nurse to shame him; he had shamed himself. Like he used to tell his boys: shame is you telling yourself that you did something wrong. Christ, he was tired. He put his head in his hands, lulled by the heat in the ICU. Let the boys in the hall sort it out, he figured.

Then came the kid's raspy voice, startling him: "Is she alive?"

Mulvaney looked up. "Is who alive, Ron?"

"Grandma."

"Why do you ask that, Ron?"

"I just wish I had some candy." The kid tugged again at the nose tube. "I couldn't take it anymore."

"What couldn't you take anymore?"

"The way she treated us. I couldn't take it."

"Explain that to me. How she treated you."

"I was constantly being yelled at for stuff. Like, my grandfather would get drunk and then we'd get yelled at for him being drunk."

"She'd yell at you and Elena for your grandfather?"

"Somebody would leave a drip of water in the sink and we'd get screamed at. Pretty much anything you could think of, we'd get screamed at."

"Why would she scream at you so much?"

"'Cause she was miserable."

"Why was she miserable?"

"I don't know."

"So Grandpa went to work . . ."

"Grandpa went to work. We went downstairs. Grandma was on the couch."

"Was she awake?"

"I don't think she really cared."

"She didn't care?"

"I don't think so. I took a pillow from the couch and put it over her face. We strangled her. Then I got a bag and I put it over her head just to be safe."

"Where'd you get the bag?"

"From the closet."

"In the hallway?"

"Yeah."

"What kind of bag was it?"

"A trash bag."

"What color bag was it?"

"White."

"Did it have a drawstring?"

"Yes."

"What color was that?"

"Blue."

"And you put it over her head? Did you tie the bag?"

"Yes."

"Was Elena in the room with you when you did it?"

"Yes."

"Did she help you with the bag? She did? When you had the pillow over your grandmother's face, did Elena help you with the pillow? She did? What happened after you put the trash bag over your grandmother and tied it?"

"I cleaned out the safe."

"What was in the safe?"

"Jewelry. And coins. Silver dollars. The big ones."

"Was Elena in the room with you at this time?"

"No. I don't know where she was."

"Did you do anything else while you were in that room?"

"No."

"Before that, when you put the pillow on your grandmother's face, I'm assuming your grandmother pushed against it and tried to get the pillow off?"

"No."

"No?"

"No. We just wanted to be safe."

"Was she awake when you put the pillow on her face?"

"Yeah."

"Her eyes were open?"

"Yeah."

"Did she talk to you at all?"

"I said something to her. And then she said something to me."

"Do you remember what you said to her?"

"Something about the weather."

"You were talking to her about the weather? And what did she say back to you?"

"She said, 'More fucking snow.'"

"What was that, Ronny?"

"More fucking snow."

"Is she making any noises or anything, do you remember?"

The kid shook his head, signaling no, or maybe he didn't want to remember what Grandma looked like or sounded like at that point in time. Mulvaney refilled the water glass and held the straw for him. Just a couple of details to iron out, and he would be done for the day. "Ronny, when you left, did you lock the door?"

"Yes."

"Did you leave by a window or did you leave by the door?"

"The window."

"Why did you leave by a window?"

"'Cause I can't lock the door."

"You had to lock it from the inside? Okay. So, after you smothered your grandmother, you got in the car. Did you call Dylan?"

"Yeah, to see if he wanted to go."

"Did you ask him if he knew of any pawnshops that were still open?"

"Yeah. It was like a gas station."

"Did you tell him what happened?"

"Course not."

"Going back to your grandmother on the couch, did you take rings off her fingers, or did Elena?"

"I did."

"How many rings?"

"Three or four."

"Where was Elena when you were taking the rings off her fingers?"

"Upstairs already."

"She was already upstairs? But she was definitely in that room with you and helped you hold that pillow over her head?"

"Yeah."

"Describe the pillow to me."

"It's a black pillow, a black cover on it."

"After you put the bag on her head, did you put another pillow on top of her?"

"Yeah, I just threw it there."

"Were you worried about somebody coming home and finding her like that?"

"No. Grandpa usually doesn't get home till midnight."

"Were you thinking about getting away?"

"No. I was thinking about dying."

"About dying? So, your plan would have ended with the overdose?"

"Yeah. But it wasn't good enough. The dope I copped. Either that or it wasn't enough, I don't know. And now I'm gonna go to jail for all those things."

Mulvaney sighed. That pretty much summed it up. One more question.

"Ron, why did you kill your grandmother?"

"I got sick of her putting me down."

"Why did Elena help you?"

"She didn't help me."

"Was she with you when it happened?"

"No, she was upstairs."

"She was upstairs when it happened? Which one's the truth, Ron?"

"I did it. Elena had nothing to do with it. Turn that off now, please."

Mulvaney clicked off the audio recorder and tucked it in his pocket.

He went to the door. It was a mistake to look back, but he did it anyway, and there was the kid, watching him, his eyes half-expecting something more, some sort of help, a word of encouragement, anything. But Mulvaney simply went out into the hallway and signaled to Hartford, he was all theirs.

A couple of detectives rushed up to him. Did he talk? Did you get it? Mulvaney nodded. "I got it."

Big smiles all around, a few slaps on the back. The lead investigator called to him as he headed to the elevator: "We sent the right guy."

Mulvaney got into the elevator and pressed the ground floor button.

I didn't get no help.

Mulvaney had tried. He really had. After the trial, he'd stopped by a couple of times to check in on the kid, driving out to that brick apartment building on his day off, ringing the bell. Once he brought him a vanilla sundae. He recalled Ronny sitting at the kitchen table, spooning up the ice cream, saying he couldn't sleep at night, he kept having bad dreams. He kept seeing the janitor's closet, the bare lightbulb hanging down from the ceiling on a string, the janitor closing the door behind him, the sound of that heavy bolt locking them in. The room smelled like ammonia, like cleaning supplies. The floor was hard tile. Mulvaney heard him out. Then he assured him that was all over now, he never had to worry again. *We got him. You got him. You did it, Ronny. He'll never* hurt anyone again. *Not you. Not any of the other kids from the neighborhood. No one.* The twelve-year-old looking up at him with those brown eyes: *But how can you be sure?* Mulvaney told him he'd been sentenced to thirty years and the kid jumped up and hugged him, held him tightly and cried onto his uniform, and Mulvaney had patted him gently on the back and tried not to rush him, had told him everything was okay now, it would never happen again, he was clear of all that forever, it was over. He gave him his home number, told him to call anytime. He gave the mother his card too. What else could he do? The professionals had his info, the social service people, they were going to follow up, they had the kid's file, they had the resources, the skills, they would do the rest. Mulvaney was a patrol cop back then, that was his job, answering calls.

His job.

The job took everything, sooner or later. It had ruined everything, his marriage, his peace of mind, his sobriety. It left nothing but scars. The thing he'd done for this kid—the one good thing he'd done on the job, the one pure act—he'd just erased it.

He came out of the hospital into the late afternoon gray. The skies were opening again, the wind kicking up. His windshield was frosted white. Snow.

More fucking snow.

---

*I've often pilfered from my experiences as a lawyer for use in my fiction. As far back as my first year law of school, I read the criminal law casebook "fact patterns" with fascination and awe for their depiction of human pathos—the shipmates in Dudley and Stephens *who killed and ate the cabin boy while adrift on a lifeboat on the high seas; the mother in* King v. Cogdon *who, "in a somnambulistic state," left her bed, fetched an axe from the wood heap, entered her daughter's bedroom, and split her head with the blade of the axe, "thus killing her." In the legal cases I've worked on, source material—depositions, interrogatories, medical reports—often tell a story as compelling as anything by Raymond Chandler. In "Snow over Hartford," I used the form of the police interview in a direct, realistic fashion to reveal a mystery and a tragedy.*

Annie Reed *is the award-winning author of more short stories than she can count. A great many of them are mysteries, although she writes in a wide variety of genres. Her stories appear regularly in* Pulphouse Fiction Magazine *and* Mystery, Crime and Mayhem. *This is her third appearance in a row in* The Best Mystery Stories of the Year, *with her stories "Little City Blues" and "The Promise" appearing in the 2022 and 2023 volumes. Reed is a multiple Derringer finalist, and her short fiction has also been selected for inclusion in study materials for Japanese college entrance exams. She writes novels as well. Her latest is* Road of No Return. *She lives in Northern Nevada.*

DEAD NAMES

Annie Reed

The kid had one of Antonia's old business cards.

He was standing on the concrete walkway outside her second-floor apartment door, waiting for her. He was wearing the unofficial uniform of teenagers who lived on the street: dark hoodie with the hood pulled up over a baseball cap and old jeans. He had on dark boots that probably came from Goodwill or one of the local charities, which told her he didn't have enough money to buy a name-brand pair of athletic shoes.

The hoodie was zipped up, and she was willing to bet he had on a few layers of T-shirts underneath. It was nearly midnight, and the night was cold and wet. It had been raining steadily since she went on shift at the diner at four that afternoon.

She was soaked from her five-block walk home after her shift ended, and she was wearing an old, supposedly waterproof parka that covered the layers of secondhand sweaters she wore over her waitress uniform, not a hoodie.

As she climbed the stairs to the second floor, her knees barking at her thanks to the damp cold, she closed her hand around the can of pepper spray she kept in the pocket of her parka. The kid didn't look dangerous—she'd known too many street kids in her time to assume they were all out to hurt everyone they ran into—but better safe than sorry. It was a hard-earned lesson.

Her neighbor had strung Christmas lights around her front window and had managed to wrap more holiday lights around the rusted banister leading up to the second floor. The lights had large bulbs, the size that had been popular when Antonia was a kid, only these were LEDs, not the old-fashioned glass bulbs that shattered when the neighborhood kids hurled them at the sidewalk.

The overhead lights that were supposed to illuminate the second floor's exterior walkway had been burned out for months. The Christmas lights made her neighbor's apartment look like an oasis of holiday cheer in the midst of a dark, damp cave. Antonia was too tired and wet and sore to have much in the way of holiday spirit, and she didn't have enough extra money to splurge on lights she'd only use once a year.

Her neighbor's Christmas lights not only let her see the kid waiting by her door, now they let her get a decent look at his face. Seventeen, she thought, or a small eighteen. The older she got, the harder it was for her to pinpoint the age of anyone under twenty. He was fine boned with huge dark eyes in a too-thin face. He held out her business card like it was a golden ticket that would get him the hell out of whatever trouble had him waiting for her in the middle of the night.

And he was in trouble. He had bruises blooming on one cheekbone. A fresh scab crossed the bridge of his nose, another one cut across his chin. Both were ragged enough that they might heal into scars he'd carry for the rest of his life, but none of the injuries she could see were life-threatening.

He must have been waiting for her for a while. The overhang above the second-story walkway provided some protection from the weather. His clothes were damp but not slick with rain like hers, and the lank hair sticking out from beneath his hoodie wasn't dripping wet. Either he had more patience than most teenagers she'd known, or he had nowhere else to go. She was betting on the latter.

"What do you want?" she asked when she reached the top of the stairs.

"They said you could help." The hand holding her business card trembled, either from the cold or from sudden doubt.

She didn't ask who *they* were. She knew. *They* were any one of a hundred nameless kids who'd fallen between the cracks of a well-intentioned system that didn't always live up to its lofty ideals.

She used to hand out her business cards like they were candy. "You have any problems or you need anything, you call me," she'd said.

And they had.

So many kids, so many problems adjusting to living on their own in a world no one had prepared them for. She'd tried to help them all. She'd cared for them like the mother so many of them never had, and she'd cried over each and every one of her failures.

On their behalf, she'd butted heads with bureaucrats who hadn't cared. With administrators who put in their time but never read the reports she'd "filed or responded to the requests she'd made or acted on her recommendations.

She'd kept at it, because the kids weren't just names on a piece of paper or numbers on a spreadsheet or line items in a budget already strained to the breaking point. They were *people*, and people always mattered.

She'd kept at it until it ate her up inside. Until doing the job broke her.

"*Please*, Ms. Gonzales," the kid said. "I already tried, and I couldn't . . . I'm not strong enough. They won't listen to me."

I'm not that person anymore, she wanted to scream. Hadn't she already done enough? Hadn't she already given enough?

Couldn't they just leave her alone?

"I can't help you," she said. "You're resourceful. You found me, and I'm not easy to find." She turned away from him. "You'll figure out how to get by."

Her feet hurt, and her hip, the one that had been so badly damaged it had to be replaced, ached with the damp cold. It had taken more effort than it should have to climb the concrete stairs. She needed a hot bath, and then she needed about ten hours' sleep before she faced the next shift at the diner.

At least tips had been good tonight. Tips were always good around the holidays. It was like some little part of most people still believed in Santa Claus, and they wanted him to know they were good one month out of the year.

She'd just slid her key into the lock on her front door when the kid spoke again.

"It's not for me," he said. "It's for my wife. If you can't help us, they're going to kill her."

The kid—he said his name was Aaron—was asleep on her couch. Antonia sat in her secondhand armchair, a garage sale find, and while her neighbor's Christmas lights cast colorful patterns on her threadbare drapes, she considered what—if anything—she could or should do about Aaron and his wife.

After she'd let him inside her apartment, she'd fixed him a can of chicken noodle soup and a PB&J sandwich. While he ate, he'd told her his story.

He was eighteen, he said, and he'd started out life as Amelia. His family had kicked him out at fourteen when he'd finally screwed up the courage to tell them he was trans.

He'd survived on his own for a while on the streets until he'd been picked up by the cops, and from there he'd ended up in the foster system.

"Everybody always called me by my dead name," he said, "but nobody cared that I wouldn't dress like a girl."

Most of the fosters Antonia had worked with were good people. They opened their homes to troubled kids—kids who'd been abandoned or orphaned or been taken away from unfit parents—and they did the best they could. But there were always fosters who were just in it for the paycheck and who treated the kids like commodities. Antonia had worked hard to weed out fosters like that, but her reports never seemed to generate any traction. As long as the kids weren't abused—and Antonia had never been able to prove actual abuse—the fosters were never booted out of the system.

Aaron had ended up with a series of fosters who'd basically treated him like livestock. No care, no love, just a place to sleep and eat and get a new change of clothes every few months. A few were outright hostile, although he claimed none of them had ever punished him because he was trans.

By the time he turned eighteen, he'd wanted *out*, even though he could have stayed in the system longer. The whole foster experience had soured him so badly that he hadn't talked to anyone about the programs available to help him adjust to life on his own. He hadn't trusted anyone associated with the foster system, which told Antonia just how desperate he was. The business card he thought would save him was for Maria Gonzales, a caseworker in the foster system.

Antonia's former name. Her dead name, she supposed, just as much as Amelia was Aaron's.

Her job had been to help kids like Aaron transition to life outside foster care. The program had funds—limited, yes, but available—to help foster kids with college tuition, housing, career counseling. All the things parents might do for their own children. She'd even acted as a liaison between foster kids and potential employers.

Aaron'd had trouble finding a job, even a part-time fast-food job. He had no prior work experience and no permanent address. Thanks to a flyer posted on a streetlight, he'd finally found a job working in a drafty warehouse putting together cheap trinkets, the kind sold to tourists. He worked ten hours a day and was paid in cash at the end of every shift.

Most of the workers were street kids like himself, none younger than sixteen, no one older than twenty. A great many of them had foreign accents and knew very little English.

Aaron's wife was one of those kids.

"Sonia," he said. "She was the prettiest girl I'd ever seen."

He said she didn't mind that he was trans. He told her he planned to get reassignment surgery as soon as he'd saved up enough money.

"She said she'd help me," he said. "That she'd give me some of the money she made. No one's ever offered to do something like that for me."

She said she was eighteen too. She hadn't been born in this country, but she knew a lot of English and was learning more every day.

Soon they started spending every off hour together. Most nights they stayed in one of the homeless shelters in the city—when they could find available space—or in one of the homeless encampments when no shelter space was available. They talked about getting married someday after Aaron had his surgery, and they both agreed to work as hard as they could at the warehouse to make that day happen sooner.

But it turned out they couldn't wait. Antonia wasn't surprised. Teenagers, even patient ones, could only wait just so long for things they really wanted.

One night they found a street preacher outside a strip club and asked if he would marry them. He'd said some words over them, had them kiss each other, and told them they were married.

Antonia didn't mention that the marriage likely wasn't legal for any number of reasons. Their marriage wasn't the problem.

The trouble had started when one of the adults who supervised the kids working in the warehouse offered Sonia a different job.

"He told her it would mean more money," Aaron had said, "so she took it. To help me."

The different job was in a locked back room. Aaron had asked if he could work back there too—more money sounded good to him, no matter what the work was—but the man had told him no. The back room was only for girls. None of the other workers were allowed back there, and the only entrance was guarded by a serious-looking man with a gun.

Aaron said he'd asked Sonia what she did in that room, but she wouldn't tell him. Whatever it was, it made her sad.

"No amount of money was worth that," he'd told Antonia, "so I told her we should just quit and go somewhere else. Find other jobs, you know?"

But Sonia wouldn't leave.

"She said she was working off a debt to the people we worked for. I told her I would pay it for her—I had all that money I'd saved up for my surgery, and she was saving up to help me—but she said it wouldn't be enough. Not to try because it would get her in trouble. But she was so sad, and I love her, and . . ."

He didn't need to say the rest. Antonia knew what must have happened. He'd tried to stand up for the woman he loved, and he'd been beaten for his efforts.

"They told me to forget about her. They called me 'boy' like it was some cuss word, the worst one they could think of." He'd swiped at his cheek with the back of one hand. "They told me they owned her until she was done paying her debt. They won't even let her leave now. I guess they're afraid we'll run away."

Antonia knew these kind of people. Aaron was lucky all he'd gotten was a beating. It could have been much, much worse.

He'd finished the soup and sandwich she'd made for him. By that time he was almost falling asleep at the little two-person table she usually ate at alone in her kitchen. She'd told him to take the sofa for the rest of the night, that she needed time to think things through.

She'd covered him with a blanket before she sat down in her secondhand chair and stared at the soft glow of her neighbor's colorful Christmas lights shining through her threadbare drapes. The lights brought back memories of the Christmases she'd had as a child. Back when she'd been safe and warm and well loved, and the hardest thing in her life come December was waiting for Christmas Day to actually get there so she could see what Santa had left for her.

She'd always had a family when she was a kid. Her parents had stayed together even in tough times, although she hadn't realized exactly how lean some of those years had been until she was much older. She'd been an only child who'd wanted a brother or sister but never had one. She could have ended up spoiled, she supposed, except her parents always took her shopping every year to buy one new toy and leave it in one of the donation bins near the front of the toy store on their way out.

"For children who aren't as lucky as you," her mother told her.

The lesson, hard at first for a child who was certain she deserved to get all the toys in the world for her very own, eventually sunk in. Picking out a new toy for someone else and leaving it behind became easier to do the older she got. Christmas wasn't all about receiving. It was about giving too. About making sure kids who had less than she did knew that someone somewhere cared about them.

That lesson was probably why she'd gone into social work in the first place and had accepted a position working with foster kids.

That's what kept her in the job so long that she'd eventually burned out.

But still she didn't leave until after she'd had a run-in with a man who exploited young men the way the adults Aaron and Sonia worked for exploited teenagers who lived on the streets, and especially the ones who were in this country illegally. Big Man D, as he called himself, was the king of his very own kingdom, a shadow world that existed out of sight of most people who lived and worked in the city.

She'd tried to help some of the older teenagers he recruited—foster kids who were trying to use the resources available to them to break away from this man's influence—but she'd failed. Big Man D caught wind of what she was doing and decided to teach a lesson to any of his people about what happened to anyone who crossed him.

One of his lieutenants had followed her home one night and attacked her in the foyer of her building. He'd beaten her badly, sliced up her belly and the skin over her ribs, and then thrown her down the concrete steps leading up to the entrance to her building.

The only reason she was still alive was because one of her neighbors had come home just in time to see her land on the sidewalk. He'd called the police, and Big Man D's lieutenant had fled.

Antonia had spent a week in the hospital. Her hip had been shattered so badly it had to be replaced, her left arm had been broken in three places, and one of her broken ribs had punctured a lung. She still had scars from the knife wounds that she tried not to look at every time she took a bath.

The message his lieutenant had delivered that night was unmistakable: stay the hell out of my business.

She had. She'd not only quit her job, she'd quit her life. She'd used some of her shadier connections to obtain a new identity. For all intents and purposes, Maria Gonzales—the woman she'd been, the name on her old business card—was dead. Antonia Merin was a waitress who kept her nose out of other people's business, and she never, ever messed with anyone associated with Big Man D.

Until now.

She couldn't turn Aaron away. He was in love, probably for the first time in his life, and he wouldn't stop trying to get to his wife. The men at the warehouse would end up killing him. To them, he was no more a person than he'd been to the fosters who'd treated him like a commodity. They'd probably dump his body somewhere as a warning to everyone else not to mess with them. Antonia would never forgive herself if that happened.

If she didn't help him, no one else would. Not the cops, not the administrators who'd never listened to her. Not the bureaucrats who'd tell her Aaron had blown his window to avail himself of any help the foster system could provide to kids who turned eighteen. To them, Aaron was just a number on a spreadsheet. Hell, some of them might even be paid to look the other way.

She couldn't go against the men at the warehouse on her own. She wasn't a killer. She didn't even own a gun. And without a threat like that, she was just one stupid old woman who still thought she could change the world.

She needed help, and there was really only one person who could help her. One person with enough clout to make the men at the warehouse listen.

The man who'd tried to have her killed.

Big Man D.

She left a note for Aaron on the coffee table in front of the sofa where he slept. She told him she'd be back and to stay put. That she'd have news for him when she got back, but he was not to try to do anything else himself.

She only hoped he'd listen to her. He'd never had an adult go to bat for him in his short life, and he might not entirely trust her now. Especially since she hadn't told him what she planned to do.

The sun wasn't up yet when she got herself a cup of coffee from a twenty-four-hour corner grocery store one block over. The store had made an attempt to decorate for the season—tattered cardboard cutouts of a smiling white Santa who looked straight out of a Coca-Cola ad were pasted onto the front windows beneath the security bars, a two-foot aluminum tree sat on the counter next to a plastic jar of pepperoni sticks, and a few paper snowflakes were suspended from the stained acoustical tile ceiling—but the results looked shabby instead of festive. Like someone had rummaged through the junk from a dead person's storage shed and grabbed whatever was free.

An old, dark-skinned man sat on a stool behind the front counter. He was skin and bones beneath a worn flannel shirt and yellowed undershirt. He rang up Antonia's coffee, and she handed him a five dollar bill and told him to keep the change.

He inclined his head just the slightest as a thank you and scraped the change into the tip jar. He had a fringe of curly white hair around his skull and white stubble on his cheeks. His one nod to the holidays was the black-skinned Santa Claus pin he wore on the navy-blue vest that identified him as an employee.

"You know where the man is these days?" she asked him.

He cocked an eyebrow at her.

"The Big Man," she said.

Now he shook his head. "You don't want to be messing with him, sister, not if you gotta ask where he's at. If he don't know you, he don't want to know you, you know what I mean?"

"He knows me," she said, which was true. "It's just been awhile." Also true.

She caught movement behind her. She turned her head in time to see two teenagers, both Black, emerge from one of the store's narrow aisles and head toward the door. Both of them were wearing black hoodies with the hoods pulled up over black watch caps. Long silver chains hung from their pockets and were attached to their belt loops.

One of them nodded at the old man behind the counter. "Catch you later, Pops," he said.

Pops didn't answer back. He just watched them carry a paper bag out of the store. Neither of the teenagers had paid, and the old man—Pops—didn't try to stop them.

"Tell you what," Pops said to Antonia after the door banged shut behind the teenagers. "You know where Silven's is?"

Silven's was an unlicensed dance club that operated off a back alley eight blocks away. Back when Antonia had been Maria Gonzales, the gang unit used to raid Silven's on a regular basis. She would usually be assigned to work with any of the street kids who'd been caught in the club and who hadn't given the cops any reason to arrest them and send them off to juvie.

"I used to," she said, and gave the old man the name of the alley. At least the name the alley had been called years ago.

"You ain't lying when you said it's been awhile," Pops said. "The kids call that alley Kingdom Road now because the king calls it home." He glanced at a round security mirror over Antonia's head, probably to make sure they were alone. He still leaned forward toward Antonia and lowered his voice. "I hear tell there's a door at the end of that alley, got a faded old dragon sticker on it. If the man's anywhere, that's where he'll be."

That didn't make sense. The last place a man like Big Man D would hang out would be next to a club that got raided all the time.

"Next to Silven's?" she asked. "You sure?"

"I know what you're thinking, but no one raids the club anymore. The kids tell me the man cleaned the place up."

"You believe them?"

Pops leaned back and shifted his butt on the stool. "I believe the cops don't raid there anymore, and that's all I care to believe. Now I think you've about used up the rest of that five you gave me, so I'll wish you a Merry Christmas and a safe New Year, you hear?"

She did. She thanked him and took her coffee. She had an eight-block walk in front of her, but at least the city streets were still just wet. Christmas was a week away, and the prospects of snow before then were slim. She'd loved the few years the city got snow for Christmas when she'd been a kid. It made everything look so pretty, at least for a little while. Now that she was older—much older—and had to walk everywhere, snow was more an annoyance than anything else. But the rain made everything look dirty and damp, especially the garbage that always seemed to accumulate in the gutters and at the base of the buildings.

She made it three blocks before a black SUV pulled up to the curb alongside her. The back door opened and one of the teenagers she'd seen in the corner grocery store got out.

She dropped her coffee and fumbled for the pepper spray in the pocket of her parka, but her fingers were stiff from the damp. The teenager got to her just as she was pulling the canister free. He knocked it from her hand, and the canister clattered to the street.

"Don't be doing that, Granny," the kid said. "It ain't polite, or don't you know that?"

Granny. Just like the guy behind the counter had been Pops. Anonymous names meant to depersonalize. The kid was just a teenager, but he was stone cold. He'd just as soon wring her neck as talk to her, but someone else was pulling his strings.

The kid ushered her to the back of the SUV and opened the door. No light came on inside the car when the door opened, and the sun wasn't up yet, so she couldn't see inside. It didn't matter. She already knew who waited for her.

"I hear you been looking for me," Big Man D said. "Why don't you climb in my office, and we can have a talk."

Big Man D got his name naturally. He was three-hundred-fifty pounds at least, and most of it was muscle. He must have been well over six feet tall, the way his legs seemed to fill all available space in the back of the SUV.

Antonia had never seen him in real life, only in surveillance photographs taken by the gang unit, and he'd looked monstrously big then.

In person?

He sucked all the air out of the SUV, or at least that's how it seemed to her. She was having trouble breathing, and all the old injuries hurt. The scars on her ribs and belly where his lieutenant had knifed her burned, and her hip was screaming.

The kid had slammed the SUV's door behind her, and the driver took off before Antonia could think about bailing out of the SUV. If she could even move fast enough to hurl herself out of the SUV before Big Man D latched onto her with one meaty hand and pulled her back inside.

This was what she'd wanted, wasn't it? To talk to the man?

She just hadn't planned on having the conversation in a moving SUV but in a building with an escape route where she had a chance of surviving the encounter.

"What's your name, Granny?" Big Man asked.

Again with Granny. "You knew me as Maria Gonzales." Her dead name sounded strange after not using it for years, but she wasn't about to give him the name she went by now.

He whistled low. "Man, I thought you were dead. How come I ain't heard you still around here?" As he said that last bit, he glanced at the man in the front passenger seat, a skinny Black man in a charcoal overcoat darker than his skin.

"She dropped off the radar," the man said. "Quit messing around your business, D. She got the message." He shrugged. "We let her alone."

Those last words chilled Antonia to the bone. They knew where she was, who she'd become. They could have reached out to her at any time. Killed her on her way home from work if they wanted to, and make it look like a random mugging. But they'd let her alone because she'd left them alone.

She had to say what she'd come here to tell the Big Man—D, his lieutenant had called him—just the right way. Make him understand she wasn't the one messing in his business now.

At least she hoped it wasn't his business. She'd find out soon enough if the sweatshop where Aaron and Sonia worked was one of his subsidiaries.

The driver made a left at the next intersection. They were headed to the heart of D's territory, they had to be. There was little traffic on the streets—too early yet for commuters who'd be arriving in the city by train, and nobody drove into the city, parking being as expensive as it was. D's eyes glittered in the scant light from street-lights and stoplights as he turned his gaze back to her.

"So I got to wonder why you here," D said.

She started to speak, and realized she'd have to clear her throat first. When she tried again, her voice came out steadier than she'd thought it would.

"Because I found out someone else was messing in your business," she said. "Working out of a warehouse in your territory—"

"Whole city's my territory," he said, interrupting her. "My kingdom be vast, my holdings many."

"They're using kids to prep drugs for distribution," she said.

She didn't know that for sure, but from what Aaron had told her, that's what made sense to her. The girls weren't being prostituted, not in a locked back room where no one was allowed to go. But grown men who exploited children always thought girls were easier to intimidate. Teenage boys, with all those hormones raging through them, would be too hard to control.

"Street kids," she said. "Immigrants." She didn't say *illegal*; the whole damn operation was illegal. "I thought you should know."

D went very still. He was still staring at her, but he was like a big black hole, taking everything in and letting nothing show.

His lieutenant had turned around enough in his seat that he was looking directly at D. He wasn't as careful with his expression. He was clearly concerned, and she'd bet it wasn't just because of what she'd said. He was worried about how his boss would react.

Which meant they hadn't known about the operation in the warehouse.

"Why?" D asked her. "Why you tell me this?"

Now came the tricky part. She couldn't schmooze this man. Flatter him and lie to him in the hopes he'd give her what she wanted. He'd see through the bullshit. With a man like him, she had to stick to the truth.

"I want to get two of the kids out," she said. "I want to get all of the kids out, but I'll settle for two. I can't do that on my own."

"And you can't sic the cops on them 'cause ICE come down on those kids like the wrath of God." D laughed, an ugly, self-indulgent sound that made the hair on the back of her neck stand up and shivers that had nothing to do with the cold run down her spine. "So you find me 'cause you know I be protecting my kingdom from people don't think they need the king's okay to set up their little business."

Now he nodded his massive head. He'd shaved his skull clean since the last surveillance photos she'd seen. His scalp had little bumps and indentations and an old scar over one ear that she saw when the SUV passed beneath a stoplight.

"You thought right," he said when he stopped laughing. "You give my man here the location of this warehouse and the names of the kids, and we'll get your kids out."

"In one piece," she said, knowing she was pushing her luck. "These kids aren't part of—"

He held up a hand, interrupting her again. "These kids, they ain't innocents or they wouldn't work sticking that shit in whatever they're packing it into."

She disagreed with that. Street kids did what they had to do to survive, just like the homeless did, but she wasn't going to argue with him.

She'd told him she wanted two kids out because she was pretty sure Aaron would be gone by the time she got back. And if he wasn't? If he'd actually waited for her? Then D's men could get another boy out. Another one who was smart enough to tell D's men his name was Aaron.

"You bring me this information, I get your kids out," D said. "Then what? You gonna snitch to the cops 'bout what we gotta do?"

He was telling her they'd terminate the warehouse operation in a lethal way. She knew her life depended on her answer, if not now, then later. But she couldn't lie.

"No kids die," she said, "I don't say anything to anybody."

She didn't have to say the rest. If any kids died, she'd go to the cops. Tell them it was D's men who did whatever he was going to do to the men who ran the warehouse operation. Who kept kids like Sonia working behind locked doors guarded by men with guns.

If D let her live that long.

He went quiet again, and she knew he was thinking things through. A man like D had a lot of assets. No doubt some of them he could burn, others he couldn't. He was the king, and the king was planning to go to war.

All because a former foster kid loved his wife and couldn't leave her behind.

As far as Antonia was concerned, the reason was worth the cost.

"Must be the damn season," D said. "All this shit about good cheer and your fellow man rotted my brain." He shook his head and slapped his thigh. The slap sounded like a rifle shot. "Rudolph and all that shit," he said again. "And one old lady who came back from the dead. If that ain't Christmas, I don't know what is."

He held out his hand to her, the intent clear. She hesitated only a moment before she took it to shake on their deal.

But before he let her go, he pulled her in close. Close enough that she could smell onions and fried food on his breath.

"You mess with me on this, you better disappear for good this time, you understand, *Antonia*?"

Hearing her new name coming from that mountain of a man shook her to her core, but she didn't let it show.

"I don't go back on my deals," she said. "And we just made one."

A deal with the devil. The lesser of two evils. All the old sayings went through her brain, but she kept looking him in the eye. She wanted him to know she meant what she said.

He laughed again as he let go of her hand. "I like you, Granny, I do. You tell me where to let you out, and my man here, he take you there."

She could tell them to take her home and they'd do that. It would save her a long walk through the cold, dark streets, but she didn't want to do that. Even though they knew where she lived, she didn't want them anywhere near her apartment. She needed her little illusions of safety. She needed her anonymity, even if it was false.

She needed her hope.

And she needed to get out of this SUV before she lost the fragile hold she had on her nerves.

"Here's fine," she said.

The SUV pulled over to the curb in front of a bus stop, and the man in the front passenger seat got out to open her door.

He gave her his hand to help her climb down from the back seat. She thought about ignoring it, then thought about how the kid—one of D's runners, no doubt—had knocked the can of pepper spray from her hand. How he'd told her it wasn't polite. When you were in the presence of a king, politeness mattered.

She took D's lieutenant's hand and let him help her down. Big Man D didn't say anything else to her, but his lieutenant wished her a Merry Christmas. She said it back automatically just like she said it to all her customers at the diner.

As the SUV pulled away, its taillights flashing red in the pre-dawn darkness, her knees finally gave out. She sat down heavily on the bus stop bench, amazed that she was still alive. Frightened by what she'd just set in motion. And scared most of all for the kids that would be caught in the middle.

Big Man D hadn't promised his men wouldn't hurt the kids, but he knew the stakes. So did she. She hoped she hadn't just shook hands on her own death warrant, but if Aaron and Sonia got out alive—if all the kids got out alive—it would be worth it.

She had to believe it would be worth it.

She was still trying to convince herself when a city bus pulled to a stop and she climbed on, ready for the bus to take her back home.

Christmas Day dawned bright and cold.

Antonia sat by herself at her kitchen table, nursing a cup of coffee, reading yet another report on her old laptop about a gangland shooting the night before. Police had been called to an abandoned warehouse shortly after midnight only to find the bodies of four adults, all killed execution style. Unnamed sources told reporters that the warehouse had been used as a distribution center for fentanyl, but police refused to comment on the ongoing investigation.

No one had seen the shooters, they'd only seen teenagers fleeing the scene.

None of the reports Antonia had read said anything about teenagers being among the dead.

Big Man D had been good to his word. He'd shut the operation down without killing any of the teenagers the men kept locked in the warehouse overnight.

Antonia hoped that Aaron had finally been reunited with Sonia. He'd been gone, of course, when she finally got back to her apartment from her nerve-racking meeting with Big Man D. Aaron hadn't left her a note, but he had locked up her apartment on his way out.

She felt empty and a little sad. She'd only been thanked occasionally by the kids she'd helped back when she'd been known by her dead name. She shouldn't have expected anything more from Aaron. Kids like Aaron lived according to their own rules, and street kids only had one rule: stay alive.

She shouldn't be drinking coffee this late—or this early, depending on how she looked at it. The diner had closed up early the night before, and she'd been back at her apartment before eleven. No snow had fallen on Christmas Eve, so no white Christmas. But her neighbor had a fully lit Christmas tree now in her living room window that was neatly framed by all the Christmas lights. It reminded Antonia of home and her parents, both long dead now, and how they'd stayed up late on Christmas Eve drinking hot chocolate and listening to her dad read the last few pages of *The Polar Express*.

Instead of going to bed, she'd bought a copy of *The Polar Express* online and read it on her computer. That's how she'd found out about the warehouse shooting. It had been headline news when she'd gone to turn her computer off and go to bed.

She really should go to bed. She was going to be dead on her feet tonight at the diner if she didn't get at least a few hours' sleep.

The soft knock on her door came as a surprise. She wrapped her sweater around herself as she went to peek out her threadbare drapes.

A teenager stood in front of her door. It wasn't Aaron but a slight young girl in a puffy hooded coat that needed washing.

Antonia's breath caught in her throat. Was this Sonia?

She opened the door as far as the security chain allowed.

The girl had vivid blue eyes and the kind of smooth complexion a teenager shouldn't have if she lived on the street without benefit of all the creams and cleansers advertisers insisted were necessary to keep skin clear and healthy. Her hair was long and ash blonde, and when she smiled at Antonia, the smile lit up her entire face.

Aaron had been right. She was the prettiest girl Antonia had seen in a long time.

"Ms. Gonzales?" the girl said.

"Just a minute." Antonia closed the door only long enough to remove the security chain. This time she opened the door wider. "That's me," she said. "Or who I used to be. And you're Sonia?"

The girl looked confused, but she nodded. "I don't understand 'used to be,'" she said. "My English is getting better, but I have trouble with . . ." She paused for a moment. "Idioms," she finally said. "Aaron, he teaches me, and I'm trying to learn."

"I think you're doing great," Antonia said, and she meant it.

Sonia shifted to glance over her shoulder. Antonia saw Aaron standing at the base of the stairs, keeping watch on the street.

"We're leaving," Sonia said. "Going to a new city. We have enough money for bus fare, and Aaron, he says we'll be safe if we start over new somewhere else."

That might not be true. Antonia hoped it would be, but she'd helped them as much as she could. The foster system wouldn't help them at all, and Big Man D had been right about one thing. If Sonia was undocumented, ICE would deport her in a heartbeat.

"We wanted to wish you Merry Christmas and to thank you," Sonia said.

"That's nice, but it's not—"

Antonia was going to say it wasn't necessary, but Sonia interrupted her by surprising her with a hug. Strong and tight, like she didn't want to let Antonia go.

Antonia patted the girl's thin back, surprised at the moisture that sprang to her eyes. "You both take care of each other for me. That will be thanks enough."

"We will," Sonia said, finally pulling away.

Antonia gave her a serious look. "Promise?"

Sonia nodded. "Aaron, he take good care of me. He's good husband."

She turned and smiled at him. The expression that stole over his face was nothing short of breathtaking.

Sonia left without another word, but Aaron gave Antonia a wave before they both disappeared down the street.

Antonia shivered as she shut her front door. The walls in her apartment building were thin, and from her neighbor's apartment, she heard the first notes of a familiar Christmas carol.

Maybe she'd make herself a mug of hot chocolate before she went to bed. She might even go to a few shops and see what decorations went on sale tomorrow. She might even find an artificial tree on clearance. She could put it away for next year. Decorate it and put it in her window.

Create a second oasis of holiday cheer in the dark cave of her neighborhood.

It wasn't like she had to hide from Big Man D and his lieutenants anymore. She wouldn't go back to using her dead name, but she could finally start living a real life.

If that wasn't a Christmas miracle, she didn't know what was.

Often an image becomes the initial spark for a story. It's usually a picture I see online somewhere, but in the case of "Dead Names" it was something I saw while I was driving one rainy December night: a single strand of Christmas lights illuminating a portion of the second-story railing of a rundown apartment building. No other part of the complex had any holiday decorations. No Christmas trees in apartment windows, no wreaths on doors. Even most of the lights in the complex's parking lot had burned out.

When I sat down to write a hardboiled story for an anthology invite, I couldn't get the image of those Christmas lights out of my mind. The holidays aren't an easy time for everyone, but someone in that apartment complex was trying. Even if it was only the one strand of lights they'd wound around an iron railing, they were trying. When everything seems dark and bleak and hopeless, sometimes trying is the best anyone can do. That thought, along with the image of those lights, gave me the start to this story.

Cameron Sanders *was born in Jasper, Indiana. He graduated from Indiana University with a BFA in creative writing. Shortly after graduating, he published his first short story, "Billowing Down the Bayou," in* The Greensboro Review. *Sanders currently lives in Indianapolis, Indiana, where he is working on editing his first full-length novel. He can be contacted at cameronsandersauthor@gmail.com.*

BILLOWING DOWN THE BAYOU

Cameron Sanders

Mama always says you can't outswim the bayou, not since The Billows came a billowing. She says the dust brewing up North meant mud clumping down South and before she knew it the rivers in these parts started looking like landslides. Unless you're a catfish, Mama says you won't be swimming long under these waters.

Mama says she ain't the smartest of mamas, but she knows an awful lot more than me, and she knew life before The Billows, so she could probably be one of them doctors she talks about—the ones she said could chop off your leg and keep you upright walking. She taught me everything I know, and she still got stuff up there that I haven't even heard of. Mama's got an answer for anything, but she don't much like to talk about life before The Billows. She says things were just as bad before the clouds started turning to dust, but at least now she's got her little duckling girl to watch over.

Mama says a night like tonight would've looked *heavenly* back then. We're only supposed to use that word for things that remind you of the Bible, something only God could make. Can you believe that the frogs used to go *ribbet*? Just like that too: *ribbet ribbet ribbet.* Loud enough to block out the crickets, Mama says. But them tongues of theirs must've stuck to too much dirt and packed them full of mud because all they're doing now is coughing like Mama does when she forgets to cover her mouth before heading outside.

The moon's doing its best to light up the night but even then the water doesn't quite do it justice no more. The water looks thick enough to walk on, but Mama says only Jesus can do that sort of stuff and that I'm not allowed to try it. She's just looking out for her Lil Duckling, and I know that. But even Jesus had a group of friends, and I ask Mama every day if I can have a little baby sister or a little baby brother and all she says is that "there aren't no more Daddies 'round here no more." Mama says too many people went swimming, and she tried to stop them, but nobody would listen. Even my Daddy must've gone swimming because I ain't ever seen him. The waters don't remember much of all it's eaten, else I'd ask if Daddy is down there swimming. Mama says nobody's down there, and if there were, the crocs would've eaten them up by now. When Mama gets real mad she says she's gonna throw me in too. Mama don't look that strong, but I know she could if she wanted. Sometimes I get to wondering if Mama threw them all over. She says they never were nice to her and that's why she don't want no more neighbors. Mama does what's right, so if God said to do it, I know she would. I bet I would too if God went around talking to me.

I think the Lord must've been listening to my prayers every night. Don't tell Mama, but I prayed for a little baby every night before bed—even wished on a star and Mama says only witches wish, but I figured God made the stars so wishing was his work too. And that's when it happened. On a night much like tonight, I saw it coming toward us—a little basket rocking back and forth across the bayou. It was bobbing in and out of the trees, and I swore it was one of my swimming neighbors finally coming up for a breath of fresh air. But no siree, that there was little baby Moe. Mama says that in the Bible the princess of Egypt found baby Moe on the river, so that must mean me and Mama are princesses. *Royalty,* she says—something so special that God would send down a little baby of our own.

I knew it must have been my baby brother the moment I saw him. I ain't ever heard a baby cry before then, but I heard his *goo*

goo and his bawling, and I swear he was trying to say, "Hey Big Duck, come and pick me up!" Mama wouldn't let me hold him. She says only mamas can hold babies and that I'm only six and that's too young to be a mama. But I think she forgot how old I am because she keeps saying I'm six every year, and I remember I started counting on two hands a while ago, so I must be at least eight. And eight is plenty big; big enough to hold baby Moe. He's a little bread loaf and Mama has me carry those around all the time.

Even though I can't carry him around even now, I still sneak a peek at him whenever I can—when he's not locked up in Mama's room. She don't like it when I call him my brother. She don't like it when I call him anything. Baby Moe's got big blue eyes, the kind of blue I think Mama talks about when she says the sky was blue before The Billows came. He's a pale little thing though: Mama says he's sick and that's why he's not like us. She says The Billows in the North must have rubbed him dry until his skin just started falling off. Moe don't look very sick. He smiles and laughs whenever I make faces at him, and when Mama takes our little boat out across the waters, I try to tell him stories. He never once cries whenever I tell him stories. Whenever I tell him about the neighbors under the bayou, he's really listening, straight-faced and all. I betcha he could tell you those same stories if he could talk, that's how well he was listening. I could even see his shriveled lips moving to match mine. He probably saw our neighbors on his way floating over here. Probably was waving to all the little fishes and the old neighbors, and I bet he learned from them what really happened. Mama says all the neighbors went swimming and never came up, but I bet Moe knows the truth. If that boy could start talking I know what he'd say. He'd say, "Hey Big Duck, your Mama went and dunked them all because she was scared they'd make things go back to normal." There's no way that boy was sick.

Mama wouldn't listen though, so I said, "Mama, baby Moe is just fine. He ain't coughing or crying, he's just a little pale baby." But she says that she's seen pale babies before and they never turn out right. That's when Mama showed me her back. She stripped down naked, and I thought she was gonna go take a bath, but she told me, "Let me see your hand. You feel that, those bumps?

What's that feel like to you, huh Duck?" Now I didn't know what to say. I'd seen these lines every time Mama took a bath and I'd always try to play tic-tac-toe with my fingers, so I didn't know what else Mama wanted me to say. But she said, "This right here was a pale baby all grown up, and they don't do much but hurt you."

Mama almost started crying when she said it too. Mama never talks about the times before The Billows. She always says things were worse back then, and she's always acting scared that I'll learn what the world was like. She's just trying to keep her Lil Duckling safe. "This right here is what happens when you aren't doing what your Mama says, you hear me, Duck?" And I heard her. She only got the switch out when I wasn't doing what I was told or when I'd try and push the boat out all by myself. Mama never liked that; she said I wasn't strong enough, but I knew I was. I'd practiced on the dock and had my own little pushing stick and all. I'd stab it deep into the mud and jump, just high enough that my feet were off the ground like I was flying, and I'd fall back down on the dock. But she still wouldn't let me, and when she caught me practicing, she spanked me harder than I ever had been spanked before. I swear I must've been bleeding for a day. That's when Mama told me all about the doctors and how they could chop off your leg and you wouldn't feel a thing. Mama wasn't no doctor. I felt everything.

The first time I heard Mama call the baby, Moe, was when she told me that she knew a way to fix him up. She still swore he was sick, but if The Billows had rubbed his skin pale and dry then The Billows could put it all back together again. It was God's plan she kept saying, *God's plan*. She picked up Moe, carried him off into our little rowboat, and had me follow along behind her. I didn't get to leave our dock often—it was my little island. The sway the boat made whenever I stepped in never got old. It makes my belly do somersaults even just thinking about it. Every time I stepped foot on that boat I saw something I never had before: a new star, a new tree, a new dock that was long forgotten. How far did Mama have to go before she found our food? She says when I'm older I'll be allowed to go out and visit the world. There's a city downriver that Mama says has all the food in the world, yet she only ever brings back scraps enough for the two of us. *A pale baby all grown up did this.* Mama thinks everything is too dangerous for me. I think Mama thinks I'm dumb. Maybe I am, but she's taught me everything I know, so I can't say for sure.

For the first time ever, I got to hold Moe on that boat ride. Mama says I got to make sure the winds stay out of his face and that he is sick enough as is. I love it when I get to wear the goggles Mama got me because I only put them on for special occasions like going out on the boat. Mama says the dust isn't bad enough around our house to need them, the trees blocking out as much as they can, but on the water, the sky can open up.

The night was getting too dark to see, or maybe it was still morning and Mama had woken me up to head out on the water before the sun had risen. The thing about the moon is that it never has as much of a glare as the sun does. It meant I could see out my goggles just fine. I was supposed to be covering up Moe's eyes too, but I couldn't help but keep that pale face of his uncovered to see those blue eyes. It got me thinking: how come Mama knew pale babies before The Billows if The Billows were what made them pale? Now that just don't make no sense to me. And you could tell Moe was studying my face just as hard, trying to figure out who I was now that I had these big honking circles protecting my eyes from The Billows. I probably looked like a swamp ghoul to him, but all he did was reach up and try and pry them off my face. Instead, he managed to grab a fistful of my curls and tried his best to pull me down to him. My little brother was tough. I bet he could push the boat way before I could. I could feel his lips moving underneath my hand, the one that was keeping the dust out. His muffled cooing didn't make much sense to Mama, but that's because his words were only for me. "Big Duck, I ain't sick. Don't let our Mama do this."

"Mama, why we taking Moe this far out?" Mama didn't quite like it when I talked out of turn like that. She said it meant I was trying to boss her around. I only gotta speak when she speaks to me.

"Hmm, what you mean, Duck? Trust your Mama, will ya? I'm just doing what the Lord thinks is right." Mama was leaning over the boat to take those huge pushes she does with her stick to move us a bit faster. Back before The Billows, Mama says she could use a paddle to row the boat. Now she's stuck to pushing us around. Mama says they do it like this in some big ol' fancy cities, where they have tiny boats filled with mamas and daddies kissing on the water. When I was a kid, she'd kiss me on the forehead telling me stuff like that. Only the best for her Lil Duckling.

"I trust you Mama, but why we out like this at night? You told me the sun keeps the bad guys away. Mama, I can't hardly see nothing out here. What if we run into some of those bad guys?"

"When has your Mama ever let you get hurt?"

She was the only person who was ever there to hurt me.

"You ain't gonna hurt baby Moe, are you?" Moe kept his mouth moving under my hand like he was whispering secrets into my palm. Moe knows that something is wrong. He won't stop talking about it.

"We are going to fix the baby, Lil Duckling. You have to trust me."

"Mama, you ain't gonna hurt my little brother, are you?" The chirping crickets held their breath waiting for a response.

"Duckling, please don't you start your crying."

"Tell me you ain't gonna hurt him."

"Remember what your Mama said about doing what you're told? Remember your Mama's back? You remember that, Duck?" Mama was stabbing at the mud now more than she was pushing.

"Mama, Moe ain't sick."

"You've never seen a pale boy like that. You don't know what sick is, Duck. Look at your own skin and tell me whether that's pale or not."

"Mama, you're wrong!"

"What did you just say to me?" She wasn't pushing the boat anymore.

"You're wrong! My little brother ain't sick!"

"That *thing* is not your brother. Give him to your Mama now." Mama was hobbling across the boat toward me, rocking it side to side as she moved. Her eyes and teeth were the only things visible against the moonlight.

I shrugged away from her, diving against the floor of the row-boat, Moe tucked under my chest.

"You listen to me now, Duck. Give me that *thing*. Else your back will look worse than mine, you hear me little girl?" Mama was pulling at my hair, trying to raise my body off the baby. The boat was swaying as much as it could atop the muddy bayou. Thick waves rolled over the sides of the boat, like dirty fingers reaching in along the edges.

"Mama, please . . ." She was hurting me. I felt strands of my hair being ripped from my scalp, one by one, as Mama's grip got tighter. The strap of my goggles was the only thing keeping her from wrenching my head back.

"Listen to your mother!"

I couldn't hold her back much longer. Tears were running down my face and my goggles were fogging from my own breath. Moe was screaming and crying for help; I know he was. Mama pounced on top of me, turning me over. For a moment I thought she'd rip Moe in half if I didn't give in to her pulling.

Mama clenched the baby in her hands. Moe was still crying as she held him an arm's length away from her, dangling him over the water.

"Lil Duckling, you have to understand. The pale baby is sick. The Billows brushed him of all his color. Let the bayou wash it all back over him. He'll be right back, dear. Just a quick dip. Like in the Bible, Duck. Don't you remember John? Your brother will be right back, brand new and fixed. Trust your mother."

Moe was right. There was something wrong. Something wrong with this night and every night. There was something wrong with Mama.

I didn't mean to hit her as hard as I did. I was only trying to make her turn around, to get her attention. She turned around all right, as if she was stumbling back around to catch her balance. Moe fell from her hands and plopped onto the floor of the boat. He was screaming, but I knew he was cheering me on, not crying.

Mama took one last look into my eyes before her heel hit the side of the boat and she started looking straight up at the stars. She hung there long enough to count all of them. And then she was crashing into the waters. The waves weren't as big as I had imagined they'd be. The mud must have contained them. Mama was shouting the best she could, but all I could think about was how the frogs used to go *ribbet*. Just like frogs, I couldn't hear her over the crickets. I was holding Moe now, rocking him back and forth, doing my best to soothe his screams. There was a bump on his head from the fall. If only we had one of those doctors Mama talked about. Maybe the town knows.

Mama had taught me everything I knew.

Most were lies.

But she was right about one thing: unless you're a catfish, you won't be swimming long under these waters. Nobody outswims The Billowed bayou.

I first started creating the Billows universe as an anthology for my university writing assignments. I loved the interconnectivity of a singular world because it was what most resembled a novel—which has always been my true aspiration. The Billows revolves around an alternate-history United States, in which an apocalyptic dust bowl interrupts the Civil War and turns most of the nation blind. I have always been fascinated by the voodoo culture that sprung out of New Orleans and wanted to find a way to blend it with the Billows in this aptly named short story, "Billowing Down the Bayou." This is my first story published, and I am honored to have it included among the stories of such incredibly talented authors.

Anna Scotti *recently began a perhaps permanent hiatus from a twenty-year teaching career, in order to focus on writing—including writing a screenplay based on the character featured in these pages. This is Scotti's second inclusion in* The Best Mystery Stories of the Year—*the first was "A Heaven or a Hell" (2022), also first published in* Ellery Queen Mystery Magazine. *In 2023, Scotti's short story, "Schrödinger, Cat" was a finalist for both the ITW "Thriller" Award and the Macavity Award, and received a third-place Readers Choice Award from* EQMM. *The same year, her unpublished short fiction collection,* They Look Like Angels, *was a finalist for the Killer Nashville Claymore Award. In addition to mysteries, Scotti writes poetry and young adult fiction. Watch for stories coming up in* EQMM *and in* Sherlock Holmes Mystery Magazine. *Find her at annakscotti.com.*

IT'S NOT EVEN PAST

Anna Scotti

Vindi whined and pawed at the door. I groaned, rolling out of Marta's big fluffy guest bed, which triggered a cloud of lavender scent to rise from too-soft pillows. As my feet sunk into Marta's adorable lemon-patterned bedside rug, I missed everything about my spare little pool house—the hard bed, the bare floor, and most of all, the privacy.

"Go on," I told the big dog. She darted into the hall without a glance backward. Vindi, my irritable and decidedly ungrateful rescue greyhound, had finally found her person. It sure as hell wasn't me; Vindi barely tolerated me, treating her brother Meme with discernible disdain when he lay at my feet or danced at the door with his leash in his mouth. No, for no real reason I could ascertain, Vindi had decided that Marta's younger son, Diego, was her personal ward. She tracked him through the house, guarded the stairs that he was too young to go up and down alone, and licked crumbs off his face and hands at every opportunity. Diego loved her back in the rather brutal way of toddlers, and I winced every time he sunk his little hands into her short coat or grasped her bony tail, trying for a ride. But Vindi showed no aggression at all, simply shaking Diego loose as necessary, then nuzzling his head or licking his cheeks. Diego's big brother, Tony Jr., liked Vindi too, but she mostly ignored him. As for the six-foot, black-haired, green-eyed master of the domain, Antonio Sr., he didn't have an opinion about Vindi, because he was stuck in my pool house with only Meme for company.

COVID had slammed Santa Monica hard; my landlord had recovered from an early bout, though his restaurant hadn't. When Chez Jason closed, fourteen employees lost their jobs. With no vaccine in sight and Marta expecting their third child, Tony had reluctantly decreed that he'd have to move in with a roomie for the duration. His job as a homicide detective simply involved too much contact with the unwashed, unmasked public. It was Marta who'd suggested that Tony and I trade houses. My employer, Kennerly Prep, had put all the teachers' aides on furlough at the start of the pandemic, and Marta didn't like the idea of my being alone for however many weeks or months quarantine might last. Besides, she'd argued, Tony would pay my rent, and I could help her with the kids. As children of an essential worker, they were eligible to attend day care, but Marta had laughed scornfully when Tony told her that.

I'd said no, initially, but Marta is a lot easier to say no to than her husband. He took my hand, gazed into my eyes, and I found myself mumbling agreement with every fool thing he said, just to get away with my honor—and my friendship with Marta—intact.

So Tony got my digs, my dog, my luxury-free way of life, and somebody to watch over his wife and kids, while I got a comfortable room, a private bath, pool access, and Marta's superb home cooking. I hated it. I loved her and the boys, but with everyone yapping nonstop on TV and the internet about an epidemic of loneliness, most days I wanted nothing more than a few hours—or weeks—alone. Tony and Marta's suite was on the ground floor, along with baby Diego's room, but little Tony was upstairs next to me, and he got out of bed several times each night, wanting a snack or a hug or needing—God help me—fresh pajamas. I tried to handle it when I could; Marta was getting big to run up and down those stairs. But my job at Kennerly had been with middle-schoolers. I'd never been around little kids much, and they require a different kind of patience.

Marta had the boys at the table when I came downstairs. Little Tony was munching happily on waffles while Diego slipped bits of his under the table to Vindi, who sat with her head resting on his plump knee.

Marta turned from the sink, one hand cupped comfortably under the mound of her belly. Just six months along, she was so slender that she looked like she had a basketball tucked under her loose T-shirt. "Morning, Cam! Are you ready for—hey! What's wrong?"

I shook my head. "Nothing's wrong. Just coffee, please, Marta."

She poured me a cup and motioned for me to sit down.

"I'm thinking of taking a little road trip. Camping. Just one or two nights. You'll be okay with the kids, won't you?"

Marta shrugged. "I'm a cop's wife," she replied, as if that were answer enough. And I supposed it was, given Tony's crazy hours. She was used to going it solo.

"But where can you go? Everything's closed, Cam. The whole country."

I nodded. "State parks are closed. But federal lands, they never close. And they're not policed. I'll just throw a bedroll in my car and I'll be all set."

Marta looked doubtful.

"I'm not gonna bother anybody," I assured her. "I just need a little space. I'll be back before you know it."

I hadn't always been a loner; once I'd had a family, a fiancé, a best friend, and a host of coworkers at my dream job at the fabled Harold Washington Library in Chicago. That had all ended when said fiancé murdered said best friend, with whom he'd been playing slap and tickle, as they say, behind my back. In the years since, I'd become someone very different from the nerdy girl whose biggest fear was defending her dissertation before a committee of PhDs. Life in WITSEC was supposed to end someday, when the government had enough on my former fiancé and his backers to put *all* the honchos away forever. Until then, I was on pause, and I'd learned to live without many of the things I'd once held dear.

I wasn't allowed to visit any of my old haunts, not only Chicago, but also all the places where I'd tried to make a go of it so far. Even my hometown was on the no-fly list, although there would scarcely be anyone there to recognize me now. I didn't care. I just wanted the road and some wide-open space.

I hopped on PCH and headed down the coast, thinking maybe I'd find a beach in Orange County and catch a few waves before heading inland.

The parking lot at Huntington was closed, but I found a spot on the street and made my way across the broad, white beach to the sparkling water. Huntington is what most people think of when they picture an L.A. beach. No homeless encampments, no CBD shops steps from the water. Just an endless expanse of clean beige sand and wave after whitecapped wave slapping the shore. There should have been surfers out; the waves were good. There should have been kids on boogie boards at the break, and families scattered over the sand, and tourists oohing at dolphins and wondering if they were sharks. Instead there was a flock of seagulls waiting at the water's edge and a single sandpiper that ran back and forth, pecking at the goodies deposited on the shore as the tide receded. A blue face mask bobbed on the water like a jellyfish. I kicked off my Rainbows and used one of them to catch it, throwing it up onto the sand to grab later.

The shore was deserted, but even an empty beach is a noisy place, with the rush of the waves and wind. I guess the solitude gave me a false sense of ease, because I didn't know he was there until he plopped down in the sand beside me.

"Cam."

I sprang to my feet, wielding a flip-flop like it was nunchucks. He looked up and cracked a thin smile. "So much for the mousy librarian." I forced my shoulders to drop, though adrenaline still coursed through my chest and temples. My handler. I hadn't seen him in nearly a year, but he hadn't changed. Plain suit pants, blue oxford shirt rolled up at the sleeves—his idea of casual, I guess. His mask matched his shirt and they were both the color of his eyes and of the sky behind him. "Marshal. What the hell are you doing here?"

He took a paper mask from his breast pocket and handed it to me. Instead of putting it on I dropped back onto the sand, more than the requisite six feet from him.

"Can't a fellow need a day at the beach?"

I eyed his black oxfords. "You're not exactly dressed for it, Marshal. Did you follow me all the way from Venice?"

He shrugged again. "You can call me Owen, Cam. I've told you that. *Marshal* seems unnecessarily . . . western."

"Is Owen really your name?"

He smiled again, but there was something automatic about it. "It's as real as yours, I guess."

He had a point. I'd been Audrey Smith, Serena Dutton, Juliette Gregory . . .

"Seemed like you were on a mission to get somewhere," Owen continued. "By the way, I believe the speed limit's still sixty-five, even on the San Diego Freeway."

Owen had a formal way of speaking that matched his clothing and his clean-shaven, square chin. I'd fantasized a few times about grabbing him and planting a kiss right on his incongruously full lips. I'd like to know if there's a red-blooded man inside that Ken-doll placidity.

There weren't many reasons for my handler to get in touch. The best possible scenario was that my ex was finally going to trial for racketeering, specifically bribery, extortion, arson, dealing in controlled substances, and . . . oh yeah, homicide.

Owen's eyes met mine, and for once I saw something other than cool professionalism. This scenario wasn't going to be best-case.

"I know it's been hard on you, Cam." He hesitated. "I guess the hardest part is being without your family. I've tried to keep you informed. But sometimes . . ."

My parents had been told I was presumed dead, per a confidential but reliable tip. That kept them from looking for me, but left the door open for me to spring back into their lives someday, posttrial. I had long ago stopped imagining what torture it had to be for them, picturing my death at the hands of the spoiled, sloppy band of miscreants Owen referred to as "the cartel." Sloppy didn't mean harmless. My ex had killed a woman right before my eyes.

Owen had explained, and I got it, that it was safer for my folks to believe me gone forever.

Owen was watching me. He seemed almost fearful. "Out with it, Owen," I told him. "As Nietzsche said, 'Nothing is more precious than honesty.'"

He winced. "I don't actually know who Nietzsche is," he admitted. "Or was. But I do know how close you were to your dad."

I waited. A pulse throbbed in my temple, in time with the waves rushing to the shore.

"Cam." He blinked. "Your father passed away on April nineteenth, after two weeks of illness. It was COVID-19. Your mom came through it just fine. She's okay now."

A long time ago, lifetimes ago, April nineteenth had been my birthday. I wondered if my dad had hung on till then, somehow hoping he might see me again. The girl my father had known was gone. She had a new name, a new birthday, and a new identity. But she still lived inside me and her hurt was filling me up, choking me and forcing tears from my eyes. "When is the funeral?" I asked. "I *will* be going, Owen. To hell with your bullshit rules. I'll wear a disguise, I'll stand in the back, whatever you want. But I *will* be there."

Owen sighed. "Cam. The funeral was at the end of April, as soon as your mom was well enough. I couldn't tell you. I knew you would want to go."

I got up and brushed sand from my clothes. He put out a hand and I flicked it away. The water had receded even farther from us. Low tide. "That leaves my mother with no one, Owen," I told him. "I don't have any siblings. Her only brother is dead."

He nodded. "I know. I've been keeping an eye on her. Your cousin Marsha does too. And there's a neighbor—"

His voice was like a swarm of annoying insects buzzing around my head. "Just shut up," I suggested.

He blinked, nodded, and walked off across the sand. Back to me, he pulled off his mask and let it dangle from one hand.

Owen was not a bad guy, from what I knew, but there was no love lost between us. What most people don't know about WITSEC is that the majority of witnesses being protected are criminals themselves, waiting to turn state's evidence against other criminals deemed more dangerous or more important by the judicial system. The marshals that run federal WITSEC—and there are multiple state versions of the agency too—are no-nonsense guys and gals who would score off the charts on a resistance to change scale. They are interested in following the rules and preserving the lives of their wards to get them to trial; comfort and happiness for said charges factor very little into the equation.

Withholding the news of my father's death until after the funeral had been Owen's job. I got it. My parents had been safer not knowing the truth. But that hadn't protected my father in the end, and I didn't know if I could forgive myself for letting him die without knowing the truth about me. I crossed the hot sand and hopped into my Versa and got on the freeway, heading north back toward Los Angeles. And toward the Oregon border.

The brick corbel-gabled house where I'd grown up was impossibly small. It hadn't seemed so at the time; I'd been an only child and I'd had everything I'd wanted—bikes, pets—and always, books. I'd been the class bookworm all through elementary school, graduating to chief nerd in high school. Didn't have a boyfriend until sophomore year at college. Scholarships had made that possible, but there hadn't been a lot left over for travel. Wellesley, Massachusetts, is a world away from Medford, Oregon—and being restricted to visiting home just once or twice a year had been good for me. I'd grown up a lot in my four years at The Blue, but I'd stayed close to my parents after graduation, flying them out to Chicago for visits as often as I could persuade them to come. My ex had made that possible, and I cringed, remembering our spacious penthouse on the Gold Coast. I'd been naive to believe the few hundred bucks I kicked in for rent covered half. Covered the cable bill, more likely, and he'd accepted even that much reluctantly. There had been a lot of red flags in that relationship, but my ex had been a very pretty boy—probably still was—and I've always been a sucker for those, even in my librarian days. Rich and charming hadn't hurt either. Of course, now I know that many sociopaths are utterly charming. Nowadays a guy tries to charm me and I run screaming out of the room.

Now, parked across the street and a few houses down from my childhood home, I felt confident no one would recognize me. Once upon a time I'd been a proper lass in straight skirts and twin sets, hair smoothed back in a tidy bun. I was close to the same weight I'd been back then, but I'd traded twenty pounds of jiggle for twenty pounds of muscle. I'd cut my hair—radically, and bleached it to an ombré blond, and I had a ring of platinum studs in my ear where modest pearl clips had once nestled. I'd worn glasses my entire pre-WITSEC life, but now contact lenses did the job and also changed my natural baby blues to an unremarkable hazel. Black Ray-Bans and tattered yoga pants the old me wouldn't have been caught dead in completed the transformation.

Laura Ashley curtains hung in my old bedroom window, faded but still pretty—tiny pink rosebuds on a navy-and-gray background that I could have drawn with my eyes closed. My canopy bed, shower curtain, and even my bathrobe had all been done in the same fabric, a gift from my parents on my fourteenth birthday, along with dozens of paperbacks and a hardcover copy of *Boston Adventure* that was one of the few treasures that made it into my life on the run.

"I remember, I remember the house where I was born," I whispered. "The little window where the sun came peeping in at morn." I stopped, feeling foolish. Odd that a poem written nearly two hundred years before my birth could so perfectly capture the melancholy of a twenty-first-century girl.

I knew that I couldn't speak with my mother or have any contact at all. I just needed to see her, to see that she was okay, somehow, although I knew she couldn't be. She and my father had been more like twins than partners. They'd finished each other's sentences, fixed each other's coffee, made the bed together every morning. It was only by knowing they had each other that I'd been able to bear deserting them.

My back was aching—I'd spent the night in my car on BLM land and then driven straight to Medford, stopping only for a bathroom break, bitter coffee, and a stale donut at the California-Oregon border. I'm not a big person, but the Versa is really not made for a comfy night's rest. I was considering hopping out of the car for just a moment to stretch my back when the front door—my old front door—opened. My mother stepped out into the early-morning light, blinking.

I sunk lower in the seat and tugged my watch cap down to meet the frames of my Wayfarers. But my mother didn't even glance my way. Like a sleepwalker, she shuffled to the edge of the lawn and picked up the newspaper. Mom was thinner than she'd been eight years before, almost frail, and her hair, originally a light mousy brown, was shot with silver. My mother had always prided herself on good posture, but now she hunched over as if she were trying to curl up into herself and disappear.

When she'd gone back inside I started the car, blinking hard to try and dissipate the hot tears that threatened to spill over. Big girls might cry, but all the tears in the world never fixed anything.

The cemetery was decently cared for, at least, but I couldn't find my father's plot and I knew better than to ask. I figured it would be unmarked—it can take months or even a year for a headstone to arrive. But there were several fresh graves and finally I just picked the one that seemed most likely. It was near a pretty Doug fir, and there was a stone bench where my mom could sit if she visited, and someone had laid a bouquet of jonquils on the grave—my mother's favorite flowers. Kneeling on the grass with my hand pressed flat to the fresh sod, I had so much to say to my dad, but the only thing that would come out was, "I'm sorry." My voice cracked and I began again.

"I've made so many mistakes, Daddy," I said finally. "I know I should be here to take care of Mom."

Something moved by the fir and I got up fast. It was a pretty harmless-looking kid, a nice-looking kid, actually. Seventeen or eighteen, dressed in impeccable black 511s and fresh Nike Air Maxes, the ones with the black swoosh. He was maskless, but far enough away for that to be okay. I nodded and he grinned, lifting one eyebrow.

Boys sure hadn't dressed like that when I was growing up in Medford.

In fact, the boys I'd seen on the streets and in the 7-Eleven here in town *still* didn't dress like that. I felt a sick thrill of fear move down my spine.

My ex wouldn't bother to post a kid at my father's grave on the off chance I'd show up to pay respects. Of course he wouldn't.

Of course he would.

I was the key witness linking him to the cold-blooded murder of my best friend, and a handful of other crimes to boot. He had plenty of money; it was scruples he was short on. It wouldn't be a big deal for him to send a soldier to spend a few weeks in Oregon, keeping an eye out for me.

The boy was definitely watching me, but that didn't mean much. I'm no Gal Gadot, but I've been told I'm fairly easy on the eyes if you like the wiry type.

A black S450 came through the big metal front gates, cruising slowly, looking for something. The driver was maybe thirty, thirty-five, wearing Persols and a black fabric mask. He motioned to the kid, who gave me a last grin before stepping out to the drive and hopping in.

I couldn't see what state had issued the plates; they were too dirty to read, although the car itself was pristine. I swallowed hard. Tried to look nonchalant as I headed back to my car. There was no point in pretending it wasn't mine; the Versa and the Mercedes were the only cars around. But if they ran my plates all they'd get would be a fake name and a fake address—there was nothing to link Cam Baker to the person I'd once been.

Nothing except a grave in Medford, Oregon, and a weather-beaten corbel-gabled house.

But as I pulled out of the lot, I saw that the Persol man and his teenaged companion weren't so sinister after all. They'd parked the Merc by a white-marble mausoleum and the man was arranging a bouquet of pink tulips carefully at its base. The boy stood, hands clasped in front, head bowed. Their wife and mother? I shrugged.

It was time to go home. I should not have broken the rules of WITSEC, and my insubordination was making me paranoid. I checked my phone and saw a couple of missed calls from Tony.

Where you at? Call me, he'd texted, and then retexted with exclamation points.

When I phoned back, he sounded exasperated. "Marta's worried about you, Cam. Why'd you take off?"

"You know why, Tony," I said. "Two little reasons. We love them a lot but they make a lot of noise."

He laughed. "Hey, those are healthy boys. Buy earplugs."

"Don't worry," I told him. "I just wanted to sleep under the stars for a night or two. I'll be back late tonight or early tomorrow."

Tony covered the phone with his hand and said something. Then he was back. "Cam," he said seriously. "If you've got trouble, I can help. *We* can help. You've got the Santa Monica PD at your service."

I smiled. "How's my dog?"

"Meme's okay. Probably lonely. I'm working a lot of doubles. Figure I might as well, since I can't be at home." He hesitated. "Don't worry. Chef Jason's letting him out a couple times a day when I'm gone."

The measure of contempt Tony managed to squeeze into the words *Chef Jason* was all out of proportion to anything poor Jason had ever done wrong. He was an arrogant, self-important young chef on the rise—or he had been, until the pandemic—but he wasn't really a bad guy. It pissed Tony off that Jason referred to my little cottage as the "pool house" when there was only a hot tub, and even that was treacherously slippery with mold. Tony expected Jason to stop by to fix leaky faucets and loose window sashes, but if he'd actually done so, he could probably have doubled my rent. I was okay with our arrangement, but after a month at Tony's palatial digs in Culver City, I could see why he was annoyed.

"Well, I care about you, Cam," Tony said. "So if—"

"Gotta go," I told him, and hung up fast. I'd pretty much gotten over my colossal crush on the ridiculously gorgeous Detective Antonio Morales—falling in love with a guy's wife and kids will tend to help that process along—but I never like to tempt fate. "Our wills and fates do so contrary run," I told myself, staring into the rearview mirror, "that our devices still are overthrown." Ah, Hamlet. I hadn't seen or even read Shakespeare in months, maybe years. I sighed for the person I used to be.

I should not have stopped at the market on my way out of town. I knew better; even in disguise, even just running in to grab a couple of protein bars and a bottle of water, it was risky. Owen had gone over the rules ad infinitum. But the market was the last stop before I jumped back on the freeway, and there were only a couple of cars in the parking lot, and I decided to chance it.

It wasn't the market I'd grown up shopping at; we'd mostly used the big Kroger in town, but I'd been in a few times over the years. Not much had changed. I didn't recognize the plus-sized woman at the register. She looked up, took in the ombré-blond hair sticking out from my watch cap, my cropped yoga pants and tee. Her eyes lingered for a moment on Piltdown man, tattooed on my right ankle. I guess I passed muster because she gave me a diffident wave and looked back to the folded magazine she held in one plump hand. Brad Pitt grinned up at her.

The aisles were empty. There was a nice selection of bars, so I grabbed a half-dozen and headed for the refrigerator in the back. I was reaching for an Earth20—bottled in Oregon!—when a soft voice said wonderingly, "Lorraine? *Lori?*"

I knew what I was supposed to do. Walk out without turning around, as if I hadn't heard. Get in my car, and drive, drive, drive, and contact Owen for instructions before I really got anywhere.

That's what I was *supposed* to do. But those instructions didn't factor in how it would feel to hear my own name, my real name, from my mother's mouth after eight years on the run. My heartbeat was an ache in my chest that I could not bear. I dropped the bars and turned to her, very slowly.

She looked even older up close, her eyes a faded blue like jeans that have been washed a hundred times, her hair a mostly silver halo around her lined face, an impossibly beautiful, impossibly dear face I'd thought I might never see again.

"*Mama.*" I hadn't called her that since I was five years old. It had been Mother or Mom since the first day of kindergarten.

She put a hand out to touch me, hesitantly, as if perhaps I wasn't real.

"Your *eyes*, Lori. Your pretty hair . . . I—Daddy." She stopped. Rubbed her eyes as if she was trying to wake up.

"Mama. We can't. We *can't*. I shouldn't be here. It's dangerous for us both." I shook my head hard. "Don't tell anyone, Mom. Someone will be in touch with you. Don't tell *anyone*. Promise."

She nodded. Looked bewildered. As I turned away, I heard a sob catch in her throat.

I'm not supposed to call attention to myself, ever, and in a high-risk situation, that rule was supposed to go double. So I probably shouldn't have left the market without buying anything, but I simply couldn't make small talk with a clerk while my mother waited at the back of the store, forbidden to speak to her only child, risen from the dead.

I got in the Versa and took off toward Jacksonville, following the streetcar route. I could have thought of fifty things I'd have rather done than call Owen and confess that I'd blown my cover, but for my mother's protection and my own, I had to. First, though, my friends. The only friends I still had in the world, in fact, and I wasn't kidding myself. I knew this was going to be goodbye forever. I thought Marta would probably keep Vindi, and if she wouldn't take Meme too, maybe Tony could find a home for him. Poor guy; it would be his third adoption since he'd escaped the hell of the racetrack.

I pushed the little Versa hard to get it close to seventy, but then I realized I might get pulled over and I slowed way down. A tiny part of me, the part that probably still believed in unicorns and Santa, wondered if Owen might let me keep my Cam Baker life if I pinky-promised and crossed my heart never to go near Oregon again. But I knew. Cam Baker was dead; as dead as Audrey Smith and Juliette Gregory. As dead as a mousy brokenhearted librarian named Lorraine Yarborough.

I waited until I was just a few hours out of town before I dialed Tony. I had to swing by my place at Jason's to grab some things before Owen whisked me off to Oz or wherever I'd be going next. I had a couple thousand in go money stashed in books on the mantel, and a silver locket my dad had given me for my dateless, pimply sweet sixteen, and my mother's diamond engagement ring, treasured but too small for her middle-aged fingers. I sometimes wore it on a chain around my neck. There was *Boston Adventure*; I wasn't leaving without that. A couple of sweet notes kids had written me at the Kennerly School.

But I wouldn't see Tony. He was too perspicacious and I cared too deeply for him for that to be possible. It had been hard, the time he'd asked me point blank if I was in WITSEC and I'd had to play dumb. Soon he'd know for sure, I figured. Unless Owen could come up with a story good enough to fool one of SMPD's finest.

"Hey, you." I kept my voice light. "If you're not at my place, I need to grab a couple of things, if you don't mind. I promise I'll wear my mask." Part of distancing was staying strictly in our own bubbles. Mine included Tony's wife and kids; his included the entire rest of the world.

Tony sighed, exasperated. "Trust me, Cam, your germs are the last thing I'm worried about. I had a drunk vomit on my shoes last night and the smell is just—"

He stopped. "I'm not home. But if you're coming up this way, I could meet you for coffee."

"Sure," I said heartily, without any intention of following through. "What time does your shift end tonight?"

"It's quiet so far," he said. "If nothing kicks in, I'll be off at nine."

I calculated fast. I couldn't make it to Santa Monica much before that. I was about to do my best friend really dirty.

"The Starbucks at Wilshire and Fourteenth has a patio," I told him. "Meet me there at nine-thirty. If I'm a little late, order me a half-caf cap." By the time Tony figured out I wasn't coming, I'd have been to the cottage, kissed Meme goodbye, grabbed my gear, and scooted out of his life forever.

I should have phoned Owen immediately, but I'd done so many things I shouldn't have already that it hardly seemed pressing. Even if my mother broke down and told one of her girlfriends or my cousin Marsha or the minister at her Presbyterian church, it would take a little time for word to get around. But she'd always been pretty good at keeping a secret. I pulled into the driveway behind Chef Jason's bungalow and went in, reviewing my mental checklist. Everything was right where I expected it to be—cash, book, notes . . . but not my mother's ring. I cursed. That was at Marta's, of course, along with my favorite clothes and my computer.

Meme knew something was wrong. He whined and pressed against my legs, trying to stop me from leaving. Finally I went to the refrigerator, found some sliced roast beef Tony was probably going to be annoyed as hell to find missing, and used it to coax Meme into letting me out the door. He started barking like his heart was breaking before I had the car in gear.

A confused-looking guy in a beige windbreaker was standing in the sallow glow of the streetlight, comparing something on his phone with a semi-folded street map. He looked up and motioned for me to stop as I backed out of the drive, but I ignored him. He'd have to figure it out old-school—I was on a very tight schedule if I was going to pull this off. Besides, I try never to chat with strangers on a lonely street after dark.

It was nine o'clock when I pulled up to Marta's. I knew the kids would probably be asleep, which would make everything easier. I glanced down at my phone and my stomach turned. Four missed calls from Owen. Maybe my mother had spilled the beans after all. He would have to wait. This was not my first time at the rodeo—once Owen determined the need to move me, it would all go like lightning. Any part of my Cam Baker life that I did not have on me when he picked me up would be lost forever.

Marta struggled to pull herself out of the soft couch cushions as I let myself in. The alarm made an urgent beep until I punched in the code: *459-1054*. I smiled. I was going to miss Tony's sense of humor. *459* is the police code for "home invasion." *1054* is the code for "possible dead body."

"I'm going out again in a minute," I told Marta. "Be sure you set the alarm again when I leave."

Vindi had padded down the hall to greet me, a first. I bent to scratch her ears, which she tolerated for just a moment before heading back to stand guard outside Diego's room.

"We missed you," Marta said sleepily. "The boys wanted Auntie Cam to give them their bath."

The smile I gave her felt like one of those garish masks people were wearing around town, the kind with a clown smile drawn on where the mouth would be.

"You okay, Marta? How's my niece?"

She patted the bulge of her tummy and smiled again. "Hungry, like always. And missing Dad." She sat up awkwardly. "I think I'll make a quick sandwich. Can I fix you one?"

I declined and headed upstairs to grab my stuff. Marta was going to have to go it alone, unless Tony moved back in, but that would put her at an unacceptable risk. Maybe her mother would come from El Paso. I thought about my own mother. The shock and hurt in her cracked voice. The hope blooming in her faded eyes before I'd walked away.

I grabbed the ring and shoved a few pairs of panties and a T-shirt into my computer bag. Tied a sweatshirt around my waist. I was ready to run when I heard a noise—very soft—from outside. It could have been anything—a possum, a creaky branch, the wind. It could have been anything, but when I glanced outside I saw a slim figure in a beige windbreaker working at the window just below mine. Diego's window.

Stealth or warning? I let my adrenaline decide.

"Marta," I yelled. "Hit your panic button! Call nine-one-one! Get up here to Tony's room and lock the door!" I was still screaming instructions as I barreled down the stairs, but she wasn't going for the alarm or calling the cops. She's a mom. She heard *Tony* and lumbered up the stairs to his room with astonishing speed.

Vindi was going wild, clawing at the door to Diego's room so hard that her paws left bloody streaks down the yellow paint. I kicked the door and let her in and there he was, the mild-mannered fellow I'd seen on the street outside my pool house, fumbling with a map. He didn't look so harmless now. He had a big ugly smile and a big ugly Desert Eagle .44 to match. It's a huge piece, way more firepower than most people need—even criminals. But there was no time to offer him a lesson in moderation. He had the gun trained on me, hammer back. The slide was racked and ready to fire. Vindi froze at my side, growling low in her throat. Diego lay in his crib frantically sucking on his thumb, staring at me. "You got five seconds to get in the car," the intruder began, swinging the gun toward the toddler.

Five seconds was more than Vindi needed. With a strangled cry, she leapt at the man and knocked the gun from his hand as he fired. At the same moment, I heard sirens blare from far away, and Marta began screaming, pounding back down the stairs. Diego opened his mouth and matched her, note for note. "Binnie! Binnie!" he wailed, arms outstretched toward the dog.

Sliding in Vindi's blood, I scooped the Eagle up in both hands. An Eagle weighs four and a half, five pounds—way too heavy for me—but I pushed hard with my right hand and pulled back with my left to stabilize it, just as Tony had taught me. With a big piece, if you let the gun wiggle it can jam. The man grimaced and hopped back out the window, racing for his car. I leaned out the window without hesitating. He'd have made great fertilizer for the Morales's lawn. Unfortunately, when I pulled the trigger, nothing happened. The next round had failed to feed.

Marta flew into the room with Tony Jr. in her arms. She slid on Vindi's blood, cried out, and leapt toward Diego's crib. But it was all over. Vindi lay silent and perfectly still, unmoved by the baby's heartbroken cries. The sirens were close. I threw the Eagle onto the high bookshelf, making sure Marta saw it. I wanted to crouch by Vindi and thank her and pet her but I couldn't. I wanted to hold Diego one more time and tousle Tony Jr.'s hair and tell Marta that I would never stop being sorry. But there wasn't time. There was just enough time to grab my bag and run out the back door. My Versa was parked in front; gone forever.

I slipped down the dark alley, smelling Vindi's blood, smoke from the Eagle, and my own rank perspiration. I was sure that Beige Jacket had taken off, but just in case I kept my footsteps light and my breathing soft and even.

I didn't stop moving until I was at least three miles from the Morales's place. I found myself contemplating the big stone steps of Beyond Baroque, some kind of literary gathering spot on Venice Boulevard. They hosted poetry readings, that kind of thing. I'd been reading about the joint since my Chicago days but I'd never been. And now I never would go.

The building was dark, with only weak solar lights in the lush garden providing any illumination. I found a shadow and sat down. I had to call Owen, but there was another call I needed to make first. My mother had to be baffled, scared, hopeful—all of the above. She'd be frantic to hear from me. I thought maybe I could let her down easy; explain that I had to stay in hiding until the trial, whenever that might be, but that I'd be parked on her doorstep the moment I was free. I imagined her soft hands touching my hair. My real name, my true name, on her lips. *Lori. Lorraine.*

But there was no answer. Her house phone rang and rang, and if my mother had joined the twenty-first century and gotten a cell phone, I didn't know the number.

Owen picked up on the first ring. "Location," he demanded. "Code orange, Cam. This is for real. The cartel is onto you. They tracked you from Oregon, goddamnit."

"No duh, Marshal," I told him. "I spent the last half-hour whupping bad guys. I've got my go bag—no car—and I'm ready to roll."

"Location," he demanded again, and I gave it to him. It was a continual irritation to Owen that I insisted on keeping tracking off on my phone. All things considered, I had to admit he had a point.

Owen told me to get low and close to the building, behind a shrub if possible, and to wait for him without using my phone again.

"Turn it off, Cam. No lights. Code-orange procedure."

"Owen, wait," I told him. "Wait. My mom—she knows. I saw her. She saw me. I'm sorry, I—"

He cut me off. "Your mother is in the hospital under twenty-four-hour guard," he said abruptly. "They roughed her up a little, but they were interrupted by the mail carrier and fled—"

I gasped.

"She's going to be okay. Now sit tight and do not move. Clear?"

He hung up without waiting for an answer.

Owen picked me up not fifteen minutes later. His car was as inconspicuous as his clothing—a Dodge Stratus, charcoal gray. What was more conspicuous was the SIG Sauer P250 he held loosely in one hand as he held the door for me, head swiveling the whole time. I didn't speak at first. There was nothing to say. I was overcome with shame. I'd betrayed Tony's confidence in me, put his wife and kids in mortal danger, gotten one of my dogs killed and abandoned the other. Because of me—my sentimentality, my inability to follow instructions, my arrogance, to be truthful—my mother had been terrorized by thugs and I was on the run again—with nothing but a few pathetic possessions that seemed meaningless now that I'd risked so many lives to get them.

Owen spoke at last, far more gently than I deserved.

"It happens, Cam," he said. "You're not the first to blow cover, and you won't be the last."

I bit my lip and tasted blood. "I'm not Cam anymore," I said finally. "I'm no one."

He glanced over at me, then back at the road. "You're Lorraine Yarborough," he said. "None of this changes that. This is temporary, and it *will* end, Lori. It will. And then this will all be in the past. Dead, gone, and forgotten."

I stared out at the dark street. "The past is never dead," I told him. I doubted he would pick up the Faulkner reference, but lately Owen had been full of surprises. He flashed me a grin. "It's not even past," he said, finishing the quote. He signaled, moved right, and headed onto the freeway toward LAX. The sky was a navy velvet cape, spangled with a thousand stars.

---

*Lori and I have been through a lot together—she's witnessed murders, fled crime scenes, and had her heart broken more than once since her first appearance as "Cam Baker" in the pages of Ellery Queen Mystery Magazine *in 2018. Over the same span of time, I've lost loved ones, survived a pandemic, weathered years of teaching secondary school, and have sometimes felt as jaded as Lori with her hand-me-down dogs, beat-up wheels, and borrowed identities. Lori is in many regards my alter ego—impatient, hapless, cynical, sometimes abrasive—but is just a bit better educated, a bit more intelligent, and more than a little bit braver than I. She works out more, too. And that's the fun of being a writer with a recurring character. Lori can snap out a quote from Shakespeare or Donne or Baudelaire while I'm fumbling for my glasses to look it up in Bartlett's. She sleeps alone in a bedroll in a national forest while I need a flashlight and pepper spray to walk the dog around the block at night. Lori is in many ways my better but, as she grows, so do I, and we're both grateful to the editors and readers who make it possible for us to keep adventuring.*

Archer Sullivan's *stories have appeared in* Ellery Queen Mystery Magazine, Tough, Reckon Review, *and* Rock and a Hard Place, *among others. A ninth-generation Appalachian who is proud of her roots and homesick for the hills, her crime fiction is hard-boiled and country-fried.*

GOOD HARVEST

Archer Sullivan

I watch my mother dig. I listen to the scrape of the shovel—a loud *SHINK*—in the moist, sandy soil. She grunts as she gets another shovelful and tosses it over her shoulder. The dirt falls in a clumpy shower.

Shink, grunt, pitter-patter. Shink. Grunt. Pitter-Patter.

My mother is strong because she is a woman who has lived her whole life in the mountains and has pulled a plow with her own body. She has carried babies and carried groceries and carried lambs fresh born and later, in pieces, from the butcher.

The night is dark but I see her in the light of the moon. Her hair is a gossamer blond streaked—already—with white and pulled back from her face with a bandanna. There is dirt on her cheek, her clothes, her hands.

I shift to look closer at the hole she is digging and my mother says, "No. Stay right there, sugar. Keep an eye on Jasper."

Jasper is my little brother. I am nine. He is four.

Jasper sleeps in the back seat of our car. His seat belt is off and he is lying down, curled up under a Batman blanket. I am leaning against the back door, watching, as my mother digs.

I do not know yet—but will figure out soon—what my mother is doing, or why. I do not know, yet, about the man in the diner, the things he said, the things my mother did.

What I see now, as I lean against the car and listen to my mother dig, is the form of a person wrapped in the blanket we always kept in the trunk of the car.

What I think is that the man in the blanket—which is a pale peach color but stained from years of use before I was even born—looks like a burrito. What I think is that I would like to go to Taco Bell.

"Mamma," I say.

SHINK. Grunt. Pitter-Patter.

"Yeah, sugar?"

"Can we go to Taco Bell?"

She laughs. It is the first time I have heard her laugh since she picked me up from Noma's—mine and Jasper's grandma—and her laugh is very soft and very tired sounding. My mother has a laugh that rolls out of her mouth like an echo of her heartbeat. *Huh-haaah. Huh-haah. Huh-haaah.*

Her laughter rolls on into the *shink*s and *grunt*s as she goes back to digging.

Eventually, she says, "Maybe."

Encouraging. Hopeful, I say, "They stay open late." I know this is true because I have seen it in commercials.

"Maybe," she says again, looking not at me but at the bottom of the hole.

I look up at the stars and try to find the Big Dipper, which I have learned about in school and from a book that we got from the library. I have learned about stars and planets and I have asked for a telescope for Christmas even though I know that they are expensive.

"Cheaper than a bike," I have said more than once. "And safer."

Shink. Grunt. Pitter-patter.

I look back at my mother. She is waist-deep in what I now understand is a grave. I feel tired but I do not want to sit down. Sitting down, for some reason, feels like a betrayal. Like I am lazy while she digs a grave.

I look over at the burrito man. I can see the bottoms of his shoes poking out from the end of the burrito like a couple of shiny black olives. The shoes look barely worn, the soles hard and slick-looking. The men I have known in my life—my uncle, Jerry, my Pop-Pop, even my teacher, Mister Davies—have all worn work shoes. Real shoes. There are treads on the bottom and there are worn-in places, faded and chewed up.

There is nothing on this man's shoes. No sign of life lived in them.

"Mamma," I say when my mother is hip-deep in the grave.

"Yeah, sugar?"

"Where are we?"

Shink. Grunt. Pitter-patter.

Shink. Grunt. Pitter-patter.

"Mamma?" I say again.

"I heard you," she says. She is breathing heavy. She pauses a moment and I look at the shovel in her grip. I think her hands must be aching. My mother has tough hands, I tell myself. They are thick-skinned on the bottoms and soft and veiny on the tops and they smell like coffee and dish soap. My mother can carry a hot, hot plate without even a pot holder. She does it every day at the diner. Every night at home. Still, I think, it has been hours.

"I feel like," she says, wiping her forehead with the back of her wrist, "it's maybe better if you don't know where we are."

"Oh," I say. *Shink. Grunt. Pitter-patter.* "Because I was thinking we're in Amber and Matthew's cornfield."

I watch my mother push down a smile and carry on shoveling.

I go to school with Amber and her brother, Matthew. My mother works with Amber and Matthew's mother at the diner and I know that Amber and Matthew's daddy is planting tomorrow. I know because Amber and Matthew got to ride along when their daddy harrowed the field and they told me today that the weather is right and that tomorrow is planting day.

"Tomorrow is planting day," I echo.

Shink. Grunt. Pitter-patter.

If we are in Amber and Matthew's cornfield, then we are not far from home. Only two roads over. I could almost walk home if I took the path through the woods. My aunt Mellie will be there, at home. Mellie is my mother's sister, who lives with us. Or we live with her. I'm not sure.

We live together.

Mellie stays up late watching shows on the laptop. She is probably watching a show right now, I think. Probably one of her cop shows. Mellie likes shows with dead bodies.

I look again at the burrito man.

I see now, when I hadn't seen before, that one of his hands is poking out from the burrito, just a little bit. Enough. On his finger is a gold ring.

I stare at the gold ring in the high, pale moonlight, and I jump because, as I stare at it, it moves.

"Mamma," I say.

Shink. Grunt. Pitter-patter.

"Mamma," I say.

Shink. "Yeah, sugar?" *Grunt. Pitter-patter.*

"Mamma, I think that man's hand just moved."

And as I say it, the burrito wobbles. A groan comes from inside it.

My mother sighs and climbs out of the hole. She is still wearing her diner uniform, minus the apron, which is a pair of black scratchy pants and a yellow scratchy shirt. The shirt is covered with dirt now. And something else.

"Look away, sugar," my mother says.

"Mamma," I say.

"Look back at Jasper," she says.

She is dragging the shovel out of the hole behind her.

"Keep an eye on him, alright?"

"Okay," I say. And I turn away.

I look inside the back seat at my little brother who has hair as gold and pretty as our mother's. He has the blanket up to his chin and he is sucking his thumb.

Behind me, I hear the *CLANG* of the metal shovel and the *SQUISH* of something wet. My heart is beating hard. My tummy hurts. I keep on looking at Jasper.

"You sure you don't wanna crawl in there and get some sleep?" my mother asks me. Her voice is thin and panting.

"No," I say. But I'm still turned away from her. "No, I want to stay with you."

I was asleep when we arrived here, in Amber and Matthew's field. I do not know where the burrito man came from, how he got to be rolled up in the blanket, lying in a turned field. I do not recognize his shoes or his hands or his smell.

Shink. Grunt. Pitter-patter.

My mother keeps on digging. She has always said any job worth doing is worth doing right. She is burying this burrito man under the moon in the middle of the cornfield and I know that she will not stop until she gets the hole deep enough so critters won't smell him. So Amber and Matthew's daddy will come out in the morning—probably only a couple hours away—and drill his sweet corn right on top.

Shink. Grunt. Pitter-patter.

I am tired and I know she must be too. She worked all day today and then picked us up, dropped us off at Noma's, went back out, came back to get us. Just like Jasper, I fell asleep in the car from Noma's, as I often do.

And then I woke up. And my mother was digging a hole in Amber and Matthew's cornfield with a burrito man lying on the ground behind her.

She is more than hip-deep now and there is a blotch like Fire Sauce on the far end of the burrito. She stops. She breathes out the word, "Okay." She crawls out of the hole again, bringing the shovel with her. She sits down for a few small, panting seconds. She looks at the shovel, the burrito man, me.

"You okay?" she asks.

"Yeah," I say.

I am nine, I think. And probably not okay. This is not the kind of thing Amber and Matthew are doing right now. But I am smarter and more serious than Amber and Matthew. This is what my mother has said and I know that it is true.

"Yeah," I say again. "I'm okay."

My mother nods and puts her hand beside her in the dirt and heaves herself up to her feet and goes to stand behind the burrito man. She heaves a sigh and kneels and gets the edge of the burrito blanket. She tugs hard but nothing happens. She tugs again, lets out a big grunt. Nothing.

My mother is tired.

She gets up even before any of the rest of us. Even when it is still sleepy early. My mother rises in darkness. She does it for us.

I push off the car and go to stand beside her. She does not argue this time. I wrap my hands around the blanket edge. Hold tight.

I had forgotten that the blanket edge is satin. Its softness in my sweating hands surprises me.

"Okay?" my mother says.

"Yeah."

Together, we pull. The burrito man budges but not much else. We both take heavy breaths. Again, I see the burrito man's shoes. The slick, shiny, unused black reflecting the night.

My mother says, "One. Two."

I grip the blanket harder, stand like my mother is standing, try to dig the heels of my sneakers into the loose soil.

When she says, "Three," we pull.

The burrito unwraps itself and the man rolls into the grave.

"Don't look, sugar," my mother says.

But I do look. I do not see his face. Only the back of his head. His hair is a plain acorn brown and he is wearing a fancy jacket like the ones the lawyers wear in my Aunt Mellie's dead body shows.

My mother says, "Oh." And she gets back into the grave and kneels and comes back up with a fat brown leather wallet. She puts it in her own back pocket, climbs out of the grave.

My mother shovels dirt back into the hole. This putting back is easier than taking out. Faster.

Skish. Pat-pat-patter. Skish. Pat-pat-patter.

My mother is rushing, hurrying on. It must be very late, I think. Maybe not even Taco Bell is open now. *Skish. Pat-pat-patter.* And the stars have shifted above. I try to find the Big Dipper again and do. *Skish. Pat-pat-patter.*

Soon, she is finished. She looks around at the messy dirt. She rakes the shovel through the area again, hacks at it a little, spreading out the loose soil. She is trying to make it all match, I think. Trying to make it look like nothing was ever dug or buried here in the middle of the night.

"Okay," she says when she is finished. "Sugar, go get in the car with Jasper."

I mind her and I watch as she picks up the burrito blanket and folds it, makes the Fire Sauce blotch disappear into the square of dirty, peachy fabric. Jasper stirs as I open the door and the light comes on.

"What . . . are we home?" he asks.

"Not yet," I say. "Almost."

He closes his eyes again as I slide into the passenger seat up front. He puts his thumb back into his mouth and says around it, "I'm hungry."

"We'll get something when we get home. Put your seat belt back on."

He falls asleep again. I get out, open his door, pull the seat belt out, pull it around him and his blanket while he whines and fights me. I click it closed and let him lay back against the seat, his head lolling onto the doorframe as soon as I've closed it.

I go back to the front.

Behind us, I listen as my mother opens the trunk. The shovel and blanket go inside. She closes it with a soft thud and then walks around to the front of the car. She slides a dark blue sweater off of the seat back and pulls it on over her dirty yellow work shirt. She gets in behind the wheel, starts the car, puts her hand on the gearshift. She is shivering.

We do not talk about what has just happened. Why. What led us here. I realize, much later, that we never will. This night is as thin and sharp as a dream. It always will be.

We pull away from the edge of the field, away from the trees under which we've been parked, and back onto the road. We drive just a little ways.

And then there are the lights.

Red and blue. Flashing.

My mother gasps. There are tears in her eyes as she pulls to the shoulder. It seems a forever long time until a man in a black outfit comes walking toward her side of the window. She has already rolled it down. She looks in the mirror and wipes a smudge of dirt from her cheek.

The man in the black outfit—OFFICER SALISBURY it says on his badge—shines a light into the car. We blink at it.

"Evening, Officer," my mother says. Her diner voice.

Officer Salisbury says to my mother that she has a taillight out.

"Oh . . ." my mother says. "I didn't know."

He looks at both of us, at Jasper in the back seat. My heart goes, *TUMTUMTUMTUMTUMTUMTUMTUM*. There are no downbeats. No calm beats. Just hammering. I am sweating. I swing my feet and feel something that I had not noticed before. A hard thing. Like a box or a case. I tell myself not to look at the thing. Only Officer Salisbury. Only smile. Be good.

TUMTUMTUMTUM.

"Out awful late, ain't ya?" he says.

My mother's mouth opens into a silent, awful *O* and she is still shivering.

TUMTUMTUMTUMTUMTUMTUM.

I open my own mouth.

"It's for homework," I say.

"Homework?" he asks.

"We're learning about stars," I say. "I was trying to find the Big Dipper. I want a telescope for Christmas and—"

But he nods and taps the roof of our car and says, "Get the taillight fixed."

And he walks away.

Tears go sliding down my mother's face.

TUM-TEE-TUM—Tee-Tum-tee-tum.

"Mamma," I say.

"Yeah, sugar."

"Let's go home."

She nods. We get home and she is carrying Jasper in and Mellie opens the door for us.

"We were here all night," my mother says to Mellie, "Except a few minutes to see the stars." It's just a statement. Like saying, "We had roast beef for dinner," but instead, "We were here all night." A lie that sounds so regular it might as well be truth.

"Okay," Mellie says, adjusting her reality around my mother's words. Behind her, on the laptop, a woman in a gray jacket is talking to a man in a blue jacket. They are looking at a dead body on a table. He is lying half under a clean white sheet. His feet are covered.

It is months later that I am sitting on the porch with Amber and Matthew. It's their porch and we are shucking corn together while Jasper catches crawdads in the creek a little ways down the hill.

Through the window, I hear Amber's mother talking to my mother inside the house.

"The police think it was some kind of drug deal gone bad," Amber's mother says. "That's what my cousin said. He said the man had a briefcase full of cash. And you know he was bragging about it on the phone in the diner that day? You heard him didn't you?"

"Yes," my mother says.

And Amber's mother says, "How he was gonna take that money, get on a plane, and fly away."

"Yes," my mother says, sounding bored as she can be. Like this missing man who had a bunch of money and then came through our town and then disappeared is nothing exciting at all.

"They think he probably switched cars here somewhere, or maybe someone picked him up."

"It sure is something," my mother says.

"Well," Amber's mother says, "He definitely ain't here anymore. That's for sure. Otherwise, someone would've seen him by now."

"You'd think," my mother says.

"You all wanna stay for dinner?" Amber's mother says.

"Nah," my mother says. "Better get home." She comes out onto the porch and Amber's mother comes with her. They watch us as we shuck the corn.

"It's been a good harvest so far this year," Amber's mother says.

"Looks like," my mother says.

I glance up at her. She is almost hurting beautiful, there in the sunshine, her blond-and-white hair glowing like one of the angels in Pop-Pop and Noma's church windows.

My mother smiles at me and I smile back up at her.

She is wearing a new dress, bright white, and new earrings too. The night before, I heard her talking to Mellie about getting me a telescope. What kind. Where to get it from.

I pull the last green sheaf from the corn in my hand with a *Ksshhh*. It smells like heaven. I put the fresh ear into the basket with the others and my mother says, "Looks like a real good harvest."

"As a kid, I spent a lot of time in the car. I don't know why, exactly, but it always seemed as if me and my single mom were always going somewhere. And the sensation—waking up in the middle of the night, AM talk radio playing to keep her awake, her drive-through coffee in the cup holder, the stars shimmering overhead, the road nothing but yellow rectangles stretching out on black tarmac—is something that remains as near and vivid as any other childhood memory. I suppose this story grew from those nights, from the sleepy conversations, questions, and dreams of better days ahead.

Andrew Welsh-Huggins *is the Shamus, Derringer, and ITW-Award–nominated author of the Andy Hayes Private Eye series and editor of* Columbus Noir. *Kirkus Reviews called his latest crime novel,* The End of the Road, *"A crackerjack crime yarn chockablock with miscreants and a supersonic pace." His stories have appeared in many publications, including* Alfred Hitchcock's Mystery Magazine, Ellery Queen Mystery Magazine, Mystery Magazine, *and* Mystery Tribune, *and multiple anthologies, including* Mickey Finn: 21st Century Noir *volumes 1, 3, and 4,* Paranoia Blues: Crime Fiction Inspired by the Songs of Paul Simon, *and the 2021 Bouchercon anthology,* This Time for Sure.

WONDER FALLS

Andrew Welsh-Huggins

My father left for good the first week of my junior year in college. As horrible as it sounds now, I was glad to see him go.

It wasn't the first, second, or even third time he walked out on my mom and sister and me. I was so accustomed to his disappearances by then that I felt almost nothing when my mother mentioned his latest abandonment in a letter that arrived, now that I'm doing the math, almost two weeks after his departure. "Oh, and your father's finding himself again," she wrote near the end of the note in her always-exquisite Palmer-style script, a missive in which she spent more time ruminating on Reagan's recent appointment of Sandra Day O'Connor to the Supreme Court than her husband's desertion. "I suppose he'll be back at some point."

Finding himself, I knew by now, was not code for what you might think. Or not exactly. Without question, my father had multiple affairs during our parents' fitful twenty-three years of marriage. My sister, Holly, was in therapy for months just to deal with the day that, at age eleven, she answered the door to find a young, bellbottoms-wearing woman in tears as she begged to see our father and make him deliver on the promises she said he made. Naturally, it was my mother who dealt with that particular mess and eventually sent the poor girl on her way. But such straying was a symptom of my father's illness, not the disease itself. In this case, "finding himself" meant once again pursuing his dream of being a writer—a real writer, not some part-time hack—which apparently entailed forsaking his responsibilities and, with my parents' meager pile of savings in hand, holing up in a cottage someplace to hammer out yet another manuscript destined to go nowhere.

And sure enough, three weeks after my mother's letter arrived, a postcard bearing a picture of the Old North Church showed up in my college PO box from my father postmarked Boston, bearing three short sentences in his equally familiar—though nearly indecipherable—handwriting. "Taking a breather out east. You probably already heard. Working on something that's the best yet—excited to show you."

And that was that. Because it was always the best yet. Except it never was.

The autumn passed in a rush and soon enough I arrived back from college in Ohio to my hometown of Winter's Falls for Thanksgiving. Once at the house, the absence of my father at the holiday table dominated the short visit even though it scarcely came up in conversation, in the same way I expect that people who live near eye-popping wonders like the Grand Canyon or Devil's Mountain go about their lives, managing the routine matters of existence in the presence of sights that make first-timers gasp at the enormity of what they're seeing. My mother hardly spoke of him at all, murmuring, "Nothing new, like always," the one time that Holly brought it up, the morning of Thanksgiving as we sat around in pajamas watching the Macy's parade on TV while the house filled with the smell of turkey. If my mother felt anything—anger, relief, exasperation—it was difficult to tell through the inscrutable mask of her Midwest upbringing. Of the tiny scar on her left cheek that hadn't been there when we both left for college in August, she said nothing at all. I do know this: despite that blemish, her face seemed softer—more relaxed—than I'd seen in a while. Living with our father couldn't have been easy for her, with as much as she tolerated. And yes, that included the occasional push, the random

shove, probably even a slap or two—obviously—that fell short of
chronic physical abuse but still constituted part of the price of
existing within the orbit of his volatile personality.

For one fleeting moment I thought she was ready to talk about
the elephant in the room, late on Saturday morning as we worked
outside, raking leaves in our enormous backyard, puffs of breaths
punctuating our conversation in the cold, western New York State
autumn air. But then our neighbor appeared around the corner of
his small barn, his own rake in hand, and my mother went quiet.
He gave us a wave, and we all waved back, and then he walked
back the way he came without a word. It seemed odd that he hadn't
approached, and when I asked my mother about it, she replied,
simply, "He misses your father," and went back to raking.

"Misses the whiskey, more like it," my sister whispered when
we were out of earshot.

His name was Doug McCurdy, but to Holly and me he was
always just "Farmer Doug," our juvenile dig at his unruly two-
acre plus spread on the edge of town, only a small part of which
contained an actual garden. Retired early from driving a school
bus, and in fact not a half-bad looking man, he nonetheless made
an easy target, with an unkempt backyard full of dilapidated patio
furniture, cracked ceramic pots, and even a car engine leftover
from some ill-advised repair. You saw his ilk a lot in small Finger
Lakes towns in those days, harmless loners—he was widowed and
childless, with only a sister in town—padding along on their own
quiet, eccentric paths.

Despite my sister's snarky aside, McCurdy and my father had
in fact been unlikely friends, dating from the moment my father
discovered that McCurdy had shelf after shelf of novels and
biographies and history volumes not just in his house but spread
into the barn itself, which functioned on the weekends as a kind
of combination flea market and used book stall. McCurdy was
not just a collector but also a great reader, and he and my father
bonded over mid-twentieth-century fiction and tumblers of
Dewar's for hours on end. McCurdy always invited our mother to
join them, since she was as much a reader—if not more—than my
father. But she almost always demurred, limiting her interaction

to shuttling over occasional pies or bread loaves or tubs of soups to McCurdy when she made too much. As far as my sister and me were concerned, he was the oddball guy who drove our school bus and we had relatively little else to do with him growing up. The only real attraction for us was McCurdy's pond, where we occasionally fished as kids in the summer and often ice skated in the winter. Until our father indirectly ruined those small pleasures for us as well.

And that was that for the first post-disappearance Thanksgiving, and on Sunday morning I headed back for the remainder of fall classes. I should probably pause and explain the irony of my destination. I attended Kenyon College, a small liberal-arts institution perched on a wooded hill in the middle of nowhere, Ohio. Despite its rural locale, however, the school had bona fide prestige when it came to the arts, and especially literature—I was an English major—and chief among those was its famous literary magazine, the *Kenyon Review*. And it was that journal, a year before my birth, that started my father on his downward path by, ironically, accepting one of his first stories.

Appearance in a publication of that standing meant something in those days, and even came with a little money—not a lot, but enough to leave you hungering for more, as was the case for my father. He was just finishing his dissertation at Binghamton University and parlayed the minor fame of that short story achievement into his first teaching job, at Oberlin College. There he met my mother, a junior who took one of his advanced English courses, and who fell prey to his charms in a time-honored student-professor fashion. In reality, given their relatively minor age difference—she was twenty-two, he had just turned twenty-six—the liaison doesn't seem all that scandalous now. Or at least compared to the subsequent family ruckus caused by her decision to leave without a degree to help my father "follow his dreams."

And then—then it all gradually slowed down until it stopped. The *Kenyon Review* success wasn't the beginning, as it turned out, but the beginning of the end. Almost three years passed before my father published another story, this time in a small Illinois literary journal so obscure and hence impoverished that it required he pay for contributor copies out of his own pocket. He struggled to finish his first novel, *Wonder Falls*—a labored allusion to our village's name—and while, to his credit, he eventually managed the task and even found a small—very small—New York publishing house willing to put it in print, it landed in the literary world two days after Nixon defeated Humphrey with all the impact of a single autumn leaf dropping to the floor of an Adirondack forest. I suspect the copy I have is one of the only surviving in the world. His star already faded by his early thirties, my father moved from college to college across the Midwest and then back east, my mother's secretarial gigs providing much-needed financial support at every stop, until we ended up, to his great, secret shame, back where he began: in a small Finger Lakes town.

Here, where Holly and I grew up, he cobbled together community college teaching gigs while pounding out a series of increasingly dense and perpetually unpublished books. My father, the literary traditionalist, insisted on hand-writing his first drafts with a fountain pen he purchased with some of that *Kenyon Review* money. Then, it was up to my mother to decipher his cramped handwriting—she was one of the only people who could translate his penmanship—and type up the results. When he wasn't writing or teaching, he conducted a series of not-all-that surreptitious affairs with older female students and younger faculty members, and passed weekends with glasses of whiskey in Farmer Doug's barn. And then, one day, he was gone for good.

Well, not entirely gone. My wife had a cousin who simply vanished one day, on his way to a suburban Cleveland mall one moment, never heard from again the next. It wasn't exactly like that. It's true that I never saw my father in person after the fall of my junior year. But from time to time postcards would arrive, usually from around Boston, occasionally from New York City, or once, oddly, from Chicago, with scant updates on his life. *Finally buckled down and read most of Peter Taylor, as I expect you already have . . . Feels like life is looking up . . . The writing's going well, for a change . . .* And so on, and so forth. Years later, married and with a family of my own, it would take numerous sessions with my own therapist to work out the anger that accumulated over his abandonment and refusal to have anything further to do with us—with me—than those notes. But at the time, I dismissed him as an insensitive kook and tossed the cards almost as soon as I read them. Obviously, I wish now more than anything that I had saved them instead.

Meanwhile, our mother moved on with her life. The following summer she accepted a new job as secretary at the high school serving our little village and three others. Within a year she was promoted to secretary to the superintendent, a post she held for twenty years until her retirement. Her pride in landing that position was evident the Christmas after my college graduation, when I arrived home from New Haven with my new girlfriend in tow, and we toasted the accomplishment with a bottle of the finest Finger Lakes sparkling white. Certainly, it was a pleasure to see my mother smile that week, her sweet grin like a sliver of sun peeking through a bank of gray clouds. The only thing that marred the visit was something not of her making, but which for years soured my girlfriend—later my wife, then my ex-wife—on my hometown.

My mother had driven up to Rochester for some last-minute Christmas shopping, making it clear with good humor it was an expedition we weren't welcome to join. We were perfectly happy with the time alone, as it gave us the opportunity when she was scarcely out of the driveway to make love first on the living room couch, gasping like teenagers, and then on my narrow childhood bed. Afterward, as snow fell in the rapidly graying late afternoon, I suggested a trip next door to ice skate; after all, I'd been extolling this bonus of my childhood to Eva for weeks. Bundled up, skates in hand, and bearing a thermos of peppermint schnapps–laced hot chocolate and two mugs, we tramped to the edge of our long yard, already snow-filled from a previous storm, and cut through the bank of lifeless lilac bushes to the path that ran along the back of Farmer Doug's property and toward his quarter-acre pond. It was cold that week, with overnight temperatures well into the teens, and thick ice beckoned. Youthful memories of better times, my father still around, flooded my mind as we laced up our skates. And then we heard him.

". . . for you," Farmer Doug shouted from a good fifty yards away, tramping toward us from the barn that served as his makeshift bookshop and antique store, the distance cutting off the full sentence. Misunderstanding the situation, I waved with a grin, which fell from my face as he approached and I saw the anger in his eyes.

"This isn't for you," he said, much closer now.

"Mr. McCurdy?" I said, uneasiness in my voice. Beside me, Eva grabbed my right arm and whispered, "What's going on?"

"This isn't for you," McCurdy repeated as he arrived at the pond, caught his breath, and stood before us in heavy tan boots, worn corduroys, and a padded vest over a flannel shirt that couldn't have been nearly enough protection against the December cold. He wore neither hat nor gloves, and it occurred to me he must have been inside the barn when he spied us through the back window and rushed out.

"I'm sorry?"

"There's no skating," he said. "Not anymore."

"Oh," I said, not certain what to say. "I thought . . ."

"You'll have to leave. I'm sorry." Though these words, put to paper, imply his tone had softened, in fact his face grew even harder as he spoke.

"I didn't realize," I said, trading an awkward glance with Eva. "Mom didn't say anything."

"This has nothing to do with Genevieve," he said, glancing in the direction of our house with a fierce expression, as if she had long ago poisoned his cat or pulled up his tomato plants or knocked over his flowerpots with the mower, and then never apologized for the deed. At the time, I was so shocked by the encounter that his use of my mother's full name—everyone else knew her as Jenny—didn't register.

We waited for more explanation but none came. As an awkward silence settled over us, we removed our skates and slipped our feet back into our boots, not bothering to lace them, and made our way back to my house, our tracks already blurring beneath the snow that was coming down even harder now.

My mother paled a little that night when I told her what happened.

"I should have warned you," she said at last, taking a larger-than-normal drink of wine. She stayed quiet for a while, as though wrestling with what she had to say.

"Warned me about what?"

She took several more moments to compose her reply.

"The fact that he blames me for your father leaving."

"What?"

Another drink of wine. "He doesn't think I was supportive enough."

"Supportive enough? You typed out his novels, for Chrissake."

She shook her head. "More like, if I hadn't said certain things, perhaps he wouldn't have left."

"Certain things like what?"

"Never mind that. I'm just telling you how he feels. Doug, I mean."

"Did he say as much?" Eva asked, curled up on the couch beside me with her own glass of wine.

I could tell my mother was put off by the question, which was fair, though perhaps not one she wanted to hear from a stranger to the family dynamic. But after a few seconds she said, looking at me and not Eva, "Not in so many words. But I could tell. Your father was over there a lot. Doug doesn't have many people in his life. Claire's pretty much it." Claire—the sister down the street.

"That's absurd," I said.

"I should have warned you," she said once more.

And there it was. Another consequence of my father's betrayal of our family: the loss of a beloved childhood activity. In the grand scheme of things, a minor calamity. But yet it was symbolic of so much—the stripping away of a memorable part of growing up in western New York State in the sixties and seventies, when that era's epic winters provided a snowy playground for months on end. And now thanks to him, and to Farmer Doug, that was gone too.

The cards from my father continued sporadically over the years, though at some point in the late 1990s or early 2000s they stopped and I had to face the fact he was probably dead. Unlike my father, though, I saw McCurdy again. Many times, in fact. As the years went on Eva and I moved often while I grew my teaching and writing career—four published novels compared to the singular *Wonder Falls*, thank you very much. I traded up one assistant professor job for another before, fully tenured, I settled us in Cleveland where we bought a house in the suburbs, had children, and then endured the long, slow dissolution of our marriage. But before that train wreck, we returned often to my hometown to visit my mother and many times would see McCurdy entering or leaving his barn, puttering in his garden, or a few times staring in our direction across his lawn. Once or twice, coming back from a jog on the nearby country roads, I waved at him, but while he might wave back, he never warmed to an actual conversation.

Though both my sister and I were long gone from Winter's Falls, my mother resisted all entreaties to leave her house and move closer to either of us. At first, she used her job for the superintendent's office as an excuse. And of course fondness for her friends, a sparse collection of like-minded readers, occasional cardplayers, and companions on the charter bus circuit. She'd always been a big one for travel, and one benefit of her husband's abandonment was the ability to finally indulge the pleasure to her heart's content. Later, in retirement, she said she simply preferred where she was too much to consider leaving. Before her health faded it was easy to see her point. Every season was special in the Finger Lakes, whether the greening springs, the temperate summers, the spectacular falls with riots of autumn colors painting the hills, or the cold, snowy winters. I always enjoyed my visits, especially with the kids, before and even after the divorce.

"I just like it up here," my mother told me more than once. "It's like the Midwest without all the hate."

But eventually the house became too much for her. Two weeks after her eightieth birthday she took a tumble coming downstairs. That led to six weeks in a skilled nursing facility, and from there a forced move to an assisted living home two towns over. She was never truly happy there—and why should she have been, really—but she did her best, joining the book club and taking trips up to Rochester to the art museum and attending weekend musical concerts in the lobby. My sister, living in Buffalo with her own divorce behind her, did her best to visit, as did I, though not as often as I should have.

The day came when the transition from an assisted living apartment to a single room on the nursing home side of the facility took place, and from there our mother's health declined rapidly. Two months after we moved her into that room, we received a call that she had taken a turn for the worse. Holly arrived before me, and when I finally walked in, I misinterpreted the funny look on my sister's face as anger that I hadn't made good enough time.

"What?"

She looked at our mother, someplace between sleep and drugged unconsciousness.

"The weirdest thing happened."

"Weird how?"

"Someone was already here when I walked in this afternoon. Just for a second I thought it might be a chaplain, sitting by her bed. But then I realized the person was crying."

"Who was it?"

She held my eyes with a directness I hadn't experienced in years; ours had not been the best sibling relationship.

"It was Farmer Doug. And he was holding her hand."

I was so taken aback I couldn't speak for a moment.

"You're kidding."

"God's truth. I didn't know what to do at first. Finally, I cleared my throat and he looked up. He wiped his eyes, nodded at me like we were old friends or something, and walked out of the room without saying a word."

"Jesus."

"I know."

My mind reeled with the idea that my mother and McCurdy had reconciled.

"Maybe he had a change of heart?"

"A big one, apparently," Holly said.

"What do you mean?"

"I checked with the charge nurse. She said he visits every day. That got me to thinking. While I was waiting for you I walked over to the reception desk on the assisted living side. The lady there said he was always around. He often had dinner with her. She seemed to think they were a couple."

I leaned against the door, staggered, looking at my mother, her features wan and drawn, her wasted, shrunken body almost childlike. "She never said anything."

"Maybe she didn't want us to know?"

"Maybe," I said doubtfully. But what other explanation was there?

We pledged to ask when we next spoke to her. But we never had the chance. We were both asleep in the hotel room down the road we were sharing for a night or two when the call came that our mother passed away a few hours after we bid her supine figure goodbye.

We saw Doug McCurdy one last time, at her memorial service a week later. I tried speaking with him, but by the time I crossed the room, he'd signed the visitor's book, gazed briefly at the rotating display of digital photos commemorating our mother's life, and slipped away, walking slowly and stiffly with the help of a cane.

Three months later, I had a text from Holly, who heard from an old school friend that McCurdy, too, had passed away. Unlike my mother, however, he went out with his boots on. Literally: he was found by a weekend tourist looking for a flea market bargain slumped in a chair in his barn, a book in his lap. And then three months later, we heard the inevitable; his house had been sold to a local developer with plans to subdivide the property, tear down the barn, drain the pond, and put up two additional houses. Though we had no claim to any of this, and McCurdy's banishment of us from his home years earlier largely put to rest our childhood nostalgia for our hometown, it was still a shock.

But nothing compared to the phone call from my sister two months after that.

"How soon can you get to Winter's Falls?"

Understand, we weren't allowed near the pond. Everything was taped off when Holly and I drove up, and a gruff sheriff's deputy—the son of someone we went to school with—waved us off and directed us to the justice center in Geneseo. And it was there, in a windowless conference room, that a plastic bin was pushed across the table to us and we looked inside to find a pair of muddy leather shoes, a belt, a watch, a pair of thick black eyeglasses and a fountain pen that even forty years on was as familiar to me as the sight of my own face in the mirror.

"Yes, that's all his," I said, my voice catching. "They were . . . ?"

"They were on or near the remains," the detective confirmed, a middle-aged woman with hard hazel eyes.

She wouldn't tell us more that day. But it all came out eventually. As the water ebbed out of Farmer Doug's pond during the initial phase of construction and redevelopment, a rusted hunk of metal emerged—an old engine, the excavator operator told police. And strapped to that engine with several loops of copper wire, what was left of the body of our father, whose flight from our family turned out to have consisted of just a few hundred yards. The depression at the back of his skull implicated a single, powerful blow from a blunt object in his death, but in truth there was no way to know for sure. There was no one left to ask.

Though we never received all the answers we so desperately sought, McCurdy's sister provided one piece of the puzzle in the end. The day after we saw our father's belongings in the sheriff's conference room, Holly and I drove back to town for a final drive past our mother's house, which still stood mostly in the same condition but to our amusement now sported a large climbing fort and swing set in the backyard. We stopped at the village diner afterward where, as we picked at soggy club sandwiches, an elderly woman approached us. It was Claire McCurdy. She greeted us by name, told us how sorry she was, and then said she had something to show us. Curious, we followed her back to her small cobblestone two blocks away. Excusing herself, she went inside, and then emerged with a book and a paper grocer's bag.

"These were in his house," she said, handing me the bag.

Wordlessly, I pulled out what I immediately recognized as two pairs of our mother's socks, along with a bra, a blouse, and a favorite necklace. Before I could respond, Claire handed me the book.

"And somehow I ended up with this," she said. "It was with Doug when he died. I didn't know what to do with them."

"Them?"

She opened the front cover and handed me the volume, but not before I realized what I was holding in my hands. A copy of *Wonder Falls*.

"Your brother was reading this when he died?"

"That's right," she said. "He so admired the fact your father was a writer."

Biting my tongue, I stared at several scraps of folded paper tucked inside the cover. Opening the first, I saw three sentences written in a familiar scribbling.

The writing's going well, for a change.

Again, in slightly different form. *The writing's going well, for a change.*

And one more time. *The writing's going well, for a change.*

"That's Mom's handwriting," Holly said.

"No," I snapped. "It's Dad's."

"Look closely. It's supposed to *look* like Dad's. See how she practiced to get it right?"

And after a moment, I did. It was my mother's handwriting but almost perfectly mimicking my father's chicken scratch. And in a rush it all became clear. A practice document, ahead of the actual fabrication on a postcard—on postcards—of her choosing. Mailed, no doubt, on all those trips that my father's death opened the door for. Our mother and Doug McCurdy, hiding the deed that allowed their relationship to persist with the simplest of literary subterfuges.

Questions leaped into my mind. Had they become lovers before or after his death? For the first time, I saw those pie and bread and soup deliveries in a brand new light. Had the blow that left the scar on my mother's face, the one I spied that first Thanksgiving after his disappearance, been the final straw? Who raised whatever object was used to protest his brutality once and for all?

And then of course the ultimate irony, like a trumpeter's note rising above an orchestra's collective sound: My mother, the sacrificing secretary, had manufactured a fiction more convincing, and long-lasting, than anything my father, the ersatz novelist, ever managed.

"Do the notes mean anything?" Claire said, interrupting my reverie as she looked at me with weary, rheumy eyes.

"No. Nothing at all." I thanked her and asked if I could keep the book.

"Of course," she said. "I wouldn't know what to do with such a thing."

After all this time, that copy is still with me on the shelf of my office back in Cleveland. I would say, without exaggeration, that I pick it up at least once a week and run my finger across the cover, like a blind man reading braille, to trace the letters of my father's name. And each time I do, I pledge to myself that one day, one day soon, I'll make the time I need, pour myself a tumbler of Dewar's, sit down in my favorite chair, and finally read *Wonder Falls*.

Although I've lived in Ohio for nearly thirty years, I grew up in New York State's Finger Lakes region in a small town reminiscent of the one where I set my story. Home was an idyllic burg where I ran free the way you did as a kid in the 1960s and 1970s and where I first put pen to paper and summoned the courage to call myself a writer. Drafting "Wonder Falls," I channeled that upbringing as I tried to re-create fond memories of place, mood, and personalities, with a fictional murder thrown in for good measure.

Stacy Woodson *is a U.S. Army veteran, and memories of her time in the military are often a source of inspiration for her stories. She made her crime fiction debut in* Ellery Queen Mystery Magazine's Department of First Stories *and won the 2018 Readers Award. It is the second time in the award's history that a debut took first place. Since her debut, she has placed stories in several anthologies and publications—two winning the Derringer Award. Her short fiction has also been adapted for animation. This is her first story selected for* The Best Mystery Stories of the Year.

ONE NIGHT IN 1965

Stacy Woodson

The date was August 26, 1965, the day I took the case that changed my life forever—at least my perspective of it, anyway.

I sat in my PI office, two blocks from the Vegas strip, eating a Swanson TV dinner, watching the *CBS Evening News*. Cronkite, the most trusted man in America, was at the news desk. A soda-straw view of the Vietnam War rolled through the screen. The audio faded in and out, too.

Someone pounded on my door.

I ignored it, my focus still on the TV. I pushed up from the couch. Looked for my cane. Gave up. Limped over to the Magnavox. Adjusted the rabbit ears. Then smacked the box for good measure.

The sound finally kicked in.

Cronkite was talking about President Johnson, how he needed more men to fight the war against communism. Which wasn't news.

The change Johnson planned to make to the draft—*this* was news.

Hours ago, Johnson announced deferments would still be granted to men who married before midnight. Tomorrow, however, men could no longer get married to avoid military service.

Good, I thought. Fewer opportunities for men to shirk their duty. I had stepped up to the plate. It was time others did, too.

More pounding.

"Jack—" Lou called. I recognized my friend's voice through the door. He was a big-deal defense attorney and a pal I'd served with in the Marine Corps. He sometimes threw me a job. Usually, to look through police reports, copies of evidence, photographs, witness statements for inconsistencies, so he could get a guilty client off on a technicality.

"Come back during office hours," I yelled.

"Damn it, Jack!"

I groaned. "Fine." I clicked off the TV, made my way to the door, flipped the dead bolt, eased it open. Lou was dressed to the nines—shirt starched, suit perfectly pressed. A sharp contrast to my boxers and T-shirt.

"Nice threads," Lou said.

"Hey—it's *me* time."

Lou eyed my stomach. "A whole lot of it, apparently."

He wasn't wrong. My belly was round. Definitely not the six-pack I had before Korea.

Before I was shot.

"Do you need something?" I asked. "Or did you come here to bust my balls?"

"Both." Lou handed me my cane. "Found this in the hall."

"Christ. I was looking for that." My mind went back to the previous night, one too many bourbons, stumbling home from The Atomic.

Lou followed me to my desk—the transition smoother with the cane. My pants and shirt were draped across my chair. I tossed them aside and took a seat.

"You know, it's only a matter of time before the landlord catches you living in your office."

I shrugged.

"He could bounce you, Jack."

"I'm not worried." I offered him a cigarette and the couch. He waved away both. I lipped a cigarette from the box, lit the tip, inhaled. "What gives? Must be something big if you're declining a smoke and a seat."

"You're going to be getting a call."

"Ain't that mysterious."

"Don't screw with me, Jack. It's a big client. Work that needs the utmost discretion."

I smiled.

Lou didn't. "I'm serious."

I could tell he was serious and nervous, too. Which was unusual. During the Battle of Chosin Reservoir, I watched him charge the enemy. He didn't hesitate. The man was fearless. This whole anxious thing I'd never seen before.

"Jack . . ."

"I get it," I said.

"Good." He folded his arms. "You do this job, you do it right, the firm will offer you a permanent position. More money—maybe enough to afford a roof over your head. At least enough for some real food."

"I have a roof over my head. And don't knock the Salisbury steak. It's better than those C-Rats we used to eat."

"That doesn't say much." Lou looked like he was about to say more, but my phone rang. He pointed at it, bug-eyed, like I didn't hear it. And I couldn't resist the opportunity to screw with him again. I grabbed an ashtray, crushed out the cigarette, my movements slow and deliberate.

"Pick it up, Jack."

"I'm working on it."

"I swear to God—" He yanked the phone from the receiver and pushed it at me.

I grinned.

Asshole—he mouthed.

I cleared my throat. "Vegas Investigations."

"Please hold for the senator from Nevada."

I frowned, covered the mouthpiece. "Senator?"

But Lou wouldn't look at me, his eyes laser-focused on the phone.

A man came on the line. "Is this Jack Taylor?"

"Speaking."

"Senator Wilkerson here. Calling from Washington. There's a bill on the Senate floor that needs my attention. So, I'll be brief.

Lou tells me you're the best. I have a family matter that I'd like you to handle."

The senator told me about his son. That he'd been drafted to serve in Vietnam. How he'd left for Vegas for an I-do-and-dash.

"At least that's what the wife thinks," the senator continued. "Thomas has an old flame who lives in Vegas. This afternoon, he cleared out his checking account, took my Ford Fairlane, left Carson City. The wife found an address for the Clark County District Courthouse in his bedroom."

In true Sin City fashion, the county's license bureau offered same-day-marriage licenses and no-wait weddings until midnight daily. Odds were the senator's wife was right.

"Even if he's planning a quick wedding, it isn't illegal," I reminded the senator.

"True. But here's the thing. The policy change, the one President Johnson announced today, I'm the one who wrote it. You can imagine how this will look for me, politically, if my son marries to secure a deferment after this announcement."

"Yeah." He'll look like every other self-entitled kid who had dodged the draft.

"I fought in World War II," the senator continued. "I understand you served in the Korean conflict. We all have a duty to our country. Don't you think? I want my son to honor his. The Selective Service board requested Thomas report for induction tomorrow. I want him to be there."

Even though the senator's motives were self-serving, he wanted to hold his son accountable, and I respected this. "What would you like me to do?"

Twenty minutes later, I was showered, dressed, and in my Buick Riviera, driving to the Clark County District Courthouse. The senator wanted me to stop Thomas's wedding and convince him to return to Carson City. If the kid refused, I was supposed to detain him until someone from the senator's staff arrived. Lou would handle things for the senator moving forward. He gave me a picture of the couple and details on the Fairlane.

My first task was to locate Thomas.

When I arrived at the courthouse, couples spilled out of the license bureau, down the sidewalk, and onto the lawn. They were young—some dressed like they were going to church, others to a protest rally.

All had anxious faces.

I tried to feel some empathy for them. But I couldn't do it. Kids who didn't have money, kids who couldn't afford to run away to Vegas and get hitched—they would be drafted and forced to take their place.

Someone always took their place.

I tightened my grip on my cane, pulled out the picture from Lou—a prom shot of Thomas and Lilly. It was a few years old. But it didn't matter. Their likeness was all I needed.

I worked my way up the line, comparing faces—one after the other.

No Lilly. No Thomas.

I continued into the license bureau.

No luck.

At the counter, the sign said the clerk's name was Betty. She looked as young as the people she served. She seemed stressed, haggard. The pace she processed paperwork determined who would make the deferment deadline, and the responsibility clearly weighed upon her. I needed to question Betty and find out if Thomas and Lilly had been here.

I elbowed my way to the front.

"Hey, pal," a kid with a flattop whined. "There's a line here."

I ignored him and tried to get Betty's attention. "Excuse me, miss."

"Ms." She corrected me, her hands still working—typing, stapling, processing. "You need to move to the back of the line. When it's your turn, I can assist you."

"I'm not here for a marriage license."

"Then you're in the wrong place." Betty looked at Flattop. "That'll be eight dollars."

Flattop elbowed me out of the way and handed Betty the money. She pushed a ledger toward him. He signed it. Then, she handed him a license. "Go through the double doors on the right. The justice of the peace will see you in the back."

"I don't know if I can do this," the girl with Flattop whispered.

His eyes went wide. "Don't you love me?"

"It's not that." She visibly swallowed. "It's just . . . we've only been dating for three weeks."

"Do you want me to die in Vietnam?"

The girl's breath caught. "God, no."

"Make up your mind!" someone in line yelled.

She started to cry.

"Tick. Tock." A man in a sports coat chimed in. "We are running out of time. Your indecisiveness is going to get the rest of us killed."

The yelling seemed to prompt a security guard to emerge from the judge's chambers. He stood near the doors, arms folded.

"Here's the thing," the girl started again, "I just applied to be a stewardess."

"You'll be married," Flattop said. "You won't need to work."

"But I want to travel."

"Do you want to save his life or not?" Betty demanded.

"Well, since you put it that way . . ."

"We'll sort it out later, okay?" Flattop grabbed the girl's hand and tugged her toward the judge's chambers.

"Excuse me," I tried to get Betty's attention again, my mind on the ledger. I needed to see it. If Thomas had picked up a license, his or Lilly's name would be inside.

Betty still ignored me.

I walked behind the counter.

"You're not allowed back here." She motioned to the security guard.

"It's my leg," I said, gripping it dramatically. "Sometimes the pain is too much, and I need to sit. There are no chairs in the reception area. Please forgive the breach of protocol."

She looked at my leg. Then, at my cane. Her face flushed. "I didn't know."

The security guard hovered over me now, so close I could smell the tuna and rye he had for dinner. "Is there a problem here, Betty?"

"I'm good, Tom."

"You sure?"

"Yeah." She nodded.

He walked away, his eyes still on me. I flashed Betty a grateful smile.

She continued to work. "How did you get injured?"

"Korea."

"Damn wars." She shook her head. "They take something from everyone, don't they?"

The conviction in her voice, the anger. I could tell this ran deeper than politics. It was personal. "Did you lose someone?"

"My brother." She pointed to a picture on her desk, a snapshot from a huge family gathering—at least fifteen faces. "Teddy is on the bottom right."

He looked young.

They always did.

"I'm sorry for your loss," I told her. And I meant it. I waited for her to finish with another couple before I said, "There're a lot of people here to manage by yourself."

"Normally, two of us process marriage licenses, but my coworker didn't come back from her break today."

"She picked a hell of a day to play hooky."

"Tell me about it."

I eyed the ledger on her desk, watched Betty work, considered my next move. If I told her my purpose, to stop a wedding and a deferment, she wouldn't help me. Hell, she may even try to stop me. I needed to take another approach, find the right angle. Something that would resonate with her. And then, I got it—the picture on her desk. Family was important to her.

This was my way in.

"Look, I know you're busy, and you've been so kind. It's just—I'm looking for my little sister. She's getting married today, and my mother is beside herself."

Betty frowned.

Crap. She thinks I'm trying to stop them.

"My mother," I paused, reworking my approach, "she can't imagine her baby taking such a big step without someone from the family being there. I'm here to support my sister, of course.

I didn't see her in your line. I'm worried I may be too late. That she's already married."

"Of course." Betty glanced at the picture on her desk and nodded knowingly. "I can't imagine getting married without my family." She wheeled an application into her typewriter. "If your sister picked up a marriage license, she or her fiancé signed for it." She motioned to the ledger. "Feel free to take a look."

"Thank you." I reached for the book, flipped through the pages—nearly one hundred entries today, so far.

None for Thomas and Lilly.

"Any luck?" Betty asked.

I shook my head. "Maybe they haven't arrived yet, or maybe one of them changed their mind."

"We've had a few of those today."

"I know you're swamped. But will you take a quick look at a picture for me? Just in case they came through your line but didn't finalize their license. I need to tell my mother something."

Betty glanced at the line of people, which didn't seem to end.

"Please," I pressed.

"Fine." She exhaled the word. "Put the picture on the desk. I'll look while I work."

"Thank you." I smiled. "I feel like I'm saying that a lot to you today." I slid the picture over.

She took money from another applicant and directed them to the judge's chambers before she finally looked. "Lilly Miller? Seriously? *She's* your sister?"

"You know her?"

"You're sitting at her desk."

"What?" I said, surprised.

"Lilly took her break. Left here with that guy in the picture. She left and never came back."

Lilly Miller's *brother* should have known she worked at the courthouse. Thankfully, Betty was too busy with applicants to notice. I quickly disappeared before she got wise to me.

I located a phone booth outside, flipped through the white pages, found Lilly's address, and headed to her apartment.

On the drive, I considered my latest development—that there was no evidence Lilly and Thomas applied for a marriage license. The assumption that Thomas had come to Vegas to marry Lilly for a deferment seemed less likely.

So, why would Thomas come here the night before his induction? Maybe he wanted one last night with Lilly in Sin City before Vietnam? I suppose this could be true. But then why not tell his parents? Why leave Carson City in such a hurry?

The Grecian was a Mediterranean-style apartment complex with open-air units that horseshoed around a pool. Lilly lived on the third floor. Navigating the stairs was an event. When I reached her apartment, sweat pooled under my arms, and my leg screamed.

I sucked in a breath. Then, another. Tried to steady my ragged breathing before I finally knocked on her door.

No one answered.

There was a light on inside. I pressed my face to the window. But there were curtains—thick, like cotton. I could only make out shapes, no details.

I went back to the door.

Knocked again.

Still, nothing.

I reached into my pocket, pulled out my knife to jimmy the lock. Reconsidered it. Tried the knob instead. It turned in my hand.

"Hello?" I eased the door open. "Lilly?"

Her studio apartment looked like it had been tossed—drawers half open, clothes strewn on the bed, costume jewelry scattered on the floor. I continued to the bathroom. The medicine cabinet was empty. Lilly's toiletries were gone. In the closet—empty hangers. No suitcase.

If Thomas had come to Vegas to party with Lilly, she'd have no reason to pack, no reason to leave her apartment in a hurry.

None of this made sense.

I raked a hand through my hair, circled the room again, found nothing. I needed to figure out my next steps. I tried to sort through the facts and the assumptions I'd made.

I knew Lilly and Thomas were together—thanks to Betty. Thomas picked her up at the courthouse. Lilly had her suitcase with her, or they came back to her apartment and packed. The order didn't really matter. They planned to disappear together—at least, that's what it looked like. But where? Canada, maybe?

This would make sense if Thomas was dodging the draft. But why become a fugitive if there were a legal way to gain a deferment?

Desperate for answers, I went to her trash cans. The bathroom one was empty. But the kitchen can was full. I pulled the bin from under the sink, the contents nearly spilling over the sides, and dumped it onto a table. Food leftovers, wrappers, bottles—everything you'd expect in a kitchen can was there.

Nothing useful.

Which meant I would need to question Lilly's neighbors. See if they knew anything. Interviews like these took time, time I didn't have.

I had to call Lou. I washed my hands. Found Lilly's phone, dialed his number.

"Jack?"

"Yeah."

"Any luck?"

"No dice."

"What do you mean no dice?"

I told him about my trip to the courthouse, going to Lilly's apartment, how I had nothing.

"I can't go to the senator with nothing."

"I hear ya, Lou. I'm not happy about it either."

"You need to give me something, Jack."

"I'll continue to look for leads. But it could take some time. If you want to move things along, have the senator call Vegas PD, report the car stolen. I know he wants to keep this a private matter, but this may be the quickest way to locate his son."

"I don't know." Lou blew out a breath. Ice dropped into a tumbler. A splash of liquor—whiskey, maybe? That's what it sounded like over the phone. Lou took a long sip and sighed. "I'll suggest it to the senator."

"Good." I pulled out a chair, collapsed into the seat, my leg still sore from the stairs. I leaned back, my eyes rested on the space under the kitchen sink, the spot where I'd yanked out the trash can. Then, I saw it—the newspaper. It must have tumbled out, and that's why I'd missed it.

"Did you hear me, Jack?"

I ignored Lou, put the receiver on the table. Made my way to the sink. Reached for the newspaper. An issue of *The Rebel Yell*—UNLV's student newspaper.

On the front, pictures of antiwar protests, students burning draft cards, an editorial encouraging students to join the campus resistance movement. It mentioned the Student Union for Peace Action, the Committee to Aid American War Objectors, and the Anti-Draft Programme—all Canadian groups willing to help resisters once they crossed the border. The name of the person who wrote the piece was circled: Arlo Stanley. His picture was included as part of his byline.

Did Lilly and Thomas plan to connect with Arlo and use his connections to make a run for the Canadian border?

I walked out the door and was halfway to UNLV before I remembered that when I'd left Lilly's apartment, Lou was still on the phone.

It was only the second week of the fall semester, and UNLV's Student Union was busier than I expected. Still, I managed to find a parking space next to the building. I walked through double glass doors that opened to a common area. Students sat at tables drinking coffee, talking, studying. I walked to the Student Union's directory, located the newspaper, and followed the signs to their office on the first floor.

When I arrived, *The Rebel Yell* was in full swing—students at desks typing copy, others proofreading—everyone seemed to be working to put the newspaper to bed.

No one matched Arlo's picture.

A pimple-faced kid saw me at the reception desk and walked over. I told him I was looking for Arlo Stanley. He turned to a group of students gathered by a desk. They were debating the placement of an article.

"The piece about Johnson's new policy should be above the fold," someone in the group said. "I know UNLV seniors that had college deferments who got married today because they didn't want to be drafted when they graduated in the spring."

"I still think the piece on substandard housing conditions is more wide-reaching for our student body," another person argued.

"Anyone seen Arlo?" The pimple-faced kid asked before the group could wind up again. "There's an old guy here looking for him."

A blonde seemed to study me. Her eyes narrowed. Maybe it was the haircut or maybe it was because I still carried myself like a soldier that set her off. But it didn't take a genius to see she didn't trust me.

"You just missed him," she said, her voice tight.

"Really?" A kid with Buddy Holly glasses thumbed toward a row of closed office doors. "I could've sworn I just saw him in the—"

"Shut up, Walter," she hissed, her eyes still on me. "He's gone for the night."

I considered pressing Walter. But the way he clammed up when the blonde yelled at him, I knew he wouldn't tell me anything in front of her.

The pimple-faced kid returned to the reception desk. "Sorry for the confusion, man." He handed me a business card. "If you want to call tomorrow, Arlo's usually here between classes."

That wasn't going to work for me. I took the card anyway and thanked the kid.

Arlo was clearly nearby. The question was where.

Outside the Student Union, I followed the sidewalk that looped behind the building until I was on the back side of the newspaper office. My plan was to peer in the windows and see if Arlo was in one of the offices.

But I didn't get that far.

Along the sidewalk, at the curb in a no-parking zone, was the senator's Ford Fairlane.

I stood there stunned. "I'll be damned."

I walked closer.

A parking ticket from campus security was clipped under a windshield wiper. I looked inside the car. There was a suitcase in the back seat. I didn't know where Thomas and Lilly were on campus, but I did know one way to slow them down.

I glanced around, confirmed I was still alone. Pulled out my knife. Slashed a tire. In case there was a spare, I slashed another. I waited until both tires were flat before I turned to the Student Union and peered through the windows.

The newspaper offices were empty.

I walked up the sidewalk, looking for Thomas. Maybe he and Lilly were at a table in the Student Union with Arlo, and I'd somehow missed them. I went through the common area again.

They weren't there.

I continued through the rear doors of the Student Union, which opened onto the quad, a wide-open space that connected one side of the campus to the other. That's when I saw them, huddled under a cluster of palm trees.

Three people—two men, one woman.

At least, I thought it was them.

Despite the lights that ran along the sidewalk and the full moon overhead, the trees still cast shadows on their faces, making their features difficult to distinguish.

I dropped behind a group of kids walking across the quad, a cloud of pot wafting behind them. I did my best to stay upwind while I made my approach. When I was closer to the trees, I shortened my gait and confirmed their faces.

Arlo was talking. His Afro was big, probably the biggest I'd ever seen, and I fought the urge to stare. He tapped an envelope against his hand. "Everything you need, man—passport, driver's license, credit cards—it's all here." He stopped talking and looked at me.

My stomach tightened. I glanced away, pretended to struggle with my cane.

"Everything okay?" Thomas asked Arlo.

I walked toward a bench. It was close enough that I could still hear while I pretended to nurse my leg.

"Sorry." Arlo shook his head and laughed. "I've been doing this for a year now. I'm still a little paranoid. Guess I still expect the feds to rush in and arrest us."

He handed the envelope to Lilly.

She looked inside, seemed to confirm the contents before she dropped the envelope into a leather shoulder bag.

Thomas handed Arlo a wad of cash. "You sure this will work? I don't want any issues at the border."

"No issues so far," Arlo said.

"None that you know about," Thomas muttered.

"There is a list of addresses in the envelope," Arlo continued. "Sympathizers, safe houses, places where you can stop if you get jammed up."

Guess I was right. Thomas was making a run for the border. The kid couldn't commit to the military or a woman. Why get married when you can buy a new identity and disappear instead?

They continued to talk. But I didn't need to hear anymore. I pushed up from the bench and walked back toward the Fairlane. My job was to ensure Thomas made it to his induction. And that's what I planned to do.

I leaned on the hood of the Fairlane and waited for Thomas and Lilly. It was secluded behind the Student Union. If I was going to honor the senator's request for discretion, this was the best place to confront them. It wasn't long before they were walking toward me. When Thomas saw me, he stepped in front of Lilly.

Kid was chivalrous. Certainly not what I expected.

"Can I help you?" Thomas asked.

"No." I folded my arms. "But you can help yourself."

"I don't understand."

"Friday, June 1, 1949."

"I'm sorry, sir. I'm not into riddles. We are in a hurry. So, if you could get off my car—"

"That was my induction date for the Korean conflict," I continued, unwavering. "I watched rich kids like you avoid the draft. While kids like me, kids with working-class parents, took your place. What makes your lives more valuable than ours?"

Thomas frowned. "What are you talking about?"

"I did my duty. Your father sent me to make sure you do yours. You have an induction date in Carson City tomorrow morning. It's my job to make sure you're there."

Thomas blinked. Then, his eyes went wide. "Wait. My dad thinks I'm dodging the draft?"

"Aren't you? I saw you with Arlo—the documents."

"Thomas." Lilly tugged on his arm. "This has gone too far. We need to tell him."

"It's not safe, Lilly."

"If he worked for them, I'd already be dead."

Thomas shook his head. "You don't have to do this."

"I'm not going to cause a rift between you and your father." Lilly stepped forward. She looked petite, smaller somehow than when I first saw her in the quad. "The documents aren't for Thomas. They're for me."

She told me about her job at the license bureau. How she also worked as a stenographer in the courts. The bribes she'd witnessed. Cops, judges, government officials—all connected to the mob. "I didn't know what to do. It wasn't like I could look the other way. So, I collected evidence, contacted the FBI. And—" Her voice cracked.

Thomas put his arm over her shoulders.

She sucked in a breath, tried again. Her eyes started to mist.

"The agent Lilly was supposed to meet was murdered," Thomas filled in. He handed her a handkerchief.

She dabbed her eyes and nodded. "I knew I needed to run. But I had no money. No car. No resources. I called Thomas."

They both stopped talking and looked at me now like they were waiting for me to say something.

"It's the truth, sir," Thomas added.

I thought about what they'd told me, compared it to what I knew. The rush to the courthouse but no marriage license. The meet with Arlo—he'd handed Lilly the documents, not Thomas. There was only one suitcase in the back seat of the Fairlane.

Thomas was never running to Vegas to avoid the draft.

He was running to Vegas to help a friend.

"Maybe if you explained things to the senator," I tried. "He could help you."

"We considered that," Thomas said. "But political circles in Nevada are small. If this leaked, if something was said in my father's office in front of the wrong person, it wouldn't take much for them to find Lilly."

Sirens.

My eyes went to the ticket still under the Fairlane's windshield, and my stomach tightened. "You need to get out of here."

"You think they're coming for Lilly?" Thomas asked.

"No, they're coming for you." I told him how I'd advised the senator to report the car stolen. How when campus security filed their parking ticket with the local precinct, it alerted the Vegas police department the Fairlane was here.

"If the police find me," Lilly said, panicked, "you may as well hand me over to the mob. Give me the keys, Thomas. If I leave now, I'll be gone before they get here. You can tell them it was a misunderstanding."

"That won't work," I told her. "The Fairlane has two flat tires."

"What?" Thomas asked.

"Take mine." I tossed him my keys. "It's the Buick Riviera in the Student Union parking lot. I'd take Lilly myself, but you'll be faster without me. I'll smooth things over with the police."

The sirens were louder.

Thomas locked eyes with Lilly. Some silent exchange I didn't understand.

"What are you waiting for?" I pressed.

She reached into her shoulder bag, pulled out a large manila envelope, handed it to me. "I trust you'll know what to do with this."

And then, just like that, they were gone.

Two weeks later, I sat on my couch in my PI office wearing my boxers and T-shirt, another Swanson TV dinner in front of me, waiting for the *CBS Evening News* to start. I wondered if Cronkite had received the envelope yet. The one with Lilly's recordings—evidence that connected Vegas officials to the mob.

After I left Thomas and Lilly that night, on the cab ride back to my office, I'd contemplated what to do with the tapes. I thought about going back to the feds, even giving the recordings to Lou. But in the end, I decided to send them to Cronkite. He was the most trusted man in America, after all. If anyone could shed light on the truth and hold people accountable, it would be him.

Lou wasn't happy when I told him that I'd found the senator's car but had no luck detaining the kid.

The next morning, I received a telegram from Thomas telling me where I could find the Buick. The kid must have used the registration paperwork in my glove box to find my address. He could have a future in the PI business if he survived Vietnam.

Truth was, I didn't know if Thomas made it back to Carson City in time for his induction date. And for the first time since I started this case, I didn't care.

During the Battle of Chosin Reservoir, Lou had charged the enemy not because of some obligation to our nation. He did it to protect the people who served by his side—his friends. No different than when Thomas risked everything and rushed to Vegas to help Lilly.

Meeting Thomas made me realize my hang-up with deferments had nothing to do with dodging the draft. It wasn't a person's lack of service that bothered me. It was their lack of character.

And just like Lou, Thomas had it in spades.

Cronkite started to speak. The audio faded in and out on my TV. A picture of the Clark County District Courthouse filled the screen. "Corruption and the mob. Early today, CBS News broke a story—"

"Jack." Lou pounded on my door. "It's me. Open up."

"Come back during office hours."

More pounding. "Damn it, Jack!"

I limped over to the door, flipped the dead bolt, turned the knob.

Lou pushed past me. "Are you watching the news? I've got a job. It's a big client. Work that needs the utmost discretion. It's about the tapes that went to Cronkite's office."

My eyes went wide.

"I need you to track down the whistleblower. You do this, Jack. And you do it right. The firm will offer you a permanent position . . ."

I looked past Lou at my TV dinner, the smell of Salisbury steak wafting in the air, and I couldn't help but think that I'd be eating them for a while.

Michael Bracken is a wonderful friend and mentor. When he was accepting submissions for Groovy Gumshoes: Private Eyes in the Psychedelic Sixties, *he asked that I write a story with a military character. I told him that I'd never written a private eye story and couldn't land on an idea that worked for me. Michael suggested looking at a PI hired to recover a draft dodger. This was the spark that inspired "One Night in 1965." The heart of the story was inspired by my father, a man who taught me to appreciate history and a Vietnam veteran who volunteered to serve.*

BONUS STORY

Yes, that **L***(yman)* **Frank Baum** *(1856–1919), the man who created the most magical and popular series of fairy tales ever written by an American, beginning with* The Wonderful Wizard of Oz *in 1900.*

Although born to a wealthy family that made its fortune in the oil business, Baum went out on his own in search of a career, first as a journalist, then as a poultry farmer. When the family fell on hard times, he struggled to earn a living for himself, his wife, and their four children. In addition to journalistic pieces for newspapers and magazines, he wrote short stories and, in 1897, a successful children's book, Mother Goose in Prose, *followed two years later by* Father Goose: His Book, *which became a bestseller. His next book was* The Wonderful Wizard of Oz *(1900), the publication of which he financed himself, launching one of the most successful careers in American literature. He wrote sixty more books, mostly for young readers, including seventeen additional Oz books (a couple of which were published posthumously and one,* The Royal Book of Oz, *credited to him was written entirely by Ruth Plumley Thompson, who wrote more Oz novels than Baum—nineteen). Many of the Oz novels were filmed, though none as successfully as the 1939 film,* The Wizard of Oz, *with its iconic portrayals of Dorothy by Judy Garland (though the studio's first choice had been Shirley Temple), the Cowardly Lion by Bert Lahr, the Scarecrow by Ray Bolger, and the Tin Man by Frank Haley. Like all of Baum's books for young readers, they offered positive, optimistic views that assured children that they could be successful by embracing the traditional American virtues of integrity, self-reliance, candor, and courage.*

It is, therefore, especially shocking to accept the notion that the same person could have written the following story, which is as diametrically opposite those sentiments as it is possible for anyone to be. It is one of the darkest stories in this book.

"The Suicide of Kiaros" was first published in a now-forgotten literary magazine, The White Elephant, *in its issue of September 1897.*

THE SUICIDE
OF KIAROS

L. Frank Baum

I.

M r. Felix Marston, cashier for the great mercantile firm of
Van Alsteyne & Traynor, sat in his little private office with
a balance sheet before him and a frown upon his handsome face.
At times he nervously ran his slim fingers through the mass of dark
hair that clustered over his forehead, and the growing expression
of annoyance upon his features fully revealed his disquietude.

The world knew and admired Mr. Marston, and a casual
onlooker would certainly have decided that something had gone
wrong with the firm's financial transactions; but Mr. Marston
knew himself better than the world did, and grimly realized that
although something had gone very wrong indeed, it affected
himself in an unpleasantly personal way.

The world's knowledge of the popular young cashier included
the following items: He had entered the firm's employ years before
in an inferior position, and by energy, intelligence and business
ability, had worked his way up until he reached the post he now
occupied, and became his employers' most trusted servant. His
manner was grave, earnest and dignified; his judgment, in business
matters, clear and discerning. He had no intimate friends, but was
courteous and affable to all he met, and his private life, so far as
it was known, was beyond all reproach.

Mr. Van Alsteyne, the head of the firm, conceived a warm
liking for Mr. Marston, and finally invited him to dine at
his house. It was there the young man first met Gertrude
Van Alsteyne, his employer's only child, a beautiful girl and
an acknowledged leader in society. Attracted by the man's

handsome face and gentlemanly bearing, the heiress encouraged him to repeat his visit, and Marston followed up his advantage so skillfully that within a year she had consented to become his wife. Mr. Van Alsteyne did not object to the match. His admiration for the young man deepened, and he vowed that upon the wedding day he would transfer one-half his interest in the firm to his son-in-law.

Therefore the world, knowing all this, looked upon Mr. Marston as one of fortune's favorites, and predicted a great future for him. But Mr. Marston, as I said, knew himself more intimately than did the world, and now, as he sat looking upon that fatal trial balance, he muttered in an undertone:

"Oh, you fool—you fool!"

Clear-headed, intelligent man of the world though he was, one vice had mastered him. A few of the most secret, but most dangerous gambling dens knew his face well. His ambition was unbounded, and before he had even dreamed of being able to win Miss Van Alsteyne as his bride, he had figured out several ingenious methods of winning a fortune at the green table. Two years ago he had found it necessary to "borrow" a sum of money from the firm to enable him to carry out these clever methods. Having, through some unforeseen calamity, lost the money, another sum had to be abstracted to allow him to win back enough to even the accounts. Other men have attempted this before; their experiences are usually the same. By a neat juggling of figures, the books of the firm had so far been made to conceal his thefts, but now it seemed as if fortune, in pushing him forward, was about to hurl him down a precipice.

His marriage to Gertrude Van Alsteyne was to take place in two weeks, and as Mr. Van Alsteyne insisted upon keeping his promise to give Marston an interest in the business, the change in the firm would necessitate a thorough overhauling of the accounts, which meant discovery and ruin to the man who was about to grasp a fortune and a high social position—all that his highest ambition had ever dreamed of attaining.

It is no wonder that Mr. Marston, brought face to face with his critical position, denounced himself for his past folly, and realized his helplessness to avoid the catastrophe that was about to crush him.

A voice outside interrupted his musings and arrested his attention.

"It is Mr. Marston I wish to see."

The cashier thrust the sheet of figures within a drawer of the desk, hastily composed his features and opened the glass door beside him.

"Show Mr. Kiaros this way," he called, after a glance at his visitor. He had frequently met the person who now entered his office, but he could not resist a curious glance as the man sat down upon a chair and spread his hands over his knees. He was short and thick-set in form, and both oddly and carelessly dressed, but his head and face were most venerable in appearance. Flowing locks of pure white graced a forehead whose height and symmetry denoted unusual intelligence, and a full beard of the same purity reached full to his waist. The eyes were full and dark, but not piercing in character, rather conveying in their frank glance kindness and benevolence. A round cap of some dark material was worn upon his head, and this he deferentially removed as he seated himself, and said:

"For me a package of value was consigned to you, I believe?"

Marston nodded gravely. "Mr. Williamson left it with me," he replied.

"I will take it," announced the Greek, calmly; "twelve thousand dollars it contains."

Marston started.

"I knew it was money," he said, "but was not aware of the amount. This is it, I think." He took from the huge safe a packet, corded and sealed, and handed it to his visitor. Kiaros took a penknife from his pocket, cut the cords and removed the wrapper, after which he proceeded to count the contents.

Marston listlessly watched him. Twelve thousand dollars. That would be more than enough to save him from ruin, if only it belonged to him instead of this Greek money-lender.

"The amount, it is right," declared the old man, re-wrapping the parcel of notes; "you have my thanks, sir. Good afternoon," and he rose to go.

"Pardon me, sir," said Marston, with a sudden thought, "it is after banking hours. Will it be safe to carry this money with you until morning?"

"Perfectly," replied Kiaros; "I am never molested, for I am old, and few know my business. My safe at home large sums often contains. The money I like to have near me, to accommodate my clients."

He buttoned his coat tightly over the packet, and then in turn paused to look at the cashier.

"Lately you have not come to me for favors," he said.

"No," answered Marston, arousing from a slight reverie; "I have not needed to. Still, I may be obliged to visit you again soon."

"Your servant I am pleased to be," said Kiaros, with a smile, and turning abruptly he left the office.

Marston glanced at his watch. He was engaged to dine with his betrothed that evening, and it was nearly time to return to his lodgings to dress. He attended to one or two matters in his usual methodical way, and then left the office for the night, relinquishing any further duties to his assistant. As he passed through the various business offices on his way out, he was greeted respectfully by his fellow-employees, who already regarded him a member of the firm.

II.

Almost for the first time during their courtship, Miss Van Alsteyne was tender and demonstrative that evening, and seemed loath to allow him to leave the house when he pleaded a business engagement and arose to go. She was a stately beauty, and little given to emotional ways, therefore her new mood affected him greatly, and as he walked away he realized, with a sigh, how much it would cost him to lose so dainty and charming a bride.

At the first corner he paused and examined his watch by the light of the street lamp. It was nine o'clock. Hailing the first passing cab, he directed the man to drive him to the lower end of the city, and leaning back upon the cushions, he became occupied in earnest thought.

The jolting of the cab over a rough pavement finally aroused him, and looking out he signaled the driver to stop.

"Shall I wait, sir?" asked the man, as Marston alighted and paid his fare.

"No."

The cab rattled away, and the cashier retraced his way a few blocks and then walked down a side street that seemed nearly deserted, so far as he could see in the dim light. Keeping track of the house numbers, which were infrequent and often nearly obliterated, he finally paused before a tall brick building, the lower floors of which seemed occupied as a warehouse.

"Two eighty-six," he murmured; "this must be the place. If I remember right there should be a stairway at the left—ah, here it is."

There was no light at the entrance, but having visited the place before, under similar circumstances, Marston did not hesitate, but began mounting the stairs, guiding himself in the darkness by keeping one hand upon the narrow rail. One flight—two—three—four!

"His room should be straight before me," he thought, pausing to regain his breath; "yes, I think there is a light shining under the door."

He advanced softly, knocked, and then listened. There was a faint sound from within, and then a slide in the upper panel of the door was pushed aside, permitting a strong ray of lamp-light to strike Marston full in the face.

"Oho!" said a calm voice, "Mr. Marston has honored me. To enter I entreat you."

The door was thrown open and Kiaros stood before him, with a smile upon his face, gracefully motioning him to advance. Marston returned the old man's courteous bow, and entering the room, took a seat near the table, at the same time glancing at his surroundings.

The room was plainly but substantially furnished. A small safe stood in a corner at his right, and near it was the long table, used by Kiaros as a desk. It was littered with papers and writing material, and behind it was a high-backed, padded easy-chair, evidently the favorite seat of the Greek, for after closing the door he walked around the table and sat within the big chair, facing his visitor.

The other end of the room boasted a fire-place, with an old-fashioned mantel bearing an array of curiosities. Above it was a large clock, and at one side stood a small book-case containing a number of volumes printed in the Greek language. A small alcove, containing a couch, occupied the remaining side of the small apartment, and it was evident these cramped quarters constituted Kiaros' combined office and living rooms.

"So soon as this I did not expect you," said the old man, in his grave voice.

"I am in need of money," replied Marston, abruptly, "and my interview with you this afternoon reminded me that you have sometimes granted me an occasional loan. Therefore, I have come to negotiate with you."

Kiaros nodded, and studied with his dark eyes the composed features of the cashier.

"A satisfactory debtor you have ever proved," said he, "and to pay me with promptness never failed. How much do you require?"

"Twelve thousand dollars."

In spite of his self-control, Kiaros started as the young man coolly stated this sum.

"Impossible!" he ejaculated, moving uneasily in his chair.

"Why is it impossible?" demanded Marston. "I know you have the money."

"True; I deny it not," returned Kiaros, dropping his gaze before the other's earnest scrutiny; "also to lend money is my business. But see—I will be frank with you Mr. Marston—I cannot take the risk. You are cashier for hire; you have no property; security for so large a sum you cannot give. Twelve thousand dollars! It is impossible!"

"You loaned Williamson twelve thousand," persisted Marston; doggedly.

"Mr. Williamson secured me."

Marston rose from his chair and began slowly pacing up and down before the table, his hands clasped tightly behind him and an impatient frown contracting his features. The Greek watched him calmly.

"Perhaps you have not heard, Mr. Kiaros," he said, at length, "that within two weeks I am to be married to Mr. Van Alsteyne's only daughter."

"I had not heard."

"And at the same time I am to receive a large interest in the business as a wedding gift from my father-in-law."

"To my congratulations you are surely entitled."

"Therefore my need is only temporary. I shall be able to return the money within thirty days, and I am willing to pay you well for the accommodation."

"A Jew I am not," returned Kiaros, with a slight shrug, "and where I lend I do not rob. But so great a chance I cannot undertake. You are not yet married, a partner in the firm not yet. To die, to quarrel with the lady, to lose Mr. Van Alsteyne's confidence, would leave me to collect the sum wholly unable. I might a small amount risk—the large amount is impossible."

Marston suddenly became calm, and resumed his chair with a quiet air, to Kiaros' evident satisfaction.

"You have gambled?" asked the Greek, after a pause.

"Not lately. I shall never gamble again. I owe no gambling debts; this money is required for another purpose."

"Can you not do with less?" asked Kiaros; "an advance I will make of one thousand dollars; not more. That sum is also a risk, but you are a man of discretion; in your ability I have confidence."

Marston did not reply at once. He leaned back in his chair, and seemed to be considering the money-lender's offer. In reality there passed before his mind the fate that confronted him, the scene in which he posed as a convicted felon; he saw the collapse of his great ambitions, the ruin of those schemes he had almost brought to fruition. Already he felt the reproaches of the man he had robbed, the scorn of the proud woman who had been ready to give him her hand, the cold sneers of those who gloated over his downfall. And then he bethought himself, and drove the vision away, and thought of other things.

Kiaros rested his elbow upon the table, and toyed with a curious-looking paper-cutter. It was made of pure silver, in the shape of a dagger; the blade was exquisitely chased, and bore a

Greek motto. After a time Kiaros looked up and saw his guest regarding the paper-cutter.

"It is a relic most curious," said he, "from the ruins of Missolonghi rescued, and by a friend sent to me. All that is Greek I love. Soon to my country I shall return, and that is why I cannot risk the money I have in a lifetime earned."

Still Marston did not reply, but sat looking thoughtfully at the table. Kiaros was not impatient. He continued to play with the silver dagger, and poised it upon his finger while he awaited the young man's decision.

"I think I shall be able to get along with the thousand dollars," said Marston at last, his collected tones showing no trace of the disappointment Kiaros had expected. "Can you let me have it now?"

"Yes. As you know, the money is in my safe. I will make out the note."

He quietly laid down the paper-cutter and drew a note-book from a drawer of the table. Dipping a pen in the inkwell, he rapidly filled up the note and pushed it across the table to Marston.

"Will you sign?" he asked, with his customary smile. Marston drew his chair close to the table and examined the note.

"You said you would not rob me!" he demurred.

"The commission it is very little," replied Kiaros, coolly. "A Jew much more would have exacted."

Marston picked up the pen, dashed off his name, and tossed the paper towards Kiaros. The Greek inspected it carefully, and rising from his chair, walked to the safe and drew open the heavy door. He placed the note in one drawer, and from another removed an oblong tin box, which he brought to the table. Reseating himself, he opened this box and drew out a large packet of banknotes.

Marston watched him listlessly as he carefully counted out one thousand dollars.

"The amount is, I believe, correct," said Kiaros, after a second count; "if you will kindly verify it I shall be pleased."

Marston half arose and reached out his hand, but he did not take the money. Instead, his fingers closed over the handle of the silver dagger, and with a swift, well-directed blow he plunged it to the hilt in the breast of the Greek. The old man lay back in his chair with a low moan, his form quivered once or twice and then became still, while a silence that suddenly seemed oppressive pervaded the little room.

III.

Felix Marston sat down in his chair and stared at the form of Kiaros. The usually benevolent features of the Greek were horribly convulsed, and the dark eyes had caught and held a sudden look of terror. His right hand, resting upon the table, still grasped the bundle of bank-notes. The handle of the silver dagger glistened in the lamplight just above the heart, and a dark-colored fluid was slowly oozing outward and discoloring the old man's clothing and the point of his snowy beard.

Marston drew out his handkerchief and wiped the moisture from his forehead. Then he arose, and going to his victim, carefully opened the dead hand and removed the money. In the tin box was the remainder of the twelve thousand dollars the Greek had that day received. Marston wrapped it all in a paper and placed it in his breast pocket. Then he went to the safe, replaced the box in its drawer, and found the note he had just signed.

This he folded and placed carefully in his pocket-book. Returning to the table, he stood looking down upon the dead man.

"He was a very good fellow, old Kiaros, he murmured; "I am sorry I had to kill him. But this is no time for regrets; I must try to cover all traces of my crime. The reason most murderers are discovered is because they become terrified, are anxious to get away, and so leave clues behind them. I have plenty of time. Probably no one knows of my visit here to-night, and as the old man lives quite alone, no one is likely to come here before morning."

He looked at his watch. It was a few minutes after ten o'clock.

"This ought to be a case of suicide," he continued, "and I shall try to make it look that way."

The expression of Kiaros' face first attracted his attention. That look of terror was incompatible with suicide. He drew a chair beside the old man and began to pass his hands over the dead face to smooth out the contracted lines. The body was still warm, and with a little perseverance, Marston succeeded in relaxing the drawn muscles until the face gradually resumed its calm and benevolent look.

The eyes, however, were more difficult to deal with, and it was only after repeated efforts that Marston was able to draw the lids over them, and hide their startled and horrified gaze. When this was accomplished, Kiaros looked as peaceful as if asleep, and the cashier was satisfied with his progress. He now lifted the Greek's right hand and attempted to clasp the fingers over the handle of the dagger, but they fell away limply.

"Rigor mortis has not yet set in," reflected Marston, "and I must fasten the hand in position until it does. Had the man himself dealt the blow, the tension of the nerves of the arm would probably have forced the fingers to retain their grip upon the weapon." He took his handkerchief and bound the fingers over the hilt of the dagger, at the same time altering the position of the head and body to better suit the assumption of suicide.

"I shall have to wait some time for the body to cool," he told himself, and then he considered what might be done in the meantime.

A box of cigars stood upon the mantel. Marston selected one and lit it. Then he returned to the table, turned up the lamp a trifle, and began searching in the drawers for specimens of the Greek's handwriting. Having secured several of these he sat down and studied them for a few minutes, smoking collectedly the while, and taking care to drop the ashes in a little tray that Kiaros had used for that purpose. Finally he drew a sheet of paper towards him, and carefully imitating the Greek's sprawling chirography, wrote as follows:

My money I have lost. To live longer I cannot. To die I am therefore resolved.

KIAROS.

"I think that will pass inspection," he muttered, looking at the paper approvingly, and comparing it again with the dead man's writing. "I must avoid all risks, but this forgery is by far too clever to be detected." He placed the paper upon the table before the body of the Greek, and then rearranged the papers as he had found them.

Slowly the hours passed away. Marston rose from his chair at intervals and examined the body. At one o'clock rigor mortis began to set in, and a half hour later Marston removed the handkerchief, and was pleased to find the hand retained its grasp upon the dagger. The position of the dead body was now very natural indeed, and the cashier congratulated himself upon his success.

There was but one task remaining for him to accomplish. The door must be found locked upon the inside. Marston searched until he found a piece of twine, one end of which he pinned lightly to the top of the table, a little to the left of the inkwell. The other end of the twine he carried to the door, and passed it through the slide in the panel. Withdrawing the key from the lock of the door; he now approached the table for the last time, taking a final look at the body, and laying the end of his cigar upon the tray. The theory of suicide had been excellently carried out; if only the key could be arranged for, he would be satisfied. Reflecting thus, he leaned over and blew out the light.

It was very dark, but he had carefully considered the distance beforehand, and in a moment he had reached the hallway and softly closed and locked the door behind him. Then he withdrew the key, found the end of the twine which projected through the panel, and running this through the ring of the key, he passed it inside the panel, and allowed the key to slide down the cord until a sharp click told him it rested upon the table within. A sudden jerk of the twine now unfastened the end which had been pinned to the table, and he drew it in and carefully placed it in his pocket. Before closing the door of the panel, Marston lighted a match, and satisfied himself the key was lying in the position he had wished. He breathed more freely then and closed the panel.

A few minutes later he had reached the street, and after a keen glance up and down, he stepped boldly from the doorway and walked away.

To his surprise, he now felt himself trembling with nervousness, and despite his endeavors to control himself, it required all of his four-mile walk home to enable him to regain his wonted composure.

He let himself in with his latchkey, and made his way noiselessly to his room. As he was a gentleman of regular habits, the landlady never bothered herself to keep awake watching for his return.

IV.

Mr. Marston appeared at the office the next morning in an unusually good humor, and at once busied himself with the regular routine of duties.

As soon as he was able, he retired to his private office and began to revise the books and make out a new trial balance. The exact amount he had stolen from the firm was put into the safe, the false figures were replaced with correct ones, and by noon the new balance sheet proved that Mr. Marston's accounts were in perfect condition.

Just before he started for luncheon a clerk brought him the afternoon paper. "What do you think, Mr. Marston?" he said. "Old Kiaros has committed suicide."

"Indeed! Do you mean the Kiaros who was here yesterday?" inquired Marston, as he put on his coat.

"The very same. It seems the old man lost his money in some unfortunate speculation, and so took his own life. The police found him in his room this morning, stabbed to the heart. Here is the paper, sir, if you wish to see it."

"Thank you," returned the cashier, in his usual quiet way. "I will buy one when I go out," and without further comment he went to luncheon.

But he purchased a paper, and while eating read carefully the account of Kiaros' suicide. The report was reassuring; no one seemed to dream the Greek was the victim of foul play.

The verdict of the coroner's jury completed his satisfaction. They found that Kiaros had committed suicide in a fit of despondency. The Greek was buried and forgotten, and soon the papers teemed with sensational accounts of the brilliant wedding of that estimable gentleman, Mr. Felix Marston, to the popular society belle, Miss Gertrude Van Alsteyne. The happy pair made a bridal trip to Europe, and upon their return Mr. Marston was installed as an active partner in the great firm of Van Alsteyne, Traynor & Marston.

This was twenty years ago. Mr. Marston to-day has an enviable record as an honorable and highly respected man of business, although some consider him a trifle too cold and calculating.

His wife, although she early discovered the fact that he had married her to further his ambition, has found him reserved and undemonstrative, but always courteous and indulgent to both herself and her children.

He holds his head high and looks every man squarely in the eye, and he is very generally envied, since everything seems to prosper in his hands.

Kiaros and his suicide are long since forgotten by the police and the public. Perhaps Marston recalls the Greek at times. He told me this story when he lay upon what he supposed was his death-bed.

In writing it down I have only altered the names of the characters. I promised Marston that so long as he lived I would not denounce him, and he still lives.

THE BEST MYSTERY STORIES
2024
HONOR ROLL

Additional outstanding stories published in 2023

Libby Cudmore, Wait for the Blackout
Ellery Queen Mystery Magazine, May/June

Eve Elliot, Hell Hath No Fury
Malice Domestic #17: Murder Most Traditional (Wildside Press)

Vasseen Kahn, Ace of Spades
The Strand Magazine, Vol. 69

David Shawn Klein, Monster Case
Mystery Magazine, December

Robert Lopresti, The Accessories Club
Alfred Hitchcock's Mystery Magazine, March/April

Chris McGinley, The Females Especially
Coal Black: Stories (Shotgun Honey/Down & Out)

Jessica Slee, Woodpeckers
Shotgun Honey Presents Thicker Than Water (Shotgun Honey)

Rob B. Smith, Our Most Sorrowful Mother of the Blessed Hardwood
Vautrin, Vol. 5, No. 1

Mark Thielman, The Experimental Theater Company of Barbed Wire
Alfred Hitchcock's Mystery Magazine, November/December

Peter Turnbull, The Extremely Pleasant and Most Helpful Lady with Three Ears
Ellery Queen Mystery Magazine, July/August